SAVING
MISSY

SAVING
MISSY

BETH MORREY

HarperCollins*Publishers*

HarperCollins*Publishers*
1 London Bridge Street
London SE1 9GF

www.harpercollins.co.uk

Published by HarperCollins*Publishers* 2020

3

Copyright © Beth Morrey 2020

Beth Morrey asserts the moral right to
be identified as the author of this work

A catalogue record for this book is
available from the British Library

ISBN:
HB: 978-0-00-833402-4
Export TPB: 978-0-00-833403-1

Typeset in Adobe Caslon by
Palimpsest Book Production Ltd, Falkirk, Stirlingshire

Printed and bound in Great Britain by
CPI Group (UK) Ltd, Croydon CR0 4YY

MIX
Paper from
responsible sources
FSC™ C007454

This book is produced from independently certified FSC™ paper
to ensure responsible forest management.

For more information visit: www.harpercollins.co.uk/green

To Mum, Dad and Ben – my first *oikos*

Every heart sings a song, incomplete,
until another heart whispers back.

Attributed to Plato

Part 1

'Let your hook always be cast; in the pool where you least expect it . . .'

Ovid

Chapter 1

It was bitterly cold, the day of the fish-stunning. So bitter that I nearly didn't go to watch. Lying in bed that morning, gazing at the wall since the early hours, I'd never felt more ancient, nor more apathetic. So why, in the end, did I roll over and ease those shrivelled feet of mine into my new sheepskin slippers? A vague curiosity, maybe – one had to clutch on to that last vestige of an enquiring mind, stop it slipping away.

Still in my dressing gown, I shuffled about the kitchen making tea and looking at my emails to see if there were any from Alistair. Well, my son was busy, no doubt, with his fieldwork. Those slippers he bought me for Christmas were cosy in the morning chill. There was a message from my daughter Melanie but it was only to tell me about a documentary she thought I might like. She often mistook her father's tastes for mine. I ate dry toast and brooded over my last conversation with her and for a second bristles of shame itched at the back of my neck. It felt easier to ignore it, so instead I read the newspapers online and saw that David Bowie had died.

At my age, reading obituaries is a generational hazard, contemporaries dropping off, one by one; each announcement an empty chamber in my own little revolver. For a while I tried to turn a blind eye, as if ignoring death could somehow fob it off. But people kept dying and other people kept writing about it, and some perverse imp obliged me to keep up to date. Bowie's death upset me more than most, although I never really listened to his music. I did remember him introducing the little animation of *The Snowman*, but when we watched it with my grandson at Christmas they'd replaced the introduction with something else. So my one recollection of Bowie was him holding a scarf and looking sombre, and for some reason the image was a disturbing one. The unmade bed beckoned, but then Leo's voice in my head as it so often was, 'Buck up, Mrs Carmichael! Onwards and upwards!'

So I went up to my room to put on my thickest pair of tights and a woollen skirt, grimacing at the putrid blue veins, and creaking along with the stairs on the way back down to fetch my coat. Struggling with the buttons, I sat down for a moment to catch my breath, thinking about the sign in the park the previous week.

My post-Christmas slump was particularly bad this year, the warm glow of festivities punctured by Alistair's departure, and with him Arthur, my golden grandson, his voice already taking on the Australian upward lilt. And it was still hard, being in the park, without remembering Leo. He was a great believer in a constitutional; enjoyed belittling self-important joggers and jovially berating cyclists. Every landmark had a dismal echo, but I was drawn back again all the same – the resident grey lady, idly roaming. There was a certain oak tree we used to visit – Leo liked its gnarled old trunk and said it was a Quercus version of him, increasingly craggy in old age. I would no doubt have spent hours standing there wool-gathering that day, but was distracted by a child who sounded like my Arthur. A boy of his age was tugging his mother fretfully as she read a notice pinned to the railings that circle each lake. Moving closer, I pretended to read it.

'Mummmmmeeeeeeee!' He had strawberry blonde locks and biscuit crumbs at the corner of his mouth that begged to be wiped away. Children are so beautiful, flawless and shiny, like a conker newly out of its shell. Such a shame they all grow up to be abominable adults. If only we could preserve that giddy-with-possibility wiring, everything greeted with an open embrace.

'Jeez, Otis, give me a break,' said the mother, in a broad Irish accent, batting him off. She had dyed red hair and I loathed her instantly. She glanced sideways at me, the old crone leering at her son, and I resumed my faux-study of the notice.

'What do you think, Oat?'

Oat? Good Lord, people today.

'They're gonna electrocute the fish! Wanna watch?'

The park caretakers needed to move the fish from one lake to the other, which required them to be stunned. Electrofishing. I'd never seen or heard of such a thing, nor did it seem particularly interesting, but maybe if I could see 'Oat' again then the tightness I'd felt in my gullet since Ali and Arthur got on the plane might ease a little. It would be something to do, after all . . .

Since that afternoon a week ago, I'd changed my mind half a dozen times, dwelling on the decision as only the terminally bored and insecure can. In the end, I decided to go so that there would be something to tell Alistair about. My life had become so circumscribed I'd grown worried he might think me trivial, and I only read the papers (including the obituaries) so that I knew what he was talking about when he mentioned a politician's gaffe, or asked which new plays were on in the West End. I could tell Ali was impressed when I went to the Turner exhibition, so the three buses in the rain were worth it.

Seeing some carp get electrocuted wasn't quite the dazzling metropolitan excursion, but it was better than nothing. So there I was, off to see the fish-stunning in my best winter coat, already drafting the email I would write on my return. Perhaps I might bump into little Otis and feed the ducks with him and queue up with his mother for a coffee, and . . . I ran adrift at this point, and nearly turned back, but by then my legs were stiffening up in the cold, and the bench by the lakes was nearest.

A small group had gathered to watch. Someone was handing out croissants, and when one was offered I took it, not because I was hungry but just grateful to be noticed. I put it to my lips and remembered a time in Paris with Leo when we'd had pain au chocolat on the banks of the Seine and then went to a book-shop where he'd disappeared up a rickety staircase while I petted a cat curled on a battered sofa, picked shards of pastry out of my teeth and worried which hand I was using to do which. They smelt of chocolate and cat for the rest of the day because we couldn't find anywhere to wash. My eyes filled with tears: Leo and I would never go to Paris again, even though it wasn't a particularly pleasant memory as I found the city dirty and unfriendly, there were no green spaces, and despite Leo speaking fluent French, they used to curl their lips at him because he never sounded anything but English and as puffed up as their croissants.

I swayed and sank onto the bench, blinking and fighting the breathlessness, until a warm patrician voice said, 'Oh my love, don't look so horrified – they're not Greggs or anything. I made them myself.' A middle-aged woman with eyes like berries was smiling down at me, waving a napkin, so I made a show of nibbling the croissant and mumbling my thanks, cursing myself for being such a distracted old bat. She carried on moving through the crowd, handing out her pastries and pleasantries, then everyone surged forwards, so I struggled to my feet again, to watch two men in waders and lurid jackets sailing across the pond in a curious-looking boat.

About four feet off the bow hung a circular contraption with small bars dangling from it into the water, like a giant set of wind chimes. Next to me, a chap was explaining the process to the woman on his other side. The device worked in combina-tion with a conductor on the hull to create an electrical field in the water wherever the boat travelled, with an on-board lever controlling the current. The men made large circles around the lake, one steering and operating the electrical lever while the other knelt poised with a net. For a while nothing happened, but then a glistening grey buoy popped gaily to the surface – the first stunned fish. 'Ooooh,' said the onlookers, clapping politely. After that they started bobbing up everywhere, gleaming and flaccid, waiting to be fished out. Every time the second man scooped one up, the watching crowd cheered and clinked their paper cups of mulled wine.

But the longer it went on, the more unsettling it became. The rhythmic 'plash' as they juddered out of the water, the slow whoosh of the net, the resulting thud as they hit the container. Plash, whoosh, thud. Plash, whoosh, thud. Then . . . flap. The stunning only lasted long enough to get the fish into the boat. Those vast, prehistoric-looking carp, covered in pond-mud, were hauled on board and immediately started writhing and flopping. Plash, whoosh, thud, plash whoosh, thud. Flap, flap, flap.

One minute you're gliding along, not a care in the world, and the next a huge prod appears and knocks you for six, and then everything is different and you're gasping with the shock of it. And there's no triumph in survival, because you're just swimming round and round endlessly in a new lake, mouthing pointlessly. I'd rather someone put me out of my misery. Ashes to ashes. The breathlessness, back. Plash, whoosh, thud. I could look the other way, then it would go away. Don't think, don't think. Thud, thud, thud. I clutched the railings, trying to ignore the looming branches above, but my skin prickled around the edges, flared, and I felt myself fall amidst reaching hands and faraway shouts as the blackness took over . . .

Chapter 2

Something rough was rubbing against my cheek, moving up my face like a scourer. Moaning, I turned my head away.

'She's coming round, move back!'

The scourer was back, rough and warm, with sour breath behind it. I could feel my nose wrinkle as the stench flooded my nostrils.

'Give her some air! Nancy, get away with you!'

Reaching out feebly, I encountered a handful of fur. Then felt the scourer on my hand. A tongue. I pushed it away and moaned again.

I must have been a bit under the weather, because when I finally came to I was lying on the bench and the woman with the berry eyes and pastries was holding a wet napkin to my forehead, onlookers peering around her shoulders. Struggling to the surface, clammy and astray, I could still feel the link with whatever underworld I'd been to, and closed my eyes again, hoping they would all go away.

'Gosh, you took a bit of a turn, my love,' the woman said, holding my wrist. 'I don't have a clue what I'm doing with this pulse nonsense,' she continued, jiggling my hand gently. 'What's right, after all? Seventy, eighty? I don't know. No, don't get up just yet.'

'Oh no, I'm fine, really.' I heaved my legs off the bench. 'Sorry to be such a bother, I don't know what came over me.' The darkness was receding, replaced by the equally cold sweat of embarrassment. My cheek and hand were coated in some sort of sticky substance and there was that urge to go and wash it off.

'Probably the weather, sweetie. It's a bit parky, isn't it? Let's just sit for a moment and look at the trees. Aren't they beautiful? Would you like another croissant? Go on, build up your strength. I'm Sylvie, by the way. And these two are Nancy and Decca.'

Still dazed, I realized she was indicating two small dove-blue dogs prancing round her feet. As she sat down on the bench next to me they jumped up either side of her, and I had to shift along to make room, wiping the back of my hand on my skirt. We sat eating croissants, looking up at the trees, and they were rather beautiful in a bleak way, stark and spiky against the pearly sky, with weak sunlight clawing through the clouds and dappling on the lake. The crowd had dispersed, although the men continued to circle, scooping the last of the fish.

'Something toxic in the water, apparently,' remarked Sylvie, nodding towards the lake. 'I do hope they survive the experience. Who's Leo, by the way? Your son? Would you like someone to fetch him?'

Leo.

I would have liked nothing more. Someone to go and fetch him, bring him back to me. He'd march up, take my hand, say, 'Missy! What have you been up to, silly old girl?' And we'd walk home together and light a fire to ward off the cold. The tears came again and I dabbed them away, the drops warm on my white fingers.

'I'm sorry,' said Sylvie, patting and squeezing my icy hand. 'I shouldn't have asked. You said his name, and I thought, maybe . . . Anyway, let's just sit here awhile, shall we? No hurry.'

So we sat, mostly in silence, but sometimes Sylvie would point out a plant or bird or dog of note, and I was able to reply adequately without worrying I was boring her or saying the wrong thing. Then I finished my croissant and dusted off the flakes, ready to get up and say goodbye to this easy, undemanding woman who had been the first stranger to speak to me in weeks. Best to end the conversation before I wanted to instead of after she did.

'Thank you so much,' I said, awkwardly holding out my still-sticky hand. 'So kind, but I must be going . . .'

'Bollocks, we missed it.'

We both turned to see Otis's red-haired mother dragging her sulking son down the path between the lakes. He was wearing a cape and had hooked a shield over the handlebars of his scooter, his russet hair sticking out in different directions. I wanted to smooth it down, then ruffle it up again.

'See, I told you they'd die without us,' she huffed, shouldering an enormous over-stuffed bag and leaning down to fondle the dogs.

'Angela, love,' said Sylvie. 'Late as ever. Fancy a coffee? I was just about to ask . . . um . . .?' She turned to me expectantly.

'Millicent,' I murmured, scarcely able to believe my luck. Would it be all right to say yes? Surely I deserved a treat? But it wouldn't do to look too eager.

'Millicent . . . to join us.'

Angela sighed and hefted her bag again. 'Go on, then. But I wanted to see some fish being killed. So did Otis, but he couldn't find his Spider-Man outfit, daft beggar.'

'Millicent, would you like to come and have a coffee with us? Or tea – don't want to get dictatorial about beverages!' Sylvie's eyes crinkled engagingly as she linked arms with Angela and held out her hand to Otis.

They seemed such a merry little band. Of course they didn't want a fuddy-duddy like me tagging along and slowing them down, so I said I had an appointment to get to, which was true in a way, and watched them walk down the avenue towards the café. The sky cleared a bit more as I headed off, feeling cheered by my outing. At least they asked. I told Leo about it, exaggerating some of the details to make it sound more dramatic. But of course it didn't matter which way I told it, there was no one there to listen, so after leaving some flowers and tidying up, I left for my empty home.

Back in my kitchen, there was the tick-tick-tick of the clock, with no other sound to drown it out, and in the living room Leo's chair was empty, and I didn't have any new friends – I would never see Sylvie or Angela or Otis again, and would have to avoid the park now in case they thought I was trying to run into them.

I cleaned the house and remembered when we had young children and it was impossible to keep anything tidy. Now everything was spotless, and stayed that way. Eating an over-boiled egg for my lunch, I read more about David Bowie, and thought of the scarf and *The Snowman*. I had made Arthur a scarf for Christmas, forgetting that it was summer in Sydney, and now the knitting needles just rolled around my cutlery drawer, reminding me of my mistake. Later, I couldn't be bothered with making dinner so just had cereal and thought about watching television, maybe that documentary, but really, what was the point? Alistair watched Australian television now, bought me Australian slippers. I turned in early, checking the cupboards and shivering as I got into bed, waiting for the blankets to warm up. '*Sibyl told me . . . before she died. I don't think she knew what she was saying.*' I blinked to banish the image of my daughter Melanie, wide-eyed in my kitchen, backing away. The guilt gnawed away at me, as it had since that terrible day. Whenever I tried to weed it out, it just took a deeper root.

So the day ended as miserably as it began. But I still felt it somewhere – that spark. The beginning of something. Or the end. Who knows?

Chapter 3

'Come closer, Missy.'

Kensington, 1942, and impervious to the booms above, Fa-Fa bent to light the spill on one of the candles, cupping huge hands around his pipe and puffing away to get it going. With each inward breath my grandfather's lined face glowed in the charring light. A crash overhead made me flinch, but I was too caught up in his stories to pay attention to the bombs, snuggled in our bunk, nestling closer under scratchy wool, with half-eaten carrot sandwiches squashed in our hands. Fa-Fa blew out a stream of smoke and settled back.

'Mesopotamia, 1916. Flies like soot around my face.' He waved at the grey fog in front of him, and I could almost see them.

'That blasted fever, too weak to brush them away . . . When I'd recovered, I was allowed home on leave. Marvellous to be back in London after that terrible heat. Your grandmother and I went out to a restaurant in – where was it, Jette? Swallow Street? – to toast my return.'

Our grandmother, sniffling over there in a dark corner. I couldn't imagine anyone wanting to have dinner with her – she barely ever opened her mouth, either to eat or speak. She gave us a watery smile and ducked her head at another skirl above. Then the gap, like thunder after a lightning strike. When it came, it was quite faint.

'We had a grand blowout, then walked back to Piccadilly to find a hackney – you couldn't whistle for one, and of course it was dark along the back roads, and we were a trifle fuddled, must admit.' He chuckled and drew on his pipe, Henry and I giggling at the thought of Fa-Fa, and particularly our grand-mother, in such a state. No beating about the bush; that was why we loved him.

'Then, in the darkness, Jette tripped and fell, and as I helped her up, a thief darted forwards and filched her purse, the rascal! I immediately gave chase.'

Fa-Fa shifted his bulk on the low stool as Henry and I gasped and clutched each other. Jette, hunched in the shadows, the mouse to his man. I couldn't see her expression in the gloom, only her hand gripping the handkerchief.

'Caught up with him fairly easily, turned him round and saw he was a young lad, too young to fight in a war but old enough to steal in one. Nothing much in the purse of value, a few coins maybe, but I wasn't going back to Jette without it. Gave him a bit of a tap, just to let him know I wasn't going anywhere. Thought that would be the end of it, but he clung on for dear life and try as I might, I couldn't get it out of his grasp. Locked fast in his fingers, he just wouldn't let go.' Fa-Fa held up a ham-fist, tendons bulging, sending a few flecks of tobacco to the floor. He stooped forward to sweep them up before he continued.

'In the end, had to give him a rare old pummelling, a good going over, but no matter what I did, his grip still wouldn't budge from the bag.'

Another draw on the pipe – puff, puff, puff – along with the slow glow of the burn. Jette's thin fingers plucked at her dress.

'Punch, jab, punch! But he wouldn't let go. Like a dog with a bone.'

Boom went the bombs. My grandmother blew her nose. We were all wreathed in the fug of Fa-Fa's smoke. It made my eyes water, but I couldn't take them off him.

'Started kicking him in the shins, stamping on his feet. He was screaming but he wouldn't let go. By the time I'd finished with him, he was curled in a ball at my feet, but his hands *still* gripped the purse. It was dirty and covered in blood as well. Realized even if I got it back, Jette wouldn't want it. So I left him there, lying in the street, mewling like a baby, with the bag still clenched in those bloody hands.'

There was a brief silence, even from above, as Fa-Fa put down the pipe and polished his spectacles, rheumy eyes focused on the job. His hands were shaking a little as he put them back on.

'Damned scamp got the bag. Admired him for it. Whatever was in it that he wanted, he got. Good on him.' Leaning forward, he licked his fingers and pinched out the candle nearest our bunk. 'And that's the moral of the story tonight. If you really want something, you hang on. Don't give up. Hang on, as if your life depended on it.'

'Even if someone beats you black and blue?' piped up Henry.

'Even if they do that!' retorted Fa-Fa, ruffling his hair. 'Even if they *cuff* you,' he tweaked Henry's ear. 'Even if they *thump* you,' he aimed a mock punch at Henry's stomach, then again a little harder. 'Even if they bash the hell out of you, you hang on!' He and Henry began play-fighting, but as the bombs started up again, the frolic became something else. Fa-Fa had Henry in a headlock, my brother's face a livid red, eyes sparkling with excitement or tears, I couldn't tell which. Jette stood, holding out her white handkerchief.

'Father! What are you doing?'

My mother had slipped in through the cellar door, unnoticed. She was unwinding a scarlet scarf from her neck, pale from the cold and angry as usual. Jette rushed forward to embrace her, but Mama ignored her, still glaring at my grandfather. Fa-Fa looked up and released his hold on Henry, who fell back on the bunk, his hands at his throat.

'When will you learn to be gentle around the children? They're not your recruits. I suppose you've been telling them awful stories again. Now, Milly, Henry, let's get you in bed, it's far too late for you to be up.' She began the motherly round of tucking us in, picking up our half-eaten pieces of bread and leaving them on the side for morning.

Fa-Fa retreated to a chair in the corner to pack another pipe, sulking, as Mama lay down on her pallet. The last thing I remembered was her blowing out the final candle, and the comforting smoulder as Fa-Fa smoked the night away. Then the ink-blot shadows on the walls sent me into a deep sleep that even the booms outside couldn't penetrate.

The next night, an SC250 landed in the road outside our house, reducing the garden wall to rubble. No one was injured although Fa-Fa's spectacles fell and shattered in the blast. After that, my mother decided we would be better off in the country and packed us off to my Aunt Sibyl in Yorkshire. But it seemed the decision wasn't so much based on the bomb as the story of the bag, which Henry recounted to Mama the next morning, provoking another tirade. Fa-Fa was reprehensible, telling disgraceful stories which probably weren't even true (Jette wouldn't confirm or deny when asked), it was high time we got some country air, etcetera. So off to Kirkheaton we went, to a draughty old rectory where we slept in the garret, searched priest holes for ghouls, made dens in the woods and mostly forgot about the war and Fa-Fa's strange habits.

We didn't forget that story though, and used to tell it back to each other, lying in those hard narrow beds under the eaves. Each time, we'd add an embellishment – a dramatic flourish, some sordid detail, until eventually we weren't sure where Fa-Fa's tale ended and ours began. Did he make it up, or did we? Did any of it happen, or none of it? As the years passed, I was inclined to believe the latter.

Still, it's true though, isn't it? If you really want something, you hang on.

Chapter 4

A week went by without anything happening that I could put in an email to Alistair. I hardly left the house, except to get a few bits – a scrag end at the butchers, a prescription from the chemist. I thought Sylvie was in front of me in the queue and bent my head so she wouldn't notice me, but it wasn't her at all, just some other middle-aged woman buying indigestion tablets.

I splashed out on a bottle of wine on the way home, though drinking on my own seemed like a slippery slope. But the evenings stretched, and a glass of something gave the synapses a sly tweak, lending a little '*entheos*' – the Greek buzz of enthu-siasm. Just the one glass, maybe two small ones, distracting myself from the rest of the bottle by poking around various rooms in the house, most of which were hardly ever used any more. What did I need a dining room for? All those dinner parties?

The dust in Leo's study gave me a coughing fit. I should really pack up the books and get rid of them, but he would have been horrified; most of them were first or rare editions and I didn't know enough about them to be sure of getting a decent price. So instead I wiped them, and read the inscriptions: 'Darling Leo, Christmas '86, with love'; 'Leo, read this and please be kind – Asa'; 'Dad – another old tome for you – Mel'. '*Tómos*,' meaning 'slice'. Each book a slice of the man. None of them were mine. I stopped reading when the children were born.

One night and another visit to the vintners later, I found myself in Alistair's room, still as it was when he was a boy. His Arsenal posters, his Lego models, his fossils. My son, the archae-ologist! The room was like one of his sites; the artefacts and remains of some revered Pharaoh. And now the next in line slept here – I smoothed the pillow where Arthur's golden head had lain. How I missed him. A gap in the shelf where the first edition should be.

The day Ali left home, we drove him to his halls, Leo chunt-ering about red-bricks, while I was speechless with the effort of not crying, smiling as we unloaded his bags and settled him in that dingy little room, as if it were just wonderful to think that he was going off into the world to make his own way. What an adventure! Just at the end though, when we said goodbye and he hugged me, I found I couldn't let go. Eventually, Leo gently prised my fingers from Alistair's sweater and gave them a re-assuring squeeze. 'He'll be back at Christmas,' he said heartily. Christmas, always Christmas – casting its fairy lights on the banality of every other day.

I went to the fridge again, then to Mel's room to pack up a

few of her books. She had her own flat in Cambridge, and it wasn't like she ever visited any more – not since that terrible afternoon. After checking the cupboard doors on my way to bed, I remembered the lights were still on in the living room, so had to drag myself downstairs again. As the room flicked into darkness, the street outside was illuminated, revealing a young couple wrapped around each other, making their way home after a night out. Her teeth glinted in the lamplight as she smiled up at him, tucking his hand more firmly under her arm as he kissed the top of her head. Lithe and blithe with most of their mistakes unmade. It might have been Leo and me, half a century ago. I closed the curtains, did another round of checking and reeled off to bed.

The next day, nursing a headache, I went to the chemist again, and again saw a woman who looked like Sylvie, only this time it *was* Sylvie. I ducked, but it was too late.

'There you are!' she exclaimed, as if I'd only been gone five minutes. 'You rushed off the other day. How are you feeling?'

'Fine, thank you.' I shuffled forward in the queue, hoping she wouldn't notice the paracetamol, which I always used to hide from Leo. A hangover was an admission of guilt. If I didn't have one, then I hadn't drunk too much the night before.

'Snap.' Sylvie nudged her box against mine. 'I've got the most god-awful monster behind the eyes. All self-inflicted, of course. Angela can really put it away. She's a hard-drinking journalist. What about you?'

She had the air of everything in life being a tremendous joke, a flippancy that made me want to kick off my shoes and talk of cabbages and kings – to be in a world where things didn't matter so much. But all I could manage was a weak shrug.

'Fancy a coffee?' She nodded at the café opposite. It looked as warm and inviting as Sylvie herself, all low lamps, metro tiles and bare wood. There was the row of workers at their laptops, bashing away; two mothers with prams, heads together as they coochy-cooed at their offspring; a couple deep in conversation, their hands entwined. I didn't belong there, amidst all that companionship and industry, and had no idea why Sylvie would offer such a thing.

'Oh thank you, but I really must be going.' I handed over my coins and reached for my paper bag of painkillers.

'All right, well, see you soon, hopefully. Millicent.' She remembered.

'It's actually Missy,' I blurted, as she pulled open the door. It tinkled merrily and she turned back with a raised eyebrow.

'I'm sorry?'

'Well, my name is Millicent, but everyone calls me Missy,' I floundered, dropping my change, feeling the heat building in my face.

'Oh, right, well, Missy it is! I'm sure I'll bump into you again, I'm always around,' Sylvie waved and exited, wielding her wicker basket like a 1950s housewife.

I left the chemist, flustered and overset. No one called me that. Not since Leo, and before him, Fa-Fa. She must have thought me completely doolally. Cheeks still burning, I found myself walking across the road towards the café. If she was there I'd jolly well have a coffee with her, stop being so silly.

The workers were still tapping away, the mothers clucking over their babies and gossiping, but the couple had gone. There was no sign of Sylvie, but I ordered a coffee anyway and sat at a table, feeling stiff and embarrassed, sure everyone was watching me, wondering why an old lady would come in here on her own. But no one seemed to notice, and gradually the warmth and noise of the place started to sink in. Someone had left a newspaper on the next table. I took it and read about Jeremy Corbyn, who lived nearby, and the astronaut Tim Peake, living much further away, and Alan Rickman, not living anywhere any more. He was in one of Leo and my favourite films, about a ghost who tries to cheer up his bereaved wife. I was a bit like Nina, the wife, wandering around my empty house in the hope of a miraculous resurrection. I always thought she was wrong not to stay with her husband Jamie, even though he was dead.

I stayed there for a while, sipping my coffee and reading the paper, and when I'd finished, the smiling waitress collected my cup, the mothers shifted their prams for me, and a man left his laptop to hold open the door. I walked home slowly, noting the pine needles that still littered the pavement but occasionally holding my face up to the weak winter sun.

When I got back, rather than embark on my usual round of cleaning, I went upstairs to the spare room and brought down an old paisley throw, draping it experimentally over the sofa. Then I went back up and fetched a lamp, placing it on a low stool to one side. I stood contemplating it for a while, then, feeling faintly foolish, went into the kitchen to make myself a cup of tea.

Later on though, when the light faded, the lamp and blanket looked rather snug. I skipped cereal for once and cooked myself some pasta, eating it off a tray on the sofa while I watched some new period drama. Leo would have scoffed at the anachronisms, but it was a relief to be pulled in by gentle domestic tribulations. I considered rounding my evening off with a glass of wine but remembered I'd finished the bottle the night before. Ah well, I could always buy another tomorrow. Who knew who I'd bump into?

I still didn't have much to write to Alistair about, but at least I'd been invited for a coffee and went, in a way. Baby steps. Old lady steps. Even if I wasn't quite sure where I was going.

Chapter 5

Down, down, down, and it's 1956 and I'm in Cambridge, kneeling on the floor trying to make a fire.

There I was, Milly Jameson, in my second year at Newnham College, miserable in a freezing room, pretending I enjoyed reading Homer. The other students were so glamorous, shrieking down the long corridors and sneaking men into their rooms. The girl next door to me was garrulous and captivating, my polar opposite. Tiny and curvy, with tinted blonde hair set in perfect waves, she kept a bottle of gin under her bed for 'Magic Hour' cocktails served to her numerous guests. Alicia Stewart and her legendary soirées – every night, I heard her gramophone and banged on the wall as she sang to the tune of 'Mr Sandman': 'Mr Barman, bring me a driiiink . . . Make it so strong that I can't thiiiink.' I had no idea how she intended to get a degree – probably by charming the exam paper into submission.

However, Alicia's fearsome cocktails were one of the few things that allowed me to unbend, so we had become friends of a sort, or at least she facilitated my drinking habit. My room had a window that opened handily onto a lean-to, serving as an escape route for those who found themselves locked in college after hours, so in return for the odd tipple, I permitted her to smuggle her gentlemen friends out. She swore there was no more going on than heavy petting, as if I were in any way an arbiter in these matters, being as far from 'necking' as I was from singing with The Chordettes.

Midway through the second year of my degree, it was becoming apparent that I was not the gift to the academic world I'd imagined. My supervisor described me as 'a skimming stone', which was fair – who wanted to contemplate the depths? In the eleven years since my father died, I'd become particularly adept at disregarding deeper waters.

Rather than wrestle with 'Catullus 85', 'Odi et amo', I was sitting on the threadbare rug that chilly February evening, trying to coax a flicker in the grate. We were in Peile Hall, a draughty old building where they had yet to install gas heating. Instead there were these metal sheets we held in front of the fireplace to draw the air – Sydneys, they were called – but there were only two to go round all of us. We had to traipse along the corridors knocking on doors to hunt one down, so when there was a knock on my own door I assumed it was someone after the Sydney. Instead it was Alicia, already three sheets to the wind, propping herself up against the doorframe.

'Milish . . . Mishilent. What's that smell?'

'Smoke. I'm trying to light a fire.'

'Why?'

'Because it's cold.'

'Is it? Never mind. There's a party. For a new poetry magazine.'

'Oh good. Have fun.'

'No. You have to come with me.'

'Why?'

'Because I can't find it.'

'I've got nothing to wear.'

'You can borrow something.'

'I don't feel like it.'

'There'll be wine. And it'll be warm.'

Which was how I found myself, wearing one of Alicia's black dresses that was too short and big in the bust, tottering through the streets of Cambridge as we searched for the Women's Union in Falcon Yard. When we finally got there, I wished we hadn't bothered. So loud and dark, with pockets of light illuminating the jazz band, and people reciting verse that made me cringe. I've always found poetry – particularly the reading aloud – excruciating. Like religion and Bongo Boards, best practised in private.

Alicia weaved off and disappeared, so I went in search of the wine she'd promised. At least it *was* warm, with all those people, all that hot air. There was a poet standing in the corner, head flung back as he declaimed to an earnest little throng – something about buttocks and crystals. Good Lord, it was awful.

I stood with my back to the wall, gulping wine, examining my lack of cleavage and wondering how soon I could escape.

And then, across the room, there he was. Like everyone else, he was drunk. But he was the only man wearing a suit, rather than a turtleneck, and that, along with his height, made him distinguished. He saw me, and grinned as though he knew me, and that moment was a homecoming. He ambled over, still smiling. Then, as he drew nearer: 'Oh, gosh, sorry! I thought you were someone else!'

Up close, he was even drunker than I thought, swaying like a great oak in a gale. But he was very handsome, big and blonde, a Labrador of a man, and I was emboldened by the wine.

'Who else do you want me to be?'

I'd always been a terrible flirt. I just couldn't do it, even with lubrication. Luckily it was so loud in there, with the jazz and the poetry and people smashing glasses, that it didn't seem to matter.

'Well, since the girl I thought you were doesn't seem to be here, shall we have another drink?'

He led me over to the long table stacked with bottles, and poured me a glass while I tried to think of something clever to say.

'It's a terrible name for a magazine, *St Botolph*. Sounds like something to do with church,' I blurted. Oh blast, he was probably one of the editors. But he just laughed.

'I know, but this party puts paid to that notion. Definitely nothing godly about it.' He dodged a wine bottle as it sailed past. 'Do you like poetry?'

'Not really. It's a bit self-indulgent for me.' I didn't know why

I was so forthright all of a sudden. Probably the alcohol, but also a strange sense that I couldn't stop myself unfurling – a flower opening up to the sun.

'Really? What do you study?'

'Classics. But I'm more of a prose person generally.'

'Tell me something you like.'

I looked around the room. 'One half of the world cannot understand the pleasures of the other.' I felt very erudite.

'Ain't that a shame,' he replied, reducing me to gauche school-girl again. Across the room there was a couple ferociously kissing, or wrestling, I wasn't sure which. I had to do something spec-tacular, *be* spectacular, so that he would remember this point, and when people asked how we met, we would be able to say, 'now, *there's* a story . . .'

Instead, Alicia Stewart chose that moment to re-enter the room, waving a glass of wine, tripping over a discarded bottle, grabbing a tablecloth to break her fall and vomiting spectacularly over her old black dress, with me in it. The poet stopped reciting for a second, looking at us curiously, then resumed his discourse on bloated knaves.

'Shit.' She lay on the floor, drops of red wine caught on her eyelashes like beads of blood. Roaring with laughter, my knight stooped to help her to her feet. In the circle of his arms she looked up at him admiringly.

'Oooh, you're nice!' Alicia exclaimed. She shifted her glance to me. 'Milly, you're covered in sick. You look dreadful. You should go home before you disgrace yourself.'

I glared at her and used the tablecloth to wipe myself.

'I shall have the honour of escorting you both,' said our hero, offering us his arms.

'Lovely,' slurred Alicia, grabbing hers like a drowning woman. 'I'm Alishia and this is Milish . . . Milish . . . Misha.'

'Hello, Misha. I'm Leo.'

'Ooooh, Leo the lion!' she crowed. 'Take us back to your lair, Leo!'

We picked our way through the broken glass, swiping a half-empty bottle of wine along the way. Outside in the corridor a girl was sobbing and being comforted by a bony young man who kept patting her shoulder, saying 'Don't worry, he was a sod anyway.' He was always going to be the friend who picked up the pieces.

Outside we could see puffs of our breath in the frigid air as we weaved through the cobbled streets. The sky had cleared, and when we emerged on to King's Parade it was swathed in a velvety blanket of stars that winked above the chapel. Even they were mocking me.

As soon as a decent interval had elapsed I dropped Leo's arm and fell behind so they could walk together. But I kept the wine. The streetlamps caught the golden tints in Alicia's hair as she gazed up at him, doing that tinkly little giggle she affected with men – her real laugh was more of a charlady cackle.

We crossed the bridge on Silver Street, and I looked down at the sluggish River Cam, remembering how I'd imagined Cambridge would be all punting to Grantchester, and cycling through quads with my gown flapping in the breeze – skimming stones that barely rippled the waters. Instead I got the bolt at

St Botolph's, following my sozzled neighbour home in the early hours, covered in her sick, while she seduced someone I saw first. '*Odi et amo*'. Draining the last of the bottle, I threw it in the river and watched it slowly sink into the depths. I suppose it's still there somewhere.

Chapter 6

The following Tuesday, there was a fight at my new café.

After my encounter with Sylvie in the chemist, I took to loitering around that row of shops, the café in particular, until the smiling waitress began to recognise me and serve my coffee with plain cold milk, none of that frothy nonsense. They gave me a little card that got stamped every time I bought a cup, eventually resulting in a free drink. The bread in the Turkish shop next door was cheap and fresh, and I browsed the children's fiction in the charity bookshop, picking up a Thomas the Tank Engine book for Arthur for fifty pence.

I'd never bothered with any of these local explorations before – I'd been busy with the children and running the household, and later, when he got ill, looking after Leo. I didn't have to worry about money then either, whereas now I spent my time rooting out meagre bargains as if it would make the slightest difference. My meanderings whiled away the hours and the pennies, but there was still no sign of Sylvie.

That Tuesday, enjoying my regular 'Americano', who should come in but Angela, this time without Otis. She was unkempt as usual, tendrils of too-red hair escaping from a topknot, smudged eyeliner, leather jacket and scruffy boots with buckles that clinked as she walked. At first I didn't notice the woman she was with, but as they sat down together in the corner I saw she was crying, and that Angela appeared to be comforting her. She was speaking quickly, persuasively, but the woman kept shaking her head, wiping at her cheekbones. She was terribly thin, with a sucked-in look that led me to conclude she was probably on drugs.

Then Angela suddenly sat back, smacked the table like she was finished, and the other woman got up and cannoned her way out of the café. Angela half-stood up and called out something that sounded like 'Flicks!' but maybe she was just cursing. The woman stopped in the doorway and turned around, mascara in streaks down the hollowed panes of her face, her mouth twisted into a snarl.

'You don't get it,' she snapped. 'You'll never get it.'

They both seemed oblivious to the other customers, who had fallen silent at the spectacle, watching over the rims of their cups as they appreciated this little soap opera scene.

'I want to help you,' said Angela. 'Please.' She held out a hand.

Like a tennis match, all eyes darted across to the other woman in the doorway.

'Then stop interfering. Leave me alone,' she spat, reaching for the door handle. What happened next was extraordinary.

Angela leapt forward and pushed the door shut, barring her way; the woman tried to shove her aside, and they grappled in the entrance, pulling each other this way and that. Occasionally one of them would say, 'no!' or 'don't', as they continued their ungainly shuffling, oblivious to the dropped mouths of the onlookers. Then the other woman suddenly lifted her hand and slapped Angela across the face. She fell back with a short cry and there was a collective gasp from the customers; one of the row of laptop-workers stood up, as if to protest, then thought better of it as Hanna the waitress hurried forwards and pulled Angela back a step. The other woman watched them for a second, chest heaving, hair askew, then wrenched the door handle and stumbled out into the street.

There was a barely perceptible sigh of disappointment as she exited – the fun spoilt when it was just getting going – but I've always found such public displays sordid. Leo and I once had an argument at a party, *sotto voce* out the sides of our mouths, lifting our glasses and nodding to passing guests. People have no standards nowadays; they just let it all hang out.

Angela, a livid mark on one cheek, sank into her seat, took a cigarette packet out of one pocket and lit up right then and there. Hanna went back over to remonstrate with her. Grimacing, Angela stubbed out the cigarette in a saucer. She sat with her head in her hands for a while, then picked up her bag and made her way to the door. As she passed my table she caught sight of me and raised her eyebrows wearily.

'Oh, hi, er . . .' Unlike Sylvie, she'd forgotten.

'Millicent.'

'Hi, Millicent. You OK?'

'Fine, thank you. Um . . . you?' To my dismay she suddenly hefted her bag on to the floor next to me and took the seat opposite, beckoning Hanna over to take her order.

'I'm fucking awful, as you can see. I'm just gonna sit here for five minutes if that's OK, stop me doing something stupid.' Pulling the bowl of sugar cubes towards her, she crunched one between yellow teeth. She was very pale, with dark circles under her eyes. Probably all that hard drinking with Sylvie.

'Of course.' I hoped this didn't mean I would have to pay for her coffee.

We sat in silence for a few seconds as she picked at the skin around her fingernails, which were bitten to the quick and flecked with chipped nail polish. Hanna delivered her coffee and she slurped it, wiping her mouth on her sleeve.

Eventually she looked sideways at me. 'You married?'

I caught my breath. 'Yes. But he's not . . . he's not . . .'

She waved away the question. 'I'm not,' she said grimly. 'And sometimes I'm so fucking relieved, you know? More trouble than it's worth.'

I was intrigued enough to venture a question of my own. 'What about your son? Is his father . . . around?'

She snorted. 'Didn't want to know. Better that way, trust me. Anyway, I'm not talking about me. You got children? Grandchildren?'

'Yes, two children. And one grandchild.'

'Boy or girl?'

'A boy. Arthur.'

She grinned. 'Bet he's a terror.'

'Yes,' I said. 'A terror.' But she'd drifted off again, staring into space, drumming her fingers on the table in time to the jazz playing in the background.

'She's got to get the kids out. And Bob. That's the trouble,' she mumbled, more to herself than to me.

I sat in silence, waiting for her to work it out. Women like her always have some drama or other. Just as I was wondering if it would be rude to signal Hanna to bring the bill, Angela leaned back in her chair, rubbed her face and heaved a great sigh.

'You're right, I can't get involved,' she said.

I inclined my head, and caught Hanna's eye.

Angela pinched the bridge of her nose and huffed again. 'Fuck.'

The expletives that pepper today's conversations are particularly unsavoury, so ugly and unimaginative, although it was more the repetition that bothered me than the word itself. Angela's curses were so frequent that they were like punctuation points, each one provoking a twinge of distaste, a sourness in my mouth and hers. Her speech was as sloppy as her scuffed shoes. I picked up my bag and put it onto my knee, ready.

Hanna brought over the bill. As she put the saucer down in front of us, she briefly squeezed Angela's shoulder, but before I could decide what the gesture meant, Angela tweaked the paper between her fingers. 'I'll get this.'

I shook my head, 'Oh no, please don't,' fumbling coins out of my purse. Angela waved them away, 'No, go on. I barged in on you, it's the least I can do.' She slapped a five-pound note on the table and gave a hovering Hanna the thumbs up.

'Well, there was no need. No need at all. But thank you.' I stood up, feeling awkward as always, on the cusp of conversations. Beginnings and endings, I'm never sure how they should go. 'Er, goodbye then. Hope you manage to . . . sort it out.' But as I backed away, she grabbed her bag and slid out of her chair. 'I'll walk with you, I could do with the fresh air.' I muttered an oath of my own.

Angela lit up again as soon as we were outside, inhaling her 'fresh air', head back and eyes closed, the bruise on her cheek already darkening. She turned to me, smoke curling out of her flared nostrils.

'Where is Arthur?'

I nearly stumbled, so discomfited – and offended – by the question that for a while I didn't reply. There was something disturbingly direct and intense about her.

'He lives with his father, my son. In Australia. They moved out there three years ago.' The words had to be choked out, everything in me rebelled against them. Angela stared at me for a second, then turned and kicked a fallen leaf.

'That's some tough shit,' she said. 'What's he like?'

The marble was back in my throat. 'He's four. He likes Lego, and football, and Batman, and all the usual things a boy of his age likes, I suppose.' I stopped, then found I couldn't. 'I don't see them often, but when I do . . . He's busy. Always playing, running, fighting. He hardly ever sits still, he's just fizzing with energy all the time, so when he does stop, you want to . . . pin him down, moor him somehow. It's so hard to keep up with him. But I want to. I want to keep a version of him at every age. He just keeps getting better and better. But I miss all the babies and boys he was, and want them all back.' I tailed off, embarrassed.

Angela nodded slowly. 'Yes, it's like that, isn't it?'

'What's Otis like?'

'Such a sweet boy,' she said. 'Nothing like me. Nothing like his father either, thank Christ. There's no side to him, no edge at all. I get scared sometimes, by the love. I used to be hard as nails – had to be, doing what I do – but he's taken it out of me, made me soft. Like when you bash a steak.'

'Tenderized,' I said.

'That's it. He's tenderized me, the little sod. I'm no bloody good at my job any more.'

I still didn't like her much, but she had Otis and I had Arthur. 'Sylvie said you're a journalist?'

'Yeah, but freelance, so you're always hustling for the next thing.' She switched into interrogation mode again. 'You're retired, right? What did you do?'

'I was a librarian. Before I had children.'

'They're closing all the libraries now,' she said glumly.

'Well, this is me,' I said, my hand on the gate.

Angela looked up. 'Fuck me, the whole house? I'm just down the road, but in the top-floor flat. Postage stamp. You've got the *whole house?*'

'We bought in the sixties. The area wasn't quite so gentrified then.' I thought of the riots, the strikes, the burglaries. The rubbish piling up in the street. We'd been pioneers.

Resigned to the fact that Angela wanted to come in, I made a last stand all the same. 'Where's Otis?' I asked, hoping she'd remember she had to go and pick him up.

'He's at the childminder's,' she murmured, still gazing up. 'The whole house. Jesus.'

Unlocking the front door, I could sense her behind me, hopping from foot to foot in anticipation. Pushing it open, we stepped inside.

The first time I went into that hallway was back in 1964. Heavily pregnant, and daunted by the wide sweep of stairs, I'd waddled left and discovered the most charming drawing room. A huge bay window sent sunlight flooding through, casting rays along the varnished floorboards; dark and light, dust particles rolling in the shafts as I wandered between them. Unfurnished – the previous owner had died and evidently the relatives had swooped in and snaffled the lot – it was a blank slate. While Leo argued with the agent about damp, the house whispered to me that it was mine.

Nowadays, of course, people would move in and immediately gut the place, stripping out and paring back so they can fill it all up again. New owners are so keen to 'put their stamp on things' – such an aggressive term, as if a house can be branded with one's personality. We preferred to let the building's own character shine through and didn't change a thing, apart from re-painting one of the bedrooms for the baby. In fact, beyond general maintenance, it was still the same as it was just after Miss Edith Crawshay passed away in it.

'Shit a brick,' said Angela, seeing the kitchen. 'This is a fecking time warp.' It was rather outmoded, I suppose – the cabinets dated from the fifties. There was an Aga, which seemed incongruous in a city house, but it worked perfectly well, and to demonstrate, I put the kettle on the boiling plate. Angela had already prowled off. I scurried after her, keen to stop her before she reached . . .

Leo's study. The door was already ajar. How dare she barge into my house and take stock like this? But as I opened my mouth to berate her she turned and her face was so transfixed with wonder it brought me up short.

'Oh, Millicent,' she breathed. 'This is *fabulous*.' She was stroking Leo's John Milton reverently. 'It's a treasure trove. *Look!*'

'It's my husband's,' I said, taking it off her and putting it back on the shelf.

'Some collector,' she observed, unabashed, wandering over to his still-dusty Dickens collection. 'Is this him?' she stopped by his desk to pick up a photo of us, taken shortly after we were married.

'Yes.'

'Very attractive,' she noted, then looked at me appraisingly. 'Both of you.' She picked up another photo. 'Your children? The son, who's in Australia. What about the girl?'

'Melanie. She lives in Cambridge.' I resisted the urge to snatch the frame back.

'Do you see her often?' She'd already moved along to the historical section.

'Not really. She's very busy. She teaches at the University.'

Once again, Melanie, backing away in my kitchen. *'What you did . . . it wasn't wrong . . . You shouldn't blame yourself . . .'*

'Who's Leonard Carmichael?' She pointed at the shelf, stacked with his books, his name again and again on the spines.

'My husband,' I said, my voice shaking only slightly. 'He wrote historical biographies. Mostly political ones.'

She stood on her thin ice and looked at me without saying anything, then the kettle started to whistle and I rushed off to deal with it. When I brought the tea into the living room she was already there, rocking on her heels and gazing around with her mouth open.

'Have you had a car boot sale or something?' She gestured around the room.

'What do you mean?'

'Well . . . It's a bit bare, isn't it?'

Apart from the throw and lamp I'd reclaimed the other night, there was very little in the living room other than a sofa, a stool serving as a coffee table, and the television on a stand. No rugs, no pictures on the walls, no knick-knacks of any kind. I loathed clutter. When the children were little I felt as though I were drowning in it, and gradually banished the lot, finding that the less *stuff* I had surrounding me, the calmer things felt. Leo didn't care one way or the other – as long as he had his books he was happy.

'There's rather a lot up in the attic.' Angela's eyes gleamed at the thought of untold treasure, but we certainly weren't opening that can of worms. So she drank her tea and moaned about a deadline. Then she said she'd do a feature on 'the houses that time forgot' and use mine as an example, as if I would consider such a vulgar thing. But as she left, running a finger along the banister and casting one last look up at the grubby chandelier above the landing, she suddenly squeezed my arm like a conspirator.

'Listen, give me your number. It's my day off on Friday and I'm taking Otis to the park. You should come. He'd like to see you. He hasn't got a grandma, or at least, not one in this country.'

It was nonsense of course. Otis had barely noticed me. But my face flamed with gratification as I tapped my number into her phone.

'Maybe,' I said. 'If the weather's nice.' I shut the door behind her, allowing myself a rare moment of triumph. At last, I would have something to email Alistair about.

Chapter 7

Angela wanted a babysitter. Of course she did.

On Thursday night I was sleepless with anticipation, checking the weather forecast online all day to make sure it wasn't going to rain, planning my outfit – trousers, in case I needed to do any bending in the playground – and wondering if I should bring a picnic for Otis in case he got hungry. But I didn't know his mother's views on snacks, so instead I put one of Arthur's little cars ready in my coat pocket, just in case.

When Mel was younger she became interested in amateur dramatics, and used to try out for roles in school plays. She would get hopelessly overwrought about them beforehand, storming around the house saying she couldn't remember her lines, didn't understand the text, hadn't had time to prepare. I had no patience with such dramas, but Leo would indulge them, bearing her off to his study to go through her monologues. Now, tangled up in my blankets, it felt like I was about to mess up an audition.

* * *

The next morning, gritty-eyed and irritable, I slumped at my kitchen table drinking strong tea for the caffeine and catching up with the news. Today's death was Harper Lee. Ten years older than me. Would I last another ten years? I was fit, in good health, *compos mentis*. But as everyone else dropped off, it felt more and more like I was outstaying my welcome. Sometimes the loneliness was overpowering. Not just the immediate loneliness of living in a huge house on my own, loved ones far away, but a more abstract, galactic isolation, like a leaking boat bobbing in open water, no anchor or land in sight. I might sink, or just float further and further out, and I wasn't sure which was worse.

I was just wondering whether to telephone Angela and say I wasn't well enough to go out when there was a resounding knock on the door. As I walked into the hall I could hear Angela outside: 'Jesus, Otis, you'll break it down at this rate.' They were both on the doorstep, Otis dressed as the Incredible Hulk, with a witch's hat perched incongruously above his mask. Unable to see his face, I felt a stirring of delight. It might have been Arthur under there.

'Hello, Hulk,' I said, twitching his hat.

A voice mumbled out from the mask, 'I'm Bruce Banner.'

'Hello, Bruce.' I led them both into the kitchen, wondering if there were biscuits in the bread bin.

'Sorry we've door-stepped you,' said Angela, hustling him in. The mark on her cheek had faded to a mottled blue. 'He was up at five-thirty and I've been going insane. Ooooh, Otis, say thank you!' she added, as I handed him a slightly stale digestive.

'Would you like a cup of tea?'

'No thanks, I'll get my fix in the park.'

I put on my coat, checking the pockets for the car, and we set off together in the winter sunshine. Otis shambled along kicking leaves and occasionally hoiking up his costume as his mother launched into a rant about the government. I noticed Otis's Hulk feet were trailing, picking up debris. We should roll them up for him in the playground. As Angela's voice reached a higher pitch, I pretended Otis was Arthur, though they were quite different, really. My grandson had a rather forceful personality whereas Otis seemed more pensive. But they both had the droll, quintessential charm of little boys.

'Anyway, it'll be fine,' concluded Angela, having got whatever it was off her chest. By then we'd arrived at the arboreal avenue that led up to the café, the few leaves that still clung to the branches bristling as the gentlest of castanets. The air was crisp and there was a pleasing freshness to the day, as if everything were newly minted.

Angela nodded towards the lakes. 'I heard a rumour that the fish all died. The shock was too much for them.'

'The electric shock?'

'No, the shock of being in a different pond.'

She went off to get her coffee while I stood with the little one watching the park's resident goats stump around their enclosure. After a minute or two of silence he said, 'Goats have rectangles in their eyes.'

I looked over at the impassive mask, two dark circles regarding me solemnly from within.

'Do they? I didn't know that.'

'Yes.' He pulled me towards the fence. 'Look!' As the darker goat passed us and snuffled its nose against the wire, he pointed at one rolling eye. Bending and peering, I saw that the pupil was rectangular-shaped, like a horizontal slit. It looked rather alarming.

'How extraordinary,' I said, squeezing his hand. 'Why is that, do you think?'

'That mean,' – he had such a quaint way of speaking – 'that mean he gets hunted. The hunted animals have square eyes. The ones who hunt them are round.'

'Our eyes are round,' I noted.

'Yes,' he agreed. 'That mean we are the hunters.' He scampered off towards Angela, who was approaching with a steaming paper cup, puffing away on a cigarette.

'You go on ahead, I've got to get this smoked before I can go in. Fucking shirty mums,' she grunted.

At this time of day the playground was sparsely populated, just a few mothers chatting as their children scuttled around. Otis immediately climbed onto the trampoline, tripping over his Hulk feet and sending the witch's hat askew. By the time Angela rejoined us I was holding the costume and Otis was jumping in his normal clothes, holding Arthur's car.

Angela stood next to me, shivering in her leather jacket. 'God, this is awful, isn't it? Half the time I'm panicking he's going to break something or get snatched by a paedophile, and the other half I'm going out of my mind with boredom. I could do with a drink, they should put a bar here or something.'

I thought it was perfectly pleasant to watch the children

playing and enjoy the fresh air, but Angela was already furiously jabbing at her phone. She would periodically dash out of the playground to greet people she knew, though she seemed more interested in their dogs. Frankly, she didn't watch Otis as well as she should have, but I suppose that was the point of inviting me. An extra pair of hunter eyes.

Every time she returned there was a new tirade. The park wardens were jobsworths, the cyclists went too fast, the joggers were wankers and whoever poisoned the pond and the fish deserved to drink their own toxic water. She held forth on a number of subjects, another cigarette perched between two fingers, despite the disapproving looks, as Otis ditched the climbing frames in favour of chasing pigeons and digging rice cakes out of his mother's bag. I hadn't warmed to Angela particularly, but true to her profession she was something of a raconteur, and I began to enjoy the stream of invective, storing tidbits of gossip for Alistair. A famous news correspondent had had his morning jog interrupted by a Cockapoo and had started a furious row with its owner: 'like he thinks his pissy little run is as important as Syria.' A Red Setter had got into the playground and his subsequent rampage had parents up in arms: 'they should shut the fucking gates then, shouldn't they?' A Retriever had run off with an old lady's wig: 'She was livid but it wasn't the bloody dog's fault, was it? It was his tosspot of an owner; too busy chatting up some tart with a Chihuahua.'

She paused for breath. 'Otis, not over there!' she bellowed. 'Tramps piss there and stuff.' She turned back to me. 'Listen, talking of dogs . . . I need to ask you about my friend. The one you saw the other day. She's in a bit of a mess and I've got this idea . . .'

'Angela, darling, why aren't you wearing a proper coat?' We turned to see Sylvie ambling towards us, eyes crinkling at the corners as she picked her way through scurrying children.

'I feel quite the adventurer in here, with no little people. Millicent! No – Missy! How lovely. I came to invite you all to lunch. I've just bought some Le Creuset and want to show it off.'

'All right,' said Angela. 'We'd better go now though. You left the gate open and Decca and Nancy have got in.'

'Heavens.' Sylvie swivelled round and saw her dogs frantically digging in the sandpit, showering nearby children, who shrieked with laughter and flung sand in each other's faces as their mothers bore down on us, fingers wagging.

'Oh, hell.' Angela grabbed a passing Otis by his sweater and pushed him towards the gates. 'Let's get out of here before one of them takes a shit on the seesaw.'

Lunch at Sylvie's; my crazy-old-lady fantasy made flesh . . . I wondered how to say no, but it seemed they just assumed I would be coming, so I picked up Arthur's discarded car and followed, feeling rather light-headed.

'Why did Sylvie call you Missy?' asked Angela, as Sylvie secured her dogs and, scattering apologies, we left the playground.

'Just a silly nickname,' I hedged, still embarrassed about it.

'It suits you,' she said, and I couldn't decide whether to be pleased or not.

Sylvie lived in an elegant Georgian house west of the park,

with a glossy wrought iron gate and an exquisite little parterre in the front garden. She led us up the flagged path, and turning back as she unlocked the front door, winked at me.

'My abode,' she said, and pushed it open.

We were immediately greeted by the smell of cinnamon, and a very grand black and white cat who weaved around our legs as we entered. The walls were papered in the same William Morris design that adorned my old college halls and I felt a sense of nostalgia as we made our way through to her kitchen and wandered amongst the artful clutter of crockery, copper pans and poinsettia, the room as homely and twinkling as Sylvie herself. Thinking of my own bare and antiquated space, I decided she must never see it.

We had the most delightful lunch, perched (in my case, rather precariously) on bar stools around the peninsula. Home-made hummus and plump olives, a quiche warm from the oven, tangy blue cheese, flatbreads dipped in a broad bean and feta concoction that was salty and moreish, all displayed on matching teal blue crockery. I'd never seen food as something to be fussed over, but there was something about Sylvie's unaffected pleasure in it all that was infectious, encouraging me to relish every mouthful. Otis lay on the sofa in the sitting room, draped in cat and dogs, hummus around his mouth as he watched CBeebies. Angela was reading *Country Living*, occasionally stabbing a page to complain about the size of people's houses, as Sylvie bustled about, arranging her smart new pots and dishes.

'How do you two know each other?' I asked, picking up an olive.

'I kidnapped her dog,' mumbled Angela, through a mouthful of bread.

Sylvie chortled. 'It's true. Four years ago. She stole Nancy from the park. I sent out a search party and found a dog walker who'd spotted her with a mad-looking Irish woman and a screaming baby. Then someone else pointed the way to Angie's garret. Found them both on the sofa eating Hobnobs and watching *Bargain Hunt*.'

'It was a mistake,' protested Angela. 'I thought she was a stray.' She reached down and fondled one of the dogs – I assumed it was Nancy, though still couldn't tell the difference. 'I *was* a bit mad, I'd just had Otis. Thought a dog would complete the family.'

As shadows lengthened on the walls, candles were lit, and – really too early – a bottle of red wine opened. I declined, but was pressured into a small glass. After that, to the accompaniment of Frank Sinatra, Angela became more raucous, knocking back her drink and fulminating again. Sylvie asked me lots of questions about myself, which was nice of her though I wouldn't bore her with any details. I did tell her a bit about Arthur and noticed her eyes flick towards Otis on the sofa.

Drifting off as I sipped my wine and admired the leaping flames in the fireplace, I found myself thinking of families and *oikos*, an important concept in ancient Greece. It's not an easy idea to describe as it can mean different things. A house or dwelling, but also the inhabitants. Home and hearth. The hearth part always interested me as I thought of *oikos* as a kind of rock – the rock upon which a family was built. But how big a family did one need to achieve it? I didn't perceive anything lacking in Sylvie, whereas my loneliness, my emptiness, was a balloon that bellied and dragged me away. But when the house had been full of my husband and children, I didn't notice, didn't appreciate my *oikos*. Or maybe I had never had it at all. Perhaps the threads of my life were always loose, always out of my control, just waiting to slip out of reach.

'Millicent. Missy,' barked Angela, rousing me. 'What are you thinking about? You were a million miles away.'

Only half a mile down the road, actually. The bottle was nearly empty and suddenly I felt I shouldn't be around for the second. I had somewhere I needed to be.

'I must be going,' Gripping the marble table top, I gingerly slipped off the stool. 'Thank you so much, it's been lovely.'

'I'll come round next week,' said Angela, picking up a corkscrew. 'I want to talk to you about my idea. And maybe you could take Otis to the park again?' She fixed her round eyes on me innocently.

Like I said, she wanted a babysitter. But when it came to that kind of thing, I was easy prey. I went through to the living room and mussed Otis's hair as he sleepily watched a Peter Rabbit cartoon.

Sylvie led me back down the hallway, switching on lamps as she went.

'You have a lovely house,' I said, picking up my purse.

'Thank you, sweetie,' responded Sylvie, helping me with my coat. 'Angie says yours is gorgeous too. Lovely to have a big house round here.'

Not if there was no one in it. 'You should come round,' I found myself saying. 'I wish it looked more like this.'

'Darling, I'm a designer – I live for that sort of thing.' She kissed me on the cheek and I could feel tears starting, so I ducked my head and walked quickly out the door, humming Sinatra to distract myself.

Out in the dusk, I hit rush hour; commuters, heads down like mine, braced against the chill, gunning for hearth and home. I walked slowly towards my destination, torn between hope and melancholy. I'd had a lovely day, but the warmth and cheer only served to highlight the dismal prospect of my lonely walk to an even lonelier place, trying to hold on to the threads of a previous life.

After my bleak pilgrimage to take flowers to the empty space that was once Leo, I headed home, trying to cheer myself up. Maybe Sylvie *would* come round. Maybe I *would* take Otis to the park. I let myself in and switched on the lights, wincing a little at the glare. Going through to the kitchen, I put the kettle on, opened my laptop, my state-of-the-art laptop given to me by my son the archaeologist, and logged into my email.

'Darling Ali,' I began.

Chapter 8

I was a virgin, of course. This was 1956 – what else could I be? An uptight nineteen-year-old, carefully reared in Kensington and Kirkheaton? I'd spent weeks hearing him traipse up and down my corridor on his way to Alicia's room, gramophone blaring, though not entirely drowning out the sound of that grating little giggle. Once I bumped into him en route to the bathroom in my robe, and nodded awkwardly, cheeks burning with the shame of rejection, though it had never even got to that stage. Thankfully, Alicia had the decency not to ask me to let him out through my window after their late-night shenanigans. But then that just went to show, didn't it, that *she* knew. I didn't drink with her any more, but found other ways to acquire alcohol.

Despite my social and seductive limitations, I was not entirely a loner. Dutifully doing the usual round of parties and gatherings, I acquired a few friends and was even asked to a play by a young man from St Catharine's. I put on my best green dress with a sweetheart neckline, my hair curled right for once, and cycled over to the ADC theatre to meet him. He was called Percy, but I wasn't sure if that was his first name or last. He met me outside the theatre and under the streetlamp I could tell he would go bald in later life. The play wasn't a play at all but a series of little skits, none of which I found very funny, though everyone else roared with laughter throughout.

After an excruciating drink in the café round the corner, Percy walked me home, which was unnecessary as I had my bicycle with me, so he pushed it while I hugged my wrap around myself and wished I'd worn something warmer. Outside the door to the porter's lodge he lunged, letting the bicycle fall to the ground in his enthusiasm. The feeling of that tongue forcing its way down my throat, his hands digging into my shoulders and ripping my dress, made me gag. He apologized afterwards. I think the experience upset him as much as me. So I apologized as well, and he picked up my bicycle like a gentleman. Then he left for his college, promising to call on me the following week, although we both knew he wouldn't.

Back in my room I cried a little and hung up my dress although it kept slipping off the hanger because of the tear. Then I got a bottle of sherry out of my desk and poured myself a glass, and another, and another, so that by the time Leo knocked on my door just after midnight, I was already well away.

'Can I come in? Sorry, I've had rather a bad night,' he leaned against the doorframe, blinking owlishly and waving a half-empty bottle of wine. I tightened the cord of my dressing gown, feeling thankful my hair was still done. Of course I let him in; I'd let him in the moment I first saw him across a crowded room.

We shared the rest of the bottle as Leo told me Alicia had finished with him, that she'd met someone else, a viscount from St John's. He was so stoic about it – 'obviously I can't compete, he's got a castle in Northumberland' – that when he kissed me, I didn't mind at all. He was so different from Percy or any of the other bumbling, self-absorbed boys I'd met. He just felt like my home.

So when he led me to that narrow, creaking bed I didn't resist, and in fact it was I who pulled him down on top of me, to feel the weight of him, mooring me. Then there was the moment he looked into my eyes and said, 'shall I?' and I nodded, fiercely, because right at that moment there was no fork in the road, no other option open to me but to pursue him, us. Afterwards, we lay together in the embers, every bit entwined, him ringleting my hair on one of his fingers, and I felt replete, complete. My song, answered.

But later, when the dawn light pierced the thin curtains, I saw the blood on the sheets, felt the pounding in my head and heart, and realized what a mess I'd made of it all. Why couldn't I be as sophisticated and experienced and elusive as Alicia and all the other girls who twirled around Cambridge as though they owned it?

While Leo slept, I sneaked out of bed to clean myself up and put on some make-up. Luckily the curls were intact. By the time he woke I was back, looking fairly decent and in control of myself despite a throbbing head. Smiling brightly, I chatted as he hastily put on his clothes. He was obviously desperate to leave and it didn't matter at all; everything was absolutely fine.

Closing the door on him, still smiling, smiling, as he assured me he'd call on me the following week, then slumping down the wall, silent tears taking the breath out of me as I thought about the blood on the sheets and the ripped dress. Jette's purse and Fa-Fa's shattered glasses – broken, ruined things that couldn't be repaired.

After a while, I picked myself up and went to my desk, opening my Latin lexicon to prepare for my supervision. *Luó; Gr λύω – to loose, untie, release, destroy.* The message couldn't have been clearer. Leo, *Luó.* I'd let go, when I should have hung on. But then, even then, I had a tiny shred of optimism, a hope against hope that he *might* call. He might.

Leo graduated and left Cambridge that summer, and it was two years before I saw him again.

Chapter 9

I was so cheered by my lunch at Sylvie's that the comfort of it carried me through the next few days, remembering the warmth of her kitchen, the camaraderie of perching on those stools together. Maybe I wasn't the social pariah I'd imagined; perhaps it would be possible to build up a small circle of friends to insulate me against the loss of Leo, and of Ali and Arthur.

Continuing my explorations, I ventured into independent shops, dropped in to the library, and visited a little redbrick church around the corner from my café. I've never been much of a church-goer – religion was an irrelevance in our family, any reference met with baffled stares. Even my Aunt Sibby, who married a vicar, rarely mentioned it. But I lit a candle for Leo all the same, and thought of whatever twilight world he was in, whether he was happy, if he remembered me at all.

So taken up with my wanderings, it was over a week before I realized Angela hadn't visited. Despite not even liking her that much, it was disappointing, as I wanted to see Otis again. As the days went by with no further contact, I became despondent. Perhaps I'd said something at the lunch that she objected to? She was very left-wing. Or perhaps it was something I *hadn't* said? I had no witty anecdotes, knew none of the mutual acquaintances they'd discussed, and most of all I was so old, so jaundiced – who would want to be friends with me? She didn't need to like me to let me babysit her son. But maybe she thought I wasn't even up to that.

Once again I retreated into my cavernous house, drifting around in my nightie, unearthing old albums and wallowing in them for hours. Me, in my gown in the gardens of Newnham after my graduation, my mother's arm around me, proud and exultant. I looked shell-shocked. We were standing next to a little stone statue of a boy holding a dolphin. He looked like Arthur – naked, as my errant grandson often is.

Then a photograph of Leo and me on our wedding day, him grinning towards the camera, and me looking up at him, my veil partly obscuring my face. I gazed at that face, my younger self; those wide eyes, unwaveringly fixed on my prize, dark hair tumbling under the net, slim in borrowed silk, unlined but not unscarred, even then.

We were married in King's College chapel, and after the photo was taken by his friend Tristan, a fellow historian, Leo swept our guests off to The Anchor pub, where everyone got very merry. I barely sipped my wine, already drunk on the prospect of being married to this flaxen god who dwarfed everyone around him. Later, my mother took me to one side and said, 'Darling, are you sure?' as if anything could be done by then. It was all settled for me the moment I saw him in Falcon Yard. *Alea iacta est*.

I was twenty-one then, and by my twenty-second birthday was nesting in our little cottage off Jesus Green, pregnant with Melanie. I made a cake, still a luxury, and we ate it on the floor in front of the fire, because we couldn't afford a sofa. The one we eventually bought, after the advance on Leo's first book, was still in my living room today. And here I was, another birthday looming, but no one to spend it with.

What was this fear, this terror of being alone, when I was never a particularly gregarious being and in fact used to go out of my way to avoid social engagements? It always felt like too much of a chore to go to one dinner party or another, where I'd inevitably have to drink to relax, or worry about staying up late when I had to get up for the children. Leo was more of an extrovert, but he had his club, his golf and his books, and was mostly oblivious to the invitations I declined on his behalf. Was there another reason I said no? The more people – the more *women* – he met, the more likely he would realize what was lacking at home. I bound him to me, but was always fearful he would loosen the ties.

When Alistair was born, in Leo's image, I thought perhaps the completion of our family and our new home – the *oikos* – might secure him, and me. But for years after, I was so tired. The dreary call of childcare wore me down, and the threads started to fray. While I struggled, he soared off – Dr Leonard Carmichael, respected historian, lauded biographer, lecturer;

jetting around the world, speaking on the radio, writing for the papers. When we were out, I felt he was always looking over my shoulder for the other person he knew, just like when we met.

I don't know why I'd allowed myself to become so maudlin. The wine, probably. Two glasses, which sounded better than half a bottle. We *had* loved each other. He didn't go in for passionate declarations, but we knew we were each other's home – knew it in the way he always set my teacup on the table the night before, ready for morning; knew it in the tender Latin poems and quotes he left around the house for me to translate; the way he called me Missy just like Fa-Fa had, and was the only one who knew *why* he was doing it. He didn't need to say it. He really didn't. Love begets love, and I had so much that there was enough to reflect back.

But now there was only the echo of it in this ramshackle old house that lacked clutter, and light, and youth, and laughter. Draining my glass and closing the album on my obscured face, I went up to bed, leaving the curtains open and watching the streetlight cast shadows on the walls until I fell into an uneasy sleep.

The next morning, my dreaded birthday, I tried to pull myself together. I'd go to the shops, buy the ingredients for a cake. Just a basic sponge to mark the occasion. Maybe I'd bump into someone on the way and could casually throw it into conversation. Just after ten, the post arrived. I ignored the bills, eagerly sifting through the junk mail to see if there was a card from

Alistair. Maybe it would arrive tomorrow. It was so difficult to judge post times from Australia – the last birthday card I sent him arrived a week early. There was a Cambridge postcard from Mel, a terse scrawled greeting, which was more than I deserved after what happened last year.

There was the merest hint of spring in the air as I made my way to the shops on the high street. I bought the necessary ingredients, then decided to treat myself to a coffee. Hanna smiled at me and said, 'for you is free today.' For a moment I thought somehow she knew, but realized she was looking at my card, which had eight stamps. I went to my usual table and sat down, on the lookout for Sylvie, or anyone vaguely familiar. I sat there for an hour, then walked up and down the road a few times without encountering anyone but heedless strangers.

Accepting defeat, I walked home with my shopping, and after lunch set about making my cake; assembling the ingredients in a haphazard way as I'd never been much of a cook, and after all it would only be me eating it. No possibility that Angela might pop round and I could offer Otis a slice. It turned out burnt around the edges as the temperature of the Aga was difficult to gauge, but I cut myself a piece and ate it with my afternoon tea, and it was perfectly agreeable. After I'd tidied up the kitchen, I picked up one of Mel's Nancy Mitfords and read for a while until it grew too dark. I was just going round switching lights on when there was an almighty racket at the door.

Angela stood swaying in the doorway, evidently drunk. As she pushed past me, I realized she was holding a lead, tugging along a dog. It followed her into the house and when we reached the living room, it sat in front of the fireplace, panting slightly. I was nonetheless pleased at the intrusion.

'Have you kidnapped him as well?' She didn't smile, but instead pushed lank hair back from her forehead and pinched the bridge of her nose.

'No. Well, yes, sort of. This is Bob. She's been staying with me for a few days.'

'She?'

'Yes, she.'

'Bob isn't a girl's name.'

Angela shrugged. 'It's something to do with *Blackadder*. Bob is a girl, disguised as a boy. Have you seen it?'

'No.' Mel was a fan, and she'd once made Leo watch an episode with her. The sight of them guffawing together had left me with a vague feeling of isolation, and chagrin. I never laughed that way with Melanie.

'Well, you should. Anyway, that's not the point. I need you to do me a massive favour and look after Bob for a bit.'

'What on earth are you talking about? I don't want a dog.' I looked at Bob, still sitting by the fireplace. She was a mongrel, coloured like an Alsatian but smaller, like a Collie. Not unattractive, as dogs go, but I've never been keen on them. Too dim and needy.

'I tried to talk to you about it the other day. My friend Fix – Felicity – is having a bit of trouble at the moment and has to go away, but she needs someone to look after her dog.'

'Can't it go to a kennel?'

Angela sighed. 'No. Bob needs looking after for a few months, maybe a bit longer, I'm not sure—'

'A few *months*?' I gripped the back of Leo's armchair.

'Like I said, she's got some problems right now.'

'Then she should find Bob a new permanent home.'

'You don't understand!' Angela shot out, sitting down on the sofa uninvited. 'She loves Bob, she doesn't want to give her away, but she has to. She's leaving her husband.'

'Well, can't the husband take her?'

'No. He's . . . not good news. That's why she's leaving. She's got children. They need to get away. She needs to get herself sorted out. But she can't take the dog. For now. So I thought . . .' She tailed off and looked at me expectantly.

'I'm very sorry for your friend, but I couldn't possibly look after her dog.'

'Why not?'

'What?'

'Why couldn't you look after a dog?' she demanded. 'You've got a big house, a garden, you're always walking in the park. What's more, you're *lonely*. Sylvie saw it straight away. We think a dog could be just what you need.'

'How dare you?' I couldn't bear that they had discussed me, the sad lonely old lady; a charity case for them to take on. Was my need so obvious? How pathetic they must think me, wandering round the park hoping to bump into someone. The gush of embarrassment and shame hit, flooding my face, and I looked down at the floor to hide my scarlet cheeks.

But Angela pressed on, oblivious. 'I could help you walk her.

Otis loves dogs, he could come round and visit. And it's only 'til Fix is on her feet again. Please. *Please.*'

I'd so hoped someone would visit me today and bring me something, but this was not what I'd imagined. Today of all days, barging into my house to insult me and suggest that the answer to my troubles was some homeless mutt? I kept my eyes down, unsure if it was anger or humiliation causing them to brim.

'Why can't you take her, if you're so desperate? You love dogs, Otis loves dogs.'

Angela sighed. 'Because my landlord won't let me. I already asked him. I ask him every time I renew my contract. He won't budge. But I'll help, I promise. I could buy the dog food, I could pay the vet's bills, whatever you want.'

I bit my lip, and with an effort met her gaze. 'I'm sorry but the answer's no. I don't want a dog.'

Bob gave a huge yawn, trotted over to Angela, bounded onto the sofa and curled up alongside her, whereupon she serenely proceeded to lick her own genitals.

Angela gave a tearful laugh. 'There's dogs for you, always inappropriate, just like me. I'm sorry, it was a stupid idea.' She clipped Bob back onto the lead and heaved her off the sofa.

'What will you do?' I asked, as I led her back to the front door. I'd absolved myself of responsibility, but not of guilt, which was now beginning to chafe.

'I don't know. Ask around the park, I suppose, maybe someone can take her. If not then it'll have to be the dog's home.' She leant forward and kissed Bob on the snout. 'She can stay with me for a few more days at least. My wanker of a landlord won't know.'

Angela went out into the darkness, Bob at her clinking heels, and I closed the door and turned back to my empty, echoing house to finish my special day.

I spent what was left of the evening polishing off the rest of a bottle of wine. What would I want with a dog, for goodness' sake? I didn't like them, was far too old, there was no sense in getting involved in a domestic drama like that. No sense at all. Dogs were smelly, stupid creatures, always bounding off to sniff disgusting things. There was literally nothing to recommend them. I remembered Angela and Sylvie's brutal analysis: *lonely*. A sad, pathetic, old woman, who should be grateful for a mangy old mutt's company. How utterly mortifying. I drained my glass and smacked it down on the kitchen table, then moved it to wipe away the sticky rings. Lonely. I swabbed feverishly until it was clear.

Later, I went around the house turning off lights and checking doors, still thinking about this Fix, and her children. I wondered where they were, what exactly the husband had done, whether they were missing Bob. Arthur wanted a dog. He often talked about it, and Alistair always said, 'next year.' Quite right, a dog was a huge responsibility, not to be taken lightly.

We had a dog once, when I was very tiny. A black Labrador called Jonas. My mother adored him and would hoot when Henry dressed him up. One of my earliest memories was of us putting her wedding veil on him and her laughing. He just sat there and let it happen. When the war began he had to be put down. I didn't know that until much later, but vaguely recall my mother sobbing as he was taken away. He wouldn't have known a thing, of course – just let it happen like he did with the veil. I was too young to be upset, but I remember my mother's stricken face for months afterwards. She once told me that she never got over it, that the death of her own father wasn't as bad as that day.

'It's for the best,' I said to myself firmly as I looked in the cupboards and under the bed. And then, once I was in it, hunched against the cold, into the darkness and silence: 'Happy birthday, Missy.'

Chapter 10

That night I dreamt about Jonas, this time an unwilling lamb to slaughter. He was bundled into a van, scrabbling and howling for my mother, her screams mingling with his barks, then an incessant scratching as his claws scraped against the door. I had to get him out. Pounding against it, my hands a bloody mess as I slapped and thumped. And then giving up, sliding down it, my back to the cold metal as I listened to Jonas on the inside, still scrabbling. Scratch, scratch. Scratch, scratch. Then a click and a thud. And then I was awake and my house was being burgled.

The noises took a while to process, in the haze of sleep and residue from the dream. It was hard to work out what was real, and even harder to acknowledge it. The quiet scraping, the dull thumps and fumbles; every sound made my whole body throb with horror. What could I do but let it happen? A defenceless seventy-eight – no, seventy-*nine*-year-old woman, alone in a huge house at two o'clock in the morning? I lay there, bound to the bed in my terror, listening to them moving quietly through the rooms downstairs, then started praying to a God I didn't believe in that they wouldn't come up. What would I do if they did? I had to let them get on with it, because the alternative was unthinkable.

I heard them creeping up the stairs – there were at least two of them – and closed my eyes tightly, grateful that the curtains were closed so it was too dark for them to see my uneven breathing. When they came into my room I stayed very still, not moving even when the flashlight played across my face. I worried they would be able to hear my heart pounding, but they didn't really care if I was asleep or not – I wasn't going to stop them. They went over to my dressing table and rifled through my jewellery box. Things Leo bought me, mementos my mother left me. Her pearls. The Regard ring Leo bought me after Mel was born. The ruby earrings he gave me for our fortieth wedding anniversary. Not the what, but the who and the why.

Concentrating so hard on lying still, at first I didn't notice one of them had moved nearer and was standing by the bed looking down. I couldn't see him of course, but I could hear him, feel his gaze. Still as I was, I stiffened, barely able to breathe, and then . . . the rustle of fabric as he reached out. I could sense his hand hovering above my hair, almost touching but not quite. That I, who so craved the comfort of human contact – a friend's embrace, a child's hand – should endure this. I lay like a corpse, so revolted that bile rose in my throat, but his companion suddenly hissed, the hand was withdrawn and he moved away.

Then they went out again, and very slowly and carefully I breathed a sigh of relief, because it could have been so much worse.

They left rather less quietly than they came in, because the job was done by then. I couldn't face going down to inspect the damage, so waited until my tears had subsided and then got up and opened the curtains, letting the streetlight in so that I could watch the shadows on the wall. When dawn came, I went down to the kitchen and saw that my new laptop had gone, and cried again, because it had all my photos of Arthur on it.

When the police came, they'd said they'd probably picked the lock on the back door, that they were good at that sort of thing nowadays, as if it was a skill people learned in school. They said not to worry, that they probably wouldn't come back now the house had been 'done', but to change the locks and consider some additional security measures. So I got out the emergency locksmith although I couldn't afford it, and he put on some extra bolts and recommended an alarm system. But the price he quoted was so extortionate that I balked, and hustled him out of the door. No men in my house, not now.

I stayed in my kitchen for the rest of the afternoon, drumming my fingers on the table to drown out the silence (they'd taken the radio). I thought about Leo, and Percy the lunger, and Fix's husband, and the burglar's hand . . . As a girl, I'd always thought of men as the protectors – Fa-Fa in particular the mammoth gatekeeper of our family – but at Cambridge I realized that they had little comprehension of the damage they could cause. I supposed guardians were by their nature ruthless, in some respects. *A monster not to be overcome . . . Cerberus who eats raw flesh, the brazen-voiced hound of Hades . . .*

As the light started to fade again I couldn't take it any more, couldn't think any more, so I put on my coat and let myself out, marching briskly down the road to the big house Angela had pointed out to me. Peering at the many doorbells, I squinted until I saw '7C. A. Brennan' and pressed it firmly. After a little while I heard a familiar voice, harsh with cigarette smoke. 'It's me. Missy,' I said. The door buzzed, and I went up, catching my breath on each landing.

Angela greeted me at her door, eyebrows raised. Otis poked his head out from behind her, followed by Bob on the other side. She wagged her tail in greeting.

'I'll take the dog,' I said. 'Just until your friend sorts herself out.'

For a second Angela was impassive, and then her face broke into an ear-splitting grin, the tiredness and worry wiped away. She leapt forwards and hugged me, too hard. But I found I didn't mind.

'You won't regret it,' she promised. 'She's the best dog.'

'I'm sorry about yesterday. It was my birthday. I was a bit depressed.' I felt shamed by both admissions, and looked away before Angela could spot the tears in my eyes, bending to scratch Bob awkwardly on the ear. She panted and nudged me for more.

Angela clapped a hand to her mouth. 'I'm so sorry! Honest, I really am, I had no idea. God, what a stupid cow, barging in like that.'

'It's all right,' I said, pinning my smile in place and straightening up again. 'I suppose you brought me a present, in a way.'

She laughed. 'Fancy a drink to celebrate?'

She led me into her flat, and as I bent again to pat both Bob and Otis, I could already hear the sound of a cork popping. Angela reappeared, holding two very large glasses. At least half a bottle in there.

'Happy birthday, Missy,' she said.

Chapter 11

With Otis passed out on the sofa, we drank Prosecco and ate leftover macaroni cheese warmed up in the microwave. Her flat was tiny – a living room with a kitchenette at one end, a minuscule bathroom off the rabbit hutch hallway and a bedroom with twin beds pushed together – one for her and one for Otis. I was a little shocked, but she assured me this was pretty good for London. As we ate the pasta, she told me about her friend Felicity and her dreadful husband.

'She met him through work – she's a journalist like me, but much more principled. Writes about climate change, saving the whales, that sort of thing. She was interviewing a local businessman about some campaign that was going on, something about cutting down trees. He asked her out, and you know. Six months later they're married and she's up the duff.'

Angela scraped a spoonful of cheese sauce out of the serving bowl and continued. 'He changed after they were married. Started slowly, just comments about her appearance and stuff. She was skin and bone by the time he started hitting her. He's really careful and you'd never suspect a thing talking to him – very plausible. But I've seen the bruises.'

'Why didn't she get out sooner?'

'The children, I suppose. Though you'd think they'd be a reason to leave. But mostly because she had nowhere to go. He threatens her, says she'll lose the kids – and she believes him because she's had years of him grinding her down. She hasn't worked in ages, she's got no money. But I've been trying to persuade her for months, and last week she finally agreed, but only after he nearly put her in hospital. Bastard.'

I took a gulp of wine. 'Where are they now?' I asked, not sure I wanted to know.

'In a women's refuge. We're trying to get her to press charges. But at least she's out. And, thanks to you, once she's sorted herself out she can have Bob back and get on with her life. She really loves that dog.' She reached down and scratched Bob, who was waiting for scraps. Angela told me I wasn't to feed her anything from the table as that encouraged begging. She had to be walked twice a day, fed twice a day and brushed regularly to stop her fur matting. Then there was worming, and anti-tick treatment, and teeth cleaning and Lord knows what else. I was regretting my decision again but then thought of Felicity's bruises, and my back door, and resolved to make the best of it.

As I gathered my things and put on my coat, Bob perked up and started prancing around excitedly. Her sudden enthusiasm was irritating.

'See, she wants to go with you,' observed Angela from the

sofa, where she was finishing her wine and stroking a sleeping Otis.

'Well, I'm not taking her on a walk or anything, only back to my house,' I said, clipping on her lead.

'She might need a wee on the way,' warned Angela. 'Oh, that reminds me.' She jumped up and went over to her poky kitchenette, rummaging in a drawer before triumphantly producing a package, which she handed over to me. 'Poo bags! You'll need a lot of those.'

This, as far as I was concerned, was the most appalling aspect of owning a dog. I couldn't imagine how I was going to cope with it, but took the package and put it in my coat pocket.

'Well. I should be going. Um, thank you,' I said, rather stiffly, when I'd got to the door.

Angela came over to me and put her hand on my shoulder. 'No. Thank *you*. You've done a great thing. I promise you'll end up enjoying it. There are loads of dog walkers in the park, a whole pack of them, and they're great fun. I'll introduce you.'

Gingerly holding Bob's lead as we walked home, I flicked through my little Rolodex of worries – what if the animal bolted? Would I be yanked off my feet? How would I stop her? Then the bewildering list of food that was toxic to dogs and must be kept away from her – chocolate, grapes, onions – what else? Toxic like the lake in the park. Recalling Angela's promise, I wasn't at all sure I wanted to mix with the dog walkers there, lonely as I was. I'd seen them, and they'd seemed a tad eccentric, always getting into fights with cyclists, and parents, and pretty much anyone who didn't appreciate their pets as much as they did. But I'd done it now, so we'd have to get on with it. Hopefully Bob would be cheaper than an alarm system. Maybe even better company.

We arrived back and I unlocked the door, listening out for intruders as we went in. Bob immediately started sniffing around the house, tail wagging, scoping it out. I went through to the kitchen and made myself some tea, then took it to the living room where I found her curled on the sofa. Angela said she'd never been allowed on furniture and I certainly had no intention of letting her adopt any bad habits.

'Off!' I said sternly, holding one finger in the air and feeling like Barbara Woodhouse. Bob stared at me and scratched behind one ear with her back leg.

She probably had fleas. I went over to the sofa and pushed her. She resisted for a second, then tipped off in a sudden flurry of limbs. Scrabbling to regain her balance and dignity, she retreated to a position by Leo's armchair and eyed me warily. She should have somewhere to lie down, at least. I looked around the room but there were no rugs of any kind, so I sacrificed my sofa throw, arranging it in a bed-shape on the floor near the fireplace. She stepped on to it, turning round and round before settling down with an inordinate sigh. It was a shame there was no fire in the grate, maybe I'd make one up tomorrow.

Picking up Mel's book, I read for a while, occasionally looking up to check on Bob, who was sprawled in a running position, snoring, nose and legs twitching furiously. It was strangely soporific, and gradually the book slid onto my lap as I dozed.

Awoken by a loud and prolonged yawn from the fireplace, I looked at my watch and saw it was after midnight. Bob was watching me, head on one side. She yawned again.

Creaking to my feet, I shuffled to the door, turning back to look at her on her makeshift bed.

'Well. Goodnight then. Stay.' Bob's tail thumped the floor.

I pulled myself upstairs to get ready for my own bed, but just as I was preparing to switch off the lights there was the scrabble of claws and a second later, her face appeared at the door.

This was not part of the plan at all. She had to be on the ground floor, deterring intruders, not lounging around in my bedroom. 'No!' I said firmly, leading her back downstairs. She followed me, tail wagging, then sat expectantly in the living room as I wondered what to do. In the end I dragged a couple of chairs from the dining room and made a barricade at the bottom of the stairs. Maybe I could buy one of those gates people got for toddlers. More expense.

I went back up to my room, and closed the door, listening out for her whining or scratching, but heard nothing. Angela had said she was a very good dog. One just had to be firm. I went to sleep thinking about where we would walk the next morning, and if we might meet Otis. He could throw a stick for her, and she could wait outside the playground while we played on the swings.

I slept deeply, and in the morning when I awoke, two things struck me at once. One: Bob was curled at the end of my bed, snoring loudly, hairs all over the covers, the door to my bedroom still closed. And two: for the first time in my life, ever since

Fa-Fa told us the story about the ripper who sang nursery rhymes from the wardrobe before he cut up his victims, I hadn't checked the cupboards before I went to sleep.

Cave canem. Beware the dog.

PART 2

Chapter 12

I t was the summer of 1958 and I was looking up at the roof of the Senate House and musing how they had got the car up there. A peculiarly Cantabrigian student stunt. It was gone by then, of course, but it took nearly a week, and in the end they had to hack it to pieces to get rid of it. It was a shame, really – I liked it perched on the apex, its incongruity somehow reassuring. Anything was possible.

I was a lofty graduate, working as an archivist in the University's Classical Faculty Library and wondering what to do next. Unlike my contemporaries, I wasn't being pressured by my family to get married now I had a degree. Henry was busy trying to break into politics, and Mama was as likely to tell me to find a husband as she was to suggest I get a tiger as a pet. As a young girl, my mother – then known as Lena Schorel – had sneaked out to hear Sylvia Pankhurst speak, and was very put out when the First World War began, because it cut short her fledgling career as a suffragist. She had also been rather disappointed when women finally got the vote, because she so enjoyed fighting the good fight.

Neither my brother nor my mother were at all interested in my marital state, and with no other family to speak of, I was left to my own devices. Perhaps my father would have had a say in the matter, but William Jameson was one of the casualties of the Second World War, and we rarely spoke of him, because the loss felt like too sharp a thing to touch. Fa-Fa had died just after the war ended, marching out one morning to buy tobacco and dropping like a stone in the street. He'd have liked that – nice and clean, no messing about. Jette had retreated even further into her shell after he died, and when she quietly passed away just after I went up to Cambridge, it was barely remarked upon. Maybe by that time we'd become inured to death. Aunt Sibby only cared about her animals, so my mother took over the house in Lancaster Villas, which became a kind of campaign base for various activists. If I'd gone back there, no doubt I'd be dragooned into joining one of her causes.

But what *did* I want to do? I wasn't sure, walking down King's Parade that evening in August, clutching a pile of books to my chest and mulling it over. Then I saw Leo Carmichael walking towards me, his golden hair fiery in the sun, and remembered he was all I ever wanted. For a second, the flood of memories nearly floored me and I swayed, dizzy with it. Whispering to my mother in the drawing room; the cold and bright light; prone in bed, staring at the ceiling, ignoring the stale sandwiches. He could not know, he could never know, how much this meant. I hugged the books tighter, preparing to look unconcerned and uninterested. As he approached, for a second I thought he didn't recognize me, but then his face cleared and he smiled with what looked like genuine pleasure.

'Milly!' he said, grabbing my hand and pumping it enthusiastically. Of course I dropped my books, and we spent the next minute scrabbling round for them on the pavement. By the time they were back in my arms, my hair was mussed and I was breathless with effort and embarrassment.

'Would you like a drink?' he asked, indicating towards the river.

I shouldn't appear too keen – let him think I have other engagements, interesting parties and interested parties.

'Yes, please.'

He took my books and we walked together towards The Anchor, a favourite haunt among students. As we approached the River Cam, I was painfully, ecstatically, aware of everything in that moment – the little toe-pinch in my right shoe, the bead of sweat on the back of my neck, my books tucked under that big arm of his as he strolled along, my still-uneven breathing. I looked towards Queens' at the punters carefully wielding their poles under the Mathematical Bridge. There was a myth that it was designed by Sir Isaac Newton, and originally built without any kind of connection at the joints. The story went that a group of students took the bridge apart, and were unable to put it together again, thus it had to be re-built with the current nuts and bolts. It wasn't true, of course, but I liked the idea anyway. I needed to build mine and Leo's relationship with a few nuts and bolts to make it secure. And above all, he must never know just how much water was under that bridge.

That summer, with a supreme effort of self-control, I channelled my natural repression and presented myself as elusive, chaste, to be chased. When we went for a drink, I left early, telling him there was a rumour some students had towed a Spitfire into Trinity Great Court. When he invited me to see *A Tale of Two Cities* at the cinema, I told him I didn't admire Dirk Bogarde. When he asked me to attend a Leavis lecture with him, I went, but made sure to bump into several acquaintances en route that I absolutely had to speak to. I kept him waiting.

Why was all that obfuscation so necessary? I felt instinctively that Leo, so straightforward himself, did not admire that quality in others. He liked guile, caprice, uncertainty. He liked a slippery fish. So that's what I was. Just before Christmas, he proposed, leaving a ring in my copy of the *Odyssey*, with a little note about my face launching a thousand ships, though I always felt less Helen, more Trojan horse. He lounged in the doorway watching me open the book, with a lopsided grin and a bottle of champagne. 'How about it?' he said, proffering the bottle, while I worked hard not to cry. We were married on a dry, chilly day in January – I was already pregnant in the photo Tristan took of us outside King's College Chapel, although I didn't know it. *Alea iacta est.*

And the problem with all of this? The flaw in my plan? Having got the ring on my finger, the baby in my belly and the little house on Jesus Green . . . when was I finally going to be able to relax, take out the bolts and see if it would hold?

Never. Having held him fast, I couldn't let go; I had to hang on.

Chapter 13

Walking Bob to the park the next morning, I felt awkward and self-conscious, as though I were an imposter. The dog seemed incongruous, trotting at my heels, and I worried that passers-by might see us and think I'd stolen her, or simply that we looked ridiculous together, like a goaty old man and his nubile girlfriend.

She was such a buoyant, unaffected presence, grinning up at me, constantly weaving off to sniff lampposts, urinate on leaves, or scratch herself at inconvenient moments. People are supposed to look like their dogs, and I imagined a dog of mine would be some sort of wolfhound – tall, grey and diffident. Not this perky, prancing thing, with her autumnal colours and sideways wink. She was the kind of dog Alicia Stewart would have had. Alicia, Leo's sparkling, vivacious first love, who capered through life expecting everyone to make way for her.

Nevertheless, we made it to the park and dutifully began a circuit, remembering Angela's lecture on the importance of exercise. The air was warmer now, with daffodils forcing their way through the cold dried mud of early spring. Looking up, I could see the delicate eruption of blossom – a brief but beautiful stage of the season. In Japan, the sakura – the cherry blossom – represents the transience of life, and they have festivals dedicated to watching it bloom; the bud is fragile and short-lived and thus one must come to terms with the inevitability of one's death. How odd, though, to sit under a tree and actively contemplate one's own demise.

My ruminations were interrupted by Bob, whining and pulling at her lead, dragging me in different directions. As we made our jagged progress around the park, we encountered another dog walker heading in the opposite direction. I didn't like the look of him or his dogs, so discreetly gave them a wide berth. They were boxers; not a breed I've ever admired (if indeed I've admired any), and their owner looked something of a pugilist himself – shaven-headed, with a bulbous nose, army jacket collar pulled up around his face, cigarette smoke in a cloud around him. But of course, Bob, in her contrary way, developed an unaccountable fancy for his dogs, tugging me over and cavorting, rolling over on her back in supplication. I pulled on her lead irritably, 'Come on!'

'She wants off.'

'I'm sorry?' I couldn't see his mouth move for collar and cigarette. Typical, on my first dog-walking day, to encounter some thuggish stranger and be drawn into conversation.

'She wants off. The lead.' He took the cigarette out of his mouth with black-nail-tipped sausage fingers, and pointed it at

Bob. 'She wants to play.' He had a thick accent – Newcastle, or somewhere up there.

I looked at Bob, still capering and yapping. 'She might run away.'

'She won't,' he put the cigarette back in. 'And if she does, she'll come back.'

Reluctantly, I unhooked Bob's lead, whereupon she immediately went into an orgy of romping with the boxers. There was much baring of teeth, but they all seemed to be enjoying themselves, and at least she was getting some exercise.

Enjoying the spectacle, my companion sucked away on his cigarette, then turned to me.

'What's her name?'

'Er, Bob,' I replied. It seemed we were expected to make polite small talk, in a tame mimicry of our dogs' interaction. 'Yours?'

'That there's Badger, and that there's Barker,' he pointed, though as with Sylvie's dogs, I had no idea how he could tell the difference. 'Bob's a boy's name,' he continued, tapping his ash on the lid of a nearby bin.

'It's from *Blackadder*,' I hazarded, hoping there would be no need to elaborate.

He frowned for a second, then chuckled. 'Aye. Good name for a dog.' I felt briefly gratified, as though it were my own achievement.

The dogs paused for breath and seizing this as my cue, I moved forwards to put Bob back on her lead, saying 'well, it's been nice to meet you . . .' But the words died on my lips as Bob chose that moment to lift herself inelegantly onto her haunches and answer the call of nature. This was the moment I'd been dreading, and now I was going to have to deal with it with him there, watching me scrabbling in the mud.

Fumbling for the poo bags, I fished out of my pocket, took a deep breath and bent to do the deed. The smell was asphyxiating, steaming slightly in the spring chill. How did one use the bag? Could I slide it along the ground and flick in the mess with a stick? Dithering, I accidentally inhaled and immediately retched. This was horrifying. I would have to take Bob back to Angela's; she'd have to go to the dog's home. I would go back to checking the cupboards. Maybe I could save up for the alarm system. The bag fell from my shaking hands to the ground.

'Want some help?' He crouched down beside me, picking up the flimsy sack and putting it over his hand like a plastic puppet. He leant forward and deftly scooped up the excrement in one fluid movement, causing me to retch again. Tying a knot in the top, he presented it to me with a courtly flourish, like a little gift. I took it with the tips of my fingers, revolted and horribly embarrassed.

'I take it this is your first time?'

'Yes,' I replied, depositing the dreadful lump in a nearby bin. 'She's . . . not my dog. I'm looking after her for someone. Thank you . . . for . . .'

'No worries,' he said. He clicked his fingers and his dogs immediately came to his side. It was quite impressive. 'I'm Denzil, by the way. I might see you around, if you need help again. It'll get easier though.' He saluted me, still holding the cigarette, and strolled on his way, his boxers frolicking around his legs. I watched him go for a second, fighting the urge to call him back in case Bob decided to evacuate again.

I turned to find her standing in front of me wagging her tail eagerly, as if to say '*what next?*'

But I'd had enough. She'd had her walk and done her disgusting business and humiliated me in the process. We could legitimately go home and lie down until later in the day when I would have to do it all over again. And again and again and again until Fix came back, or I died.

It'll get easier, he said. Things do, don't they. Most things, anyway.

Chapter 14

So began a strange and largely unwelcome kind of routine for Bobby and me. I heard 'Bob is a boy's name' too often, and unfamiliar with her namesake, felt unqualified to explain the reasoning. Bobby sounded rather more feminine, and she didn't seem to mind. Angela had given me a book on canine behaviour from the library, and in one chapter the author suggested that dogs responded better to two-syllabled monikers. Renaming her, however marginally, established a little more authority and ownership, though I was the most reluctant of owners. More of a caretaker, perhaps.

We muddled through our two walks a day, mud being the operative part of the word, as she always seemed to be coated in it on our return. I'd gritted my teeth, held my nose, and managed to pick up all the 'left-behinds', as Sylvie put it. I still couldn't do it without gagging, but was getting quicker and more dexterous, which limited the damage to my gullet. We saw Denzil most mornings, and he saluted me as his dogs (Bodger? Barker?)

enjoyed a brief frolicky greeting with Bobby. I'd met a number of other dog walkers who were friendly and full of advice, wildly contradicting each other as they offered their words of wisdom. A crowd of them assembled at a particular picnic table near the tennis courts at the same time every day and I'd been too shy to join them, but one morning we bumped into Sylvie with Decca and Nancy, and she'd strolled over so insouciantly that I felt bound to follow.

As she sauntered amongst them, addressing both dogs and humans by name, I struggled to keep up, nodding and smiling as everyone nattered away, blithely unaware of their charges as they romped and ran amok. The main thing I'd observed about dog owners was that they weren't nearly sorry enough. Their dogs barged in front of joggers and cyclists, knocked children over, defecated in front of walkers, raised their legs on pram wheels, stole sandwiches and God knows what other misdemeanours, and their owners seemed either oblivious or only tepidly remorseful. Whereas I felt like going round with a sign that proclaimed a profuse and catch-all apology. *Mea culpa*, or rather, *canis culpa*. I mentioned this to Angela one day when she came to visit and she scoffed at me.

'The dogs have as much right to be in the park as anyone!' she said, ruffling Bobby's mane. 'You worry too much.' Whereas the only thing that seemed to concern Bobby was whether I fed her, at exactly 8 a.m. and 8 p.m., and walked her, at exactly 9 a.m. and 4 p.m. She had an extraordinary internal clock and would present herself at precisely the appointed hour, sitting bolt upright and looking at me sideways, then uttering a yelping little bark until I capitulated to her demands. How reassuring to have such simple priorities, and be able to express them so effectively.

Now, for example, it was 3 p.m., and I had only an hour of Angela and Otis's company before she would force me out of the house. Otis was watching a cartoon on my new computer, which had arrived that morning, ordered by Alistair from his office in Sydney. He'd been horrified by the burglary and insisted on replacing my laptop immediately. He'd even promised to send a 'memory stick' with lots of photos of Arthur to replace the ones I'd lost. You just plugged it in, apparently. If only memories were that easy to access, and contain.

Angela was drinking tea and pontificating as usual, while I made some biscuits for Otis. They were cooling on a rack, with Bobby sitting below, drooling. Although I never fed her from the table, or anywhere but her bowl for that matter, this did not stop her begging and scrounging at every opportunity – Sylvie said she must have some Labrador in her, such was her appetite. She'd wolfed down a chicken bone by a bin on our walk that morning – vile creature. The sofa throw I'd sacrificed as a dog bed was coated in its own blanket of hairs, and smelled like a sour old sock.

'And they claim they'd spend it on the NHS, but we all know that's bullshit!' huffed Angela, as I tipped the biscuits onto a plate and put them down on the table. Eyes glued to the cartoon, Otis reached out a hand. Angela took one and opened her mouth to continue, but was interrupted by a knock at the door. Bobby immediately started barking like an idiot.

'Be quiet, for goodness' sake!'

When I'd agreed to take her, this was exactly what I'd hoped for, but she'd turned out to be less of a guard dog and more of a very loud doorbell, howling in a frenzy whenever she heard someone outside, but retreating under the table when anyone actually entered the house. Still, I supposed the noise might put off an intruder. Or the smell.

As I got up, Angela said, through a mouthful of biscuit, 'that's Sylvie.'

Sylvie greeted me on my doorstep by handing me a large bin bag. 'For you,' she said, as she swept past me, and halted in the hallway. 'Oh my,' she murmured. 'Oh my.'

I turned, my arms full of black plastic, to find her gazing up at my chandelier, and the sweep of the staircase. 'Angela was right,' she observed. 'This *is* a treasure trove. Oh, I'm going to enjoy this.'

Sylvie was a successful interior designer, and also taught design at Chelsea College of Arts. A couple of times she'd mentioned in the park that she might come round and give me a few pointers, but I'd mostly dismissed the idea, as now I knew she did it for a living, it seemed an effrontery to expect her to do it for me for free. But, as Angela lounged in the doorway to the kitchen, her mouth still full of biscuit, Sylvie turned to her and exclaimed 'My dear, you were entirely right. This is wonderful. What I could *do* with this space!'

'Told you so,' drawled Angela. 'What's in the bag?'

'Oh, it's a present for Missy, for Bobby really.' Sylvie ran a finger down the banister. 'From the dog walkers. They had a whip round.'

Opening up the bag, I looked inside. At first it looked like an enormous pillow, soft and luxuriously fleecy, but as it fell to the floor I saw it was a dog bed.

'Cool,' said Otis, pushing past his mother to join us.

'That's nice,' said Angela. Not wanting to miss out, Bobby scampered over and started to sniff the bed. She circled it once or twice, then clambered on and settled herself with a huff.

'The dog walkers got me this?' I said, croakily. 'Why?'

'Well, they heard you didn't have anything, and that you were looking after Bobby as a favour to Angela and her friend, and they thought you'd like it. One of them gets a discount at some posh pet shop in Highgate.' Sylvie sounded completely unconcerned, as if strangers bought each other expensive gifts every day. To hide my confusion, I shifted Bobby off and took it through to the living room. Picking up the stinky throw, I stuffed it in the empty bin bag, and put the new bed down in its place. Bobby immediately lay down in it again, uttering a huge sigh. Within seconds she was snoring with one eye open.

'She likes it,' said Angela.

I stared at Bobby and the bed. 'Will you . . . tell them thank you from me?' I asked Sylvie gruffly. 'It's lovely.'

'You can tell them yourself,' returned Sylvie, now wandering round the living room. 'Good Lord, this is amazing.'

'Needs brightening up,' said Angela. 'It's a bit of a mausoleum.'

Still overwhelmed, I found myself saying, 'There are some things. Up in the attic.' All three of them turned to me, expectantly. I started to regret it, but they'd bought me a present and were eating my biscuits and filling my empty home, so . . . 'There are quite a lot of things up in the attic,' I said again. 'They might be useful. I could show you.'

'Cool,' said Otis again. 'Let's go.'

Chapter 15

L eo and I *did* intend to do the place up a little, make it our own. But by the time the sale went through and we'd moved in, I was so heavily pregnant that beyond shifting our furniture around and repainting a room in time for Alistair's arrival, Miss Crawshay's house stayed the same. Leo had his new job at UCL, and I had children to look after and a household to run – that was what one did in those days. Everything else fell by the wayside.

We bought the house in 1964 with the proceeds from the sale of our Cambridge cottage off Jesus Green, and the money my mother left me. The year before, Henry, my brother, had died very suddenly – a heart attack, like Fa-Fa. We were both hit very hard by it, but a light faded in Mama. And then she wrote me a letter: 'Darling, there's no easy way to tell you this, but I rather think I have cancer.' Always very sure of her own opinions, she didn't bother with an official diagnosis, and I don't think she even minded that much. When Henry died, all the fight went out of her. She was so far along by the time she told me that she was already very ill indeed and didn't want me to see her, but I went anyway, and Aunt Sibby and I fussed over her as her light went out.

Afterwards, we sorted out her things and I found one of her banners, 'Votes for Women' stitched in violet, white and green, and wept into it, yearning for those days when she would come home to us from a march or a meeting, flushed and triumphant. Mama would never have given up a career to run a household. She marched to the beat of her own drum, whereas I seemed to listen out for everyone else's. Mainly Leo's. He suggested we move to Lancaster Villas, but there were too many memories, and I didn't have a stick to contain them all. My father, Fa-Fa, Jette, Henry, and then my mother. The threads unpicking, one by one, leaving me untethered.

We needed a new start. Leo had finished his PhD and when the London job offer came it seemed fortuitous, if anything could be called so at that time. Sibby and I agreed to sell the Kensington house, and with my share plus the money from our Cambridge place, we had a good budget for our new London home. Although we wanted a big house, I was determined to find a bargain. So we searched in unfashionable areas and eventually found what we were looking for in Stoke Newington. In those days it was scruffy and insalubrious, full of what Fa-Fa would have called 'shady characters', but we saw the house on a sunny day and felt nonchalant about our ability to integrate into the community. In reality of course, Leo lost himself in his work, I lost myself in childcare since I'd given up my work at the library when we left Cambridge, and neither of us really bothered with the community at all, just let them run riot outside our huge house.

Inside, as the children ran riot, all I ever did was clear up mess, spending my days drearily wiping noses and bottoms and tables and floors, wondering why I'd wanted so many rooms to clean. As Mel and Ali grew older, all they seemed to do was scatter debris in their wake, toys and clothes and books and God knows what else for me to pick up. I would occasionally buy an item for the house, or we would be given something, and after a few weeks of them knocking it over, or spilling something on it, or simply because I was irritated by the presence of yet another *thing* to clean, I would inevitably shove it in the attic, out of the way.

All my mother's belongings had gone straight up there, ready for when I felt able to deal with them. But when that time came, I simply didn't *have* time, because I was too busy wiping and picking up and shouting and, at the end of the day, collapsing and pouring myself a drink.

I was containing the tide downstairs, at least on the surface, but up there things were getting out of hand. Yet I found I could mostly ignore it, pretend it didn't exist. When Melanie and Alistair left home and I finally had the opportunity, I couldn't bring myself to go up and sort it all out. And then when Leo got ill, I was taken up looking after him, wiping and picking up and shouting all over again until, when he was gone, the silence enveloped and overwhelmed me. Such crushing silence. It seemed like my whole life had been a cacophony, a constant buzzing and background chatter, and then Leo went and there was suddenly total and absolute stillness. Stillness, and silence and space. What I'd supposedly craved all those years, and it was the worst, most cloying thing I'd ever experienced. I thought I'd go mad with it, so that's when I had to get out. To go to the park again, to hear the trees waving in the breeze, the birds sing, a dog bark – anything to avoid the hush of my empty home.

When I went to the attic with Sylvie, Angela, Otis and Bobby that day, it was for the first time in years, and I was both comforted and disturbed by the company. We traipsed up to the first floor together, Sylvie exclaiming the whole way, Angela and Otis less interested because they'd already explored this bit, Bobby just along for the company. When we got to the landing Angela looked up at the ceiling.

'Where is it?' she asked.

'Where is what?' I followed the direction of her gaze.

'The loft hatch?'

'There's no hatch. There are stairs.' I led them through to what looked like a cupboard at one end of the landing. Unlocking the door with a key I kept in the kitchen, I pulled on a cord and a light came on, revealing a tiny wooden staircase curving up.

'Wow!' said Otis, scampering forward.

'Careful!' I called, but he'd already disappeared, followed by a scrabbling Bobby. Angela and Sylvie followed and I brought up the rear, clinging to the little rope banister.

At the top of the stairs I found Sylvie and Angela standing

together, staring. Not having been up in there for so long, I marvelled anew at the size of it. There were two huge spaces, both with sloping ceilings either side, separated by a doorway. Each room had a dormer window that looked out over the roof onto the street, and at the far end was another little round window, mired in years of grime. Every bit of floor space was covered in furniture and boxes; boxes and boxes, stuffed with bric-a-brac, odds and ends, books, toys, clothes, and of course, all my mother's things.

'Jesus Christ,' said Angela, her hands on her hips.

'Gosh,' murmured Sylvie. She reached out and squeezed my hand.

Otis appeared, his hair covered in dust, clutching a toy train. 'This is cool!' he said, and went back into the far room to continue his explorations. Bobby trotted over, a worn teddy bear in her mouth.

'No, that's not for you.' I removed it, tapping her on the snout.

Sylvie took it off me. 'This is a Steiff,' she said, turning it over in her hands.

'Yes,' I replied, patting off the dust and resisting the urge to clutch it close. Arbuthnot. Arbuthnot Bear. 'It was mine as a child.'

Angela found an old trunk and began rooting around in it. She pulled out a dress and held it against her, twirling in front of us. It was a delicate green silk, with beading and feathers – a flapper dress.

'Is this an original?' she demanded.

'Yes,' I said again. 'It was my grandmother's.'

'Shiver me timbers,' said Sylvie. 'I think I've died and gone to heaven.'

I suddenly wanted to go downstairs again. 'I think I'll take Bobby for a walk.' I said, grabbing her by the collar. Her ears pricked up at the word.

'I'll come with you,' said Angela, laying the dress back down with a final stroke of its soft plumes. 'I want to buy some wine from the offy. Can I leave Otis with you, Sylvie?'

'Yes, fine,' said Sylvie absently, settling herself down by a box.

Down in the kitchen, I collected some poo bags while Angela fetched her purse. Bobby's afternoon walk was a shorter one, and we tended to just circle the block to a patch of common ground where she could sniff and do her business if she felt like it. There was an off licence on the corner and Angela disappeared inside, emerging a few minutes later holding a paper-wrapped bottle.

'Listen,' she said as she rejoined me. 'I know you don't really like us up there.' I started to protest but she waved the bottle at me dismissively. 'No, I know you don't like it, but you've got to let us help you. It needs sorting out, and we can all do it together, and Sylvie can make your house look nice and then you'll feel better. About your husband, and everything.' She threaded her arm through mine as we turned back. 'When Sean, Otis's dad, left, I sat in my flat for months. And then I stole Nancy and sat with her and Otis on the sofa while Sylvie banged on the door. I thought I could block it all out. But I had to let her in eventually.'

I didn't reply, as Bobby was squatting in the gutter along the road outside my house. I picked it all up and dropped it into a nearby bin.

'You're getting good at that,' said Angela, watching me from the gate. 'Quite the expert.'

I snorted, taking the bottle off her as I pushed past. 'Come on, then,' I said, unlocking the door.

We spent the rest of the evening drinking and rummaging. Otis discovered a chest of toys and delved in delight, driving trains through the dust and lining up Dinky cars; Angela tried on my grandmother's old dresses, hats and shoes, parading in her finery, glass in hand. She looked surprisingly pretty when she wasn't dressed in those clumpy androgynous outfits she usually wore. Sylvie unearthed pieces of furniture and fabrics, exclaiming and making notes. I sat in an old leather armchair, reading my mother's letters to my father, sent during the war and returned with his belongings when he was killed. Beside me, Bobby lay, quietly panting. I read with one hand on her back to feel the rise and fall of her breathing. Whenever a detail upset or unsettled me, my hand would go back; up and down, up and down. Her fur was warm and springy like the dog bed.

'Right, that's it, I'm ordering a takeaway,' said Angela, when we'd finished the wine and she'd exhausted the contents of Jette's trunk. I relinquished my letters and tucked them back into their little folder. Sylvie looked up, putting down a vase she'd been examining.

'I think I might have to come and live here,' she said. 'It's wondrous.'

We trooped back down and Angela got on her phone to order the takeaway. From the familiar way she spoke to them and the specific nature of her requirements, I gathered this was not her first time. I wasn't sure I really liked curry.

'Missy,' said Sylvie, pulling out a chair to join me at the kitchen table. 'You must do me the most tremendous favour. Let me go through everything up there. I'll sort it all out. I'll tell you what's valuable, bring things down to cheer up your rooms here, throw away the junk. You've got to understand, this is a dream for me, like discovering the attics at Knole . . . Never mind,' she continued, registering my bemused expression. 'The thing is, let me do this. Please.'

Standing up to put the kettle on the boiling plate, I pondered. I didn't want to sort out the things up there; I lacked the necessary physical and emotional energy – but this would get it done with minimal effort from me. Moreover, by granting Sylvie access to my house, I would be granting myself access to Sylvie – her *joie de vivre*, her easy charm and her cheerful consumption of food, books, people. In many ways, she reminded me of Leo. They shared a sun-like quality that encouraged people to circle, and with both of them I wanted to be at the perihelion, the closest point in the orbit. It was a tug I couldn't ignore.

'Very well,' I said. She clapped her hands in delight while I busied myself making the tea. The idea that these two vibrant, diverting women wanted to spend time with me was as gratifying as the gift of the dog bed. I'd never really had female friends before. I told myself not to be so naïve, that Sylvie had a professional interest in my belongings and Angela had a professional interest in me looking after her son. But the fact remained that here we were, eating a curry together in my kitchen, foil dishes littering the table, as Bobby drooled underneath. Otis and I shared some mild creamy chicken and I enjoyed it very much, mopping up the sauce with Indian bread and laughing as it dribbled down our chins.

Even when they'd left, a drowsy Otis clinging like a koala to his mother, Sylvie promising to pop by later in the week to start her audit, the house didn't resume its usual crushing silence. After clearing up the remains of our dinner, while Bobby sloppily lapped water from her bowl, I went back upstairs to have a last look at the attic before it became Sylvie's domain. Surveying the boxes, chests and trunks – the leftovers of lost lives: Fa-Fa, Jette, my mother and father, Leo, even Alistair and Mel, since they'd begun new lives elsewhere – I fancied I could hear the echo of them all in their things. Fa-Fa's stories, Jette's Singer pumping away, my mother chanting her slogans, Leo chortling at Radio 4, Ali brum-brumming as he clattered his cars around the hallway, and Mel, playing her guitar. I could hear it all, and it was bitter-sweet, but it was better than nothing.

I switched the light off and went downstairs again with Bobby at my side, locking the door behind me. When I reached my bedroom, she sat down on the landing, looking at me expectantly. Every night so far I'd barricaded her on the ground floor and every morning had found her inexplicably at the foot of my bed. It seemed churlish – and pointless – to continue barring her in the face of such uncanny and, well, *dogged* determination. So I opened the door, said, 'Oh, come on, then!' and watched her plumy tail weave its way through to my room.

Like Angela said, I knew I'd have to let her in eventually.

Chapter 16

'Not until you sit properly. Sit!'

I held the bowl above my head, while Bobby capered around, yelping and nudging me with her wet nose. Dogs are particularly demonstrative creatures, which was perhaps the reason why they had always made me uncomfortable. To be open with one's emotions, to reveal one's devotion so obviously, seemed reckless, as if inviting a knock-back. Bobby's expressions and body language were so vivid and explicit that I'd begun to reply to her unspoken demands, mostly in the negative. But as the days went by, I came to look forward to our 'conversations', thanking her for reminding me to lock the back door, rebuking her for not telling me her water bowl was running low, and laughing at her grumbling when I pushed her off the sofa. We would wonder what the weather would be doing tomorrow, decide to go to the park, or treat ourselves to a biscuit. She would interrupt me moping over photos and I would tell her about Leo. I couldn't talk to anyone else about him, but found I could talk to her.

Bobby was doing her breakfast dance when Sylvie knocked a few days later. Picking up a thick cream envelope from the doormat, I found her outside, notebook in hand, dressed in overalls, her hair wrapped in a forties-style scarf, like an eager schoolgirl about to embark on a science experiment. While the dog noisily ate her biscuits, I made Sylvie a coffee and thought she might like to settle for a chat before our walk, but she was clearly itching to get going, so I gave her the keys and left her to it. She was up there all day – occasionally there would be a crash followed by 'it's fine!' floating down the stairs. She emerged just after we got back from Bobby's second walk, covered in the layered muck of decades, scarf askew but berry eyes shining.

'It's just marvellous!' she said, plonking herself at the kitchen table and reaching for a teacup. 'May I? Your mother, or your grandmother, or whoever it was, had excellent taste. There are some real gems. That gorgeous little vase I found, it's Murano, and there's a divine little Maple & Co. writing bureau that will look wonderful in your living room. And what were you doing leaving an Aubusson rug up there? You're lucky it isn't completely moth-eaten.'

That rug was a wedding present from one of Leo's aunts, but I kept tripping over it, and then one day I tripped *and* Alistair was sick on it, so I rolled it up in a fury and banished it. A wedding present . . . I fingered the morning's post, still lying on the table and Sylvie eyed it curiously. 'What's that, an invitation?'

I hesitated. I'd been brooding over that envelope all day. 'Melanie, my daughter, is getting married.'

Sylvie bounced in her seat. 'How exciting! You never said.'

'I didn't know. She and her partner have been together for years. I don't really know why they're bothering.'

'When's the wedding?'

'In two weeks. I don't know if I'll go.'

Sylvie stared. 'But . . . your daughter's wedding?'

I put the milk back in the fridge to avoid her eyes. 'I'm not sure she really wants me there. That's why it's so last-minute. We don't get on all that well.' The shock of Mel's accusation – *you never wanted me* – still reverberated. My own Greek chorus, ever-present, however much I tried to ignore it. How could I go to her wedding?

'She sent you an invitation.'

'Probably just to be polite, to let me know it was happening.' I didn't want to talk about it any more, felt like the envelope opened up my failings as a mother. Sylvie could obviously sense my unease because she changed the subject.

'I'm a bit worried about Angela,' she said, sipping her tea.

'Why?' I hadn't seen her since the night of the takeaway.

'I don't know really, she just seems a bit down in the dumps. It's hard for her, raising Otis on her own.'

'Does he ever see his father?' I felt sorry for Otis having no male presence in his life. Mel and Ali had adored Leo, although he hadn't been around that much once all the conferences and book tours started taking off. But they lived for the days when he came back, the conquering hero, dropping his suitcase in the hallway and opening his arms for their hugs. Children need a father.

'No, never. I think he came back once after Otis was born, to meet him. Otis won't remember, of course, which is probably for the best. But Angela . . . she thinks she failed, not giving Otis a decent dad. Thinks she should have known better, judged better.' Sylvie stirred her tea slowly, and licked the spoon. 'Men, eh? They never have to clear up the mess.'

I thought of Denzil, with the poo bag puppet on his hand. Maybe he was the exception. It was true that during all the wiping and picking up and shouting, Leo was squirrelled away in his study, engaged in his great work. He never once came out and offered to help, not even when I turned my ankle on the Aubusson that day and Ali was sick. I had to lift him up with one arm, weeping with the pain of it, while I used the other to mop up, then limp to the attic to dump the damned thing, while both children wailed downstairs.

Not usually inquisitive, something about Sylvie inspired confidences, so I dared to ask. 'Did you ever want to get married?'

She laughed. 'Not my thing. I'm quite happy as I am, pleasing myself.'

I nodded. Sylvie was a modern-day Atalanta, the virgin huntress, and she didn't need any apples slowing her down.

'So tell me about your Melanie. Who is she marrying? Some terribly dashing academic?'

'Sort of.' Picking up the envelope again, I took out the invitation and turned it around in my hands. Mel had scrawled *'bring whoever you like'* rather carelessly on the back of the card. 'I don't really enjoy going to these things on my own.'

Sylvie set her cup down. 'Why don't you ask Angie to go with you? She's excellent value at a party. No chance of you being a wallflower with her around.'

I sat up, struck by the idea. 'Otis could come too, we could make a day of it. Cambridge in the spring is rather nice.'

'That's a lovely idea,' said Sylvie approvingly. 'Do.' She got to her feet. 'Well, I must get going. I've had such a good day, what a treat. Thank you.'

Following her to the front door to wave her off, Bobby immediately shot between us, panting excitedly as if we hadn't just got back from her walk. She was a relentless opportunist.

'Calm down, we're not going anywhere, you lunatic.'

I wondered what we should do with her on the wedding day. I'd have asked Sylvie to take her, but the dog had a deep-rooted and almost cartoonish loathing of cats. Whenever we saw one in the street her hackles would rise and she would emit a kind of strangled growl as if the feline's very presence tore at her insides. It was a strange mixture of aggression and fear, for if the cat ever hissed back she would cower against me, still growling but also shivering. She really was a ridiculous animal. Anyway, it meant that Sylvie's house was a no-go area for her, since her cat Aphra very much ruled the roost.

After Sylvie had gone I went back into the kitchen and opened the envelope again, re-reading the cursive script.

Melanie and Octavia
invite you to attend the occasion of their marriage
On Saturday, 14 May 2016
At Newnham College, Cambridge

That they were doing it at my alma mater seemed an imposition somehow, although Octavia was a fellow there. But they could have chosen Girton, where Mel studied, or Clare, where she taught now. Or just a registry office and a restaurant. I hadn't been back to Newnham in decades, not since an alumni dinner in the early 90s, where I hadn't seen a soul I knew, and all anyone asked me about was my husband, the famous Dr Carmichael, whose blistering new biography of Disraeli everyone seemed to have read.

I used to deliver the occasional lecture, when I was working at the University Library before we moved to London. Nothing like Leo's grand orations of course – students flocking from miles around to hang on his every word. But my talk on the Sinope Gospels was quite well received. Then I 'devoted' myself to being a housewife, quelling the brain-buzz with scrubbing. By the time I'd finished, everyone had moved on, Leo most of all, off to his conferences and book events, while I waited at home with supper in the oven and my apron on.

No wonder I drank to forget; to forget I had forgotten; *was* forgotten. No wonder Mel, who revered her fond and absent father, was more critical of her fractious and ever-present mother, who all too often had a glass in her hand. Alistair, with a boy's blitheness, was oblivious to it, but as I poured myself a gin & tonic at 'Magic Hour' (another thing to thank Alicia Stewart for), I would feel the heat of Mel's accusing gaze. She disliked weakness, since she had none – as sure of herself and her opinions as my mother. She never mentioned her sexuality – unless you counted a rather unnecessary speech at her thirtieth birthday party; poor Leo certainly did. I'd known, of course, particularly after we saw her in that *Calamity Jane* production, but preferred not to discuss it.

Mel and Octavia had lived together in wholly unrepentant sin for years now, and there was no reason why they should suddenly decide to get married. What was she, fifty-six, fifty-seven? Still . . . Children loved weddings. We took Ali and Mel to Leo's friend Tristan's nuptials when they were small, and we all danced together, Ali wearing my hat and sticking his tongue out as he jigged away to 'Do You Know the Way to San José'. I remembered the four of us holding hands and careering round the dancefloor, widening our little circle and then rushing towards each other. That's what the *oikos* should be – expanding, contracting, but always connected. Sometimes it took a wedding to make you see that.

It might be fun. It might make things better. I thought of the words I'd exchanged with Mel here in my kitchen. 'Some things are better left unsaid,' I murmured to Bobby, and she put her head on my knee.

When Angela dropped Otis off the next morning so she could grab an hour to meet a deadline, I plucked up my courage and showed her the invitation. She read the card and then looked up at me quizzically. 'Octavia?'

'Yes,' I replied, refusing to indulge her. 'They've been together for years.'

'An Oxbridge wedding, fancy that!' she exclaimed. 'Obviously I'd be delighted, give me a chance to gawp at all the bluestock-ings. Can Otis come? It'll broaden his tiny mind.'

'Of course,' I said, tucking the card back in its envelope. 'I thought we'd get the train up, no need to stay the night as it's so quick.' I didn't want any extra expense as there was already the wedding present to consider. But here Sylvie stepped up, or rather down, from the attic the following week with an old black and white photograph, which she put on the kitchen table in front of me. I saw myself, aged twenty-two, with a baby Melanie in my arms, my mother with her arms round us both, in front of the house on Jesus Green. I was smiling down at Mel, and Lena was smiling down at me. It was the only photo I'd ever seen of the three of us, and I'd had no idea it existed, couldn't recall the moment it was taken. For a moment I couldn't speak.

'I thought you could frame it for her,' said Sylvie gently. I nodded, swallowing the thorn in my throat, and thinking again how grateful I was that she was doing this, acting as a kind of intermediary between me and the emotionally-charged contents of those rooms above my head. I hadn't been up there since that first night, preferring to let Sylvie get on with it and deal with the results when she was finished. But I resolved to give her the Murano vase when she was done. Some things were worth letting go.

Chapter 17

'What's her name?'

My mother bent over the bassinet, dark hair falling down, blocking my view of the baby. Our tiny cottage on Jesus Green was dark, even in the harsh winter sunshine, and despite the fire in the grate there was a chill in the air. I'd seen an advert for gas central heating the other day, but in 1959 that felt like an unimaginable luxury, even with a new baby to keep warm.

I shrugged. 'I don't know. We haven't fixed on anything.' Then, sullenly, 'Leo says he wants to call her Venetia.'

Lena was tickling the baby's cheek with one finger but at this looked up, amused. My mother was often amused by my husband. 'After the novel Disraeli wrote?'

I scowled. 'He's joking, of course. He hasn't come up with anything sensible.'

'Well, don't you have any ideas?'

I looked away, and realized I was blinking back tears. Where did they come from? My nipples tweaked and fractured, leaking milk onto my blouse, already stained with my baby's posseting. Her eyes flicked and fixed on me; immediately, the screaming started, incessant and maddeningly rhythmic. Chuckling, my mother burrowed into the cot and gathered her up, enfolding and nuzzling with an ease entirely alien to me. The screaming continued, all the same.

'I think she's hungry.' Lena held her out and I took her, awkwardly, craning round to sink onto the chair near the fireplace. Its back was hard and unyielding, but we had no sofa.

Cocking her head towards the space where it should be, Lena said, 'Would you like something from the London house?' But I didn't answer, because I was manhandling this squalling infant into position, desperately squeezing an aching breast into her gaping black hole of a mouth in the hope that she would latch on. And when she did, spurting milk and tears with the pain of the release. It was like nothing I'd felt before, hideous pricks around my areolas, a tiny shark feasting with its thousand pincer teeth. She kept guzzling, the milk kept coming and so did my tears, sliding silently down my cheeks as my mother watched us both speculatively. I wanted to wipe them away, but my hands were tied. So much liquid oozing from every orifice, all that lost blood draining out, desiccating me, until all that was left was a husk.

'Did I ever tell you,' Lena said, settling herself on the floor at my feet, 'about the woman who taught me to breastfeed?'

Sniffling, I wrenched one hand free, to wipe my nose. 'Taught?' I had visions of a schoolmarm pointing to a blackboard.

'Why, yes. It was a week or so after you were born, and I was having a terrible time, and you were losing weight, and I felt perfectly wretched, but then I had a visit from a midwife.'

'My midwife just tells me off,' I mumbled, wincing. 'Says I should get out more.'

'Oh, so did mine,' returned my mother merrily. 'But this was a different midwife. One I hadn't seen before. She was French. She was *wonderful*.'

I opened my mouth to reply, but no sound came out; my throat was parched. Seeing my distress, my mother leapt up and returned with a glass of water. She held it to my lips and I gulped gratefully. When I finished our eyes met, briefly, and she squeezed my shoulder before returning to her place at the foot of the chair.

'Where was I? Oh yes, my wonderful French midwife. Well, she saw what a state I was in, the room in darkness, me in a mess of sheets and sweat, and you wasting away in your crib. And do you know what she did? She poured me a glass of wine! It was eleven o'clock in the morning!' She threw back her head as she laughed, and I laughed too, although I'd forgotten how, and it came out as a wheeze, like a barking seal.

'Anyway, the wine was very relaxing, and while I drank it she opened the curtains, and arranged some flowers in a vase in the window, and when the room was bright again she came and sat on the bed with me and took my hand, and this is what she said.'

My mother took my hand and looked hard at me, serious and spirited. 'You are an excellent mother and you are doing a fine job, and when I show you how to feed your baby, you will have learnt a precious skill that is not always as instinctive as people think.'

I licked my cracked lips. 'And did she show you?'

My mother smiled. 'She did. I never forgot it, and it would be my great honour to show *you*. May I?'

I nodded, and she moved up until she was nestled next to us both, her rippling hair tickling my cheeks where the tears tracked.

'Now, tuck your little finger in her mouth to get her off, then we'll do it properly.'

And gently, with infinite tenderness, she showed me how to get my baby to suckle; how to roll her head up at the exact angle; how to get her mouth to cup from below. How to insist on the right attachment every time, because if you don't get it right from the beginning, it will always be off. The lesson to end all lessons.

Then, all of a sudden, I got it, and she fastened onto me, and for the first time ever it didn't hurt; that terrible splintering pain didn't come, and I was crying again, but with the relief of it, the blessed absence. My mother was patting and encouraging, and I saw that the warrior in her was tempered with the nurse, and felt as grateful for it as my throat was for the water. We sat on that hard chair together, rocking and patting, and finally, when the baby fell off me, replete, I turned to my mother and breathed, 'What was her name?'

A tiny frown appeared. 'Whose name?'

I was impatient, had to know. 'The French midwife.'

Her brow cleared. 'Oh! She was called Mélanie.'

I looked down at the sleeping baby. 'Melanie,' I said, tentatively. She gave a little snore.

'Melanie Carmichael,' said my mother, thoughtfully.

I pondered. 'I suppose she'll have to have Emmeline as a middle name?'

'Melanie Emmeline *Jameson*-Carmichael?' suggested Lena the suffragist.

I laughed, remembering how. 'I'm not sure Leo would approve. Unless it was Melanie Emmeline *Venetia*.'

My mother stood and held out her hands to me, to us both. 'Come on. I agree with your midwife. You need to get out more. Let's go and get Melanie some fresh air.'

And together we went out into the front garden of our little cottage on Jesus Green, to show my daughter the sun.

Chapter 18

Saturday dawned bright and clear, a perfect day for a wedding, and I felt quite chirpy as I dressed in what I hoped was a suitable outfit. Mel was often determinedly low-key, and might scorn me if I turned up in frills and finery, so I settled for a navy crêpe dress (something blue for the bluestockings), pinning one of my mother's brooches – another of Sylvie's finds – on the collar. Gazing in my dressing table mirror, I saw Bobby reflected behind me, head on one side. 'How do I look?'

She came over to me and put her paw on my knee, leaving dog hairs on the crêpe.

'Right, you can have a good brush.'

Putting the photo, framed and wrapped, in my bag, I clipped a newly-groomed Bobby on her lead and set off to Angela's flat to pick her up.

The dog had been an issue. We couldn't leave her behind, because we would be back late and Angela said she shouldn't be left on her own for more than four hours. I'd stuck religiously to this rule, until the other day when I'd had to dash back from my John Lewis shopping trip to buy Mel's picture frame. I'd been distracted by the children's toys and couldn't resist buying a little Batman Lego flashlight for Arthur, and then another for Otis. I arrived back after 4 p.m. to find that Bobby, in her desperation, had widdled on the floor in the kitchen. She looked so guilty that it was hard to be angry and besides, it had been my own fault for getting back so late. Rather than clean it up immediately, I went to her 'treat tin' – just a Tupperware full of kibble next to the Aga – and gave her a handful. She wolfed them like she hadn't been fed in months. Afterwards she licked my hand, and I tried not to worry about the germs.

In the end I called Mel. As she told Octavia to turn the television down I could hear Octavia's *'really?'* and felt a stab of guilt. The brief, stilted phone conversations we'd had since our row had been instigated by my daughter.

'I have a dog now,' I said to Melanie, after we'd dispensed with the how-are-yous.

'Righto,' said Melanie. 'Good for you.'

'I can't leave her behind on Saturday,' I began, but Mel interrupted me.

'Bring her along,' she said briskly. 'More the merrier.'

'But, they don't allow dogs at the college, do they? Not unless they're guide dogs and, well, I don't think we'd get away with that.'

'Don't worry,' replied Mel. 'Octavia will get a special dispensation from the principal. At least she's a girl.'

As usual, I couldn't tell if she was joking or not. 'Thank you.'

'What's her name?' asked Mel. 'For the place cards.'

'Bob,' I said, forgetting my amendment.

'That's not a girl's name.'

'It's from *Blackadder*.' I winced, waiting for the inevitable quote. Mel spent her thirties reciting snippets of the scripts, though I didn't remember a single line apart from her saying, 'fortune vomits on my eiderdown once more' whenever anything didn't go her way.

'It's a funny name for a girl but it's a perfectly normal name for a strapping young dog,' she said immediately.

'You know I've never watched it,' I said tetchily.

'Then why did you name your dog after a character in it?'

'It's not my dog, I'm just looking after her for someone and . . . it's a long story.'

'Well, bring her along and you can tell me about it on Saturday. And you've got two other guests, haven't you, of the human variety?'

'Yes,' I replied. 'I sent you their names – that's all right isn't it?'

'Of course,' she said. 'It's nice you've got friends coming. I've been worried . . .'

'See you on Saturday then,' I said hurriedly, and hung up, unable to bear her sympathy, which would inevitably turn into some sort of censure.

So here we were: the old biddy, the single mother, the super-hero and the adopted mongrel, on our way to see my daughter marry her girlfriend. I suppose we made an odd spectacle as we got off the bus at Finsbury Park station. Otis was dressed as

Iron Man, Angela had insisted on tying a white velvet bow 'for the suffragettes' round Bobby's neck, and she herself was dressed in an extraordinary black sequined jumpsuit, which I didn't think entirely suitable for the event. She was shivering like a whippet, for one thing.

On the train, Angela opened her capacious bag and, Mary Poppins fashion, produced a series of enormous toys including a plastic car park, to entertain Otis, who ignored them all in favour of two toilet roll tubes he'd stuck together to make a set of binoculars. He spent the journey looking out of the window as we rattled our way out of London towards the Fens. Occasionally he would comment on the scenery – 'Sheep!' 'Cows!' 'Yellow carpet!' – while Angela rolled her eyes and muttered 'You can take the boy out of London . . .' as she played with his Etch A Sketch.

Bobby curled up in the aisle and then jumped up, mightily offended, whenever any fellow passengers tried to get past her, as I resigned myself to the idea that the day was going to be varying degrees of stressful and mortifying. At least it was a relatively short journey and I enjoyed the views, lulled by the rhythmic clunk of the carriage.

We arrived in Cambridge in good time and queued for a taxi to take us to the college. Alas, we had to wait for a driver who was happy to have Bobby in the car. Several shook their heads and beckoned the next in the queue. Time was getting tight, Angela was covered in goosebumps since Cambridge is always a degree or two colder than London, and Otis was beginning to get bored, hanging off his mother's arm and moaning that he'd left his 'nocklars' on the train. I started to wish we'd left Bobby behind; I could have put newspaper down on the kitchen floor.

Finally a taxi zoomed up in front of us, the elderly male driver leaned across and bellowed through the open window, in an Eastern European accent, 'You have dog? I love dogs!' We all piled in, me in the front seat, Otis on Angela's lap in the back and Bobby panting in the footwell beside them.

During the agonizing stop-start journey to Newnham, we learned that Jakub's family bred greyhounds back in Poland and he missed them every day. He kept leaning back to fondle Bobby's ears, making me worry that he wasn't keeping his eyes on the road.

Familiar sights flashed by as Jakub inched his way through the heavy traffic, describing the intractability of the breed. The Botanic Garden, Sheep's Green – places I'd picnicked and walked in as a student – the languid River Cam, punters already out in force; Newnham village and then suddenly we were roaring up Sidgwick Avenue and I could see the elegant red-brick buildings ranging on my left. I tapped Jakub's arm and he screeched to a halt, catapulting us all forwards in the car. He seemed so fond of Bobby that I considered asking him to drive her round the city with him for the day. But she was on the guest list now.

The ceremony was due to start in five minutes, but the porter's lodge wasn't where I thought it was, and when we finally found it we had to negotiate a series of corridors and dead ends. Nothing was where it used to be and I started to panic. Why couldn't I remember? Eventually a student approached us and asked if we were lost. I wanted to say 'I was here before you; this place is more mine than yours', but it wasn't true any more; Cambridge sucked you in, consumed you, and then spat you out to make way for a new flavour. By now we were late, running, dragging a whining Otis, Angela's huge bag clanking against her hip. Bobby, delighted to adopt a quicker pace, broke into a brisk trot and, as we approached our destination hearing the strains of some jazz singer, she suddenly ducked out of her collar, and, joyfully unshackled, bounded towards the ajar door, nipping in before anyone could stop her. Angela and I looked at each other in horror and rushed after her. The three of us erupted into the room, sweating and breathless, eyes rolling in search of my errant dog. The music stopped abruptly, and the seated occupants of the room turned as one to stare at us as Bobby hurtled between them towards Melanie and Octavia, who were standing together at the far end. As the dog careered towards her, claws scrabbling on the parquet, my daughter calmly bent and caught her by the scruff of the neck, pulled off the white bow and looped it back around as a makeshift lead. Octavia gave me a little wave. I wondered how much Melanie had told her about our argument. Stumbling forwards, I secured Bobby back in her collar.

'Clucking bell,' said Mel, handing me the ribbon. 'This must be Bob.'

'So sorry,' I murmured, scarlet with embarrassment. 'Do carry on.' I backed down the aisle, dragging a reluctant Bobby, to join Angela, who was wheezing with laughter, her head in her hands.

Sinking down beside her, I yanked Bobby under my seat as

the music started up again and Mel and Octavia joined hands. Their celebrant stood in front of them, dressed in tails, vaguely recognizable – an actor, perhaps. Mel said they'd done the official registry office thing the day before, and this bit was for their friends, for show. At least Bobby had contributed to the spectacle. I breathed in and out very slowly to calm myself.

'Why is it two girls?' asked Otis, loudly. Angela clapped her hand over his mouth. 'For Chrissake,' she hissed, 'you're from Stoke Newington! Get a grip.'

As the actor started a little speech introducing us all, I drifted off, eyes wandering again, remembering the seminars and concerts I'd attended here, sixty years before. This, at least, hadn't changed, and the familiarity was reassuring. Melanie was wearing a long cream dress, her hair in a chignon. She looked like me, though of course in a more youthful incarnation, which was one of the reasons she made me uncomfortable, like I was the ancient, corrupted attic version. Octavia, shorter and squatter, was wearing a mauve velvet suit and kept turning and pulling faces at her friends in the front, who already seemed to be getting stuck into the wine. My hand itched for a glass.

Several people got up to read and it immediately felt like we were back in Falcon Yard at the St Botolph's party. At the touch of love, everyone becomes a poet. Excruciating stuff – one of the women actually kept her eyes closed throughout her reading, like Little Miss Chatterbox. I could feel Angela's shoulders shaking again. Bobby yawned widely. Otis was under his mother's chair, playing with the plastic car park. Then the actor said, 'and now, let us sing,' and sat down with a flourish at the piano. I recognized the tune a little, some folk song. Someone in front of us turned and handed us a piece of paper with the lyrics printed on it, and as the words crystalized in front of me, the small crowd around us stood and began to warble, timidly at first; then, as more joined in, with an added confidence and clarity. As the chorus began I suddenly remembered the song, one Mel used to sing as a teenager in her room, tapping her guitar, the untouched toast I'd made on the bed next to her. The memory roused me, and I found myself singing along with everyone, with no need for the piece of paper I held:

'Every day I need to say I love you.'

Melanie and Octavia were smiling at each other as they sang, Angela was bellowing along beside me and Otis was piping up occasionally from under the seat. Even Bobby was panting along in time, her brown eyes gazing into mine.

'I love you.'

Did she say it, or did I imagine it? Leo never said it. He never called to say it, nor said it before he left home every day, nor said it in bed, nor even wrote it in Latin for me to translate. And because he never said it, I felt I shouldn't either. Should we have? Would it have changed anything? Some things were better left unsaid, particularly between Mel and I. But the way she and Octavia were looking at each other, it didn't look like there was anything unsaid between them. Whereas I'd spent most of my life not saying things I wanted to. *I love you. Stop. No. It was a mistake. Please don't go. I don't want to. I wish I hadn't. I didn't know what else to do. I love you.* Why did I hold it all in? Maybe Bobby had it the right way round after all.

Blinking back the tears, I gave myself a shake as the song finished and the guests sat down again. Mel and Octavia exchanged rings, made the promises, and it was all over. Two waitresses appeared with trays and everyone surged forwards to grab a drink. We all mingled together and I was grateful I'd brought Angela and Otis, and even Bobby, so I didn't have to stand with my back to the wall, sipping too quickly because there was nothing else to do. With them around me, I was able to smile at passers-by, and even exchange a word or two. Several guests bent down to chat to Bobby and of course she lapped up the attention, snaffling several canapés as she charmed everyone.

Eventually I made my way to congratulate my daughter and her new wife. Mel turned as I approached, both of us eyeing each other warily. Our first meeting since those terrible words in my kitchen – she hadn't even come down at Christmas last year when Ali and Arthur were over, citing long-standing plans with friends up north. She and Ali had never been particularly close anyway, and her remote affection for Arthur seemed confined to cards or vouchers on special occasions. Had I passed on my coldness, and in turn deprived Arthur of his aunt?

'Thanks for coming,' she said, as I hesitantly stepped forward to kiss her cheek.

'It was a lovely ceremony. Sorry about Bobby.' I gestured to my dog, who was wolfing a cocktail sausage. Hearing her name, she looked up and wagged her tail.

'That's all right,' said Octavia. 'It was a diversion. She's a gorgeous dog. Have you had her long?'

'Just a few weeks,' I replied. 'We're still getting to know each other.' Bobby coughed as the sausage stuck in her throat, her hacking tramp-yack echoing across the din. I considered giving her a kick.

'I love dogs,' said Octavia.

'So do I,' seconded Mel. 'But you never did, as I recall?' She looked at me curiously and I felt myself redden again.

'I'm looking after her as a favour to a friend.' I gave Bobby a faux-affectionate pat and simultaneously yanked her lead as she craned towards a passing waitress.

'Well, she's very welcome,' said Mel. 'We're having dinner in College Hall later, she's got a bit of space next to you to sit. Try not to let her escape again though.'

'Thanks, I'll manage,' I replied, wondering how she'd behave around all the food. I returned to Angela, who was holding a glass of champagne and picking her teeth with a cocktail stick.

'I'm having a great time,' she announced, snatching a sausage roll. 'That guy who did the ceremony, he's in *Midsomer Murders*, he's got all sorts of gossip. And that woman over there does documentaries for BBC Two. And I just overheard two people quoting Chaucer to each other. The collective IQ of this room must be through the roof.'

I glanced around. 'Where's Otis?'

'Some professor took him off to the library, said she'd show him a secret staircase,' she said, draining her glass. 'Come on, let's see the famous gardens.'

We went through the French doors at the far end and out onto a small lawn.

'This is shit,' said Angela, gazing around with a curled lip. 'I thought they'd be much bigger.'

Wordlessly, I led her further until we came out into Newnham's sprawling, ravishing grounds. Slowly we wandered around, our feet crunching on the gravel paths as we admired the sunken rose garden, the apple orchard, the wild flower meadow, the rigorously pruned parterre, all set against the burnt amber of the Queen Anne buildings, bathed in late spring sunlight. Angela sank into a wooden swing bench, gazing at the great oak tree that dominated the main lawn. Bobby lay down on the grass and wriggled ecstatically on her back, paws waving gaily.

'Yeah, this is all right,' she said. She looked sideways at me. 'Must be hard, finding somewhere nice to live after all this. Even your house is a bit of a dump by comparison.'

I squinted at the glinting windows of Peile Hall. 'The rooms aren't that nice, or at least they weren't in my day. Cold. Not many home comforts. Bit of a mausoleum, you might say.'

Angela grinned. 'Is this where you met your husband then?' she asked, drawing patterns in the shingle with her foot. She was wearing wedge heels rather than the usual boots.

'No. Newnham is a women's college. Leo went to King's,' I said, walking away from her and back towards the wedding party, who were now milling on the lawn taking photos. Otis came running out of one of the buildings. He cannoned into me and I caught him in my arms, smiling down at him as he beamed up at me.

'I saw a secret room!' he said. 'It was a bit like your attic, but with books. I looked at some of them, they were really boring.'

'I'm not sure Plato's *Republic* is really his thing,' said the woman who was following him. She looked exhausted.

'No,' I agreed, 'He's more of a *Goodnight Moon* man.' Thanking her, I led Otis back to his mother, already deep in conversation with a small woman who in profile looked nearly as old as me. As we drew nearer, and she turned around, I felt a stab of shock. The years rolled back and once again I was the gauche student on one side of the wall, listening to the tinkling laugh and the clinking glasses and the gramophone and watching a girl leaning against a boy under the stars. *Odi et amo*. It was Alicia Stewart.

Chapter 19

Alicia had aged well; her hair still golden, though peppered with pale grey, her eyes that startling cerulean, though now behind wire-rimmed spectacles. The fine network of wrinkles across her face added character to the rather flimsy prettiness.

'This is Dr Hargreave,' said Angela. 'She said she was at Newnham during the fifties. I thought you might know each other.'

'Yes,' I replied. 'I think we might.'

So often I'd brooded over Alicia Stewart and her Marilyn sashay, even though I hadn't clapped eyes on her in nearly fifty years. The beginning is the most important part of the work, and Leo and I hadn't had the best, with that platinum spectre hovering. What if she'd never met the viscount? Would she and Leo have swanned down the aisle, would she have looked after his children, put her career aside, mopped up after him and played the dutiful wife? Was it her heart that whispered back to him?

I bumped into her once, in London, sometime in the late sixties. I was shopping on Oxford Street, she came out of Selfridges and we both hailed the same taxi. I only hailed it because I wanted to escape, but when she saw it she wanted it, and waved, and naturally the driver stopped for her. When she saw me her arm dropped, she smiled and said, 'Milly Jameson! How funny to see you here.' I held my bags in front of my body and said, 'Milly Carmichael now.' She looked confused for a second, but then her brow cleared.

'Of course! Leo! What a dear man, how lovely.'

I'd thought: she doesn't even remember what happened. It meant so little to her, and yet for me, and for Leo too, I feared, their brief relationship had a clanging echo that was still reverberating, like a stuck gramophone. So I took the taxi, and didn't tip the driver when he dropped me off at my big house, the one I shared with Leo and our children, and never saw her again until that moment in Newnham gardens, when Angela unwittingly introduced us, and we gazed at each other, both searching for the girls we used to be.

She held out a hand, as blue-veined as my own, and I took it.

'Milly Jameson,' she said, and this time I didn't correct her.

'Why are you here?' I blurted, then caught myself. 'I mean, how do you know Melanie?'

'I don't, not really,' she replied. 'But I supervised Octavia when she was at Clare and we stayed friends. I'm so pleased for them, they're such a wonderful couple.'

The idea of Alicia – tinkly little Alicia, falling over drunk at parties – as a Cambridge fellow was disconcerting. I'd assumed she'd married her viscount, or some other member of the aristocracy, settling down to a lifetime of giddy soirées. Yet here she was – an academic. Feeling sands shifting beneath me, Bobby pulling on her lead, I made an excuse about her needing a walk, and moved away to collect my thoughts. Sinking down onto a bench once I was out of sight, I pressed my temples and tried to focus, then felt Bobby lick my hand.

'It was someone I used to know,' I muttered. 'Someone I didn't like much.'

Bobby put her head on my knee and growled in an experimental way.

I laughed weakly and ruffled her fur. 'No need, thank you.'

Alistair often tried to get me to join those 'social media' sites where people post pictures of themselves – he said it was a good way of keeping in touch, knowing what everyone was up to. But I looked at some of the pages he showed me, and they were dreadful, a virtual room full of people boasting and angrily agreeing with each other's political opinions. People my age relied on cards and letters to keep up to date, though of course in reality we never really bothered, except at Christmas – I suppose those ghastly round robin letters are our equivalent, crowing to the masses in the hope someone might be interested or impressed.

So I had no real idea how my contemporaries' lives turned out. I assumed many of them went on to have illustrious careers – Cambridge is like that, and sometimes it was better not to know as it could make one feel inadequate to hear of so-and-so winning the Booker, or getting a CBE. But I didn't know the personal details either – who married who, whether they had children, where they went on holiday, when they got ill. All those women I lived with for years, sharing bathrooms, cooking, studying together in the Cambridge bubble, and then a starting pistol popped and we all scattered. Not for the first time I felt ashamed of my limited interest in the outside world – in people who weren't Leo. I should have known about Alicia. It would have saved me the pain of so many bitter assumptions. I always felt the only reason she didn't want Leo was because she was after a title. But it seemed Dr Hargreave was the only title she was interested in.

The photographer tapped me on the shoulder, shaking me from my reverie, and I put on my best mother-of-the-bride smile, though I must have looked shaken and distracted, holding limply to Bobby's lead. Once the photos were done, we were called back into the College Hall for dinner. The Hall was exactly as I remembered, the side facing the lawns spanned by huge leaded white mullioned windows, intricate cornicing picked out in white on the walls, and the far end dominated by enormous oil portraits of Newnham's great and good – other people who'd achieved far more than I had.

Throughout the dinner I could see Alicia further down the table, talking animatedly, eating and drinking profusely. There was a certain look to Newnham women – the 'gimlet eye', Leo called it, which was apt given Alicia's love of cocktails. She had it and I suppose I did too, despite us being such different breeds. I was disturbed by the affinity, didn't want to feel it. But, making my way down several glasses of wine, I began to remember things I hadn't thought of in decades – the night we climbed out into the gardens to walk in the wet grass in bare feet, passing a bottle of pilfered Black & White between us and hiccuping with laughter over the tale of its acquisition; her habit of miming putting her head in a noose whenever we saw Newnham's gorgon of a housekeeper stalking its corridors; the flick of her wrist as she wiped lemon rind around a martini glass. These memories, bubbling to the surface as the *entheos* took hold, while the old animosity sank into the depths.

Kicking off my shoes and stroking Bobby under the table with my foot, I watched my nemesis.

'Just an old friend,' I murmured, passing Bobby a morsel of beef. She reared onto her haunches to snatch it from my fingers.

As if aware of my gaze, Alicia's eyes roved across the table until they met mine. She inclined her head and raised her glass, and then, after a second's hesitation, she stood up and moved across to join me.

'I wondered,' she said, 'if you'd like to go and see our old rooms?'

We walked along the long corridor together, Bobby trotting at my heels.

'I've lived in Cambridge for years and never been back,' Alicia explained. 'At least, I've been back for meetings and pudding seminars and whatnot, but never gone back to Peile. Cedric, my husband, and I taught at Clare and – well, there's been no reason. But seeing you, it made me remember. There might be no one in, I suppose, but it's worth a try.'

So we knocked on the door of Alicia's room and no one answered. Then we knocked on the door of mine, and it was opened by a student who was nonplussed to see two old ladies come to visit, but gamely let us in and even went off to the Junior Common Room while we stood in the doorway and looked around.

It was in better shape than when I lived there, but similar enough to spark a blaze of nostalgia – the thin high windows that the gentlemen used to climb out of after curfew, the narrow creaking bedstead, the scratched writing bureau, the smell of furniture polish and old 'boring' books. Days and nights spent in this room, shivering and reading under a blanket and lying awake watching the trees and hanging up a ripped dress in the cupboard. That fleeting, explosive period was so intense, it seemed a lifetime of formative experiences were crammed into that room. Even after all those years, it still felt like home.

We stood and stared for a while, soaking it in, and then Alicia, looking straight ahead, said, 'I was so sorry to hear about Leo. Such a lovely man. Quite brilliant.'

'Yes,' I said. I couldn't look any more, so turned and walked back down the corridor. She shut the door and followed, and as she caught up with me, she began to sing:

'Mr Barman, bring me a drink,
Make it so strong that I can't think,
Give it two shots, and I'm in clover,
Then keep 'em coming til the night is over...'

She finished with the demonic cackle I remembered so well and I found myself snorting with laughter.

'You always were a lousy singer,' I said. 'Bloody awful din.'

'You always were a lousy drinker,' she replied. 'You could never keep up.'

'No,' I said slowly, 'I never kept up with you. You said you and your husband taught at Clare?'

'Yes,' she said. 'He's a mathematician. Terribly clever, nothing like me!' She cackled again. 'We're both retired though, now. Pottering around Cambridge like a pair of old fogeys.'

'So you didn't marry the viscount,' I mused, to myself as much as her.

She glanced at me, confused. 'The viscount? Was there a viscount? I don't remember one. What about you? Did you put that glittering degree of yours to good use? I imagined you as a professor by now.'

I was silent for a second, letting that other life play out. Alicia a viscountess, me an illustrious academic. 'Not quite. Children got in the way.'

She laughed. 'That happens, of course. And it requires another kind of mental rigour. Here we are.'

We'd arrived back at the Hall. The tables had been moved against the walls and people had started dancing, Angela jigging energetically with Otis. She beckoned me over. 'Come and dance!'

So I did. I drifted around the room, dancing and talking, for once entirely unselfconscious. Everything had been unpicked, and re-sewn, and the patterns were clearer, the threads mingling as they should. Every now and then my gaze would fall on

Alicia, sitting at a table with an elderly gentleman who must be her husband Cedric, the mathematician. They kept bending their ears to hear each other over the music. Two old fogeys, just like Leo and I should have been.

Angela, Otis and I joined hands and circled the dance floor as Bobby, tied to the leg of one of the tables, waited patiently, enjoying the occasional scrap from a sympathetic guest. Then I retreated to sit with the dog while Angela and Otis danced together. We drank more, and ate wedding cheese, and my hair fell out of its bun, and Otis said I looked like a witch, so I made my fingers into claws and dug out a wand from Angela's bag and pretended to cast spells and he ran off, shrieking with laughter. When we finally tore ourselves away from the party, flushed and dishevelled and giggling, it was nearly ten o'clock.

A friend of Mel's called a (dog-friendly) taxi for us, as Otis flopped in his mother's lap, exhausted. As I put on my coat and gathered my things together, Melanie appeared, Octavia hovering behind.

'I opened your present,' blurted Mel, sounding uncharacteristically embarrassed. 'It's beautiful. I had no idea. Where did you get it?'

'From the attic,' I replied, gratified. Mel rarely expressed approval, least of all to me. 'My friend Sylvie has been sorting through a few things.'

'Well, it's lovely. Thank you. And for coming and bringing your friends. It's good to see you.' She held out her hands and clasped mine tightly, stilling their trembling. Our previous words still echoed, but I fancied they were a little fainter.

'It's good to see you too.' I paused, unsure how to say it. 'I wish your father could have been here. He would have been . . . very proud.'

She nodded, her eyes glistening. 'The speech would have been epic.'

I smiled as I unhooked the dog from the table. 'I'm glad I could be here. I'm sorry Bobby was nearly a lawful impediment.'

They both laughed.

'You seem . . . different,' said Mel. 'Better.'

'Yes,' I said. 'I am better. A bit, anyway.' Her mouth opened again, but I wasn't ready yet, so shook my head and she stopped. Instead she stepped forward and hugged me awkwardly.

'I'll come and visit,' she whispered in my ear. 'Soon. Mainly to see Bob, of course. I'd like to get to know my new adopted sister.'

'I'd like that, too.'

Angela, carrying Otis, said the taxi had arrived, so we made our way to the door. Before we left, I cast one last look around the hall and caught Alicia's gimlet eye. She raised her hand in farewell; I nodded and we walked out, down the corridor, onto Sidgwick Avenue and into the night.

Chapter 20

Melanie. From the Greek μελανία, meaning 'blackness'. I'd had an easy pregnancy – young, healthy and in love, a ship in full sail. Always rather angular, in body and mind, pregnancy plumped me out, smoothed away my corners and suffused me with serenity. During that summer the sun had shone and the days were long and full of expectation.

Everything changed with the birth.

No one warned me how awful it would be. Leo started out in the room with us, but quickly retreated when he saw all that heaving flesh, the midwives holding me down as I writhed and reared, dripping hair plastered to my face. I could see it in his eyes when he came back in to meet her. He crowed and cuddled over his 'little hedgehog' and then he looked at me and I felt like he was thinking '*what a fuss she made.*' I'd failed an important test; Leo was expecting a First and all I managed was a measly 2:2. He gave me the 'Regard' ring that was stolen by the burglars. The gems spelled out the word – Ruby, Emerald,

Garnet, Amethyst, Ruby, and Diamond. It came with one of his Latin notes – '*Sicut mater, ita et filia eius*' – as is the mother, so is the daughter. I felt deflated. Regard, not love. And '*sicut mater*' didn't feel like a compliment.

From the second she came out, Mel was angry – a tiny, fist-waving fury whose mouth was constantly contorted into a scream. There was nothing I could do to placate her; she leeched the blood from my throbbing cracked nipples (even following my mother's advice), pummelled me as I rocked her, glared at me with her dark shark-eyes as I changed her. She was always cross, a cross I had to bear.

This was not what I had imagined, bustling around our little cottage, readying myself for motherhood. I supposed I would do exactly the same things I'd done before – a walk into town, a museum visit, a leisurely drink in a café – but with a tiny bundle in my arms. But I couldn't take her anywhere because of the screams and disapproving stares. Instead I wearily traipsed round empty parks in the driving rain of that endless winter, trying to ignore the blood-curdling squawks from within the pram.

During pregnancy I bloomed – now I withered, limping through the days and months, wishing my life away and hers. Nowadays I'm sure I would have had some sort of diagnosis, with the necessary drugs and therapy prescribed. Back then it was different. But when my doctor suggested a new pill to prevent pregnancy, I wanted to embrace him as I was so terrified of doing it all again. Leo, who adored Mel and didn't have to look after her, started angling as soon as she was toddling and

I agreed because I hadn't told him about the pill and thought I could just pretend to be as surprised as he was when nothing happened.

Alas, I became rather lax about taking it, placing too much faith in its ability to keep me in my blessed barren state. And I was distracted by the letter from my mother announcing her illness, so didn't recognize the signs. I was always rather bad at recognizing the signs. I just felt so tired. Then I took Melanie to London to see Mama, and for a few weeks I was exhausted by the business of death, nursing and cleaning and sorting, even with Sibby there to help. After my mother died, I fell into a kind of torpor, back in our messy cottage, placating Melanie with biscuits, both of us growing fatter and fatter. In the end I went to see the doctor again. He looked at my belly, and then at me, as if I was dim-witted. I realized that I was almost hoping for a different diagnosis – an illness, like my mother, rather than what it so obviously was.

As my pregnancy progressed I roused myself a little and when we saw the house in Stoke Newington that late summer of 1964 I felt the faint stirrings of life and light for the first time since Melanie was born. And then when Alistair came along, everything changed again.

This time it was easier. I felt more focused, as if my efforts weren't going unrewarded. He came out quietly, round eyes blinking, arms waving to find me. He suckled immediately, gratefully. The midwives patted and congratulated. Leo stayed with us. I'd got my First, on the second attempt.

We took him home to our big new house and Melanie, who

was of course outraged. Even she grew to love him though. He was so obliging, so simple. He was the image of Leo, big and golden, with a kind of infant glow about him. He chuckled, babbled, did all the things other ordinary babies did. As the months went by, I could take him to cafés, and little playgroups, and no one stared. Everyone was mourning Churchill, but Ali and I were in our own cocoon, oblivious to the world's ills. He healed me – my failure with Mel, Henry and my mother dying and other evils best left unsaid – they all ceased to matter so much because I had produced this buoyant, glowing boy. The God I didn't believe in was smiling on me, after all. Mel was my cross, Ali my balm. It's wrong to have a favourite, but I felt absolved because for Leo it was the other way around. He found Alistair's straightforwardness rather pedestrian, preferring Mel's more complicated, challenging psyche. So they both had a doting parent and a disparaging one, which I supposed was character-building. That was our *oikos*; the yin and yang, the whole greater than its assembled parts. I made up for Leo's failings and he made up for mine. But now he was gone, and I was going to have to come to terms with them, and try to make amends.

Clackety-clack, clackety-clack . . . The lurch of the train synchronized with my heavy lids on the way back to Finsbury Park that night, suckered in by the city, Otis lolling in Angela's arms as she drunkenly snoozed, Bobby flat out under the seats, while I gazed at the blackness clattering past. I could see myself reflected in the dark window, the future Melanie – gaunter, greyer, bitter. Of course I found her difficult because I saw myself in her, all my faults blown up in my face, along with all the strengths I didn't possess. Melanie was the Missy that Leo could love without restraint. She'd tenderized his heart in a way I couldn't quite manage. Now I was sobering up, *entheos* fading, I wondered if the brief amity we'd shared on my departure could last. There was always the residue of that terrible day, that terrible fight . . .

At Finsbury Park, Angela lumbered out of the station with Otis over her shoulder, while I dragged Bobby, who developed an infuriating obsession with the urine-drenched lampposts of Seven Sisters Road as we wandered around looking for a taxi. Luckily we found a driver who deemed the dog's presence acceptable, but I was headachy and despondent by the time he dropped us off on our street. Waving goodbye with her free arm, Angela headed towards her flat as I lugged Bobby home.

When we went in, I saw a light on in the living room but didn't think too much of it, remembering that Sylvie had said she might pop by briefly to sort out a few things from the attic. She had a key, and had probably forgotten to switch everything off when she left. I went into the kitchen to make myself a cup of tea to combat the impending hangover. Bobby whined at the back door to be let out and I unlocked it, tutting as her plumy tail weaved off into the darkness of the garden. Turning back to the kettle, I poured my tea and was about to settle at the kitchen table when I remembered the light. Better save the electricity.

Even as I approached, it was clear something had changed.

The light itself was different – a softer, warmer glow than usual emanating from the room. Pushing open the door and registering the transformation, I stood rooted, gripping the doorknob in astonishment. Sylvie had worked her wonders, and I no longer lived in a mausoleum.

As a child, I used to read *A Little Princess* avidly, over and over again until my copy fell apart. I was entranced and appalled by it, taking delight in the lavish descriptions of Sara Crewe's life, her Papa's extravagance, then gleefully recoiling at her subsequent fall from grace. I was struck by the notion that life can turn on a sixpence – that one moment she could be tending to a doll as sumptuously dressed as she was; the next, bedraggled on the street, feeding buns to a beggar.

But the episode that intrigued me most was when the sympathetic gentleman next door decides to refurbish Sara's room in secret. While she is asleep, he sends his servant across the roof and in through her window, and one morning she wakes to find her bleak attic transformed into a magical boudoir, filled with exquisite home comforts. As I looked around the living room that night, I felt like the Little Princess, dazzled by the bounty and overwhelmed that someone cared enough to do it.

There was the Aubusson rug, back in front of the fireplace, its vivid red echoing the twitching embers of the fire. The writing desk was in the corner, along with a carved wooden chair upholstered in soft sage chenille. Green-flowered linen had been used to make new curtains and matching cushion covers, my paisley throw washed and re-arranged along the arm of the sofa. Another lamp had been unearthed and set on a low table by Leo's chair.

Alongside it, the Murano vase filled with Anemone. Anemone for the lost Adonis.

Photos and pictures everywhere, on the walls, on the mantelpiece – every surface had its own memento. Some were works of art I'd forgotten, including a fine oil portrait of my father, painted just before he went off to war. I paused under it, looking at that sensitive, thoughtful face. William Jameson. He had been a pacifist, though too scared to say so. My mother rarely spoke of him, except to say he was the finest man she had ever met, and I was sad that I didn't remember him at all, just knew that he was the reason I was called Missy, ever since my brother mispronounced my name in his hearing. After he left, Fa-Fa picked up on it and it stuck, though he and my father were the only ones to ever use it, before Leo came along. The letters to my mother that I'd read up in the attic had signed off, 'Love to all, esp. Henry & Little Missy.'

What was it Sara Crewe said? 'The Magic that won't let those worst things ever quite happen.' They do happen, though, don't they – fathers go off to war and don't come back, loved ones get sick, grandchildren move away, and much worse besides – the worst things that you can't even think about. But then there are life's pick-me-ups: lunch invitations, dog beds, pretending to be a witch at a wedding.

What an email the tale of today would make! But as I turned to go back to my laptop in the kitchen, I changed my mind and decided to write a good old-fashioned letter instead. After letting Bobby back in, I settled myself at my old bureau, all handily stocked with the necessary equipment, pulled out a fresh piece of paper and rummaged for a pen. The newly installed clock on the mantelpiece chimed one in the morning, but what I had to say couldn't wait. With Bobby snoring on the rug, I started to write, knowing the words would flow easily for once.

'Dear Melanie', I began.

Chapter 21

It's strange how quickly things can change. Just a few months ago it was so cold, frozen grass crunching underfoot, sky leaden with unshed snow, an arctic whistle in the wind, a few solitary flakes refusing to melt on the pane. Whereas in early June I looked out and could feel the heat of the sun on the glass. Under the blazing periwinkle, tarmac softened on the scorched streets, commuters gradually shedding their clothes as they marched to and from the tube station.

In addition to Bobby's twice-daily walks, my days began to be taken up with other activities – coffee with a dog walker who happened to be free, another lunch at Sylvie's, a trip into town to see a cheap matinée Angela had recommended. I regularly babysat in the mornings for Otis, who was a delight. He came on walks with me and we'd go to the playground, Bobby waiting patiently at the gate while he went on the swings and the long slide and hid in the bushes waiting for me to find him.

When I became a mother I assumed I was no good with children, since I was no good with Melanie, but as the years went by I realized the only prerequisite was to *want* to be good with them. I never did with Mel because there was always something else that needed doing; I suppose her outrage was an awareness that my attention was elsewhere. It's hard to accept, when you have children, that your time isn't your own any more – it belongs to them, every precious second. When I saw Otis pulling on his mother's arm as she checked her phone I wanted to shake her. But we all make the same mistakes, whether it's phones or cleaning or looking out the window come rain or sunshine, waiting for your husband to come home. So Otis and I played, and he climbed on logs, and brought me bugs in the palm of his hand and ate the biscuits I baked, and every second was spent watching him, and paying attention and responding to the endless questions, because I knew it wouldn't last forever, but we would both remember it. I didn't do it for Melanie, and I couldn't do it for Arthur, so I would do it for him.

Angela still annoyed me, with her scattiness, smoking, swearing and constant harping on about politics, but she was entertaining, and whenever she picked up Otis she would inevitably end up staying for tea and a diatribe. She would march around my kitchen holding Otis's wand like a cigarette, delivering her tirade in that husky Irish accent. It mostly went over my head as I busied myself providing sustenance for them both, admiring my newly-adorned mantelpiece and slipping Bobby the odd crumb of biscuit, after I'd picked out the chocolate. Her tail would thump in thanks as she dribbled on the Aubusson rug. She was quite a nice old girl really.

'Screw the lot of them,' concluded Angela, as she finally drew breath. 'This room looks amazing. Sylvie is a bloody genius. That reminds me, there's this quiz at the pub on the twenty-second. She and Denzil want to make up a team. You up for it?'

Obviously, I was pleased they'd thought of me. How Leo would have scoffed though. He found trivia . . . well, trivial. But that was the kind of knowledge I had, I supposed – skimming stone snippets, garnered here and there throughout my long life.

'Who will look after Otis?'

'I'll get a babysitter, it's only round the corner. Sylvie's a fiend when it comes to quizzes. She'll actually lynch you if you get anything wrong. I'm not going to answer any questions just in case. I thought I'd just get drunk and shouty.'

'Why change the habit of a lifetime?'

'Fecking cheek. You in then?'

'Is the pub dog-friendly?'

I'd got into the habit of taking Bobby around with me, in addition to her usual walks. She'd sit, tied to a lamppost outside the butcher's shop, ears pricked, sniffing my bag when I returned. The owner of the charity bookshop was happy to let her wait by the children's section while I browsed, and as the weather was warmer we could sit outside the café, where Hanna would bring a bowl of water for her. Bobby was an undemanding companion, happy to accompany me and lie by my side, quietly panting as I read the papers. She was a handsome creature with her ochre colouring, and passers-by would often stop to admire and pat her, which was rather gratifying.

A week or so before the quiz, a package arrived from Melanie. It must have been sent a few days after she received my letter, which hadn't been as easy to post as it was to write, and had travelled around in my bag for a while before I could pluck up the courage. How to undo those brutal words between us? 'Dear Melanie', when I'd never really treated her so. I viewed the parcel with some trepidation, but when I opened it, there was just a DVD and a note that read, 'So Bob can learn about her pedigree.' It was the second series of *Blackadder*.

I'd never watched a sitcom before; Leo and I caught the odd documentary or film, but apart from that the television was just a redundant box in the corner. Leo used to pride himself on the fact that he didn't really watch it, and it was one of the few rows he and Mel had, about the medium's cultural significance. I remember waiting for them to thrash it out, realizing that the set was coated in a layer of dust and dashing off to find a tea towel.

At first I found it stagey and affected, with the elaborate Tudor costumes and crude set, but then relaxed into the silliness of it all, enjoying the deft wordplay and absurd caricatures. Once Angela and Otis dropped by to join me; Angela brought over fish and chips and we sat drinking wine and giggling as Baldrick's next cunning plan was unveiled. I was thinking myself quite a fan until the last episode, which I watched on my own, with Bobby on the sofa next to me, her head in my lap. It was all as ridiculous and enjoyable as usual but then the ending came, with the characters all murdered, their corpses littering the floor, and for some reason it was quite upsetting. I went upstairs to bed and for the first time in months checked the cupboards, then slept badly, waking and watching the shadows on the walls, listening to the dog snoring and snuffling and finding comfort in her presence. In the early hours of the morning I finally fell into a deep sleep, my hand on her head.

I awoke late, to hear Bobby down in the kitchen drinking noisily from her bowl. Dressing quickly, I followed her downstairs and clipped on her lead. We made our way round the park, though since it wasn't our usual time we didn't see as many familiar faces. We sat outside the café for a while, watching the deer, Bobby growling at a paper bag blowing in the breeze.

Returning home, I had a bowl of soup and listened to the news on my new radio while I went through a box from the attic that Sylvie had left for me to sort. They were mostly letters my mother had kept, which I stowed away to read properly another time. I binned some old documents relating to the sale of the house in Kensington, though kept a photograph of it, taken shortly after the war. There was also a little box that looked like a jewellery case, but inside I found two milk teeth and a rolled up piece of paper. Unfurling it, my mother's handwriting read 'Henry 1940, & Milly 1944'. I'd never done that with my own children. Rolling up the paper again, I put it carefully back in the box along with the little ivory gems. A neutral voice on the radio told me an MP had died, stabbed in the street by a constituent. She had children too.

Ludwig and his bloody dagger, indiscriminate slaughter. A mother who saved her children's teeth and another who didn't. A parent killed and another kept alive. Live, die, love, don't love; it was all so arbitrary and random that the unfairness and unpredictability of it took my breath away. Again I loathed myself for choices I had made, things I said, and things I didn't say. I wished Leo were there to hold my hand and tell me it would be all right, but his chair was empty so instead I sank my fingers into the dog's lustrous fur and felt her breathe, up and down, up and down.

'Live,' said Bobby, and I started in shock, but she was just doing one of her yelping yawns.

I ruffled her mane and gazed around my cosy living room, with the pictures of my family glinting in the lamplight, my father smiling down at me: how lucky I was, how monstrously lucky. It had started to rain, a proper downpour lashing against the pane. Bobby's walk would be a wash-out tomorrow. She nuzzled me, turning on her back to show me her white belly.

'I'm glad you're here.' I tickled her soft fur and she wriggled nearer for more.

The magic doesn't stop the worst happening. The worst happens all the time, every day. And then life goes on. And you just hang on and hope that you can keep whatever crumbs and tiny white teeth are left.

Chapter 22

'Question number seven: The Greek Military Junta, also known as the Regime of the Colonels, ended in which year?'

'Oh balls, was it 1972? 1973?'

'1975, surely?'

Bobby's head was on my knee, willing us to do well, and I could have told them, but I was swept away, back to a night almost fifty years ago when the Colonels were still in power, and Leo and I had the fight that nearly made me tell him everything.

It was 1970 and there had been ghost-fingers of leftover snow on the ground that evening when Leo and I returned to Cambridge to attend a dinner at a hotel near Queens'. It was some tourist thing we'd been invited to, something to do with Greece, but I barely paid attention when he told me about it because I had a demanding five-year-old intent on wrecking the house and Melanie was ten going on twenty-three with a hundred dramas a day. So that afternoon I just put on a dress that didn't have their dinner on it, and we got on the train, and then into a cab, and rushed into the River Suite, because Leo said we had to get there early for some reason. On the way into the hotel, I noticed a small crowd of people staring at us, and one of them shouted something that sounded jeering, but I didn't think anything of it at the time as we were in such a hurry.

I couldn't see anything particularly Greek about the affair, just a few of the town's illustrious personages standing around quaffing, but it was obvious when we arrived that something was wrong. The waiting staff had a harassed air, shoulders tense as if expecting an eruption from the kitchen. Already anxious at events like this, while Leo began his perambulation of the room, I stood with my back to the wall and before I knew it, had consumed three glasses of champagne. When he finally returned to my side, everyone had developed a kind of echo body that overlaid their own, and at first I thought the noises I could hear were just in my head. Shouting voices were filtering in from outside, the waiters looked more worried than ever, and guests were starting to whisper to each other behind their drinks.

'There's a protest out front,' muttered Leo, swiping a glass and downing it in one gulp. 'Tristan says they've been gathering for quite a bit. Lucky we were early.'

'Who?'

'Students, mostly.'

'Protesting what?'

'Greece. The junta.'

My Greece was an ancient one: myths and metaphors, mountains and magic, and the harsh reality of a modern dictatorship felt vastly at odds, as did this suddenly-ridiculous dinner.

We took our places, although a few seats were still empty, and the first course was brought out and presented with noticeably shaky hands. Olives and peppers, fried squid rings and numerous dips with strips of flat bread curling at the edges. Everyone around me began determinedly chatting about the various tavernas they'd frequented, to prove their sophistication. As if to further enrich the Mediterranean tone, music suddenly blared into the room, causing some to cover their ears in consternation. Several people looked around to determine the source but it seemed obvious to me that this was no gentle acoustic counterpoint to our evening. With that, and the continued shouting outside, the event was rapidly becoming a farce.

After a whispered discussion with Tristan and a hovering waiter, Leo turned back to me. 'Someone's set up speakers outside.'

'How obliging of them,' I replied, sipping my wine.

After that, some dignitary got to his feet and attempted to make a speech about the wonders of the Greek coastline, to the booming accompaniment of 'Zorba's Dance'. Leo's shoulders were shaking; he and his friend Tristan were egging each other on. The shouting was now coming from all sides and eventually the speaker gave up and tailed off, shrugging helplessly at his colleagues.

The waiters were visibly sweating and gesticulating at each other, the chanting outside getting louder, diners becoming more disturbed and distracted. And then a stone hit one of the long windows that looked out onto the river. It was only a tap really, but everyone was so on edge that one woman actually screamed. It was all we needed to tip us over. A waiter dropped a tray of avocado slices with a crash, another stone followed the first, the window of the River Suite smashed, and two young men charged into the room waving placards. They were immediately set upon and bundled out, but everyone leapt up and started bunching towards the entrance, jostling, though no one seemed to know where we were going, and then, *then*, all at once, I was enjoying myself more than I had in years.

I wasn't at home on my own with two whining children; someone else was doing the wiping; I was in a nice frock and my husband's hand was clasped firmly around my own. By then the shouting was deafening both inside and out, men bellowing instructions at each other and women squealing and clutching their skirts as if rape and pillage were on the agenda. There was something aptly bacchanalian about it all, and as Leo hustled me out of the room, I swiped an open bottle of champagne from a wobbling tray and gave a little wave to the bemused waiter.

Out in reception it was no better, staff milling around in all directions and no one taking charge. A man who looked like he might be the maître d' kept clapping his hands vainly, but no one took any notice. Several of the women were hysterical, though in fact, apart from the noise, nothing had really happened.

How swift we were to descend into panic and mayhem! I began to giggle as I surveyed the dramatic scenes, and took a slug of champagne. Leo was engaged in an intense discussion with Tristan, but when he turned and saw me, he grinned across the room, and once again I was the girl hugging my books by the Mathematical Bridge. We were still holding, him and I. Despite everything.

Leo walked towards me, still smiling, and I offered him the bottle. He took it and drank from it, and when he handed it back to me, I noticed he had my coat.

'Well,' he said, 'it seems everyone is going upstairs to hide out until this is all over.'

'Hmmm,' I said, eyeing him and my coat speculatively.

He held out his arm like a gentleman. 'What do you say we make a run for it?'

I hung on and, chuckling like a pair of school children, we swept past the twittering guests, gunning for the exit. Just before the door we paused, girding our loins.

'Ready?' Leo asked, turning to me with a wicked glint in his eye.

'Ready,' I replied, and we ducked out.

Immediately, we hit a wall of heaving bodies, a seething mass of anger and exhilaration. I could see several policemen in the midst, vainly pushing against the crowd, but there must have been hundreds of people there in that tiny cul-de-sac, and they didn't stand a chance. We plunged into the throng, hands intertwined, heads down. At first it was hard to make any progress and I worried we would just get pummelled and pulled backwards, but gradually Leo threaded his way through, never letting go of my hand. We were almost there when it started to pour with rain. At least, that's what I thought it was, but the deluge was too heavy – in seconds I was drenched, like everyone else, and looking up, we saw a man in the first-floor window of the hotel, smirking as he sprayed us with a fire hose. Pandemonium broke out, people shoving this way and that, the paint on the placards drizzling and blurring. But throughout it all, Leo's hand was in mine, palms firmly pressed together, fingers entwined. He wouldn't let go.

Then all at once we were out, running down a side street towards civilization, attracting curious glances from pedestrians as we squelched past, laughing helplessly. When we finally came to a halt on a small side street that backed St Catharine's, we were both dishevelled, panting, triumphant. I passed Leo the bottle again and he handed me my damp coat.

'What on earth were we doing there?' I gasped, shrugging it on and squeezing out my hair.

Leo took a swig and spluttered. 'Tristan invited me, he's half Greek. I thought we might get a free holiday out of it!' He clutched the college's wrought iron gate, wheezing with laughter, then snatched my hand up and again we were running, through the dark cobbled streets.

'Where are we going?' I puffed at one point, as Leo led me down an alleyway off King's Parade.

'Somewhere I used to know,' was all he would say.

The night was dark and cold, with the lights of the colleges twinkling as we rushed past and for a second I missed it all, that cocoon of academic life, the delicate unpicking of words in dreaming spires, rather than the brutish earthiness of motherhood. I got a First Class degree, in the end. How might my life have been, I wondered, if all my children had been unborn? But then, Leo's hand in mine, pulling me along, and I was dragged through a graveyard with the Round Church on our left, until a Gothic red-brick building loomed in the gloom. The Cambridge Union debating chambers. Students were milling about, but Leo didn't break stride, carrying on in, bearing me along several corridors and then turning down a small set of stairs. As we descended I could hear music again, but a very different kind.

We emerged into the cellars, a place I wasn't familiar with, but could see that this murky set of underground rooms had been turned into an impromptu jazz club. The band was at one end, dimly-lit, with a few couples dancing in the middle, and others ranged on tables round the edge. Leo looked around for a second, then sighed in satisfaction.

'Just as I remember,' he said fondly. 'Do you want a drink?'

We found a table and I sat down while Leo went in search of refreshment. After a moment, he reappeared with a bottle of wine.

'This is much better,' he said, sitting down and pouring us both a glass. We clinked them and I thought how lovely it was; how we'd never done this before, because he was always too busy and I was always too ground down, but maybe, here in this dingy basement, I was finally surfacing into the light. Maybe in the end, it would all be worthwhile, and everything I had to go through, everything I gave up to get here was just a test designed to make the reward more satisfying. As the children got easier, and he settled into his career, Leo and I would spend more time together, and he could learn to love me in the all-encompassing, single-minded way I craved.

'Dr Carmichael!' A dark-haired, bespectacled young man was standing before us, blushing and stuttering. Leo immediately got to his feet, pumping his hand and exclaiming.

'Dawson!' And they were off, Leo borne across the room to a group of students who welcomed him enthusiastically, the conquering hero returned, while I was left at my table with my bottle and no one to share it with.

He was gone for nearly half an hour of chat and back-slapping, by which time the bottle was empty and I was ready to stage my own protest, with banners and chanting and lashings of self-righteousness. When he finally ambled back, tie askew and eyes alight with flattery, I was stony-faced, arms crossed and entirely drunk. Leo slumped at the table and raised his eyebrows at the dregs.

'Put it away, did you?' he observed, re-tying his shoelaces.

'Nothing else to do,' I muttered, tapping my foot and waiting for an apology.

'Sorry, darling, you know how it is.'

We sat in silence for a moment, as he saluted various admirers, and finally I couldn't stand it any more.

'You just . . . you just don't understand,' I said, wincing at my own inadequacy.

He turned to me, surprised. 'What?'

'How hard it is. You. With your . . . PhD. And me, with my

. . . coffee mornings.' Nothing would come out right; I was too drunk. But it was spilling out all the same. Some of the anger from the demonstration had infected me, lit me up inside, and now the fires were raging and wouldn't be put out. 'It's not fair.'

He was baffled. 'What's not fair?'

'You get to do everything. And I don't get to do anything at all. Just sit rotting at home.' I was slurring now, and it was awful, but I couldn't help myself. He was the dictator, I was the disgruntled populace and this was my coup, badly prepared and already out of control. But off I went anyway.

So he sat there, bored and irritable, drumming his fingers as I railed at him, and I could tell I wasn't even touching the sides, nothing was hitting home because he could just tell himself I was drunk and it didn't matter. It *wasn't* fair. So many years spent blunting my brain and making endless sacrifices, large and small, that he had no idea of, couldn't even comprehend, while he suited himself in every possible way. That complacency – that sublime self-absorption – had scratched away until the wound was red-raw. The urge to land a blow was overwhelming, and I found myself wanting to say it, wanting to tell him the thing I'd spent so many years burying, the one thing that must never be said, must never even be thought of, because that would be the end of everything. Before I could stop myself, it was out there.

'You have no idea what I've done for you. What I did. It can never be undone.'

Even as it left my lips I wanted to recapture it, stuff the words back in until they choked me. Leo, who'd managed to score a whisky, paused with the glass against his lips, finally engaged, frowning.

'What have you done?'

I was teetering on the abyss, but immediately started scrambling back, petrified by the depths.

'Nothing.'

'You were about to say something. What did you mean? What can never be undone?'

'Nothing, I don't know what I meant. Nothing.' I closed my eyes, to banish it. 'I'm sorry, I've had a bit too much to drink.'

Leo put down his glass and took my hands, then lifted my chin to make me look at him. 'Missy, is there something you wanted to say to me?'

With a supreme effort of will, I looked back at him and smiled into the clear blue of his gaze. 'No, Leo. I'm sorry. I'm just tired. It was a bit overwhelming back there.'

He squeezed my hands. 'I know.' Then he grinned, devilishly. 'Fun though, wasn't it?'

I managed a laugh, as he pulled me to my feet. 'Mrs Carmichael, even with dripping hair, you look very beautiful tonight. Would you like to dance with your husband?' His blue eyes crinkled at the corners as he looked down at me.

The band was playing a slow tempo number I didn't recognize. He drew me into his arms, I leaned my cheek against his chest and we swayed together, the soles of our shoes clinging to the tacky dancefloor. I could feel him nodding above my head to his comrades, still barracking for an audience, and the words of the song bled into my brain as we circled: *'Keep your head, and keep your calm . . . that way you'll keep your guy.'*

'Bertie,' I whispered. In the noise and darkness of the cellars, no one could hear me, or see the tears that trickled down my cheeks as I contemplated how close I came to ruining it all. Shattered into a million pieces, like that window in the River Suite.

Bobby licked my hand encouragingly. 'It's 1974,' I said, jolting myself out of my reverie and tapping the answer sheet Sylvie was scribbling on. They all stared at me.

'The junta.' I elaborated, pleased I could finally contribute.

'We know, dipshit,' said Angela, through a mouthful of crisps.

'We're on the year of Saddam Hussein's birth now,' said Denzil. 'Keep up.'

Dave, the quizmaster, was a middle-aged northerner who fancied himself as a comedian and kept saying things like 'look at your phone, you'll be on your way home' and engaging in banter with the team tables, who were mostly made up of rather nerdy-looking men. Sylvie tutted every time he attempted a gag, and Angela, already tipsy, kept shouting 'Bingo!' at indecent intervals. Denzil kept the drinks coming, though would occasionally slip Sylvie an answer out the side of his mouth.

Bobby returned from an under-table raid, and I smoothed my hands either side of her silky ears and breathed in her doggy smell, shaking off the memory hangover. Gazing into my eyes, she burped gently, and I recoiled at the stench.

Most of the questions went over my head – in the TV and

Film round I had barely even heard of the programmes mentioned, and although I knew some of the films, the questions were too obscure to attempt an answer. The name of the boat in *Jaws*? Sylvie was furiously making notes. Angela leaned across and scribbled something, and they both dissolved into giggles. I reached for a crisp and held it out under the table. Seconds later I felt a tickle of fur, and it was gone.

'Hey, Missy,' said Denzil. 'You OK?'

I shrugged. 'I don't know anything.'

He gave me a lopsided smile. 'You have untapped potential. That's why you're here.' I met his gaze for a second and thought what a kind man he was; so far removed from the shady stranger I'd tried to avoid on Bobby's first walk. That's what the dog did for me; got me past that first awkward hurdle. I could do the rest. Or at least, I was learning.

As we went into the final round, Dave tapping the microphone and everyone wincing at the feedback, I looked around the table at my friends, and thought if only I could answer one question, just one question that no one else knew, then I could go home happy. Just let me tap into my potential.

'Final round, ladies and gents,' coughed Dave. 'And this one's on . . . DOGS.'

The nerds groaned. Our table cheered.

'Yessssssss,' crowed Angela, giving our neighbours a V sign. Denzil rubbed his hands together and Sylvie twirled her pencil and winked at me. My celebrations were rather more muted; despite Bobby resting her head in my lap, it wasn't my strongest subject.

'This round's a bastard,' announced Dave. Then he dropped his microphone and said, 'shit' into it as he picked it up.

'Full house!' yelled Angela.

'Get a move on,' snapped Sylvie, arranging her pencils.

'Question one,' said Dave, 'what is the name of Hagrid's dog in *Harry Potter?*'

I knew this (Fang). But then, so did everyone else. And so it continued. Adam Bede's dog (Gyp), Mr Rochester's dog in *Jane Eyre* (Pilot), Dorothy's dog in *The Wizard of Oz* (Toto). They knew dogs I didn't know, like the name of Elliott's dog in *E.T.* (Harvey) and the dog in *Back to the Future* (Einstein). We were doing well – we could tell from the pained looks on the tables around us as we gathered momentum and became more and more exultant. We got the name of the dog in *Peter Pan* (Nana), and then came the final question, and Sylvie said it always came down to that one, that quizzes were won or lost on this last chance, so we had to get it right.

Dave cleared his throat and belched into the microphone. Bobby wagged appreciatively.

'Last one, ladies and gents,' he said. 'Make it count. What's the name of Odysseus' dog in the *Odyssey?*'

There was total silence for a second, and then someone snorted in derision.

'What the fuck?' said Angela. She looked at Sylvie, who shrugged and looked at Denzil, who shook his head. Then they looked at me.

Heady with gratification, I leaned forwards and whispered quietly, but with total confidence, 'Argos.'

Angela pulled a face. 'The shop?'

'Odysseus' dog,' I replied firmly, as Bobby licked my hand in support.

'Very well,' said Sylvie, marking our answer sheet. 'You'd better be right. My reputation is at stake.'

'Tap, tap,' said Denzil, knocking the side of his head with his knuckle and grinning at me.

I sat back, flooded with an immense satisfaction. Dave and the barmaid retreated to tot up, and Denzil went to get more drinks. Scumbag College, the reigning champions, kept sneaking us suspicious glances. It was going to go down to the wire. After an agonizing wait, Dave returned to the microphone, holding the sheaf of answer sheets in one hand and a pint of beer in the other.

'Well, it was a close one, chaps,' he announced, taking a sip. 'But the winners, by just one point, are . . .' He looked down at the sheet. 'Votey McVoteface!'

Sylvie erupted out of her chair, turning towards the crushed-looking Scumbag College with her fists raised in jubilation.

'In your FACE, IT Crowd!' Angela roared, as Sylvie did a victory turn of honour and narrowly avoided being hit by a paper aeroplane. There were several boos. No one likes a bad winner.

I fed Bobby a crisp as Denzil went up to collect our prize. We won £42 and a signed Jeremy Corbyn colouring book, which Angela clutched to her chest in ecstasy. Several of the other teams came up to congratulate us and to stroke Bobby, and Sylvie told all of them I'd been the only one of us to know the name of Odysseus' dog. Just one other person in the room had known, an elderly gentleman from a team called Mason and the

Argonauts, who tipped his straw fedora in my direction as he left. We spent £30 on more wine and staggered home with it, frittering our last £12 on fish and chips, which we shared leaning on the wall of my front garden, feeding Bobby bits of the batter and reliving our victory. I felt like a student again, holding a greasy paper bag and laughing as Angela did impressions of the computer geeks hunched around their answer sheets.

'You were all magnificent, especially me,' concluded Sylvie, licking chip oil off her fingers. 'I must go home and pop an anticipatory ibuprofen before bed. It's been a pleasure, my darlings. Toodle pip!' She sailed off into the night, back to Decca, Nancy and Aphra.

'You're all right, Missy,' said Denzil, saluting me drunkenly, turning and weaving his way in the opposite direction.

Angela hiccupped and tipped herself off the wall. She began to lurch down the road, then suddenly turned back to me, holding up a finger. Her eyes were struggling to focus. 'Don't forget to vote tomorrow,' she warned, and veered off towards her flat.

I opened my gate, letting Bobby through to the garden for a last sniff and looking up at the sky, velvety and remote, a few stars twinkling despite the city lights. Eventually she returned and lay at my feet, the noble hound.

'He fulfilled his destiny of faith,' I said to her, dashing a tear. 'He hung on.' But she'd gone again, weaving her way into the rose bushes until all that remained was rustling.

'Argos,' I whispered. He was me, and Leo was Odysseus, and, despite everything he'd done, and I'd done, I would always wait for him, no matter how long it took.

PART 3

'Friendship always benefits; love sometimes injures.'
Seneca

Chapter 23

I knew Leo was having an affair before he did. He started waking earlier, helping to get breakfast ready, even taking Alistair to school occasionally. He was cheerier than usual, as if suppressing a kind of glee, and most of all, he was more focused. Leo frequently had a distracted air, 'away with the Tories', as his great friend Tristan always said, his head in his books. But in those days he was more present than I had ever known him, spending less time in his study, suggesting day trips, even making dinner a couple of times, leaving the kitchen in an almighty mess. He was trying harder, and I couldn't work out why, until one day I saw him looking at himself in the mirror above the mantelpiece. He smoothed back his hair, then caught me looking at him and grinned guiltily. He was guilty.

He used to smooth his hair like that when he was with Alicia. I saw him once, outside her room, preparing for his entry. He caught sight of himself reflected in the window, and did the same gesture, flattening the unruly tufts at his temples. I became constantly on edge, searching for signs of him straying. Whenever he went away to a conference, convinced he was with her, I looked through his receipts for clues, checked his pockets, read his appointments diary. There was nothing incriminating to be found, but it made no difference.

And then we met her one day, when we dropped by his office to pick up his bag on our way to the theatre. His secretary handed it over, fussing over some papers, and as we left, a girl carrying a pile of books walked past. He greeted her, rather flustered. 'Carrie! I didn't know you would be here.' She turned, feigning surprise, and I knew immediately. She was small and red-haired and of course she was one of his students. I could tell from the way they were with each other that nothing had happened; they were at the circling stage, a consummation devoutly to be wished. That expectation, the holding back, must have been thrilling for them both. 'We mustn't hurt Millicent, or the children.' To imagine yourself a martyr, in the grip of a grand passion, and then to finally give way – what a rollercoaster ride! They were at the top of that first hill, anticipating the summit. There was no way anyone could stop them going over.

So I didn't say anything in the end, just let them ride it out. He was never so crass as to buy me flowers, but at the height of his little peccadillo, he did take me out to dinner at a smart new restaurant in Islington. That night, sitting in a kind of atrium, all dim lights and discreetly piped classical music, I watched him fiddle with his cutlery and thought how much

I loved him, despite it all. He caught my gaze in the candlelight and his eyes crinkled at the corners in the not-quite-a-smile he reserved just for me. I believed he felt particularly well-disposed towards me throughout the whole sordid episode, probably grateful for having such an obliging wife who looked the other way and didn't make a fuss. Not making a fuss was one of the hardest things I've ever done.

We had a few months of him doing odd jobs around the house, replacing a broken banister spindle, clumsily pushing the hoover round the house a few times and one day, absurdly, bringing home an enormous rocking horse for Alistair. Poor Ali was too old for it, but the sight of him politely thanking his father made my heart contort with the pity of it. It was a handsome thing, hand-carved with a real horsehair mane and a velvet saddle. I could never bear the touch of velvet, it made my skin crawl.

Then all of a sudden it came to an abrupt halt. Leo arrived home one night looking deflated, said something about feeling tired and that he'd been working too hard. Then he disappeared into his study and started writing his new book and we all went back to normal. The hottest love has the coldest end. I saw her on Gower Street a few weeks later, arm in arm with someone her own age. After it had gathered enough dust in Ali's room, I gave the horse to a children's home in Highbury. When I told Leo, he prepared to object, and then stopped himself – as good an admission as any. He liked to think of himself as fundamentally decent, and it can't have sat well with him, all that sneaking about. I was always much better at dissembling.

As the years went by I came to terms with it and even believed that in some ways it strengthened us. Perhaps stepping so close to the edge made him realize he didn't really want to jump off. The affection he felt for me during that time lingered, while his infatuation passed. As the children grew older, they didn't take up so much of my time, and I become less exasperated, able to concentrate more on being a wife. After I got used to Ali leaving home, it was rather nice being just the two of us, pottering about together. He ventured from his study for dinner and we would talk about his research, and enjoy the occasional outing – Oxford, Bath, Brighton – Leo in the bookshops and me whiling away the time in galleries and cafés. We'd invite friends for dinner, go to the theatre, take the odd trip abroad. Like our huddle on the dancefloor at Tristan's wedding, expanding the *oikos* and then contracting again, but always staying connected, humming along to our song.

We were coasting, idling along the tracks, the ups and downs behind us. But then Leo got ill and everything went off the rails altogether.

I was thinking about Leo's illness the morning after the quiz, as I got ready to go out and vote, feeling quite upbeat after our stunning victory, and having dodged a hangover. It was a dull day after the balminess of the night before, with the threat of rain, so I took my umbrella and set out with Bobby, who was in fine fettle, skittering this way and that.

After a quick circuit of the park, saluted by Denzil and

sympathizing with Sylvie's headache, I made my way to the polling station in the school hall round the corner from my house. As we neared our destination, though, my pace slowed and I became more thoughtful. After all, Leo was a Eurosceptic. *Skepsis* . . . ancient Greek for doubt. Maybe it would be nice to let him have his say, in absentia. It wasn't as if it would make a difference – ultimately, this was a precipice I could jump off on his behalf, safe in the knowledge that everyone else would catch me.

As my steps became more deliberate, Bobby looked up at me enquiringly.

'I'm deciding whether to stay or go,' I told her.

She pulled on her lead, dragging me forwards, which seemed like an endorsement. Securing her to the railings outside the hall, I noted with amusement that bringing one's dog to vote seemed to be something of a tradition amongst Stoke Newington residents. She sat patiently panting alongside a Border Terrier and a Labradoodle with a Remain sticker on her collar. If anything, it reinforced my decision. Carthage must be destroyed.

I went inside and took my voting paper. In the flimsy little booth, I stared at it for a second, letting the question settle, then picked up the pencil on a string and marked my cross. Feeling sated, I posted it in the box, smiling at the clerks as I made my way out to be met by a euphoric Bobby. Her greetings were always excessive, rearing up on to her hind legs, whining in ecstasy and mouthing at my wrists in her joy and relief. To Bobby, everything was black and white. If I left, it was forever;

when I came back, it was for good. She worked in a world of absolutes.

That's what everyone said about picking sides, that it was a stark choice, yes or no. Hang on, or let go. But it wasn't that simple. There were other considerations in play; shades of grey where you didn't necessarily agree or disagree but instead believed that one side summed up your feelings more than the other. I wanted to give Leo a voice, but more than anything I just wanted things to change, to stop feeling sad and bitter and lonely. That small act of rebellion made me feel I could change course even in the closing seconds of the race. Life in the old dog yet.

So I left the polling station with a spring in my step, despite the increasingly heavy skies. Rather than take Leo the usual flowers, I took my poll card and left it with him as a kind of offering. As I reached home with Bobby, the first fat drops of rain were falling, and we only just made it indoors before the heavens opened. I dried her in the hallway with an old towel and she sat obediently, lifting each paw for me to rub. When I finished I found myself kissing her on the snout, and she returned the favour, licking me on the nose.

It was so dark inside that I had to switch on the lights, once again relishing the artful clutter of my refurbished living room. Dear Sylvie, hopefully her headache was better. I bustled about making tea and replenishing Bobby's bowl of water, then settled on the sofa for a read while she twitched and snorted on her bed nearby, her jaws a whisker away from the squirrels scurrying through her dreams. We had an early night, lulled by the relentless drum of the rain on the windows, Bobby in her usual place at the foot of my bed.

In the park the next morning, the rain had made way for bright sunshine, the dawn of a new day, though I had to traipse through huge puddles that Bobby lapped at eagerly. Apart from a couple of rather glum nods from fellow dog walkers, we didn't speak to anyone. Angela texted me on my way back home, suggesting we meet at our café and, craving warmth and chat, I accepted. We met at 11 a.m., when the early morning rush had passed. She was slumped at our usual table, Otis perched on the chair next to her sucking furiously at a milkshake. Hanna came to take my order and I noticed her eyes were red, as if she'd been crying. Probably boyfriend trouble.

'I can't believe it,' said Angela, stirring her coffee and twiddling the spoon in her fingers in place of a cigarette. 'How could they? Imbeciles. Do they not realize what will happen? The economy in shreds, every racist and bigot in the country coming out of the woodwork, funding down the fucking toilet, it'll be impossible to travel anywhere, God knows what else. What were they thinking? The mind boggles, I tell you, the mind boggles.'

'What on earth are you talking about?'

She stared at me incredulously. 'The vote, of course!'

'What do you mean? What happened?'

She leaned across to the next table, grabbed a newspaper and shook the front page in my face. I took it from her and read the headline. The words blurred in front of me, then came into sharp focus. I blinked.

'I can't believe it.' I kept my head down, still reading so she couldn't see my expression.

'You'll see how it all unravels, now. All this bollocks about global trade and sovereignty. What a crock of shit.'

Hanna brought over my coffee and I thanked her, pushing aside the paper. People tended to over-dramatize, so all this talk of recession and deporting foreigners would no doubt come to nothing. I busied myself adding milk to my coffee and nibbling the little almond biscuit they served with it, realizing it never occurred to Angela to think I had voted anything but the same way as her, the same way as everyone we knew. I resolved that she must never know what had happened in that voting booth, how far I'd strayed. Like other unmentionable things, it must be rolled up, stuffed away and forgotten.

We made our way to the playground, Angela still grumbling as I helped Otis collect twigs to make a bird's nest. I watched Bobby trotting back and forth, tail waving as she sniffed and frolicked here and there. I'd grown used to her company on these walks, used to the other company we found as a result. In the few short months she'd been with me, I'd talked to more people here than in the fifty years before. The realization shamed me, just as the headlines had earlier.

I watched Otis on the swings, kicking his legs to propel himself higher and higher, and wondered what opportunities would be lost as a consequence of that vote, what chances would be denied him, what he would miss out on. Maybe it would be fine, maybe it would be a disaster, maybe something in between. Whatever the outcome I'd have to live with it, and my part in it. Just another cross for me to bear.

Chapter 24

June gave way to July and the sun scorched the grass in the park until it withered and yellowed. Bobby wilted, spending her days flopped in the hallway where the tiled floor was cooler. Her fur was so thick, I considered taking her to the groomers to get it clipped, but when I suggested the idea to Angela she was horrified.

'She's like Samson, it'll take away her strength!' she said, clapping her hands over Bobby's pricked-up ears. But there was no doubt she felt the heat, and I took to walking her earlier in the morning to escape the worst of the sun's rays. I rather liked ambling around the park on our own before anyone else arrived and took possession. The beginning of a summer's day bristled with possibility, and unlike Bobby, I relished the heat seeping through my veins, firing up my cylinders – I didn't feel quite so stiff and old in summer.

Mel came to visit one Saturday, her first time back to the house since our fight, and we were both surprised to find that we enjoyed each other's company, even in the very same room where we'd rowed so viciously the year before. After lunch, we went to take flowers to Leo together, which although a sober event, at least felt companionable. On the way back, she broke the sombre silence brought on by the visit.

'I miss him.'

I stared at the huge gnarled trees that lined the broad avenue we were walking along. 'I miss him too.'

'Sometimes I talk to him as if he's still there. As if he's going to say 'buck up, hedgehog! Onwards!'

I tried to laugh, but it came out as more of a sob. 'Did you . . .' I was going to ask if she got my letter, but all of a sudden it felt like too much. 'Did you go to look at that place on Eltisley Avenue?'

Mel and Octavia were thinking of buying a bigger flat as they had too many books, but they couldn't decide between one near Midsummer Common and another closer to Newnham. She outlined the benefits of both, then mentioned she was worried about her research funding being cut as a result of 'Brexit'. Like Angela, she never questioned my own role in it all. I didn't tell her, not being so stupid as to knock down the wobbly bridges we were building, but did suggest that Leo might have voted differently if he'd been able to.

Mel stared at me in astonishment. 'Of course he wouldn't have voted to leave! The very idea!'

'But . . .' I wanted to make my case without giving myself away. 'He always used to moan about Brussels bureaucrats . . .'

Mel snorted. 'Yes, and he also used to moan about Disraeli's crappy novels but that didn't stop him thinking he was a genius.'

It compounded my shame to think I'd voted to give Leo a voice and ascribed him the wrong one. Every day brought a new story to add to my overloaded conscience. Angela told me that Hanna the waitress had returned home one day after work to find that someone had daubed 'Poles go home' across her door. The economy was in free-fall, everyone said, the pound losing so much value that it would soon be worth about as much as the sticks Bobby brought me on our walks. What would happen to my pension? Money was tight enough as it was, every day brought more bills for me to ignore, and the other day I'd had a phone call from Horace Simmonds, our bank manager. He was an old friend of Leo's, so I placated him with some half-hearted assurances. I knew I shouldn't ignore it but it felt like too big an issue to deal with – easier to roll it up and stash it away. I couldn't tell Mel any of it – she'd start up again about me downsizing – so instead suggested we take the dog for a stroll.

When we arrived back at the house we found Angela waiting for us at the gate with Otis and a black bin bag. Remembering the bag that Sylvie brought me, I thought of the dog bed in my living room, coated in a layer of hairs, reeking of Bobby's sour old sock stench, a smell I was gradually learning to live with. Once again she was drooping in the heat. As we drew nearer, Angela put her hand in the bag and pulled out something blue and plastic, which she shook in our faces triumphantly.

'Got a hose?' she asked, grinning. It was a paddling pool.

We took it to the lawn in the back garden, and Angela began blowing it up while Mel got the hose out of the shed. It was only a small pool, with three plastic rings, but seeing it there reminded me of summers when the children were small and I used to set up a sprinkler for them, watching them shriek with delight as they ran backwards and forwards. I was touched by the recollection, an oasis in the desert, as I had a depressing tendency to think of those years as endlessly miserable and exhausting. Like dwelling on a single criticism in a sea of gushing compliments, I recalled my failures rather than my triumphs: for every sprinkler snapshot there seemed to be a whole album of snappy early starts rearing up to rebuke me. We had some lovely times, Mel, Alistair and I. I just had to work a bit harder to remember them.

Once the pool was inflated, Mel filled it up while Angela helped Otis put on his swimming trunks as he hopped from one foot to the other in excitement. Bobby circled the pool, tail wagging warily, and then sat watching and panting as Otis put his toe in the water. It took him about ten minutes of dipping and screeching to finally immerse himself, but then he was off, splashing and shouting, skinny little body glistening in the sunshine. We drank the Pimm's and lemonade Mel had brought with her, and sat on Sylvie's green, flowery cushions, watching him enjoy himself. After about an hour he started to get cold, so I fetched a towel and he sat on his mother's lap, snug as a bug in a rug, while we idly chatted and Bobby lay with tongue lolling.

Eventually we went indoors to find some shade, Mel exclaiming over my new living room and admiring the portrait of her grandfather, William Jameson, and Angela persuading her to stay for a takeaway. They went off to find the menu, and after putting the kettle on, I went back outside intending to use the paddling pool water to give my plants a much-needed drink. But as I stepped out the back door I was brought up short by the sight that greeted me.

Every now and again, some inner demon in Bobby's brain would unleash a brief but intense frenzy. Sylvie called it the 'funny five minutes'. We'd observed it on a few occasions in the park, when she'd sniffed something interesting, met a dog she particularly liked, or simply when the mood took her. It didn't happen often, but when it did it was monumental. She would race around in a furry whirlwind, barking on every about-turn, carving up the ground with her claws, a tangle of limbs and teeth, until she'd exhausted herself, and then she'd flop down, eyes rolling, looking to be congratulated on her performance.

Now the paddling pool had instigated a fully-fledged session. In and out of the pool she jumped, splashing with abandon, leaping out to shake herself and race around the garden. Then back in for another demented dip, out for a shake, race round the lawn, and repeat. As it went on, the spectacle became more and more amusing, and I started to giggle. Angela, Otis and Mel joined me at the back door and soon we were all laughing helplessly, wiping tears and splashes from our faces as Bobby's antics drenched us as well as her. Finally she skidded to a halt in front of us, panting vigorously, the wet fur plastered to her body making her look half her usual size.

'She's mental,' said Otis admiringly, as Bobby stood for one last shake and settled down to dry in the early evening sun.

Bobby's deranged romp had depleted the pool but there was still enough for me to give my roses a good soak while we waited for the takeaway to be delivered. Wandering amidst my flowers, I watched Bobby's crinkling fur and spread-eagled paws twitching, and felt envious of her ability to let herself go like that. She was such an avid, simple creature; she had no secrets, nothing to be ashamed of, nothing to apologise for – she just let it all hang out.

The pool was still half-full, lapping gently at the sides after my onslaughts with the watering can, so I slipped off my sandals and stepped into it. Cool and silken between my toes, I gazed down at the abiding blue swilling around my weathered feet. I wanted to wash away my sins, shed them like an old skin and step out refreshed and unblemished, a clean slate. As if shuffling round a paddling pool, recently vacated by a mad mongrel, could achieve that. I could already see the dog hairs gathering round my ankles.

One of my earliest memories was my mother taking me to the Parliament Hill Lido when I was tiny. I remember watching her swimming in the pool, dark hair swarming behind her. She whipped round and swam back towards me, then held her arms out of the water. 'Milly! Come!' I was standing on the side in a little knitted costume that itched at the shoulders and the water would stop the itch, but I couldn't jump because there was a spider in the way. At least, it wasn't a spider, just a crack on the poolside tile, but it might have been a spider. It might. I couldn't get past it, just in case it moved and then it *was* a spider. So I just stood there, desperate to take the plunge but stuck at the side. Eventually my mother couldn't resist floating away.

Bobby huffed herself onto her haunches and wandered over to look at a fly scrabbling on the surface. I noticed earlier that she seemed very fond of Melanie, who took every opportunity to fuss her and tell her she was beautiful. Surprised to find myself feeling a little jealous, I pulled one of her ears and sighed. 'She reminds me of things I've done wrong.' I thought of our argument, the guilt that made my rage all the more encompassing. Rage that had now dissipated, but still hung in the air like static. Despite the fact that Mel and I had brokered a kind of unspoken peace, I preferred not to think of that day; if I could ignore it for long enough maybe the lack of thought would make it fade like an old photo.

'Mum, what on earth are you doing?' It was Mel at the back door with a loaded paper bag in one hand and a poppadum in the other. I hastily got out of the pool and shuffled back into my sandals.

'Just trying it out,' I said, taking the poppadum off her and sliding past. Shaking her head, she followed me inside, a still-damp Bobby squeezing through between us. I'd have to save my funny five minutes for another day.

Chapter 25

Lancaster Villas
Kensington W8

21st September 1942

My dearest Will,

I had a letter from Sibyl the other day. I was surprised because you know she is not one for lengthy epistles or indeed any form of communication for that matter. Too busy with her chickens. Anyway, she wrote to say that Henry & Milly are doing very well, they are at school up there and enjoying the countryside by all accounts. Best of all Sibby included a note from Milly herself! I can't bring myself to send it to you in case it gets lost so the following is inscribed verbatim:

Dare Mama

I lov you. Ar room is hiy. Ther ar sheep.
Milly

Isn't that fine! I'm so glad Sibby didn't try to correct any of it, I wouldn't have enjoyed it nearly as much. There was also a picture, which I think may have been one of the sheep. I won't try to recreate it here.

Things are pretty much the same in London. Father has stopped going down to the cellar during the raids. Says he'll either die or he won't and going downstairs won't make a difference. Mother has started sewing again, always a bad sign.

With the children (and you) away I am glad to have my work. The ambulances make pretty heavy driving, but I am getting used to them. My usual hours are six at night'til eight in the morning. We have to go out as soon as the bombs start dropping, otherwise there is no one left to save. At first it was daunting but nowadays we're usually too busy to notice. The other night a bomb hit a theatre in Tottenham Court Road. The show was packed with soldiers home on leave – many of the casualties were in uniform. They'd been laid out in the road with a rug over them, and we had to check if they were all dead so we knew whether to take them to hospital or the mortuary.

I found one chap who was alive amongst them and held his hand for a while as I waited for him to pass. He said, 'Tell Elsie I love her,' and I said I would. We loaded him and the others up and drove them to the mortuary, but they wouldn't take them without a doctor's certificate. So we had bodies in the car but nowhere to put them. In the end we had to leave them in a back street. None of us liked it but what could we do? There were others who still had a chance and we had to help them.

On my days off I've been meeting with a few other women in Fitzrovia who are thinking of setting up an Equal Pay committee to push for better rights. The discussions are pretty lively and the other night we were so taken up with arguing that by the time we'd finished we emerged onto the street to find the blackout in full force and I had to use the white kerbs to grope my way to the bus stop. The driver was no good either, too heavy on the brakes. It was past ten by the time I got home. Mother was quite hysterical.

I must finish this as my shift starts soon, but I'll write again as soon as I am able. I'm hoping to get some leave to go up to Yorkshire in the next month or so. Maybe I'll get your little Missy to write you a letter of your own. Wouldn't that be delightful?

I remain
Your darling
Lena

I found the letter from Sibyl in there too, along with my own note, grubby and creased from re-reading, with the picture of the sheep at the bottom. I thought it looked more like the sun behind a cloud, but I suppose it depended which way you looked at it. All those years I thought that the worst thing was Jonas the Labrador being taken away.

The thing I really can't bear is that she did come up to see us, and she asked me to write to my father, but I never did, because we were too busy playing with Aunt Sibby's animals. I thought, as Bobby nuzzled me and licked the tears off my cheeks, that if only I could go back, I'd go up to that attic bedroom and write him the longest, most misspelt letter I could manage.

I remain

His darling

Missy.

Chapter 26

On Melanie's thirtieth birthday, Leo had insisted on throwing a party. She didn't want it, and neither did I; couldn't be bothered with the hassle of invites and venues, and the awkwardness of hosting an event in Cambridge. Ali was off travelling so couldn't help, and after making the grand proclamation Leo went off to a conference and it fell to me to organize it all, ringing round everyone and booking a room at King's, while Mel grumbled and said she'd rather just have dinner at the Peking.

On the morning of the party, I woke with a hangover, having indulged in several strong gin and tonics while I was dealing with last-minute RSVPs – 'No, of course, it's not a problem *at all*' – and trying to get through to Ali's hotel to see if he would make it back from Egypt in time. The headache was incessant, prodding at my temples, and the late summer heat didn't help, blasting through the house as I scurried about wrapping Mel's present (a Wollstonecraft first edition her loving father picked up from Bonhams at vast expense) and calling the caterers. Then Leo arrived home and started putting his oar in, asking about wine choices and saying we should have gone for an outside do. By the time we got in the car we were both sweaty and irritable, barely exchanging a word during the drive up.

In King's Hall, the waiters were setting up tables in the wrong place, so Leo went off to remonstrate with them while I escaped to the cool of the chapel and sat leaning my head against one of the pews, wishing it was all over.

'Hi, Mum,' Mel took the seat next to me and picked up one of the hymn books, thumbing through it abstractedly. 'Did you manage to speak to Ali?'

'He missed his flight,' I sighed, pressing two knuckles to the sides of my head. 'He sends his love.'

Mel snorted. 'Typical. I might have known.' She slapped down the book on the shelf in front of us and crossed her arms. She and Ali had a cordial enough relationship but they were very different beings.

I closed my eyes. 'It's not his fault, he got caught up in his dig. You know how it is.'

'I do indeed. How many people *are* coming?'

'About a hundred, I think.'

'God, how monstrous. Cowpats from the Devil's own satanic herd.'

'What I love about you, Melanie, is how grateful you are.'

'Mother, we all know there's very little you love about me.' She said it in her usual droll way, but found her mark all the same. I was too jaded to spar with her though, so instead stared at the painting above the altar, *The Adoration of the Magi*. Was that what Mel wanted? Adoration? Whereas I'd given her canapés and a live band, at her father's request.

Mel got to her feet. 'Let's get on with it, shall we?'

Back in the Hall, the tables had been rearranged and people were carrying flowers and candlesticks around. A drinks table had been set up at one end and I went to inspect it and pour myself a surreptitious glass. It was five to six, after all. Surveying the room, I thought how curious it was that Leo was so keen to celebrate Melanie's birthday but not our anniversary. Thirty years this year too, since we were married right here. But he was away on the day and when he came back he brought me a Navajo Indian pendant. A pretty thing, but turquoise; not right at all. Thirty years is Pearl. I bought him a letter opener with a mother-of-pearl handle and when he opened it, he said, 'what a funny thing!' as if the significance was utterly lost on him. Yet Mel got King's Hall, its oak panels, oils and echoes.

Halfway down the glass my headache started to subside and as the first guests arrived and the food came out, I rallied. Ali would be back soon, and there would be other anniversaries. Leo was playing the attentive host, bottle of champagne in hand, while Mel was surrounded by old friends from her college, all patting her on the back as if they were congratulating her on something more than simply existing for three decades. My back to the wall, I allowed the waiters to keep me topped up, and started counting down the minutes.

Then Leo was in front of me, beckoning as the band started

to play. I took his hand and the last of my headache melted away along with everyone else; it was just us, his hand at my waist, eyes crinkling as he looked down at me. I knew that some of this was for show – proud parents on display – but while I was in his arms it didn't matter. We could both hear our song, and for once it drowned everything else out.

'Well done,' he said, twirling me round. 'It's a good party. Even the wine's not bad.'

I laughed. 'Not the '59 vintage, I'm afraid.'

'I know you worked hard. I'm sorry Ali couldn't be here.' He kissed my cheek. 'I'd better get ready for my speech. Make sure you stand at the front, Mrs Carmichael.'

The heat and noise was intensifying, and when Leo tapped his glass and we all jostled to one side to listen, I felt crushed and disoriented after our moment alone, unable to focus on his words as he congratulated himself on having such an accomplished daughter, with her PhD and her research fellowship; following in her father's footsteps . . . I drifted off; turquoise, the talisman of kings, the Turkish stone to protect you from falls. Maybe it was better than pearl after all. I gazed at Leo, still addressing the throng, and smiled when he raised his glass to Melanie, and then he joined me in the crowd as Mel made her way to the front, her friends hollering and whooping. At first, so pleased to have him by my side, I didn't notice she was leading someone by the hand. Her friend – Octavia? Jolly woman, winked a lot. And suddenly I realized what was about to happen and stepped forwards as if to stop it, but this fall from Leo's grace was one I couldn't prevent.

So I stared at the rim of my glass, while my husband stiffened beside me.

Mel's speech was short and to the point. Octavia stood next to her beaming, and the reaction from the crowd was mixed – roaring approval from her friends, polite bewilderment from ours. I could feel Leo's consternation emanating from him, trying to look jovial and relaxed, as if this wasn't the most immense shock. So oblivious, locked away in his ivory tower – I could see his dream of her marrying some eminent professor and having wildly overachieving children dying before his eyes.

Amidst cheering and some bemused clapping, Leo, his face fixed in a grin, nodding to guests, hissed at me out of the corner of his mouth. 'Did you know?'

I shrugged, burying my face in my glass.

'Why didn't you tell me?'

I swallowed my wine, and waved at Tristan's wife Isabel, who was raising a puzzled toast in my direction. 'I wasn't sure. She never said anything.'

'You should have warned me. What am I supposed to do now?'

'It's not my fault. We'll just have to make the best of it.'

'You mean *I* will.'

He moved away, shaking hands and squeezing shoulders as he strode towards his daughter. I saw him jerk his head in the direction of the door, and they both sidled off, stopping to be congratulated by various groups as they threaded their way out. Just as they exited, she looked back at Octavia and rolled her eyes, and I couldn't help but feel a thrill of satisfaction – Mel had crossed the Rubicon, the alliance splintered. I put down my wine and followed them.

Out on the lawn by the river, they were arguing furiously, hands waving in a symmetry that belied their hostility.

'How could you?' Leo was saying. 'In front of all those people? Our friends?'

'I'm not ashamed!' Mel shot back. 'Are you?'

'That's not the point. You should have told me you were planning to . . .to . . . It wasn't supposed to be about that.'

'Then what was it about? You toasting the continuation of your legacy?'

He was silent for a second, and I had to suppress a smirk at such an effective skewering. I thought of our gift, nestling amongst the others on the table in the hall. *A Vindication of the Rights of Woman.* I had gone out there to smooth things over, but they didn't notice me – as usual – and I started to back away again, leaving them to it. Maybe this was just what they needed – not a severing of the link between them, but a fraying. And once it was done, I could be there to pick up the pieces, to comfort Leo and maybe even, for once, be the more tolerant parent. So I drifted off back to the party, and nodded appreciatively when people told me Mel was terribly brave, what a courageous young woman, going her own way.

Gradually, guests started to say their farewells, the staff discreetly began to clear up, Mel and Octavia got swept off to King's bar to carry on their celebrations. In the end, it was just Leo and me in the car again, back seat loaded with leftover bottles and flowers. In the darkness he leaned his head against the steering wheel for a second then looked across at me.

'I'm sorry,' he said ruefully. 'I know it's not your fault. I just wish . . .'

I put my hand on his shoulder. 'I know.'

He sighed. 'A few years ago there was this nice chap at Caius who wrote to me for advice about Disraeli, and then we met at Alan Taylor's eightieth, and I thought, "*that's* the kind of man . . ."' He tailed off and stared into the distance.

'No use wondering what might have been,' I murmured, sliding my hand up to rub the back of his head, my fingers moving through the still-lustrous greying locks.

'But you hope, don't you . . .' He looked sideways at me. 'That they'll find . . . what *we* found.'

There in the dark, in our cold car, my heart inflated like a party balloon. I wanted to say . . . so many things. To ask him exactly what we found – had we found the same things? To tell him what *I'd* found – my home, my *oikos*, my song answered. I wanted to savour this moment, and enrich it, and soothe him, but there was too much to say, so I stumbled over it. 'I'm sure this Octavia is very nice and clever as well.'

Wholly inadequate. He straightened in his seat, rearing away from my wandering hand. 'She's from *your* old college,' he said, slightly accusingly. And as he started the engine to back up onto King's Parade, the car stalled and jumped, and—

—and I was awake, in Angela's living room again, the clock on the wall showing it was nearly eleven. I blinked and uncurled on the sofa, my joints stiff and unyielding. As I creaked to my feet, the key turned in the door and Angela herself came in, barefoot, holding her shoes by the straps. When she saw me she raised her eyebrows enquiringly.

'All fine,' I said, rubbing my eyes. 'He was asleep by eight. Your tree surgeon? Was he nice?'

She pulled a face. 'It turns out trees are really boring.'

'That bad?'

'We had a pizza and split the bill, I put a tip down and he picked it up to cover the cost of my Pinot Grigio.'

'Oh dear. I'm sorry.'

'Not to worry. Other fish in the sea. Or trees in the forest. I'm just going to check on Oat.'

I followed her in as she padded through to the bedroom. She pushed open the door, and Otis rolled over, blinking.

'Hello, Mummy,' he said drowsily. 'Missy told me a story where everyone was murdered with arrows.'

'Sorry,' I said from the doorway. 'It was the story of Achilles.'

Angela flashed me a grin over her shoulder, and turned back to Otis. 'Did she now? Lucky you. Now back to sleep before she tells you another one.' She patted the duvet around him and tucked his hair behind his ear. Otis didn't need to be dunked in a river by his heel to protect him; there were no gaps or weaknesses to begin with. Men and women, women and women, mothers and sons, even old ladies and dogs. Love was just love, that was all. Flawed, uneven, complicated, overlapping, but still essential.

'Sorry,' I said again, as we went back into the living room. 'On reflection, it probably wasn't all that appropriate.'

'That's OK,' she said, rubbing her eyes. 'Nobody's perfect.'
She noticed the empty bottle on the coffee table. 'Not a drop
left, you fecking bastard.'

I smiled and started to gather my things, but at the door I
turned back, my fingers on the latch. Angela was slumped on
the sofa, bare feet propped on the table, munching leftover
pretzels.

'Just so you know,' I said. 'Otis doesn't need a father. He's fine
as he is.' And I slipped out and closed the door behind me
before she could reply.

Back home I let myself in to Bobby's rapturous welcome and
realized I hadn't opened that morning's post, so went through
to the living room and settled on the sofa to flick through it. It
was mostly bills as usual, but last of all was a thicker envelope
postmarked Cambridge. I slid a fingernail into the slit and
dragged it along. Inside were a couple of photographs and a
scrawled note from Mel: 'Thought you'd like these.'

They were both photos from the wedding. Melanie and
Octavia, still going strong, nearly thirty years after that party.
The first photo I remembered, taken on the lawn with Bobby,
just after we'd met Alicia. I was standing between the happy
couple, looking stiff and self-conscious, Bobby tugging at her
lead, mostly out of shot. But the other one had been taken
unawares, just as we were leaving. We were walking down the
corridor towards the photographer, Bobby pulling ahead, grinning
towards the camera, all of us bathed in the light spilling out from
the party. Angela was carrying Otis, his smiling face against her
shoulder; she was turning towards me saying something, and my

head was flung back as I shouted with laughter. What was it she'd been saying? I couldn't remember, but I'd never seen myself like that before.

The first photo summed me up, mostly, but the second had exposed my other self, the tiny part of me that could laugh like that. I wanted to poke my way into that part like I'd delved into the envelope, widen and open it up so that it overwhelmed the stiffness and self-consciousness and all the other weaknesses I despised. To be that relaxed, animated woman, put her on display and leave the other one stuffed away.

But then, like Angela said, nobody's perfect. Not Leo, not Melanie, and certainly not me. I propped the photos on the mantelpiece, the first tucked behind the second. Tomorrow I'd find frames for them both.

Chapter 27

In September, Otis started school and as the weeks went by, I found myself at a loose end. I'd grown used to our mornings together; more often than not they stretched into the afternoon, or Angela would stay for tea and a gossip when she came to pick him up.

Bobby and I still had our strolls, met other dog walkers for coffee and occasionally went round to Sylvie's for a chat, but I missed Otis, and the anchor of his visits to look forward to. Angela said he was doing well at school and one day she even took me to collect him. We stood outside the classroom and when the door opened promptly at three-thirty he came hurtling out, his book bag swinging as he flung himself into her arms. Then he turned to me, said, 'Missy!' and put his arms round my knees. We took him to the library and I read him a story while Angela went to look for Maeve Binchys. On the way out she pointed at the noticeboard.

'Look, you should do that.'

It was a notice advertising for readers at the Children's Storytime on Thursday mornings.

I shook my head. 'I don't think so. That's for out-of-work actors. They won't want an old dear like me.'

'Bollocks,' she replied. 'You're really good at reading. You've got one of those voices.'

I harrumphed and shrugged, yet found myself thinking more and more about it at home. Leo always said I had a nice speaking voice, and back in the late 1950s when I was working at the University Library, a charity approached me to record a talking book. But reading to a group of over-excited children was a different matter, and I wasn't sure I had the necessary temperament. Still, it stayed in the back of my mind and the following week when on my wanderings I found myself outside the library again, after a great deal of dallying, I went in. The notice was still there.

'Can I help you?'

A middle-aged woman with Iris Murdoch hair, glasses on a string round her neck, was peering in my direction. I indicated the noticeboard.

'Are you still looking for a reader?'

She beamed. 'We are indeed! Would you like to volunteer?'

I don't know why I signed up for it, but I felt that my laughing alter ego would have thought nothing of offering to read for a group of rowdy children. Of course, it led to a series of restless nights, watching the shadows and then dreaming that I'd gone out without any clothes on.

Later that week, I took Otis's copy of *Glenys the Itchy Witch* to the library, quaking and cursing myself for being so foolhardy. By that point, the party animal in the second photo from Mel's wedding had been thoroughly banished by the withered old shrew in the first. The last night had been the most sleepless, tossing and turning until even Bobby was disturbed, jumping off the bed and retreating to the floor in a huff, where she proceeded to fall asleep again and snore loudly, doing nothing for my insomnia. I lay and made shapes out of the silhouettes, wishing Leo was there to buck me up. Remembering Mel's auditions at school, encouraged and buoyed by her father, I really had been very unsympathetic.

In the morning I couldn't keep anything down but dry toast, and was ravenous by the time I arrived. The lady with Iris Murdoch hair, who was called Deirdre, greeted me with a cup of tea and a custard cream, then compounded my nerves by saying some of the children had already arrived. By the time I sat down in the story corner, my hands were shaking and my throat was arid. The children and their parents – mothers – were standing in the main part of the library, running around and chatting, respectively. Deirdre had set up little chairs and cushions in rows in the children's section; she stood next to me and clapped her hands.

'Sit down everyone, we're about to begin!'

The children filed through and sat down on the cushions, still twittering away, while the mothers ranged themselves at the back. Why had I said I would do this? There was still a low hum of noise and I had no idea how to get them to be quiet. I took a deep, shaking breath.

'The owl swooped down over the witch's hat,' I croaked.

Deirdre nodded encouragingly, and the children subsided, fingers twiddling, eyes sliding but occasionally focusing on me.

'And with his beak he tweaked her plait.' I had inadvertently worn my own long hair in a plait and remembered Otis calling me a witch – with Halloween coming up, it seemed appropriate. I flicked it, the children giggled, and then – finally – the laughing me woke up and started to take over.

'The witch gave a hiss and flicked her cane, turning him into a weather vane!'

And so I continued, my voice carrying over the little corner and drawing in the children and their mothers as I switched between the characters in my story. I saw to my delight that they were transfixed, gazing at the pictures I held out towards them, whispering and pointing. The mothers were smiling at their little ones, Deirdre mouthing along. As we progressed, everyone joined in for the 'Hiss!' refrain and as I dived into the final lines finishing with a wicked whisper – 'and with a snap of her cane, she was never seen again!' – I looked up to a smattering of applause from the mums. Deirdre asked if I had another story, and I didn't, but of course we were in a library, so we found a *Hairy Maclary* book and I read that too.

Afterwards some of the women congratulated me and Deirdre gave me another biscuit and asked if I'd like to go for lunch with her. We went to a café round the corner and over a baked potato she asked if I would like a job. It wasn't much – she was particularly apologetic because by then she knew my employment history – but they needed a new Library Assistant. I was overqualified, and over the moon. I said I would think about it and walked home hugging myself, wanting to tell someone who wasn't Bobby. I thought about texting Angela or Sylvie but didn't want to sound hubristic. In the end, I emailed Alistair and texted Mel, who replied promptly and with typical pragmatism:

That's great news, well done. You'll need to get to grips with the new IT systems, maybe they can give you training?

Maybe it was a silly idea, to start working again at my age. All the technology had moved on, I was bound to make a fool of myself, with my Rolodex and Greek Lexicon. Bobby sat looking at me with her head on one side, listening to my monologue as I came back down to earth. Scratching her behind the ears, she gave a low grunt of appreciation. I'd better take her on a walk – now that the nights were drawing in, we had to get it done earlier – but as I picked up her lead, my mobile phone pinged again and a text from Angela popped up.

Emergency, stuck at work, Otis at school. Could you poss pick him up? Password is Batman. Sorry and tx!

We made our way to Otis's school, the dog slightly sulky at the deviation from her usual route. Tying her lead to some railings outside the school gates, I went inside, and in reception encountered another woman coming out with her children.

She smiled at me. 'Hello! You were so good today, Bella really enjoyed it, didn't you Bel? Loved the Welsh dragon.'

I blushed and stammered my thanks, catching the door as she held it open. Otis came barrelling out, his teacher handing me a sheaf of papers covered in his scribbles. He'd been making cheese straws and proudly handed me one; it was pale and limp like a dead man's finger. When I nibbled the end it tasted of dry flour.

'Marvellous,' I said, taking another bite. 'Delicious!'

He skipped alongside me telling me about his day. He'd built a rocket with his friend Ethan, a girl was sick outside the toilets, and Belinda his teacher had taught them 'k' 'k' 'k' – he made a pincer movement with his fingers. I wasn't sure I approved of phonics. In my day we just learned to read.

We took Bobby briefly round the block and then went home where I made pancakes for Otis while he ran round the house, having tucked a tea towel in the neck of his jumper by way of a cape. When Angela knocked on the door later, we were crouched on the rug in the sitting room playing with the Dinky cars from the attic.

'Sorry, sorry, sorry,' Angela followed me in waving a wrapped up bottle of wine. 'Absolute nightmare. God, I hate my job.'

I took the wine from her. 'You didn't need to do that, you know I love having him.'

'But it's an imposition isn't it? I don't want to be one of those mothers.' She squatted on the rug with Otis and ruffled his hair. 'Were you a good boy?'

'Yes,' he said. 'There was sick outside the toilets, but it wasn't me.'

'You must have one of his cheese straws,' I said.

Over wine and dead man's fingers, Angela moaned about her latest commission ('Have Baby Boomers had it too easy?'), and then asked about my reading. I told her about Deirdre, and the job offer. 'That's amazing!' she said, clinking her glass against mine. 'When do you start?'

I shrugged. 'I'm not sure it's a good idea. I'm a bit old, and there's Bobby to think of.'

'Bullshit,' Angela snorted. 'You'd be great. Stop doing yourself down and go for it.'

I traced a finger round the rim of my glass. 'It's just . . . it's a long time since I worked. Everything's changed. They computerize everything, I'm bound to get it all wrong.'

Angela reached for her phone and started jabbing away at it. I sat back, slightly offended, but she shook her head and continued. When she put it down again she slapped the table with both hands.

'I just texted Denzil and told him to be on standby to help you. He's the bollocks when it comes to tech, he made a fortune selling his internet start-up and now just swans around with those boxers of his, spending money on art. He'll sort you out. See?' As her phone chimed she held it up and I saw his reply.

Will do. Tell Missy well done.

'Right. Any more excuses?' Angela had a glint in her eye – she had something of the gimlet about her – and I shook my head. Maybe I'd tell Deirdre I'd think about it for a bit longer.

'Are you going to Denzil's party?' continued Angela, brushing cheese straw crumbs off her jeans.

'I suppose so,' I frowned. 'It sounds terribly fancy.' We'd all had proper invitations in the post – it made a welcome change from bills, but I felt a little too old for a dress code.

Angela sniffed. 'Don't take any notice – last year Sylvie saw someone in white tie, and someone else in paint-splattered overalls. He likes artists – they're all weird. I heard he's got a Damien Hirst in the basement.'

She and Otis left soon after, and I pottered about my kitchen putting the leftover wine back in the fridge and heating up some soup for my supper. Bobby wolfed her dinner, collar jangling against her bowl, a sound I'd come to appreciate. I ate in the kitchen, feeding her scraps of buttery bread and browsing on my laptop. Checking my email, I saw a reply from Alistair. Arthur was doing very well at school, already writing his name beautifully and talking about becoming a policeman. Emily had found an Aboriginal shell midden – I had no idea what that meant – and he'd been asked to attend a conference in New York later in the year. I wished it were in London. Finally, he said he thought the job sounded wonderful and just like the kind of thing that would suit me. 'You have so much to offer,' he said. 'Dad would be so proud.'

Did I have much to offer? Six months ago I'd have said I had very little, but lately I'd felt a sense of optimism creeping up on me – the idea that there were things to look forward to, that I had options, was a heady feeling. Yet I worried my newfound zest was a flimsy thing, as brittle and crumbly as Otis's cheese straws. Would Leo have been proud? He would probably have grumbled about me being out all the time – he liked having me around, even when he was closeted in his study. He used to say he could feel my presence in the house even if he couldn't see or hear me, and that it was comforting. I felt the same. But *he* wasn't around any more, and I had to live with that.

'What do you think, Bobby?' I asked, as she began the process of turning and settling onto her bed by the fireplace. 'Is it a foolish thing to do at my age?'

Bobby's eyebrows twitched as she thought it over.

'The professional equivalent of jumping in a paddling pool,' I added, rubbing her head.

Her tail thumped.

I decided I'd take the job. There would always be spider-cracks on the tiles to put you off, but sometimes you had to take the plunge anyway. I had a feeling – a hope – that, like Bobby, it could turn out to be just what I needed.

Chapter 28

Autumn began to ripen into winter, the days contracting as the leaves turned a luscious array of bronze and vermilion. On Bobby's walk one bright morning in early November, the wardens were dismantling metal fences and clearing up the rubbish from the Bonfire Night fireworks, and while Bobby sniffed the lingering scents, I trampled over spent sparklers and looked forward to Christmas.

My obsession began as a child during the war, when the whole family would gather for the festivities at my Aunt Sibyl's in Kirkheaton. Fa-Fa would go out on Christmas Eve and come back with a towering spruce, Aunt Sibby would berate him and then we'd all decorate it together, exclaiming over the exquisite little ornaments, mostly hand-made by my grandmother Jette, who was good at that sort of thing.

On Christmas morning, we'd troop to the church next door to hear Uncle Randolph give his sermon, Fa-Fa grumbling under his breath throughout, then back to the house to eat one of

Sibby's chickens, its neck wrung especially for the occasion. We would listen to the King's Speech and after that we could open our presents. In those days of course they were paltry things, hand-knitted mittens or a pinwheel made from flimsy paper, all very *Little Women*, but I don't remember feeling disappointed. Then my mother would play the piano and we'd all gather round to sing carols. I loved the sad ones best; they tweaked my soul in a pleasingly painful way, like rubbing an aching muscle.

At the end of the war, Father was killed, and Christmases were never the same, but as I grew older I tried to recapture the spirit of that golden, glimmering time. When my own children were small I was very strict about it and even Leo knew he must emerge from his study and join in the rigorous celebrations. Perhaps a little *too* strict, never letting the children help me decorate the tree in case they made a mess of it. I was more lenient nowadays and intended to let Arthur run riot with the tinsel this year.

They came over from Australia for two weeks every December, the high point in my calendar, particularly since Leo had gone. I thought we might have a change from the usual turkey and maybe try a joint of beef or even a goose, though I had never cooked one before. I felt unusually cheery, making plans for Ali and Arthur's visit, which was why, when I bumped into Denzil and he asked me about his pre-Christmas party, I said yes rather than demur and worry that he'd only invited me to be polite.

'You've got to dress up, mind. Glad rags and all that. This is a swish do, innit.'

Denzil had been wonderfully kind to me since I started working at the library, helping me with Talis, a kind of cataloguing system we used to track items, orders, bills and the like. With his help I was slowly getting to grips with it, and now found that going into work each morning wasn't quite the nerve-wracking experience it had been in the beginning. In fact, I was rather enjoying it, and could now greet some of the regulars by name, know which authors they favoured, and point them to the right shelves. So much had changed since I'd first embarked on my career, but some things stayed the same. People still read books, and liked to talk, and saw the library as a meeting place and in some cases, a refuge.

I had a pleasant and productive couple of weeks, busy at work and with Bobby, but on the day of Denzil's 'swish do', I realized I had nothing appropriate to wear. There was no money for a new outfit, even with my modest library salary, particularly now the bills were piling up and the ignored letters and phone calls from our bank growing increasingly frequent. I had answered one a few days before without thinking, but as soon as I heard Horace's plummy voice say 'Is that Millicent Carmichael?' I assumed an Irish accent like Angela and said he had the wrong number.

That afternoon Bobby found me scattering clothes around my bedroom, holding dresses against myself and rejecting them. She gazed at my frowning reflection in the mirror.

'I'm trying to find a party dress.'

She wagged her tail encouragingly.

'I want to look glamorous for once.'

Bobby darted under my bed, claws scrabbling. For a second all I could see was her back end, tail waving, then she emerged, shuffling backwards, with Arbuthnot, my old Steiff teddy bear, in her mouth. I thought of Angela parading in my grandmother's gowns. Of course. Tweaking the bear from her jaws, I went up to the attic, much clearer now Sylvie had sorted it all, and dug about in the old trunks until I found a black flapper dress with a dropped hem, capped sleeves and a delicate lace neckline. Putting it on then and there, I surveyed myself in an old mirror propped in the corner. In the dim light and dust I looked like Jette. Perhaps I should cut my hair; it would look neater but Otis might not like it, as he was fond of my witch's plait. Rummaging around again, I found a cream fringed shawl to cover my wrinkled arms, and stepped back to survey myself once more. Bobby appeared in the frame, tail wagging.

'More sad rags than glad rags,' I said, remembering my grandmother's melancholia. 'Will you be all right on your own?'

She looked at me with her head on one side and I could tell she was thinking of lazing on my sofa.

'Uh-uh. Out of bounds. But I'll give you a liver sausage before I go out.'

Denzil's house was as impressive as Angela had promised; a grand, imposing building with wrought-iron gates, huge white-fringed bay windows and two stone dogs standing guard outside. I pressed the doorbell, feeling self-conscious in my hand-me-down garb. Denzil opened the door wearing a dull crimson satin smoking jacket and waving me in with a cigarette holder clutched between his massive fingers. His bald head gleamed in the light of the hallway chandelier and I felt quite dazzled.

'Entrez,' he said, saluting me as I handed him my home-made plum and walnut cake, which seemed absurdly rustic in this setting. Turning towards the chatter and thumping music, I found myself in a vast living room with floor to ceiling windows at each end. The walls were decorated in greys and dark blues, with dramatic lighting and several enormous and unusual artworks. Denzil must be very rich indeed.

As a waiter popped a glass of champagne in my hand, and Angela bore down on me, already drunk, I relaxed and let my eyes roam the room. Sylvie was in the corner, with a short man who appeared to be dressed in a toga. He was talking animatedly and jabbing a finger in her face. Seeing me, she winked and bent to whisper in his ear. Seconds later, she arrived by my side holding two glasses.

'Party trick,' she said. 'Carry two glasses and whenever you're trapped in conversation with some plebeian, you simply say "must go and deliver this!" and escape forthwith.'

Angela cackled. 'I'd never manage it, I'd just keep drinking them both.'

'Where's Otis?' I asked.

She took a slurp of wine. 'Managed to fob him off onto a school friend for a sleepover. So for once I'm footloose and fancy free.' She held out her empty glass to the passing waiter.

'Nice dress,' said Sylvie. 'Jette's?' I nodded and she clinked her glasses with mine and sailed off. Angela said she was too drunk to stand up so we sat on a chaise longue upholstered in navy silk, and I sipped my champagne while she pointed out party-goers and gossiped about them. Because the music was so loud, she had to shout to make herself heard, with the dubious result that she may also have been audible to her targets.

'That over there is Desiderata Haber, who is an historian but really controversial. She's writing a book about how Elizabeth I was a secret lesbian. I quite fancy her, she looks like Nigella Lawson. Desiderata, not Elizabeth. Though I'd quite fancy Elizabeth I too if she wasn't dead. Feck, this champagne is good.' She nudged me, spilling some of it. 'Look, there's Denzil's boyfriend Miguel. He is so hot.'

'Denzil has a boyfriend?' A dark-haired, snaked-hipped man in black jeans was gesticulating at the Nigella-lookalike historian as she nodded and smiled, swaying rather seductively to the music.

'Yes, they've been together for years but they never see each other because he lives in Spain and Denzil doesn't like flying or leaving the dogs. He's a choreographer. Phwoar, wouldn't mind him choreographing me.'

'I don't think he's that way inclined,' I replied, noticing Miguel's eyes slide towards Denzil, who was rocking on his heels by the marble fireplace.

Angela nodded. 'All the best ones are gay.' She gulped the last of her wine, and grabbed another glass. 'Come on, let's take ourselves on a tour of the place.'

'Are we allowed?'

'No one will notice, they're all too plastered.'

Giggling, we tiptoed down to a polished concrete vault to ogle Denzil's treasures, including the famous Damien Hirst. Enclosed in a glass case, it was a boiled sweet jar containing a heart cast in resin with a steel dart through it. A little sign underneath said, 'Love Struck.' Angela stared at it with the intensity of the very drunk.

'That's what it's like,' she said finally. 'A piercing that never heals.'

'That's awful.'

'It *is* awful.' She reached out and traced a finger across the glass, along the line of the dart, ending in its point. I thought of the story of Achilles I'd told Otis when I babysat him that night. What a mother's love could lead her to do. It had been the wrong story. Or too much the right one, maybe. Sometimes it was better not to find your mark.

We turned to go back upstairs and Angela began another tirade, this time about the price of art, and whether it *was* art, and that Denzil should have spent his money on something else, like funding art in schools, or saving Syria or rescuing dogs, and then she tailed off, because coming down the stairs was a man, and as he emerged into our silvery crypt we both saw how good-looking he was. When he saw us he stopped short, embarrassed, but also interested, his gaze lingering on Angela. She was wearing the same outfit she wore to Mel's wedding, and looked very pretty despite the squinty eyes and dishevelled hair.

I smiled at him. 'Have you come to see the Hirst? We were just admiring it.'

'Yes,' he said. 'I was curious.' He had an American accent and reminded me of Clark Kent in those Superman films. I saw with amusement that Angela was fluttering and fiddling with her hair, and looking down, I realized I was holding both our glasses.

'Well, must go and deliver this!' I said merrily, and left them to it. Going back up the stairs I heard Angela emit a little Alicia-esque tinkly laugh, and chuckled to myself.

Several glasses down, I was having a lovely time. Knowing enough people to keep myself entertained, and sustained by a well-built waiter, I talked to Simon, a dog walker whose wife Maddie had just given birth, and who'd been sent out to tell everyone about their new baby, Timothy. 'He's beautiful,' he kept saying. 'So beautiful. How could I have thought we wouldn't love him as much as Tiggy?' Tiggy was their Border Terrier. I chatted to another dog walker, Phillip, who told me about his Retriever Dexter's latest misdemeanour, jumping into the river after a swan, right in front of a park warden, concluding 'but he's a lovely boy, really.' In my opinion, Dexter was a sociopath, and Phillip was spineless, but I'd seen them together in the park one day, playing with an old piece of rope, both tugging away, and they looked so happy together I'd stopped to watch them. Sometimes love didn't pierce the heart, but cushioned it.

Later in the evening, I found myself standing next to Miguel, his gaze roving over the assembled party, foot tapping to the music. He was extraordinarily lithe and taut, with a coiled, feline grace. So different to Denzil and his boxers, but maybe that was the point. As if aware of my scrutiny, his amber-coloured eyes slid round to mine and he looked me up and down appraisingly.

'Nice dress,' he said. 'Original?'

I nodded, rearranging my shawl, which had slipped a little. 'It was my grandmother's.'

'She had good taste,' he said. His accent was lilting and exotic, almost affected. He was incredibly stylish, and slightly over the top, like the gold-tipped lilies in the vase next to him.

'She did,' I agreed.

'What was she like?'

I turned, surprised at the question. 'She was . . . depressed, I suppose. She used to make things. Sewing, mostly. She made this dress. But it was a kind of therapy, I think. When she felt sad, she would make something.'

'What was she sad about?'

'Nothing, particularly. And everything.'

Miguel nodded, his eyes back on the milling guests. 'When I feel that way, I dance. What do you do when you feel that way?'

I thought for a second. 'I walk.'

'You're lucky you can.' He smiled sideways at me, wickedly, and, like Angela, I saw why he'd pierced Denzil's heart.

We danced later, he and I, a proper old-fashioned tango, cheered on by our fellow party-goers, who surrounded us, whooping and applauding. Sylvie was there, clapping delightedly, and as we twirled, I saw Angela emerge in the doorway, still with Clark Kent. Her mouth dropped open when she saw me, and then she grinned and leaned against him to watch. I could feel my old bones creaking and protesting as we swerved this way and that, but like Miguel said, I was lucky I could still do this. Denzil, his cigarette holder tucked behind his ear, was looking at Miguel, with the quizzical half-smile of an indulgent father. Badger and Barker sat either side of him, like security guards, daring anyone to approach.

The music finished and everyone cheered. Miguel bowed to me and kissed my hand and I retreated, breathless, to the chaise longue to recover. Angela dashed over, dragging her new beau.

'You were amazing!' she declared. 'I had no idea you could do that!'

'Leo and I used to dance occasionally,' I replied, fanning myself with a napkin. 'It's one of my many hidden talents.'

'What are the other ones?' asked Angela's companion, smiling.

'Knowing when to retire gracefully,' I said, getting to my feet. 'I think I might take myself home. I'm rather tired.'

'We'll get you a cab,' said Angela, turning and beckoning Denzil.

'No, no, it's not that far,' I said weakly, because it was, particularly at that time of night.

'Nonsense,' she said, conferring with Denzil, who nodded and started to tap on his mobile. After a second he looked up. 'It's on its way.'

Ignoring my protests, they bundled me into my coat, and Denzil escorted me out himself. As we stepped out onto his porch, flanked by the stone dogs, I could see a car pulling up outside the house. Denzil waved to it and turned to me.

'Nice dancing,' he said. 'See? I told you it would get easier.'

I smiled and patted his hand. 'Thank you. For everything.'

He grinned. 'I should be thanking you. You provided the entertainment.'

'I like Miguel.'

'So do I,' he replied serenely, stroking one of the stone dog's heads.

I worried about the expense of a cab on the way home, but when we arrived the driver wouldn't take my money, saying it was on Mr Joseph's account. I was so grateful and glad I'd had a nice night out that I tangoed my way up the path to the front door, laughing at Bobby's capering as I let myself in. I'd left the lights on in the kitchen for her, and now they provided a welcoming glow as I pottered about finding her a late-night treat and making myself a cup of cocoa.

Just before we went to bed, I checked my email, and was delighted to find a message from Alistair. I settled down with my warm drink to read it, anticipating a few Christmas plans, things we might get up to while they were in London. I had already ordered a case of his favourite Doom Bar beer.

'There's no easy way to say this,' the email began. Emily had had a miscarriage. She was ten weeks' pregnant. A blighted ovum, the doctors said. I thought of the pierced heart in the glass case. I read on, the tears dribbling down my cheeks as Alistair explained that they wouldn't be coming to London after all, and were going to stay with Emily's parents until she'd recovered. He talked about maybe coming to visit the following summer. Another six months, at least, without seeing him, or Arthur. I pushed the laptop away, and sat, blinded by tears, as I contemplated Christmas alone.

'I should have known,' I sobbed to Bobby. 'I should have known it would turn out this way.' She leaned against me and I sank my fingers into her fur, pressing her warm body against my legs and staring at the first drops of rain fluttering against the kitchen window.

Once, after a particularly lucrative book deal, Leo took me on a trip to the Seychelles. It seemed to me to be a fairy tale place and I couldn't quite believe it was real as we flew over the islands by seaplane. We stayed in a tiny resort, our little island hut constantly stroked by turquoise waves, and while Leo read his research notes I sat burying my toes in the molten sand and looking out to sea. I found the coral fascinating – from above, it just looked like a dark shadow, dull as ditchwater, but dip your head underneath and it transformed into a vivid and glorious other-world, tiny electric-hued fish darting about while the sea skeletons danced around them. One day we donned snorkels and had a swim, but I found the intensity of it all too overwhelming; when I glanced towards the reef and caught a glimpse of the depths beyond, I became disoriented and Leo had to drag me to the surface, and hold on to me as I gasped with the awe of it.

On the last day, we were sitting on the beach again, ankle deep in the ocean froth, and I was admiring the way the sea made my skin look luminescent, when suddenly the undersea breeze lifted, the sand shifted and there was the round outline of a creature, a stingray, subtly shuffling its way along the shoreline. That frightful flap of fish wings unnerved me and I backed up the beach drawing my feet up to my knees and thinking about the way the sea life by the coral pirouetted and spiked, a pretty dance of death, always waiting for the predator to pounce. I was transfixed by that tail, missing me by millimetres as it slithered slowly past. Leo didn't even see it. Afterwards I realized it was always with me, that threat. Always waiting for the axe to fall. Waiting for the sting in my own tale.

Chapter 29

'Will you fasten me?'

The light was fading in our bedroom as Leo and I got dressed, shifting past each other irritably as we buttoned up. He was wearing a tie, which he never liked doing, harrumphing as he adjusted it in the mirror, while I pulled tights over my raddled legs and tried not to let my recently-painted fingernails snag. The coq au vin was bubbling in the Aga downstairs and it would go dry if we spent much longer primping, but Alistair insisted we had to be smart. I turned and presented my back to my husband in my grey chiffon. He smoothed his hair and attended to me, distractedly. He would rather have been in his study with Disraeli, but we had no choice in the matter. This was the Girlfriend Dinner, and everything had to be right, despite my reservations and Leo's lack of interest.

She was younger than Alistair. At least ten years. Ali didn't say so, of course, but from certain details he let drop, I was able to ascertain she was in her early thirties and did something called Experimental Archaeology, which sounded supremely silly to me, probably involved dressing up and role-playing famous battles. He'd never bothered introducing us to anyone in this way before, and I was simultaneously flattered and daunted by what that meant. When we spoke on the phone the previous week he said they'd drive down from Birmingham and stay the night, which threw me into a whirlwind of preparation, making the spare room ready, ordering a chicken from the butchers and buying myself a new outfit. Leo hadn't commented on it yet. He'd straightened himself up and was looking extremely distinguished, golden-silver hair brushed back from his forehead, very much the eminent Professor. Perhaps he intended to intimidate this Emily woman for his own amusement – which would be just fine by me.

'Let's bloody well get on with it, then.'

Downstairs, I put the final touches to the dining table, adjusting the damask cloth and neatening up the special occasion cutlery. The dresser drawer it lived in had stuck, and I had a bruise on my hip from wrenching at it. I checked the coq au vin and potato gratin, both sizzling nicely, and then called to Leo in the living room to pour us a drink. When he handed me my gin and tonic, I grimaced at its weakness.

'That dress new, is it? All for the golden boy?' Even then, Leo teased me for my favouritism, although our 'children' were nearly fifty and forty-five respectively. But I wanted to look elegant for Alistair and his please-let-it-not-be-fiancée. I wanted her to like me, and then meet someone her own age and forget the old lady she fondly imagined might be her mother-in-law.

I don't know why but I knew she wasn't The One. I must be charming and slightly forbidding, and I expected this would come fairly easily.

Right on time, unusually for Alistair, we heard the door knock and Leo went to answer it while I arranged myself casually on the sofa, then immediately got up to go and lean against the fireplace. Then back to the sofa, legs crossed, drink in hand, supremely relaxed and welcoming, but not effusive. Should we play some music? Something discreet and sophisticated – Mahler, maybe. Perhaps the 8th Symphony. But then Alistair came into the room with Emily and in that moment everything changed because I could see immediately that here was a woman he loved more than me. I'd lost, before the game even started. Berating myself – snap out of it, Jocasta – I moved forward to greet them.

She was young, and of course beautiful, in an understated way, blonde hair drawn back in a severe ponytail, thick-fringed blue eyes hidden behind serious glasses. What a handsome couple they made, framed in the doorway together, his hand on her elbow, ushering her forward. She came to me, the matriarch, first, her hand held out. There was no ring on the other one, thank God. I shook it briefly and indicated our cabinet in the corner.

'Hello, my dear. Would you like a drink? Was it a good journey down?'

'I'd love one, thanks. Yes, gin and tonic would be great. Traffic was terrible!'

Australian. She was Australian. I could see Leo flinching at the inflections as he picked ice out of the bucket, and remembered his shock and dismay when Melanie introduced Octavia as her girlfriend all those years ago. Now it was my turn. I tried to think of the girl I imagined for Ali, the equivalent of Leo's Caius scholar, but the truth is there never was anyone, even in my head, who measured up. I was always going to disapprove, but the sight of this bronzed Amazon disguising her magnificence with scraped-back hair and spectacles was even more galling than I feared. As my son strode towards me, the image of his father, I smiled, trying not to let my adoration show.

'Ma,' Ali kissed me on the cheek and I resisted the urge to clutch his collar. 'You look great.'

'She hit Upper Street hard this week,' quipped Leo, and I glared at him as he handed me my second drink.

We stood for a moment in the inevitable awkward silence, and then Leo said something about Michael Vaughan and New Zealand, and he and Ali were off. The cricket pitch was their only common ground. So I was left with this Emily, who looked annoyingly comfortable, sipping her preprandial and gazing round our living room.

'So, Ali tells me you work at the University.'

She shook her head. 'Not really. I was seconded there for a term, but now I work on a farm near Kinver Edge.'

'A *farm*?' It was hard to keep the dismay out of my voice. Alistair's girlfriend, the farmer.

She laughed. 'Yes, we run it along Iron Age principles. So we can learn more about the agricultural and domestic economy of the era. It's really fun.'

'It must be . . . fascinating.' I had visions of her in sheepskin, wielding a scythe.

'I love it. I like getting my hands dirty.' She turned to the men, who were still talking sport. 'You only won because you had a Saffie on your team.' They both chuckled appreciatively, and Ali's pride was palpable.

I smiled brightly through gritted teeth. 'Shall we go through?'

The coq au vin *was* too dry, the gratin too salty, but at least the wine was plentiful. Alistair and Emily did that thing of finishing each other's sentences, starting to say the same thing and then breaking off to grin at each other. They were both eating with just a fork so they could hold hands under the table. It was unbearable. My conversation became more and more monosyllabic with every 'No, *you* say it!' and I knew it was the wrong way to be – I should be winning her over and finding subtler ways to disentangle them, but the way he was looking at her was intolerable, Leo never looked at me that way, and she wore the adoration nonchalantly, like a woman who expected to be worshipped. Of course that reeled Leo right in; soon he was quizzing her about hill forts and blushing when she said she'd read his latest book.

I served clafoutis, home-made, because it was Ali's favourite, but he didn't even mention it, just munched heedlessly, cueing her up to tell their 'do you remember whens', as Leo roared with laughter and poured her more wine. She was every woman I'd ever resented, a whole hemisphere of bitterness and insecurity directed towards those too-white teeth glinting in the candlelight, that long neck thrown back, their fingers constantly entwined.

Abruptly getting to my feet, I collected their bowls and took them to the kitchen to recover my composure. Cleaning the dishes, ferociously wielding the washing up brush like a weapon, I jumped as I felt hands on my shoulders. Ali, come for the 'so, what do you think?' talk.

'So, what do you think?' he whispered, picking up a tea towel as if he was going to help.

I swallowed and managed, 'She seems nice,' aching with love and longing because I'd always given him the approval he craved, and then, at the most important time, I couldn't give it my all, or even an approximation. But luckily, or unluckily, he was oblivious, blinded by his own infatuation. My tepid endorsement was perceived as fervent, and he started sharing all the things that were great about her; the way she was so committed to her work, coming back covered in chalk, how she went out running on the heathland at dawn, that she spoke Spanish, why she loved spiders, because she thought they were cute compared to the ones back home.

Then he sighed and ran a hand through his hair, just like Leo. 'Of course, one day she'll want to go back.'

I was barely listening, so focused on looking like I was listening, but this pierced through. 'Go back where?'

He flung the towel on the counter and looked forlorn. 'Australia.' And that one word opened up a light shaft as I began to understand what he was saying. This relationship had a shelf life. It would be fun while it lasted, but the end would come. And I would need to be there to pick up the pieces. The weight lifted, I felt like I could soar around the room and hug this spider-loving, Spanish-speaking, dawn-running girl who'd bewitched my son, but would break the spell eventually.

'Ah,' I said, picking up the tea towel and beginning to dry the plates so he couldn't see the elation on my face. 'Well, I suppose it is her homeland. And she must have family there.'

'Yes,' he said. 'I knew you'd understand. You get it. I knew you would.' He came up behind me, squeezing my shoulders again, and together we made the coffee and took it into the dining room.

Later on, when they'd gone to the spare room, and Leo and I were back in our bedroom unbuttoning again, me massaging my aching feet and him peering at his increasingly bushy eyebrows in the mirror, he caught my eye in it and raised them.

'So?'

I shrugged. 'She's nice enough. Bit of a hippy.'

He grinned. 'You're taking it very well, I must say.'

'What do you mean?'

'The whole Australia thing.' He hung his tie over a chair and started turning down the covers.

I arranged my face in a sympathetic expression. 'It'll be hard for Ali, of course. But he'll meet other girls. And he can't ask her to give up all that for him. It's the other side of the world.'

Leo paused in the act of plumping pillows and looked at me quizzically.

'Missy.'

I slipped my rings off and started applying hand cream. 'What?'

He stared at me soberly for a second and then shook his head. 'Nothing. Let's see how it plays out.'

'Of course.' I got into bed beside him and he reached to turn the light out. 'Goodnight.'

'Goodnight, Mrs Carmichael.'

In the darkness, listening to his even breathing, I wondered what he had been going to say.

Chapter 30

I wanted to stay indoors licking my wounds, but Bobby wouldn't let me. I may have been contemplating a lonely and miserable Christmas, wondering if I'd ever see my son and grandson again, but my dog wanted to know when she was going to be able to evacuate her bowels, so out we went, on a grey, drizzly day when the wet cold seemed to creep into my bones, still aching from dancing the night before. I couldn't bear to be bright and post-party cheery, comparing inebriation notes and joshing about Miguel's snake hips, so kept my head down against the rain and didn't see anyone until Bobby had crouched for her last wee and I was hooking her on the lead again to trudge home.

'Well, if it isn't Shimmy Carmichael.' Sylvie, with Decca and Nancy prancing around her in their Barbour jackets. I tried to smile but it came out as a grimace. I couldn't bear Sylvie's sympathy; she knew how much I'd been looking forward to Ali and Arthur coming home.

'I was hoping I'd bump into you,' continued Sylvie, reaching into her pocket and pulling out her phone. 'You were asking about turkey versus goose for Christmas dinner? I have a suggestion.'

My face still fixed in a twisted smile, I moved forwards, feigning interest, all the while working out how to extricate myself. It seemed a lifetime ago that I'd asked for her advice. When I thought I'd have guests. When I didn't know I would be alone. If only I could go back to that time and forget last night's email.

'You were telling me about those Christmases in Yorkshire,' said Sylvie, scrolling furiously. 'And I thought: what about a really good chicken? You're right, turkey *is* dry – all that brining and primping to make it palatable. I've found an organic farm not far from Hebden Bridge, near where your aunt lived. What could be better than a couple of nice plump Yorkshire hens?'

It was perfect, such a wonderful, thoughtful suggestion, and it made everything so much worse. But Sylvie must not know, so I smiled and nodded and made my excuses, walking away as quickly as possible, worried she would be offended by my hasty exit. They were all so kind, Sylvie and Denzil, and Angela when she wasn't drunk and ranting, and all the dog walkers who bought me Bobby's bed. At least my tears weren't visible in the drizzle.

Back at home I made myself a hot water bottle, ready to huddle on the sofa for the rest of the day, or at least until Bobby's afternoon walk. I made up a fire while she curled round and down onto her bed, then sat and fretted, thinking about the way things always went wrong.

I spent several days like this, calling in sick to the library and not bothering to go out except for dog walks, which I got over with as quickly as possible, marching briskly, head down, tramping round the park for the requisite hour and returning home to brood and work my way down the Christmas sherry, ignoring the various envelopes that came through the letterbox because they were only the usual bills. Angela texted a few times, but Sylvie didn't, which I supposed meant she must have been offended by my brusque response to her Yorkshire hens. I worried about that for a while but then thought what did it matter? The outcome was always the same, alone in my barren old house, thinking of the people who'd gone.

Eventually I dragged myself out and ventured to a few shops to stock up, but winced when I saw the tinsel-fringed windows, the looped festive pop songs blaring away inside. So I retreated again into my shell of a house and sat hunched on the sofa, reading Mel's Nancy Mitfords, surrounded by my old albums, the photos of us all, 'held like flies, in the amber of that moment', while I was borne, inexorably, further and further away from those days.

I was sitting like that one Saturday afternoon, in semi-darkness, with the embers of a fire dying in the grate, when there was a loud banging at the door. Knocking back the last of my sherry, I went to open it, Bobby barking at my heels, eager for a distraction – she'd been rather bored by my inertia. I was greeted by a mass of greenery, the fronds of a fir tree pushed up against the doorframe – my very own Birnam Wood. After a great deal of rustling, Angela's head emerged.

'Well, don't just stand there, fecking help me!' she grunted, hefting the tree through the doorway. Nonplussed, I grabbed one of the larger branches, and hauled it into the hallway, shedding pine needles everywhere. Bobby whined and scuttled back to the living room. Together we manoeuvred the tree into a standing position and Angela held it in place, panting and red-faced with the effort. Otis slid in behind her and immediately headed to the kitchen to look for treats. Angela eyed me triumphantly.

'What do you think? I did a deal with Mrs Anthony, the grocer! Two for fifty quid! This one's yours.'

I stared at her, confused and irritable. It was true I'd talked of getting a tree and letting Otis decorate it, but that was when I was expecting guests and now the idea seemed preposterous. A lonely old woman had no need of such frivolities.

'I don't want it.' I slapped at one of the fronds, scowling at the shower of pins that would need clearing up.

Angela stared. 'What? But I dragged it all the way from Highbury Barn!'

'Well, you can just take it back again. It's much too big and besides I can't afford it.'

She huffed. 'You don't have to afford it. It was supposed to be my Christmas present to you.'

Tears prickled. 'And I suppose Otis can stay to decorate it while you make a deadline?' It was out of my mouth before I could stop myself.

Otis came out of the kitchen with a biscuit in his hand and loitered in the doorway watching. Angela glared at me as more needles fell to the floor.

'Fine.' She hefted the tree onto her shoulder, opening the front door with her free hand. 'I thought you might like to have a tree for Arthur but if you're going to be like that . . .' She began to lug the tree back out again. 'Come on, Otis, we're going.'

'He's not coming.' There it was.

Angela turned and peered at me through the branches but I couldn't meet her eye. 'Why not?'

I shrugged, gesturing towards Otis. 'It's complicated.' I brushed away a tear that had made its way down my cheek, but it was too late.

'Otis, go and play with Bobby,' said Angela, dropping the tree and shutting the door again. Otis started to protest but she held up a finger and he scampered off. She pushed me into the kitchen and immediately clocked the almost-empty bottle of sherry on the table.

'What's going on?'

'They're not coming for Christmas after all,' I muttered, busying myself putting the kettle on the hot plate and hiding the bottle in a cupboard.

'Why not? You were so looking forward to it.'

'Emily.'

'Who?'

'Alistair's wife. She had a miscarriage.'

Angela sank down into a chair. 'Oh my God! How awful. Is she OK?'

'Um . . . yes, I think so.'

'You *think* so? Have you spoken to her?'

I hesitated. 'I'm not really that close to Emily. I'm not sure she likes me very much. Anyway, they're not coming now.'

I wasn't looking at Angela but could tell she was watching me and could hear her fingers drumming on the table.

'She's quite a bit younger than Alistair. They met and married very quickly. We don't have much in common.'

'You have Arthur.'

'Yes.' She'd given me my adored grandchild.

The kettle boiled and I poured out two mugs, setting one in front of Angela. She cupped her hands around it. I could tell she was building up to a lecture and steeled myself.

'You never talk about Emily,' she said, finally. 'All the time I've known you, you talk about Arthur, and Alistair, but you've never once mentioned her. At one time I thought that they might be divorced, or even that she might be dead.'

I swallowed. 'I blame her.'

'For the *miscarriage*?'

'No, of course not. For them moving. She's Australian. If Alistair had met a British girl, they would be here. I would have Arthur. Instead, he's thousands of miles away, going to school and growing up and forgetting me. He has an accent now, did you know? He doesn't even sound like my Arthur any more. I'm seventy-nine years old. How much longer do I have to enjoy him? And that time, that precious time, it's been taken away, and I'm left with emails and Skype calls. It's not enough. It's not *enough*.' As I rattled on, my voice broke and I took a deep breath. 'It's not enough.'

She put her hand on mine. 'I know,' she said. 'Sometimes I

lie awake at night worrying about Otis growing up and leaving home. Leaving me. It's inevitable. And I can't bear it. But you know what they say. You have to "Let It Go."' She sang the last three words, as we'd been singing to Otis all summer, and I managed a wan smile.

Angela wasn't finished. 'I suppose he has grandparents over there, in Oz?' I nodded. 'So one of you had to lose out. And it's you. It's fucking horrible but there it is. You think of yourself as Arthur's grandmother, and Alistair's and Mel's mother, and, I guess, still Leo's wife, but you're much more than that. Own it.' She stood up. 'Now, I'm going up to your attic to get those decorations you told me about. And then Otis and I are going to decorate your tree. Because I don't have a deadline.'

'I'm so sorry. I don't know what made me say that. You know I love Otis.'

She grinned. 'I know. You can be a bitch sometimes though. Go and take that dog of yours on a walk, and pick us up something on the way back. None of that sweet sherry shit.'

At the 'w' word, Bobby came skidding into the kitchen. I gathered her lead and my purse as Angela collected the attic key and bellowed for Otis to come and help her.

Outside, braced against the December chill, we made our way down the road to Bobby's little wasteland so she could do her business. Afterwards I tied her lead to a lamppost and went into the off-licence where I bought a bottle of wine and some chocolate for Otis. As we made our way back, my pace slowed and I looked into the various houses en route. People put up their Christmas trees earlier and earlier every year, but I rather liked it, beckoning in the season and relishing the anticipation a little longer; the sweetest and most rewarding part. Each was a window into a different world and the tree a reflection of it, whether adorned with the most eclectic and clumsily hand-made of baubles, or bedecked in tartan-themed finery. As the lights twinkled at me, I absorbed their glow and felt the faint stirrings of hope.

'Maybe I'll be all right on my own after all,' I said to Bobby, as she sniffed some weeds between the cracks of the pavement. She looked up at me with such affection that I felt quite over-whelmed. 'You're right. I was never going to be on my own. I have you.'

Later, watching Angela and Otis unwrap Jette's darling little decorations, exclaiming and draping, I thought about all the other things I was. A classicist, a librarian, occasionally a witch (and a bitch), a walker and a dancer, and – for now, at least – Bobby's owner. As I sipped my wine and pointed out empty branches to Otis, Angela turned to me and smiled: perhaps I was a friend too. Or at least I could try to be.

While Otis and his mother hung the last knitted dolls and painted candy canes, I slipped back up to the attic and rummaged around until I found what I was looking for. In the spare room I discovered some leftover paper and quickly wrapped up two presents, then went downstairs again and shyly held out my offerings.

'You're in Ireland for Christmas, aren't you? So you may as well have these now, in case I don't see you before then.'

Otis darted forward eagerly, Angela following more slowly to receive her parcel. Inside Otis's box were his beloved Dinky cars, a bit bashed about, but still raring to go. He shouted in delight and was off, roaring and brumming into the hallway. As the bow fell from Angela's gift, Jette's green flapper dress was revealed, silken and gorgeous, glittering with tiny beads, delicate feathers fluttering. She stared at it for a second and then looked up at me, her face flushed in the firelight.

'You shouldn't. It's your grandmother's. And it must be worth a fortune!' She clasped it to her chest.

I shrugged. 'Not a fortune. Anyway, this is better than selling it to some faceless collector. Wear it. Dance in it. Get drunk in it. Seduce someone in it.'

She grinned wickedly. 'Not in Ireland. My mother would go batshit crazy.' She hugged me. 'Thank you. I'm sorry I won't be around at Christmas. But you'll be fine.'

'Don't worry about me. I've got Bobby,' I gestured to her, snuffling by the fire. 'We're going to eat pigs in blankets and play Canasta. What happened to your Clark Kent, by the way?

Angela, still stroking the dress, looked up. 'Who?'

'The American? At the party? I thought he seemed nice.'

She shrugged and started to pack up her dress in its wrapping. 'Jack? He had to go back to New York. It was fun while it lasted.'

'Oh. Well, plenty more fish in the sea. Or superheroes in disguise.'

They left, Otis pushing along one of his cars, Angela clutching her dress, and I closed the door behind them, smiling. My smile faded though, as I turned back to my empty house. There was no denying that the prospect of Christmas alone was daunting.

But then I saw the lovely tree in my cosy living room, Bobby sleepily opening one eye and thumping her tail as she saw me return, and I sat on my sofa thinking that together we would make the best of it.

I went through to the kitchen to make some cocoa and saw my laptop on the table. Classicist, librarian, a witch (and a bitch), walker, dancer, dog owner, friend. And mother-in-law. Sitting down, I pulled it towards me, opened it up and logged onto my email.

'Dear Emily,' I began.

Chapter 31

With nothing to look forward to, Christmas edged in more slowly than usual. Typically, I would have been swept up in preparations, nights tightening like a drawstring as the big day approached, but this year, the days rolled by idly. I went to visit Mel in Cambridge since she was going to Italy for the holidays, to see Octavia's parents. She was briskly sympathetic, but she and her new wife were busy buying their new flat, and didn't really have time for my Yuletide lament. So instead I took myself out and wandered around the city, walking the cobbled streets and admiring shop windows, then venturing into quads to look up at the lights shining from the rooms tucked away behind those Michaelmas creepers, wondering who was reading and talking and falling in love in them.

Boarding the train back, I thought *what the hell*, and bought one of those dreadful little bottles of wine like some scantily-clad girl off to the races. I must have looked strange, sitting there with my plastic cup, my mongrel beside me, but I'd learned not to care, and sat fondling Bobby and watching the inky landscape flash past.

Back at Finsbury Park, I made my way to the taxi rank and managed to find a black cab with a driver who didn't mind taking a dog. In fact, he had one of his own, a giant Schnauzer called Stanley who was scared of Christmas crackers and cringed whenever one was brandished. He showed me a picture on his phone of a handsome black dog, his inscrutable expression shadowed by a fringe of crimped fur. When we arrived home, my dog-loving driver leapt out of his seat to open the door for me, and gave Bobby a good ruffle on the head as she jumped out.

I let myself into the house, still chuckling at the thought of Stanley the schnauzer quaking at crackers. *Cosaques*, they were called originally, after the Cossack soldiers who fired their guns in the air – no wonder the dogs got scared. I wondered if Bobby would be. Leo made me a cracker once, in the old bon-bon style, with an almond and a Greek poem in it. It took me a while to translate, because it was unfamiliar to me, but I was glad when it was done. I found the handwritten paper, along with my scribbled notes, up in the attic the other day, tucked in one of the photo albums.

> *I can only sing because you loved me*
> *all these years.*
> *in the sun, in the sun's shadow,*
> *in rain, and in snow,*
> *I can only sing because you loved me.*

Since you kept your hands on me
that night when you kissed me,
since then, I'm fine as an open lily
And I have a quiver in my heart,
only because you kept your hands on me.

A quiver in his heart. That's what I was. I kept my hands on him and didn't let go.

Back home, I picked up the post and went straight to the living room to switch on the tree lights, which cast a warm glow over my various trinkets. Sitting down, I started to weed out the inevitable bills, but amongst them found a thicker cream envelope with my name and address in beautifully elegant handwriting. Inside was what looked like a Christmas card, a lovely little pen and ink drawing of an Islington-ish square with a tree in the middle and a crowd singing round it. But when I opened it, instead of the usual festive greetings, I read:

Ms S. Riche
Requests the pleasure of
Mrs M. Carmichael's company (and Bobby's)
On Sunday, 25 December 2016
At twelve o'clock
14 Lennox Square

The most fervently-worded love poem would not have made a sweeter read. 'Bobby!' I gasped. 'We've had an invitation!' She trotted over to look, sniffing the card warily and wagging her tail. I hugged her in delight, then began to fret. Could I accept? Would it not be a terrible imposition? What would Sylvie do about Aphra, her impossibly bossy cat? I picked up my mobile and called Angela. She answered on the first ring.

'Don't tell me. You've had Sylvie's invite and you're worrying about whether to say yes.'

'Yes.'

'You almighty eejit. Say yes.'

'But . . . who else will be there?'

'I don't know. Ask her, she always invites a mixed bunch. You'll fit right in.'

As usual with Angela, I didn't know whether to be pleased or offended. 'She's invited Bobby too.'

'Great, it'll be like one of those old cartoons, all the animals chasing each other.'

'I might say yes,' I said.

'Thank fuck for that. Merry Christmas.'

Chapter 32

I spent the next few days in a glorious frenzy, consulting Sylvie, buying and wrapping presents (thankful for my library salary, tiny as it was), searching in the attic for a dress to wear, and giving Bobby an extra good brush, despite her protestations. On Christmas Eve, I went to bed feeling the familiar tingle of expectation, soaking up that magical spark in the night air that sends children into raptures. It turned out I could relish it, even on my own.

The following morning, we both set out looking very fine, Bobby's silky-smooth tail waving. Under my old black coat I was wearing one of my mother's frocks, made for her by Jette: a scarlet tea dress with a flared skirt and holly leaves embroidered on the hem. She wore it one Christmas up in Yorkshire; the skirt fell over the piano stool as she played 'O Come All Ye Faithful', and I sat at her feet and fingered the holly berries. The contents of that case were a sartorial memory stick, each garment unleashing a torrent.

We stopped briefly en route to take flowers to Leo. I tied Bobby outside the gate and she waited patiently, as she always did, while I went in to leave my offerings and sit for a while, contemplating his oak tree and trying to think of something to say. Like Melanie, I felt the urge to speak to him, so occasionally I would tell him what we were doing, or simply reminisce. Today, I told him a story about a Christmas past, when Mel had stopped believing in Father Christmas, and fell into a huge sulk which only lifted when she opened her present. Chosen by Leo, it was a handsome mahogany guitar, and her squeal of glee when she opened the box made Alistair wail. Christmases were very noisy then.

Retrieving a panting Bobby, we continued on our journey and arrived at Sylvie's little Georgian terrace on the dot of twelve. There was a layer of frost covering her parterre and the eucalyptus wreath on her door, and I could see the warm yellow lights of her tree glinting in the window. Feeling apprehensive, I lifted the knocker, and a moment later Sylvie appeared, wearing a Mrs Claus apron edged with white fake fur, huge bauble earrings dangling from her ears. Decca and Nancy pranced at her feet, both wearing reindeer antlers. It was so over the top that I burst out laughing. She beamed and held out her arms.

'Darling, do come in, we're about to open the champagne,' she said, sweeping off down the corridor. 'This was a present from Denzil,' she continued, gesturing to her apron. 'I love it.'

'Are you sure about Bobby?' I asked. 'Where is Aphra?'

'Don't worry, she's at my next door neighbours', living it up with a Siamese called Tyson. She'll be having a whale of a time.'

Denzil and Miguel were already in the kitchen, Denzil brandishing a meat thermometer, while Miguel folded a pile of snow-white napkins into swans. Handing Sylvie a bottle of champagne and my latest and most successful home-made panettone, both were exclaimed over, and my holly dress admired. Then Sylvie's other guests started to arrive, firstly Desiderata Haber, the historian who'd been at Denzil's party, and secondly Hanna, the waitress from my favourite café.

'I didn't know you knew Sylvie,' I said, when she came over to say hello.

Sylvie sailed over to fill up our glasses. 'I teach a design course in Chelsea and Hanna was one of my star pupils.'

'I study at the Royal College of Art now,' said Hanna. 'Sylvie got me the job at the café to help fund my work.'

I looked across at Sylvie, weaving her way through her guests, pouring and pressing her concoctions on everyone, just like she did when we first met. Initially she'd reminded me of Leo, but really it was an unfair comparison. Leo was jovial and kind enough but his interest in other people was fleeting, as mine had been. We existed in our own bubble, floating along without ever really being bothered enough to probe deeper or – heaven forbid – pierce our protective film. But thinking about that made me feel ashamed and sad, so I drank my champagne and smiled at the last guests who'd arrived and were being introduced – Desi's husband Simeon, who'd been parking their car, and their teenage son Sam, who looked utterly horrified to be there, though marginally less appalled when he was handed a glass of champagne.

We milled around Sylvie's kitchen, munching canapés, drinking and gossiping, as Ella Fitzgerald serenaded us, and Sylvie herself bustled about basting, stirring, keeping up a constant flow of food and chat. The dogs sat drooling under the peninsula, occasionally snapping up a slice of smoked salmon or a morsel of cured meat. At one o'clock, Sylvie clapped her hands and we all filed through to her dining room, papered in a dark forest green and lit with dozens of candles, strands of ivy trailing off the mantelpiece. I found myself sitting between Miguel and Simeon, a bespectacled bookish-looking man who stooped slightly and kept looking across at his wife. I thought he might be disappointed to be next to me but gradually realized he was merely very shy and uxorious.

Sylvie and Denzil brought in the first course with much fanfare – a chestnut soup zigzagged with cream and scattered with parsley. We pulled crackers – cossacks firing – and the dogs immediately retreated to the kitchen while we rustled through the booty. Wearing golden crowns, we feasted, congratulating the chef who was, as usual, immensely pleased with herself. Sylvie had a wonderful capacity for 'philautia', that boldest of Greek loves, the love of the self – a much finer quality than narcissism, which it's often mistaken for. The way I saw it, with narcissism, you were just gazing at your reflection in a lake; with philautia, you were frolicking in the lake and inviting people to join you. People who truly liked themselves seemed to have a greater capacity for friendship, for letting people in. Perhaps that's why I, in the past, was always rather solitary. But I liked to think I was starting to dip a toe in the waters.

It was a noisy, convivial and delicious lunch, punctuated with jokes and compliments, a roar of approval going up when Sylvie brought in two plump chickens from the Hebden Bridge farm, reclining in tawny roast potatoes. When I took my first bite I fancied it brought back those days in the Kirkheaton rectory, Aunt Sibby hovering in her apron as we tucked into Elspeth or Marigold or whichever poor hen had been sacrificed for our festivities.

Simeon had to rebuke Sam, who'd had a little too much of the Pouilly-Fumé, but once he'd dealt with his son I asked him about his job and was delighted to discover he was an archae-ologist, who knew of Alistair and had even read one of his research papers. My cheeks burned with pride, and I told him all about Ali's fieldwork. Miguel and Denzil were arguing about Miguel not eating his potatoes, so Desiderata came and sat with us. She was startlingly attractive, with tumbling dark hair, sleepy almond eyes and a beguiling, languorous air; I could see why Simeon was so besotted.

'Sylvie tells me you are the wife of the famous Leonard Carmichael. I'm a great admirer of his work,' she said, sipping her wine.

I felt a flicker of unease. How much did she know about him? If Leo had been here he would have definitely been an admirer of hers. But he wasn't, so instead I helped myself to more gravy and tried to recall Angela's gossip at the party.

'Angela Brennan said you were writing a book about Elizabeth I? It sounds very interesting.'

She laughed and flicked her hair away from her face. 'The

lesbian thing? My agent told me to write it, might get me a BBC series,' she drawled. 'One must make one's mark.'

'*Was* Elizabeth a lesbian then?' asked Sylvie, topping up our wine.

'Maybe. Maybe not. I'm sure we're all on the spectrum,' replied Desiderata, picking a last roast potato out of the dish with beautifully-manicured hands, and eating it like an apple. Her son was scarlet with embarrassment, choking on his water, so I thought I'd better change the subject.

'Did we do the cracker jokes?' I asked, and everyone delved back into the glittery cardboard rolls.

'What does Santa suffer from if he gets stuck in the chimney?' asked Denzil.

'Don't tell me!' shrieked Sylvie, shoving the wine back in the cooler. 'I'll get there!' She sat down and put her fingers to her temples, eyes closed. After a second's ruminating, she opened her eyes wide. 'Claustrophobia!' she exclaimed triumphantly.

'Correct,' he said, tossing his paper back on the table.

'What do you get if you cross a snowman with a vampire?' asked Simeon.

'Easy. Frostbite,' returned Sylvie. 'Next!'

Then it became a game trying to get to the pun before Sylvie could, but such was her capacity for wordplay, she bested us all.

'What do you call Santa's little helpers?' asked Desiderata.

'Um . . . Elf workers?'

'No. Do you give up?' she teased, waving the paper.

'Yes,' said Sylvie. 'I want to go and get the pudding.'

'Subordinate Clauses,' said Desiderata, smirking.

Sylvie stood up. 'That's too sophisticated for a cracker. You damn well made that up, you cheat.' She swept out in mock-anger.

The smirk broadened into a smile. 'I might start a career sideline. Erudite cracker jokes.'

'Wisecrackers,' said Simeon, deadpan. Desiderata reached over to cup his cheek with her hand and Sam flushed with mortification again.

Sylvie came back in, buckling under the weight of an enormous dish. '*Sufganiyot*, in honour of our Jewish friends,' she said, bowing towards the Habers and Hanna, putting down a plate of bronzed and sugared doughnuts. I took one and bit into it; cinnamon-flavoured custard oozed down my chin. Reaching for a napkin, I thought better of it, instead scraping up the excess with one finger and licking it off. I noticed Bobby had crept back in now the cracker bangs had subsided and was panting at my feet, so after my second mouthful I offered her a scraping of custard and she lapped at my finger eagerly.

Next we moved onto the cheese, tucking into an oozing Brie and a nutty, salty Comte, along with oatcakes and quince jam. Then we all trooped, groaning-full, into the living room where the tree lights and flames of the fire glowed brighter against the fading light outside. There we opened presents to the croon of Nat King Cole, while the dogs snuffled around the discarded wrapping.

Sylvie was delighted with her Murano vase and immediately went off to arrange some white chrysanthemums in it. I'd bought Denzil some of his favourite cigars, and Miguel a biography of

Ninette de Valois, whom I particularly revered because my mother had seen her dance at the Royal Opera House in the 1920s. I gave Desiderata a signed copy of Leo's Disraeli biography – one historian to another – and Simeon a bottle of port because Sylvie said he liked it. She said not to bother with Sam because teenagers hated everything, but I didn't like to leave him out so with Angela's help bought him a little gadget that turned his mobile phone into a wall projector. I'd got Hanna a sequinned scarf, just a small thing, but she had tears in her eyes when she hugged me. They all seemed so pleased with their presents that I felt the agonizing had been worth it. In return I received a wonderful haul – cashmere gloves from Sylvie, silver earrings from Miguel, a beautiful new leather collar for Bobby from Denzil, a book called *Baking for Dogs* from the Habers, and a box of almond biscuits from Hanna. Even Bobby got a bag of Bonios.

Sam set up his new phone projector and projected a YouTube video of cats jumping at cucumbers onto Sylvie's living room wall. Bobby in particular was entranced, cocking her head and growling as she stared at the flickering images. I looked round the room, watching everyone huddled and laughing, enjoying the presents I'd bought, and couldn't remember a more resplendent Christmas. Last year I was so worried, checking everything was perfect, constantly panicking about food and whether everyone was having fun and dreading it all being over, washing up and stripping beds in that horrible silence.

Sylvie put on some more music and we danced a little, and drank coffee with home-made truffles and slices of my panettone, which had turned out just right. Then Desiderata and Simeon made their excuses, as Sam was drunk, and Denzil and Miguel said they'd better be going because Miguel had a flight the next morning, and Hanna left because she had an early Boxing Day shift. So in the end it was just Sylvie and me clearing up. I helped her load the dishwasher, and when it was gurgling away with her crystal glasses in it, we sat down for a tot of brandy in the kitchen, surrounded by leftovers in foil.

'How was that, do you think?' asked Sylvie, picking at a bit of chicken.

'It was lovely,' I sighed. 'Thank you so much. What a wonderful day.'

'I think Bobby enjoyed herself,' observed Sylvie, indicating with her foot. All three dogs were piled onto one bed, Nancy and Decca's grey mingling with Bobby's brindle as they snored and twitched together.

'She wants to stay for a sleepover, but we'd better be going,' I said, getting to my feet. Bobby lurched groggily, opening one eye, then rolled over and up when she saw I was on the move. She came to me, nosing my hand, and I gave her an affectionate pat. Sylvie led me to the door and helped me with my coat and scarf.

'Excellent panettone,' she said. 'And thank you again for the Murano. Gorgeous.'

'Thank you,' I said. 'For everything.'

'It was my pleasure,' she replied. I turned on the pathway between her parterre and looked back at her, bathed in the light of her hallway.

'What did the sea say to Santa?' I asked.

She grinned. 'Nothing; it just waved.'

Back home after another meandering walk through back streets and squares, I switched on my tree lights and sat on the floor next to another little pile of presents I'd accumulated. I gave Bobby hers first – she nibbled off the wrapping to reveal a floppy, enticingly soft stuffed rabbit. After staring at it intently, paws splayed either side, she nosed it and looked at me enquiringly.

'Yes, my darling. Merry Christmas.' I looked around my living room, lights twinkling on the tree Angela bought, illuminating the artful clutter created by Sylvie, the pictures of my family, the gifts under the tree. 'You deserve it. You got me the best present of all.' I gazed at her, a haze of browns and golds, with her flash of teeth and whorling nose. My Bobby, who sauntered out into the garden in the mornings, her nose lifted to the breeze to smell what the day might bring. Whose haunches nestled in the small of my back every night, defying the demons. Who listened like no one else ever had. She was vivid, present, warm, vital. The best gift anyone could ever have.

She gazed at the rabbit resting between her paws, then pounced, and immediately bore it off to be destroyed. As she lovingly mouthed her new toy on her bed, I attended to the rest of my pile. Mel and Octavia had bought me a pair of wellington boots and a takeaway coffee mug with a Blackadder quote on it. Alistair had sent me a beautiful dark blue parka with a fake-fur hood. I tried it on and looked at myself in the mirror above the fireplace. As I slipped my hands into the pockets I discovered another wrapped up present. Pulling it out, a tag read 'To Grandma, love from Arthur' in spiky child's handwriting. When I opened it, I discovered the long-promised memory stick. Still wearing the coat, I went straight through to the kitchen and plugged it into my laptop.

It took a little while to find the files, but eventually I unearthed a whole folder of pictures. Not just the ones that I'd lost, but new ones too; photo after photo of Arthur enjoying his life in Australia. On the beach, on the terrace next to a barbecue, sitting on the sofa alongside a giant stuffed bear, round the dinner table with his Australian grandparents, Emily's mother looking just as dottily devoted as me. In all of them he was beaming away, bathed in love and light. Then more photos of our Christmas together last year, him sitting on the sofa with me watching *The Snowman*, my hands stroking his hair, as I gazed down at him. And finally, one last picture of Alistair, Emily and Arthur unfurling a banner on the beach that read 'Merry Christmas Grandma!' all bronzed and glowing, grinning at the camera. I drank them all in, thinking how tragic it was that Emily had lost the baby, but also how lucky they were, because how perfect – how utterly, heart-breakingly perfect – was the boy they had already.

Closing my laptop and blinking back the well in my eyes, I switched off the lights and made my way upstairs, Bobby at my heels. I patted the bed and she jumped up, ready to snuggle. We curled up together, and, putting my hand down, I realized she'd brought her stuffed rabbit with her. It seemed our family – our little *oikos* – was now three.

PART 4

Transit umbra, lux permanet – 'Shadow passes, light remains.'

Chapter 33

On New Year's Eve I agreed to dog-sit Decca and Nancy, who were scared of fireworks, while Sylvie went to a party in Maida Vale. I wasn't particularly upset at the idea of spending that night alone, since I've always considered it to be an overblown affair – too much expectation, not to mention the staying-up-'til-midnight requirement, which seemed to me to be an aggressive kind of party etiquette, like telling guests what kind of wine to bring or forcing them to move two places down the table during dinner.

I was quite happy to sit with the dogs on the sofa, watching television and eating the shepherd's pie Sylvie had brought over as a thank you. Everyone seemed glad to see the back of the year, as if all the terrible things that had happened to the world would evaporate on the stroke of midnight. But it had been such an auspicious twelve months for me personally that I rather wanted to hang on to it. Perhaps if I was asleep when the clock struck twelve, I might carry over some of the magic with me.

That evening, as I was feeding the dogs and clearing up, there was a knock at the door, sending Bobby into her usual frenzy, with Nancy and Decca providing the accompaniment. Angela stood on the porch, looking rather thin and pale, her hair in a messy topknot, holding a bag that smelled of vinegar.

'Do you mind if I eat these with you? My mother's come back with me, and she's driving me mad. I poured all the milk down the sink so I could go out to buy more. Mam has to see out the year, and everything else, with a cup of tea. Can I come in?'

'Of course.' I moved aside to let her in and she followed me into the kitchen, where I continued washing the dishes while the dogs noisily ate their food. Angela opened her bag on the kitchen table and sat, dipping her chips in ketchup and contemplating Otis's numerous pictures taped to my fridge.

'How was Christmas?' I asked, stacking my plate on the sideboard.

'Tense,' she mumbled, through a mouthful. 'My mother's only happy if she's telling me about people who've died, and what's more, she's teetotal. Like, she last had a Babycham in 1992 and says anyone who drinks on their own is an alcoholic. Plus she thinks I should have married Otis's father, Sean, even though he's a useless twat. But he's a useless twat from our village, so ideal marriage material. And now she's come for a visit, so I'm sleeping on the sofa and she's asking why I haven't bought a house yet. "Is it because of all the immigrants?" "Jesus Christ, I AM an immigrant," I said. And she said, "Don't take the Lord's name in vain."'

'Oh dear,' I said, trying not to laugh. 'Do you want a drink?'

'No,' she sighed. 'She'll smell it on my breath and there'll be hell to pay. It's like being a teenager again, but without the illicit sex.'

I hung up the tea towel and went to sit at the table with her, while the dogs, having polished off their own meal, roamed around hoping for scraps.

'Sylvie off at her party?' Angela indicated Decca and Nancy, slavering at her knees.

I nodded. 'I'll turn the radio on when the fireworks start, poor things. Do you have any resolutions?' Leo and I used to make them together, three each. His were always the same: to finish writing one book, start another and give up chocolate – he was particularly partial to Toblerones and used to bring them back from his work trips. He generally managed the first two, never the third. Mine changed every year, and usually centred around new hobbies I intended to take up. One year I decided to learn the cello and even went as far as looking at one in a shop on Church Street, but the price put me off. Leo used to tease me about it, calling me Jacqueline and asking how I was getting on with the Elgar. I'd still like to learn.

Angela swallowed and sucked her greasy fingers. 'Give up smoking,' she said. I smiled indulgently. She'd been trying to give up ever since I'd met her, wielding various implements in place of her beloved cigarettes. The implements came and went; the cigarettes stayed. 'What are yours?' she asked, tossing a chip for Decca, who snatched it out of the air and moved away from Nancy to enjoy it in peace. Bobby panted patiently, waiting for her turn.

I hesitated. 'I don't know. I think . . . I'm all right at the moment.' Angela, throwing Nancy her chip, turned towards me, eyes narrowing.

'That's good.' She threw a chip to Bobby, who snapped her jaws into thin air, letting it fall to the floor, where it was immediately snatched by Decca. 'Oh dear, poor Bobs. Here you go, girl.' She held out another and Bobby took it gingerly.

'She's never been very good at that,' I observed, getting up to put the kettle on.

Angela laughed and ruffled Bobby's lustrous mane. 'What will you do,' she asked, 'when Fix wants her back?'

I kept my back to her as I filled the kettle and turned to put it on the hot plate. The clock on the wall ticked. Bobby chomped on her chip under the table. The tea towel was hanging slightly off-centre and I moved it back into place.

'Well?' said Angela, gently.

I turned to face her. She looked concerned – worried, even – with Bobby's head on her knee, hoping for more.

'I . . . hadn't really thought about it,' I faltered. '*Does* she want her back?' I hoped Fix might have decided to move on in her new life, without a dog, while I moved on, with one. Ships that passed in the night, with Bobby the lifeboat between us.

Angela sighed and rubbed her nose. 'I don't really know. I hardly ever hear from her, and then not many details. Originally she said she needed several months, a year even. But the plan was always to give her back, eventually. She's Fix's dog.'

But I looked at Bobby, licking her chops and thought: she's

not; she's mine. And realized in that instant I would do anything to keep her.

'I'm sorry,' Angela said, registering my expression. 'I shouldn't have brought it up. It's just . . . I didn't expect it all to work out this well. You're so good together. It's a shame – well, you know what I mean.'

The kettle whistled and I went to pour the tea.

'Try not to worry,' said Angela. 'Fix might not want her back for months, longer, even. No need to panic.' She seemed to be reassuring herself as well as me.

We drank our tea, and Angela talked about Otis, who was looking forward to his second term at school, but I couldn't concentrate on the conversation, thinking of my mother and Jonas the Labrador, and the day we got Leo's diagnosis. The marble was back in my throat and I kept noticing flecks of dirt on the kitchen units, itching for disinfectant to distract myself from the looming branches crowding my vision. Bobby, my Bobby, my *oikos*.

Eventually Angela said she'd better go, or her mother would send out a search party, so she wished me Happy New Year, threw her vinegary bag in the bin and disappeared into the night as the first fireworks started up. The dogs began to pace restlessly, ears flattened against the bangs, so I decided to call it a night. I washed my face and brushed my teeth in the bathroom, intently watched by three pairs of eyes, Bobby in the middle with her rabbit in her jaws. Switching on the radio to drown out the noise, I climbed into bed and patted the blankets. All three of them jumped up and started arranging themselves, turning and curling their way to comfort, with little heed for mine. My legs heavy with dog, I lay listening to the distant pops and squeals, only slightly deadened by Classic FM. They were playing Elgar. Not the cello concerto, but the Enigma Variations, which I've always loved, particularly 'Nimrod'. Now though, the strains of the theme sounded uncomfortably portentous, heralding the New Year and whatever it might bring. When the bongs of Big Ben chimed, I was still awake, eyes fixed on the window as the odd firework flickered across the black. 2017, my eighty-first year on Earth.

Sensing my unease, Bobby, nuzzled her head against my arm. I put it around her and caressed the soft fur, breathing in her warm scent, lulled by the gentle sighs and snores that surrounded me. Last year I'd so longed for things to be different, but now I wanted everything to stay the same. *Semper eadem.* That was my resolution, right there. Carry on as we were.

Chapter 34

After Sylvie had picked up her dogs, I took Bobby for a piece of toast in the park café on New Year's Day. We sat outside on the veranda, watching the passers-by, and I fed her buttery crusts and remembered my lonely walks there a year ago, when I was mourning my lost life and planning a visit to a toxic lake to watch some fish being stunned. Now here we were, tucked up together, greeting acquaintances, both human and canine, planning the day's activities, looking forward to the week ahead. Frolicking in our lake and inviting everyone in.

Pushing thoughts of Bobby's departure out of my mind, I enjoyed getting into my routine again. Angela went back to work, Otis went back to school and I went back to the library, logging books, reading to the children and helping members find what they needed. I also listened to Deirdre's woes, as she was worried about funding cuts and how they would affect services. She was quite fiery on occasion, quoting statistics, telling me that there were 280 million library visits in Britain every year, that people went to libraries more often than they went to football matches, theatres, A&E and church combined.

A library visit every nine seconds, she said. I liked to think of it, and would sometimes sit in my chair in reception counting the ticks of the clock and imagining people entering libraries up and down the country with requests like the ones I heard every day. 'There's a book someone recommended, I can't remember the author or the title . . . How do I use the computer . . .? Could you help me fill in this form . . .? I need something to help me understand Shakespeare . . . Have you got that new film with the shark in it? Not *Jaws*, another one.' My very own set of Enigma Variations to decode.

The weather turned colder and wetter and I was glad of my new coat and wellington boots, as Bobby's walks became increasingly sludgy. We started to recognize the fair-weather dog walkers, or at least notice their absence when the rain came. Denzil always turned up, though he was missing Miguel, who had gone back to Spain. Maddie and Simon came out with their Border Terrier and their new baby, Timothy, though they both looked grey and exhausted. Tim wasn't a great sleeper: 'we've decided we prefer Tiggy after all.' I saw Phillip and Dexter, though not at the same time. Dexter raced past first, ears flapping, with what looked like a dead rat in his mouth, and Phillip followed, puffing, a while later. 'Have you seen him? Where did he go?'

Then we would head home, where there was always a treat to be found, a fire to be sat in front of, or a visitor to be greeted, whether it was Sylvie popping in for a gossip, or Hanna, who'd taken to coming round for a cup of tea and a chat, to improve her English. We didn't see so much of Angela, but she was busy with work – or maybe didn't want to admit that she hadn't kept up her resolution.

I pottered about quite happily, taking down my decorations, sorting out the last few things in the attic, sending Alistair the occasional update, and retrieving Bobby's stuffed rabbit from whichever incongruous corner she'd left him. Named Bruce Bunny by Otis, Bobby's toy now had one ear missing and was looking rather grubby, but was a permanent fixture, carried around tenderly in her jaws and dropped in various places for me to find. After 'burying' him under cushions, rugs, beds, and forgetting where she'd put him, she would wander round the house whining until Bruce was unearthed, whereupon they would have a passionate reunion and he would be borne off to her corner for a thorough going-over. She was an odd dog and I loved her dearly.

One night when we'd lost and found Bruce, and I was just settling down with some pasta to watch a new period drama, we were interrupted by a phone call from Sylvie.

'Have you seen Angela lately?' she asked.

'No,' I replied. 'She's been working a lot, I think. Why?'

'She just called me, and sounded strange.'

'Maybe she was drunk?'

'No, it wasn't that. She was tense. It was like . . . she'd called me about something, and then decided not to talk about it after all.'

'Do you want me to go round?'

'Would you? I'd just be easier in my mind.'

So I put on my new coat and boots, collected Bobby's lead because she didn't want to miss the outing, and we marched down the road to Angela's flat. A light was on at the top of the house, so I pressed the doorbell. For a while nothing happened and then I heard her voice, low and rough through the intercom. She buzzed me up and we embarked on the lengthy sets of stairs, Bobby squeezing ahead and turning to wait for me every few steps. By the time we reached the top I was breathless and slightly dizzy, so when Angela opened the door I had to push past to go and sit on her sofa to recover.

'What are you doing here?' she asked, rather abruptly.

I coughed. 'I just thought I'd drop by as I haven't seen you in a while. Are you all right?'

'I'm fine.' She was still holding the door open, and after a second she closed it, a little reluctantly.

'Where's Otis?' I looked around.

She frowned. 'He's asleep. It's nearly nine o'clock.'

'Oh,' I said, coughing again and stalling for time. She looked unkempt, with a hint of grey roots, and her eyes were red, as if she'd been crying. 'I just wondered . . . would you like to come on a walk tomorrow?' It was a Saturday, and she and Otis often joined me at the weekend.

She started to object, then thought better of it and shrugged. 'OK then.' I lingered to see if she would ask me to stay for a drink, but she just stood by the door, clearly waiting for me to leave.

I struggled to my feet, still a little breathless. 'I'll pick you up at ten, shall I? We could go for a coffee.' She nodded and followed me as I went back out on to the landing, leaning against the door as I clipped Bobby on her lead. I waved goodbye but she was already turning away, so we made our way slowly back downstairs and headed home.

'Something wasn't right,' I murmured, as the dog trotted by my side in the darkness. Bobby paused, sniffing a lamppost, and hacked up a cough that suggested she had a chicken bone stuck. I supposed it was as good an observation as any.

The next morning I dutifully went back again to pick up her and Otis. We waited at the gate and they appeared a few minutes later, both bundled in winter coats as it was an icy day, a thick frost covering everything the sun hadn't reached yet. Angela was so well wrapped I could barely see her face, scarf covering her mouth and hat pulled down low. Otis had the necessary gear on, but it was a precarious arrangement, scarf already trailing, coat falling off his shoulder, hat askew. Usually Angela would be stopping to re-zip, re-tie and re-position but today she didn't seem to notice, and it fell to me to straighten him up while she stared at the ground and scuffed stones with her shoe.

We walked wordlessly, which wasn't unusual, but today it felt different. Our silence was usually companionable, unforced, no real need to break it with platitudes. But now I felt compelled to gabble, comment on the weather, anything to provoke some sort of response from her. Otis, at least, was oblivious, dashing this way and that, fetching sticks, chasing birds, and stamping in puddles.

I opened my mouth to indulge the urge, then closed it again, remembering Jette's silences, and my mother once telling me talking made no difference; to my grandmother, it was just empty noise, the buzz of an untuned radio. So instead I looked at the stark, bare trees, and thought of sitting on the bench with Sylvie when we first met, not really talking, just eating croissants and watching the ebb and flow of the branches above. I went into the café and bought us both a coffee, and Otis a biscuit, then we stood in the playground while he jumped on the trampoline, crumbs all over his coat.

'I need you to look after Otis for me.'

I frowned, confused. Angela was staring straight ahead at her son, who was still bouncing.

'Of course, whenever.'

'I mean, I need you to have him for the night. Just one night. Could you do that?' She turned towards me, and there was a martial light in her eye that disturbed me.

'Yes, I could have him for the night. Which night do you mean?'

Angela turned back and watched as Otis climbed down from the trampoline and moved on to the swings, pushing himself backwards and forwards, skinny little legs like pistons, his breath making puffs of vapour in the air.

'I don't know. Just a night sometime soon.' She wrapped her fingers more tightly around her coffee and blew on it. 'Is that OK?'

I paused, thinking of various questions and rejecting them all. 'Yes,' I said finally. 'Whenever you want.'

'Thank you,' she said. And it felt like we'd made a pact, but one that we wouldn't discuss further, so we called Otis and said it was cold, and he moaned, and Angela said he could have a hot chocolate at home, and we all walked back. I left them at their gate, watching them disappear into the house, before making my own way home, wondering what it all meant.

'A whole night?' I asked Bobby. 'What could that be about?

But Bobby had no more of an idea than I did. I texted Sylvie saying I'd seen Angela and she seemed all right, because although she obviously wasn't, somehow it felt like a betrayal of trust to say otherwise. I worried about cold winters and gas ovens, but then reassured myself with the thought that Angela couldn't possibly mean to do something stupid, when against all the odds she'd clearly managed to keep up her resolution. She hadn't smoked once during the whole walk.

Chapter 35

15th February, 1955

Dear Sibyl,
I'm afraid I couldn't bring myself to tell you on the telephone, which
is wretchedly cowardly, and I can hardly bear to write it, but we
always agreed to tell each other everything. Mama didn't have a
stroke, as everyone is saying. There was a letter of sorts. When Henry
and I found her, she was clutching her old buttonhook in one hand,
and a piece of paper in the other: 'All this buttoning and unbut-
toning.' It's a quote, I believe, from someone else who gave up on
things. I'm terribly sorry, though I suppose it's not too much of a
surprise since Father died – or at all, really. She always was in her
own winter's tale.

Henry is hushing it up – says it would do no good at all for people to know. I'm not sure I agree with him though – Mama never talked about it, and perhaps that was the problem. But we all prefer to do things our own way, and hers was a private one, so maybe it's for the best. Let us remember her, though, through the things she made and loved – I enclose her favourite thimble as a token, but you must come down and collect anything else you'd like.
Your loving sister,
Lena

The buttonhook and the thimble were up in the attic along with the letter. I stroked the brass metal cap with its tiny indentations; Jette's fingertip shielded from the prick of the needle, while the rest of her had no protection from the constant stabs and skewers of life, until she couldn't take it any more. Punch, jab, punch. There was only so much therapeutic sewing a woman could manage. But was it really any different to my mother, succumbing to an illness that might have been cured?

When Leo got ill, he considered it, and even hinted at me helping him, but I wouldn't listen, and then it got too late and we missed the boat, as it were. After he went, I considered it myself, but something kept me from it – some shred of optimism, I suppose, which was always what Jette was lacking, making beautiful things, but never seeing the beauty in them. All this buttoning and unbuttoning. Either your own, or someone else's. I could see how it could all become too much.

Much easier to be like Fa-Fa; less introspective, getting someone else do the hard grind, only concerned with where his next pipe was coming from. Or like Aunt Sibby, the vicar's wife who only cared about her chickens, but was still prepared to wring their necks when it suited her. Peace of mind took a certain ruthlessness, as well as a lack of imagination. Because it wasn't just about being content with *your* lot, was it? It included not worrying about anyone else's. As soon as you started, the floodgates opened.

I didn't hear from Angela again until nearly two weeks' later, in early February, when she turned up on my doorstep one evening, puffy-faced and red-eyed, and asked me to look after Otis the following night. She wouldn't come in, just shook her head and lurched off back down the path. I spent a sleepless night watching the shadows on the walls and then a frantic day cleaning the house in preparation for his arrival, re-making Arthur's bed with its dinosaur duvet cover, baking a batch of cookies watched by a drooling Bobby, and dropping by the library to pick up a DVD that Deidre had recommended.

I picked him up him from school at three-thirty, wondering what Angela had told him about this impromptu sleepover, but he seemed happy enough to go with me, and resisted my tentative questions about his mother's mood. Given that he was unable to remember what he'd had for lunch that day, it was unlikely he'd give me any valuable insight into her frame of mind. We walked quickly around the park with Bobby, as the light was fading, and then went back home where I settled him in front of the television with biscuits and milk, and soon heard him chortling away at the film while I prepared sausages and a baked potato. I wondered if I'd hear from Angela, but there was nothing, not even a text. Otis ate his dinner in the kitchen, waited on by Bobby, and seemed to enjoy it, though he objected to my home-made apple pie as it had apples in it. I'd seen him eat apples on a regular basis but it seemed he thought cooking them was an abomination. So he ate the pastry and custard and then we went up to the attic and played with Henry's old train set until it was time for bed.

We skipped his bath, as that felt a bit beyond me, but I supervised his teeth-brushing, helped him get into his Minions pyjamas, then led him to Arthur's room where we snuggled up to read a new book from the library about a dragon who was desperate for a job. His eyelids grew heavy as I read, and afterwards I kissed his forehead and sat in a chair in the corner until he'd gone to sleep. He slept like he'd fallen out of an aeroplane, on his front, star-shaped, dark eyelashes fanning his cheeks, thumb in his mouth.

I quietly let myself out of the room and found Bobby on the landing, sitting bolt upright, staring at me. It was her, Bruce and me as far as she was concerned, and the change to the status quo made her wary. So I took her downstairs, gave her a bit of sausage Otis had left, and settled her on her bed. I ate in the living room, flicking through an interiors magazine Sylvie had left on her last visit. Then I fed Bobby and cleared up, listening to the sound of her new tag clattering on the bowl as she ate. Denzil told me that you shouldn't put the name of the dog on the tag, because that just helped dog-nappers, so you put the name of the owner instead. As Angela had reminded me, I wasn't her true owner, but all the same I'd gone to the cobbler's and got them to engrave 'Carmichael' on one side, and my phone number on the other. I liked the sight of it glinting on her Christmas collar.

After her dinner, Bobby felt frisky, and brought me Bruce for a game of tug. I sat on the sofa and pulled at the frayed and damp rabbit as she mock-growled and pounced. We were still engaged in this game when my mobile rang. Dropping the rabbit, I picked up the phone abstractedly, watching her as she darted forward to snatch her toy, shaking it until she was sufficiently convinced she'd 'killed' him. Then she tenderly placed him on the floor and licked him thoroughly.

'Hello?'

'It's me. I'm outside. I didn't want Bobby to bark. Can you let me in?'

I went to the door and opened it, grabbing Bobby's snout to smother the outraged woof. As I straightened up to look at Angela's tear-stained face, I thought of her odd request, and the not smoking, and not drinking, and suddenly it all became clear and I cursed myself for being so stupid, so infuriatingly blind. I, of all people, should have seen the signs, should have prepared better for this moment. Opening my arms, she fell into them, sobbing.

'I'm so sorry. I'm so sorry,' she mumbled against my shoulder. 'I didn't know where else to go.'

'Hush,' I said. 'Hush.' I led her into the sitting room, and found some tissues, and sat with her while she blew her nose. Then I left her on the sofa with Bobby while I made some cocoa, which she didn't really drink, just held, letting the heat warm her fingers as she stared into the dying embers of the fire. Later on, I made a hot water bottle and took her up to the spare room, where Alistair and Emily usually slept when they stayed. It was a bit bare and cold, but I retrieved the paisley throw from the living room and wrapped it around her as she shivered in bed. Then I sat and held her hand and thought about all the things I wanted to say but couldn't. I couldn't find the right words, wanting to confess but not able to dredge up the right confession, even now.

'I voted Leave.'

She blinked and looked towards me, blankly. 'What?'

'I voted Leave. In the referendum. I haven't been able to tell you, and I feel so bad about it, it was a stupid thing and I was wrong and feel so awful, about Otis not being able to travel, and Hanna's door, and Mel's funding and everything else that's gone wrong. I'm so sorry.' I trailed off, biting my lip, unable to meet her gaze.

After a second, she started to laugh, weakly at first, and then properly, wheezing, new tears starting in her eyes, but better ones.

'You fucking idiot,' she said, finally. 'What were you thinking?'

'I thought it was what Leo would have wanted. But it wasn't, Mel said.'

'I should bloody well hope not,' she huffed.

'I'm sorry,' I said again. And she squeezed my hand and lay

down with her eyes closed. I didn't let go, and long after she'd gone to sleep I was still there, still holding her hand, thinking about Bertie and what I did all those years ago.

Chapter 36

I called him Bertie from the moment I realized I was pregnant, that summer of 1956, when Leo had gone and I was back in Lancaster Villas for the holidays, supposedly preparing for my third year at Newnham. It took me a while to comprehend it, maybe because I didn't want to, but eventually the nausea, which wasn't limited to the mornings, made things very clear. I spent a few weeks being sick in secret, sneaking off to the bathroom to grip the basin and cough up the bile from the back of my throat before collapsing, clammy and shaking, onto the tiled floor. Even when the sickness passed, I gagged with the misery and dread of it, contemplating the abyss of confusion and hope and horror I'd fallen into.

Downstairs, my mother and her cronies were busy organizing their latest crusade, distributing leaflets, making placards, going on marches. She'd thrown herself into the campaign for the abolition of the death penalty, devastated and outraged by the execution of Ruth Ellis the year before. So she was often out parading in front of HMP Wandsworth, or Holloway, and didn't notice her wraith of a daughter quietly retching round the house, waiting to be found out. In the end I had to tell her, as I had no idea what else to do. She stood in our drawing room, still holding a placard that read 'Thou shalt not kill', while I whispered my confession, unable to look her in the face. The silence of that moment after, as I cringed and wept, and then the blessed relief as she put down the sign, and I felt her arms around my shoulders. 'Hush,' she said. 'Hush.'

I never doubted my mother's warrior-like qualities, and in the following days she channelled that fiery energy for me. Money was found, discreet enquiries made, appointments booked. But, alongside the single-minded ferocity with which she dealt with it all, was a tenderness and absolute acceptance that humbled me, made me feel more guilty than ever, because I didn't deserve it. Part of me wanted her to rail and condemn, just as another part of me wanted her to tell me I should keep the baby. It was Leo's child, after all. Bertie, even though I would never find out if he was a boy. Bertie, even though he would never be born.

I saw two psychiatrists, and my mother said it was necessary for me to appear mentally unhinged. This I had no trouble with, as by that point I was delirious with sickness and lack of sleep, going into rooms and forgetting why I was there, twirling my hair round my fingers and pulling it out in great clumps.

I saw them on separate days on the same street in central London. They both asked me a few questions, making notes so they didn't have to look at me. The first time, I couldn't breathe properly, and had to put my head between my knees to quell the dizziness. The second time I fell into a kind of abstraction and stared into space, barely aware of the voice prodding my eardrum, an echo in my head. I wasn't sure if any of it was real, or simply the bravura performance that was essential to get me out of this mess. Leaving the second office, I caught a glimpse of the doctor's notes: 'history of mental illness in the family.' Like Sibby wringing the necks of her beloved chickens, my mother was prepared to make sacrifices.

We got a cab to the clinic out in Ealing, where I remembered very little except white sheets and the smell of disinfectant. When my mother asked and I told her she said, 'Thank God'. I had pain and bleeding for a day or two, much less than I deserved, and spent that time lying flat on my back in bed, staring at the ceiling, feeling euphoric and wretched, hopeful and despairing, cramped and unravelling. My mother brought me tea and toast with the crusts cut off, which I didn't eat, but let dry out on the bedside table, thinking of the stale carrot sandwiches in the cellars. Then, after three days, she told me to get up and start studying: 'There's a reason we did this.'

I got a First in Classics, which no one at Newnham expected, least of all my bewildered tutors. But that was my gift to my mother, my refuge in adversity; it was the one thing I could do, having put her and myself through all that. I slogged away, staying late in the library, attending every lecture, devouring every book, conjugating every last verb. No longer the skimming stone, but the boulder, shouldered and pushed up the hill, even if it all meant nothing without Bertie.

I left Cambridge with my splendid degree and empty womb,

my mother's arms around my shoulders, proud and validated. But when Leo came back and we got engaged, she was horrified. How could I marry this man, given our history? She pulled me aside at the wedding – 'darling, are you sure?' – and I nodded because he was my Odysseus, my destiny. From the first time I saw him, I knew that we belonged to each other. You couldn't insulate yourself against misfortune – an arrow would always find its way in somewhere – but with the right person, when life knocked you down, you would be able to get up again. Onwards and upwards, as Leo used to say. When I married him, I felt like I was finally making amends – picking myself up – and when I next conceived, Bertie would rise again.

How did I keep that knowledge to myself for all those years? What kind of marriage was it? An uneven one, as I'd always known it would be, weighed down by my love and my secrets, while he was unencumbered. But we bobbed away, he and I, the anchor and the buoy, and our whispered song was never entirely drowned out. I still heard it then, though it was very faint, as I sat in our spare room, holding Angela's hand, mourning her lost child and mine, as my dog listened patiently to my confession.

Chapter 37

The following morning I let Angela lie in, and got up with Otis at an unholy hour, feeding him cereal and letting him watch far too much television, keeping the door to the living room closed so as not to wake her. I didn't tell Otis she was there, instead embarking on the tricky process of getting him ready for school, retrieving socks, hunting down his school bag and wrestling him into his clothes while he tried to play trains, draw a picture of a monster, and wrap Bobby in his scarf. When we finally got out of the house, I was sweaty and breathless with the effort, and it was only after I'd dropped him at school and he'd scampered off, bag flapping against the backs of his knees, that I realized Bobby was still wearing the scarf. I took it off her and stuffed it in my pocket, taking the opportunity to scratch her neck.

When we got back from our walk, Angela was down in the kitchen drinking tea and listening to the radio. She was still pale, though less pinched than the night before. She leaned down to fondle Bobby's ears and looked up at me slightly shyly.

'Did you sleep well?'

She nodded, sipping her drink. 'Not bad, considering. Thanks for taking Otis to school, how was he?'

'Fine. He gets to set the table at lunch today, apparently that's a huge privilege.'

She smiled. 'Funny how they manage to turn chores into treats. I can never manage that myself.'

I poured myself some tea and ate some cereal, because I hadn't had time while I'd been chivvying Otis, all the while surreptitiously watching Angela to gauge her mood. The spell of the night before had been broken, and her shields were up again. When I finished my breakfast, I got to my feet and deposited the bowl in the sink.

'Hanna says her boss has made the café dog-friendly. I thought I'd take Bobby for a coffee – would you like to join me, or would you prefer to rest?'

That fired her up, as I hoped it would. 'I'll come with you,' she said, going to fetch her coat.

It was a beautiful clear day, with a light cold breeze, and we walked slowly towards the café, Bobby pulling ahead, dragging me this way and that as she was compelled to sample the aroma of every lamppost, bin, weed and twig in the vicinity. Angela walked with her hands in her pockets, head down, staring at her clinking boots.

'Why didn't you tell Sylvie?'

She looked up, eyes narrowing at the question. 'What?'

'She said you called her to talk about something, but then decided against it.'

She hesitated. 'Because she's too nice. And she's never wanted children.'

'Wouldn't that have been helpful?'

She shook her head, and we walked on in silence for a while. Then, as we approached the café: 'I so wanted Otis to have a brother or a sister. I'm an only child and I never wanted that for him. But when it came to it, I couldn't do it all again on my own. I just couldn't.'

I thought of that day when Ali was sick on the rug, both children screaming and crying, the burning in my ankle, suffused with rage and frustration, the tightly-wound impotence of the moment when everything became too much. When it came to children, two was more than two; with just one parent, I could see why it was an infinite and unthinkable number.

'Did you tell . . . the father?'

'Jack? No. He's in New York, it was never on the cards. It should never have happened, it was a stupid, stupid mistake.' She took a deep breath and re-tied her ponytail. 'Shall we get that coffee?'

We went into the café, as warm and welcoming as ever, and sat at our usual table. Bobby, excited to be in a new place, immediately started sniffing, her nose on a puppet string around the cake shelf. I pulled her back, tucking her under my seat where she lay down with a disapproving sigh, eyebrows twitching.

'Was Leo a good father?' Angela bit into a sugar cube, cupping her palm underneath to catch the falling grains.

I paused, stirring my coffee. 'No, I suppose in many ways, he wasn't.' A tingle of shock and relief at the admission. 'He was great fun, knew how to play with them, which I was never very good at. But there was a limit to his patience. He didn't want to get involved in the details and if it ever got boring, or messy, then he would just retreat to his study, or go off to a conference. And I would be left to clear up and carry on. But then, I'm not sure I was a very good mother either. The most I can say is that I was always there.'

Angela's eyes glistened with unshed tears. 'Trust me, sticking around is as good as it gets.'

'You're still young, you could easily have more children. Otis doesn't have to be an only child, and if he is, well, there are worse things.'

'I'm thirty-seven. Sean and I were together, on and off, for thirteen years. I don't think I can be bothered to get to know someone all over again. Do that thing of pretending I'm not insane, or that I don't eat like a fucking pig.'

I thought of how carefully I'd played Leo, declining invitations, all that holding back and furtive application of make-up. I felt quite glad that I was far too old to go through all that again.

'Maybe next time you could, oh, I don't know, just be yourself?' I suggested.

She stared at me for a second and then we both giggled.

'The very idea!' she gasped. 'Hell's bells!'

When I stopped laughing I felt washed out, as if I'd had a good cry. 'It'll be OK,' I said. 'You'll be OK.'

We finished our coffee and then Angela felt tired, so we paid the bill and left, Hanna's effusive boss, Ahmed, taking the opportunity to pump our hands, give Bobby a pat and assure us that dogs were welcome in his establishment.

'So you know,' said Angela grimly, as we wandered towards home. 'We're going to have to talk about Brexit sooner or later.' She raised her eyebrows and dug her hands deeper into her jacket as she stared me down.

I stalled on the pavement, Bobby tugging impatiently at her lead. 'I wish I'd never told you,' I sighed, eventually. 'I know how you feel about it. But, on the day of the referendum, I just wanted things to change. It had nothing to do with the vote, not really. It was more like . . . firing a shot in the air, to startle the pigeons.'

Angela huffed. 'More like shooting yourself in the foot. I thought you were better than that. You're an educated woman. You lived through the war, for Chrissake.'

'I know. I feel terrible about it. I'm sorry.'

'Don't say sorry to me; say sorry to the *country*.' At that point I sensed a tirade coming and realized Angela must be feeling a little better. 'This poor country, which is going to go to the dogs. Sorry, Bobby,' she patted her head. 'I'm all right, I've got an Irish passport, but the rest of you are doomed, I tell you. Doomed to sit on the sidelines as some second-rate, two-bit lost empire. Sovereignty, my arse. It makes my blood *boil*—'

Then Angela's step suddenly faltered and her breath caught in her throat. Following the direction of her gaze, I saw a tall, solidly-built man standing with one hand on her front gate, looking at us.

'It's Adrian,' she breathed. 'Fix's husband.'

We approached warily, Bobby lagging behind to sniff. When we reached him, Angela nodded stiffly.

One hand rested lightly on the wrought iron railing, but there was a kind of suppressed tension in his body, like a cat before it pounced. Adrian's eyes passed across me, barely registering my presence, before resting on Angela with an inscrutable expression. Even in the strong winter sunlight, I couldn't see the colour of them, they seemed to be all pupil, all black. Hunter eyes. He didn't say anything, just kept looking at her.

'Adrian. I didn't expect to see you.' Her hands were shaking slightly, so she thrust them in her pockets and stood very straight.

He breathed in, slowly, nostrils flaring. 'I came to see Felicity.'

'She's not here. What made you think she was?'

'I've been everywhere else.' The hand holding the railing tightened slightly.

'I don't know where she is,' said Angela. 'But I'm sure she'll be in touch if she wants you to know.'

Adrian chuckled. 'Well, now, you see, I don't think she *does* want me to know. But I do . . . very much . . . want to know.'

'I'm sorry, I can't help you.' Angela was frightened; I could see the tension in her trembling frame. I thought of what she'd just gone through, how vulnerable she was, and was horribly afraid for her.

'Oh Angela, I'm sure you *could* help me, if you really wanted to.' Now both of his fists were gripping the railings, knuckles glowing white against the black.

A fury began to build in me. How dare this man turn up at Angela's home and intimidate her, like some villain in a soap opera, with his silly insinuation, playing the hard man. I might be afraid for Angela, but all of a sudden my rage boiled over, overriding everything else. And for once – unlike that terrible day, shouting at Melanie in my kitchen – I was going to get angry with the right person, at the right time, in the right way.

'Oh, go away,' I said, stepping forward and putting my own hand on the gate. He blinked, as if seeing me for the first time, and watched in astonishment as I pushed past him. He wasn't *that* tall.

'Not until I've seen my wife,' he said, turning back to Angela.

'Well, she's not here, so you can bloody well leave us alone.' I pivoted on the pathway, one step up so I could look down on him from a distance. He was all those self-serving, empowered men that I'd grown so sick of: the feckless Sean, the burglars who raided my home, Angela's tip-stealing date, Percy the Lunger all those years ago. He was even, in some dim recess of my mind, Leo, who'd retreated when he should have stepped up.

'I can't stand men like you,' I spat. 'Turning up like you own the place, like we should all get in line to give you what you want. I'll tell you what *I* want. I want you to get the hell away from Angela's house, this instant, or I'm going to call the police.'

'And what are you going to tell them?' Adrian replied softly, doing the proper menacing thing now, fists gripping the gate.

I put my head on one side. 'I'll tell them that you did *this*.' I grabbed the front of my blouse and ripped it downwards, pearl buttons popping and scattering down the path. Then I started to twist the skin around my collarbone, hard. 'Old ladies bruise so easily,' I murmured, enjoying his shocked expression.

He stepped back, perplexed. 'You're insane.'

'Yes,' I grinned like an old witch. 'And I can't be bothered to hide it.' I bent and rubbed some soil across my brow. 'Oh dear, I fell over. I think I might have wrenched my arm.'

'I just want to see my wife.' He turned back again to Angela, almost pleadingly.

'And it all got a bit out of hand, didn't it?' I replied, pulling strands of my hair out of its plait, mussing it up.

'You stupid bitch,' he hissed, turning back to me. But as he grabbed the gate, there was a snarl and Bobby appeared between us, teeth bared, straining at her lead. Adrian fell back; recognition flashed across his face and he looked back at me, flushed with rage and confusion.

'That's my dog,' he spluttered, pointing.

'No.' I shook my head. 'She was Felicity's dog, and now she's my dog. So get the FUCK out of here before I set her on you.'

With Bobby still growling, I held out my hand to Angela, who stumbled up the path towards me, while Adrian watched, unsure what to do next.

'Ten seconds to make your mind up, sunshine, then I call the police,' I said, getting out my phone. I started my countdown, shaking with anger and euphoria and also uncertainty, as I really wasn't sure what I would do if he didn't leave before I got to zero. But at six, he slammed the gate closed with both hands and stepped back.

'Fine, I'm going,' he said. 'No need to get your knickers in a twist.' He turned and marched back down the road, shoulders hunched in his jacket, and we both watched him go, making sure. Cheap shoes with built-up heels; Achilles' heels, vile little man. I turned back to Angela and put my arm around her.

'It's going to be OK,' I said, squeezing. 'You'll be OK.'

She looked up, torn between tears and laughter. 'Fucking hell,' she panted, lowering herself onto the steps of the porch. 'Fucking hell, Missy. You were . . . amazing.'

'It was nothing.' Feeling suddenly very wobbly myself, I sank down to sit with her, looking down at my ripped blouse and wondering if I could sew the pearls back on if we found them. Bobby stood in front of us, wagging her tail, and we gave her a big fuss – she had been magnificent. We sat for a while, crying and laughing together, while Bobby licked our faces and nudged us for treats, then Angela said I should stop indecently exposing myself to all of Stoke Newington, so we stood up, brushed ourselves off, and went inside to look for wine and Bonios.

Later on, after Angela had fetched Otis from school, he was back in his own bed, and we were eating pizza and watching some pleasingly frothy drama, she looked shiftily at me over her glass.

'Earlier I said I didn't talk to Sylvie because she was too nice,' she said. 'I felt bad about that, because it implied you weren't.'

'I'm not,' I agreed. 'Not nice like Sylvie.'

'No,' she nodded. 'But sometimes you need more than nice. And that's what you were today. And last night.'

'That's one of the nicest things anyone has ever said to me.'

She laughed. 'Don't get used to it. But I tell you one thing. That vote of yours – you can strike it off the record. We're good.'

I grinned at her, feeling a weight lifting. 'Thanks.' Then more seriously. 'What will you do if he comes back?'

She didn't miss a beat. 'Punch myself in the face and call the police.'

'Good girl.' We were just pouring out the last of the bottle when there was a flump from the bedroom followed by the patter of tiny footsteps.

'Mummmeeee,' said Otis, rubbing his eyes. The front of his pyjamas were soaked through.

'Sweet Jesus,' said Angela. 'I forgot to take him for a wee before bed.'

'Clear up and carry on,' I said, knocking back my glass. I would have helped her, but I wasn't that nice. So instead I thought about Adrian and how satisfying it had been to take the little shit down a peg. When the bedroom had been silent for a while and Angela hadn't come out again, I went in and found them both asleep, Otis curled in his mother's arms in his single bed. I tucked the duvet around them and tiptoed out again, clicking my fingers to Bobby.

We clattered down the stairs together, her claws scrambling for purchase, and she turned to grin at me halfway down, pink tongue lolling. Nothing was insurmountable when she was there.

'I think *you're* more than nice,' I said. And together we slipped out of the flat, down the flights of stairs and back along the road, her tail waving alongside me as we made our way home.

Chapter 38

We spent a week or so on edge, wondering if Adrian would come back, but then Angela got a message from Felicity saying she had decided to press charges. At the same time, I received an email from the police officer who visited after my burglary the year before, saying the crime had been investigated 'as far as reasonably possible' and the investigation was closed 'pending further investigative opportunities becoming available'. Once again, I was passionately grateful for Bobby's presence, and hoped Fix fared better with her own case.

A few days later, I found a bunch of flowers on my doorstep, with a note attached, from Sylvie. 'You ARE as nice as me,' it read. Purple gladioli, from the Latin *gladius*, meaning 'sword'. I enjoyed Sylvie's penchant for plant symbolism; it was like our own secret language, and I hoped it meant Angela had told her the whole story, not just part of it.

March came, bringing with it the burgeoning spring, and once again the park burst back to life, the cold mud drying out, buds blossoming, the green gradually edging back in. Our walks became warmer and more leisurely, no longer huddled against the chill. There were more people to talk to as we ambled round, not to mention marathon runners to dodge, as they all upped their training. Now I was a bona fide (or should that be Fido?) dog lover, I was perfectly happy to snap back when they barged through us, tutting as they dodged the pack, or shouting when a cyclist flashed by too fast. We dog walkers were the self-appointed police of the park, the benevolent bobbies who patrolled and informed the wardens when there was an injured swan in the lake, or a wasps' nest swarming in the fallen logs.

I loved those mornings, gathering at the picnic table for a coffee and a chat, as the dogs frolicked and romped. Philip and Dexter had enrolled themselves in a training class in Finsbury Park and Dexter had run off with the trainer's clipboard; Maddie and Simon had called in a sleep consultant to help them with Timothy – they'd spent £250 and he'd slept through three times before reverting back to his usual screaming, but they felt the money had been worth it for a few blissful nights. Denzil had tried to buy a light switch at a Martin Creed exhibition, before discovering that it was, in fact, just a light switch: 'saved me ten grand.' Sylvie had redesigned a housewife's living room with artificial turf instead of carpet: 'she said "bring the outside in", silly mare.' We carolled under the tentative spring sunshine, amidst swaying hindquarters, and then Bobby and I would saunter home, waved off by hands and tails.

One Saturday after a companionable stroll, Sylvie suggested a trip to Upper Street, and after dropping the dogs off at my house, we caught a bus and made our way along the bustling high street. To my surprise, Sylvie took my arm and marched me into a very smart-looking hair salon. When we arrived in the reception, the lady behind the counter smiled and handed me a glass of champagne. 'Good morning, Mrs Carmichael.' I turned back to Sylvie, bewildered, and she winked. 'This is my treat.'

I was led to a twirling leather chair, where a very hip young man with several piercings introduced himself as Barnaby. 'What are we having today, darling?' he asked, sitting me down and spinning me round to face myself in the mirror.

'I don't know.' I gazed at my puzzled reflection.

'I do though,' said Sylvie, lurking behind me with her own glass of champagne. 'Cut it all off.'

Ignoring my protests, Barnaby rubbed his hands together and stuck a comb behind his studded ear. Sylvie put her hands on my shoulders and looked at me in the mirror. 'Trust me,' she said. 'It's time for a change.'

So I fell silent and let Barnaby put a gown over my arms. He and Sylvie had a brisk discussion about blunt cuts and waves and lowlights, then she left us to it, waving as the lady from reception brought me a brownie on a tiny white plate. Barnaby swung me this way and that, releasing my hair so it fell around my shoulders, putting his fingers to my temples and looking into the mirror intently. Then he swept me off to the basin, and feeling the warmth of the shower water trickle onto my scalp, I drifted off.

The whole experience was intensely soothing. Barnaby didn't

talk because he was busy, pulling me one way and then the other, chopping and pinning, folding foils, and such was his concentration that I found myself unwinding like my plait. *Luó; Gr λύω – to loose, untie, release.* It was more than two hours later that I suddenly came to, hearing the sound of clapping. I blinked, and saw Angela and Otis in the mirror, both grinning.

'Well,' said Angela. 'You're a sight for sore eyes.'

Confused by their sudden appearance, I was nonetheless entranced. My hair had been chopped into a short, blunt bob, the natural wave enhanced to a slight curl. He hadn't tried to hide the grey, just added a few darker strands to even it out a little. It made my eyes look greener. I looked distinguished – chic, even. Behind the sags and wrinkles, I looked like my mother, and Jette, and Melanie, and somehow more like me than I'd ever felt.

I smiled at Angela in the mirror. 'Not bad for an old crone.'

'Not bad?' she replied. 'I've said it before: Sylvie's a genius! Now, follow me.'

Then Angela took me shopping, to a charming boutique I'd never been to before, would never have dared go in. She marched about, grabbing items off the rails, barking instructions to the sales assistant who had started off haughty. We closeted ourselves in the dressing room, while Otis played with his cars just outside, and Angela handed me a pair of black trousers and an olive-hued chiffon blouse. She went off to look for accessories, while I put them on.

I paid very little attention to the clothes, because I was so distracted by my hair, shaking my head and tucking strands behind my ears. Leo always liked it long and on the few occasions I'd grown tired of it and suggested a chop, he'd protested so vigorously that I'd abandoned the idea, flattered by Leo's strong emotions on the subject. I wondered what he would say if he saw me now.

Angela burst back in with various garments over her arm and looked me up and down. 'Yes,' she said. Then she turned me away from the mirror, helping me into a cardigan and shoes, and putting something around my neck, adjusting and tweaking.

'Right, you'll do.' She spun me round and we both admired the new me. Tall, and rather sparse as ever, now there was a new elegance to my disposition, the sharp twenties hairstyle, the tailored trousers, cut slightly short to reveal green suede block heels that matched the softly draping pale green cardigan with the darker blouse beneath. I looked neat and put-together in a way I'd never managed for myself before – ding, dong, the witch was dead.

Just before Aunt Sibby died, I went to see her, withering away in her bedroom in Yorkshire. She was nearly ninety by then, a grand old age, but it was still pitiful to see. A lot of the time she didn't make much sense, drifting in and out of lucidity, one minute asking who was looking after her animals, the next talking to her husband Randolph, who'd been dead for years. But one thing she said stuck with me. 'I hate how ugly I am,' she rasped. 'I'm so beautiful on the inside; why can't the outside be the same?' As I grew older, skin sagging, the flecks and crevices of dotage creeping in, I saw what she meant. There was part of me that believed I should still look like the adoring bride who gazed up at Leo all those years ago. I'd lost those versions of myself – the girl in the cellars, the student, the wife, the young mother – but now I could see traces of those previous selves etched in the lines on my face, and felt a fondness for them all.

I fingered the jet-black beads at my throat. 'It's lovely, but I couldn't possibly afford all this.'

'Nonsense,' replied Angela, firmly. 'The haircut was Sylvie's treat, and this is mine and Denzil's. Mainly Denzil's. But he doesn't like shopping.'

'But . . . but . . .' I gestured to the outfit. 'It's too much.'

'Bullshit,' she said, gathering up my old clothes. 'Otis wants his adopted grandma to look cool. I'm just following orders.'

As we emerged from the dressing room, Otis dissolved into tears.

'It doesn't look like Missy!' he wailed, his lip trembling.

Angela was conferring with the delighted sales assistant, so I knelt by him and took his hand.

'It's still me,' I said. 'Just a bit more dressed up.'

He sniffled and wiped his face on his sleeve. 'You're still a witch though?'

'Of course. Always will be. This way, it's our little secret. No one else will know.'

He nodded, satisfied, and we left the shop with my old clothes in a bag. Outside we were met by Sylvie, looking even more twinkly-eyed than usual.

'Marvellous,' she exclaimed, tweaking my beads. 'You look sensational. I don't know about you but all this grooming makes me fancy a spot of lunch. How about it?'

Angela said she knew a little place around the corner, and linking arms, we made our way there, Otis skipping ahead. Gripped firmly on either side, I wondered what had provoked Sylvie and Angela to embark on a Missy-makeover like this. And then, as we pushed open the door of the restaurant and a huge roar went up, it became apparent.

We were greeted by a crowd of people, all holding glasses, milling around and shouting. Denzil and Miguel, Deirdre from the library, Hanna from the café, Simon and Maddie with baby Timothy, Philip, numerous other dog walkers and finally Mel and Octavia, who were holding hands and beaming. Turning, astonished, towards a smirking Angela, I saw a huge banner had been hung along one wall:

HAPPY 80TH BIRTHDAY!

'Surprise!' shrieked Sylvie, thoroughly overexcited.

Lost for words, I thought back to the other me sitting dejectedly on the sofa a year ago, and it seemed impossible that I could be standing here now, in my finery, with all these people. Once again I felt a lump in my throat, but this time it was a joyful nugget, a heralding of happy tears. So I swallowed it down, and smiled at everyone, as they surged forward to congratulate me.

We had a splendid lunch, all piled onto one long table, making far too much noise and drinking far too much red wine. It seemed everyone had bought me a present – candles, books, bottles and chocolates galore. I opened and exclaimed, and toasts were raised, mostly to Sylvie, who loved to drink to herself on every occasion. And then it was my turn. I stood up, waiting until they fell silent, groping my way to a script.

'I didn't expect this,' I began, to laughter. 'I didn't expect any of this. I feel so very grateful that you're all here, but also sorry that someone else isn't.' I thought of Leo, of Alistair and Arthur, so far away, but for once I didn't mean any of them. 'I'm sorry Bobby isn't here, because she is the reason I know you all so well, the reason you're all here. So I'd like to toast her.'

We all clinked our glasses: 'To Bobby!'

Afterwards, Angela sidled up to me and said, 'Bobby isn't the reason,' handing me a parcel. I opened it and found a small string of pearls – the buttons that fell from my blouse the day I confronted Adrian. They'd been re-strung as charms in a delicate little bracelet with a tiny silver clasp. I held it in my hands, fingering the ivory baubles like rosary beads, thinking of them scattered down Angela's pathway and imagining her scooping them up.

I turned to Angela, who looked embarrassed. 'Thank you,' I whispered. 'This is perfect.' And she ducked her head, grabbed a passing Otis, and made a show of rubbing chocolate off his face.

Melanie and Octavia approached, both flushed and slightly tipsy.

'Mum, I'm so sorry but we've got to go. We're moving tomorrow and have to finish packing up. What a lovely lunch.' Mel stared at me appraisingly. 'You look great.'

I patted my hair. 'Thank you. And thank you both for coming. I really had no idea.'

Octavia grinned and hugged me and they both turned to leave. But as they got to the door, Mel swung back, all at once self-conscious and determined.

'That letter you sent, last year. I just wanted to say . . . It meant a lot. I never knew you felt that way, but I'm glad you told me. And glad things seem to be changing.' She gestured towards the assembled group, still laughing and carousing. 'I'm happy for you,' she said. 'You've got some nice friends.' She reached out her hand to me and I took it in both my own.

'More than nice,' I said, squeezing. 'More than nice.'

Chapter 39

Melanie and I had our big row on my seventy-eighth birthday. She came over to try and make a thing of it, but with Leo so recently gone I was in no mood to celebrate. Yet the occasion demanded some sort of marking, so instead of a party we had a fight. Emotions, noise, memories – just the wrong kind.

I watched her bustling around my pristine kitchen, quietly seething, then decided I didn't want to keep quiet about it. Once again she was rabbiting on about this big house, how would I cope, and why didn't I think about getting somewhere smaller. My house was the only link with Leo left, and she wanted me to offload it along with everything else that was precious to me. The rooms where Alistair and Arthur stayed, the attic full of my family, the garden I tended, the space where light pierced my heart for the first time since I lost my baby. So after glowering at her for a while as she cooked her silly quinoa, which wasn't any kind of birthday dinner, I decided to make her as angry as I was.

'It must be wonderful to be so sure of yourself, I'm sure Octavia enjoys it. No doubt you both have your eyes on such prime property. You probably think you'd be very comfortable here, but I'm not prepared to give it up just yet.'

Mel swung round, dark green eyes glinting. 'What on earth are you suggesting?'

I shrugged. 'Oh, get the tiresome mother to shuffle off and make way for your new London lives. I'm sure I'll be fine in some shabby little flat while you play Lady and Lady in your Stoke Newington palace.'

'How dare you? The very idea of it! Octavia and I are happy in Cambridge, thank you very much. We have no desire to live in this old wreck.'

'Oh, a wreck, is it? Then it should suit me very well, since I'm such a crumbling old vessel.'

Mel snorted. 'Oh, come off it. I just want you to be comfortable, and this house is . . . unmanageable.'

'And we all know how you like to manage things.'

'That's not fair. I only want what's best for you . . .' she tailed off, aware how trite that sounded.

'What would be best for me is if you just leave me alone. All . . . this' – I gestured to the quinoa, which smelled of very little – 'nonsense. Leave it. Take it home to Octavia. I don't want it. I'm fine on my own. I don't want you.'

She flung a wooden spoon on the table and stood with her hands on her hips. 'No, you don't, do you? You never did, in fact.'

I didn't want to continue the conversation, but we were

wrestling on a precipice, and the momentum was carrying us over, even though this would end badly, disastrously. The air crackled with it. I licked my lips, which felt dry and sore.

'What do you mean?'

'You never wanted me. You only wanted Dad, and Ali. And Bertie.'

It was like a firework had gone off in the room, whizzing and cannoning around, enveloping us in the aftershock. My chest was tight, my field of vision narrowed until all I could see was her unshed tears and hunched shoulders as she recoiled from her own blow. Bertie, Bertie, Bertie. I hardly ever said his name except in my head, all the time, an echo in an ancient buried cave. Now Mel had lit a match and revealed the walls were decorated with endless tiny handprints. That spark was all I needed to send me over the edge.

'Get out.' It came as a hoarse whisper, out of my mouth before I knew it. 'And don't come back.'

She slumped. 'I'm sorry . . . I didn't mean . . . Sibyl told me . . . before she died. I don't think she knew what she was saying. She said . . . your mother told her.'

'I don't care. Get out. You're right, I never wanted you. So you can go.' The thrill of saying it was somehow purifying. The rage finally had a channel, and it was going full tilt. 'Go on, go!'

She was still for a minute, then picked up a tea towel and arranged it neatly on the bar of the Aga. She took the pot off the stove and set it in the sink, which sizzled slightly on impact. The clock ticked.

'I said, go.' I couldn't resist twisting the knife. It felt awful, which was better than nothing.

She turned to me, breathing slowly and evenly. I loathed her self-possession. Where did it come from? I could barely keep myself in check – she had to leave before I lost control.

'I'm going. But I just want you to know. What you did . . . it wasn't wrong. Sibyl said you never forgave yourself but . . . there was nothing to forgive. You shouldn't blame yourself.'

This was worse than anything else she could have said. The anger overflowed and erupted out of the dark corner where it lurked, ready to scorch everything in its path. I got to my feet, unsteadily, placing both palms on the kitchen table.

'I don't blame myself,' I said shakily. 'But I do blame you.'

Her brow furrowed. 'What does it have to do with me? I don't understand.'

'When you were born.' I made sure to enunciate every syllable. 'You weren't him.'

She backed away towards the door, eyes wide, then grabbed her coat with shaking hands, not bothering to put it on, picked up her bag and turned the latch on the door. For a second she leaned her forehead against it, then pulled back and looked me in the eye.

'Happy Birthday,' she said, and then she was gone.

I ate the quinoa, which tasted how it smelled, and sat drinking the red wine Mel brought with her, shivering in my bare living room and deliberately not thinking of anything at all. The cave was dark and empty again, and I could almost ignore the echo if I put the radio on, or had another glass, or scrubbed the Aga, which was flecked with those stupid grains. By the time the phone call came my hands were cracked with bleach and my head was fuzzy, but when I answered I could tell she was as drunk as I was.

'Don't hang up,' she said. I didn't say anything, but didn't put the phone down either. Suddenly I didn't have the energy any more. The anger had found its outlet and now there was nothing left.

'I just wanted to say I'm sorry. Again. I shouldn't have said anything, not my business, it was wrong of me to bring it up. But I wish you . . . had told me . . . I wish you . . . would say . . .'

But I couldn't. Like Leo couldn't, or wouldn't. Regard, not love. *'Mother, we all know there's very little you love about me.'* So I sat there in silence listening to the catch in her breath, looking at my empty glass, until I heard the click as she quietly put the phone down, then the dial tone that just went on and on.

Chapter 40

23B Garrod Street,
Cambridge

15th May 2016

Dear Melanie,

Such a strange way to begin a letter, when I've never really treated you so. You were never 'dear' to me, were you? From the beginning, I acted as though you were an aberration, and I suppose in a way you were, because you weren't Bertie.

What is so painful to me is that you knew it. So I am doubly guilty. You said I shouldn't blame myself, but a lifetime of blame is hard to shake off, and it tends to spill over into other things. Into blaming you. I treated you as though you were somehow complicit, which of course is absurd. What I said to you that day was unforgivable, and I said it because I was angry — so very,

very angry – with myself, with your father, with life itself. But not with you.

I'm not angry any more. I'm sad, and sorry, and I know I should have been a better mother to you, my Melanie, instead of being the mourning mother of Bertie. When I saw you today, standing with Octavia, I felt very glad that you have managed to find the kind of straightforward happiness that eluded me.

But getting Bobby – that ridiculous, beribboned hound who very nearly ruined your wedding – has opened up something in me. It's a beautifully uncomplicated, direct relationship, unhindered by dark secrets or lopsided requirements. We both need something from each other, and we're both giving it. So far it's proved wonderfully beneficial. I wish I could have been as open with you, my dear.

Congratulations on your marriage. You have my blessing, and were he able to give it, you would have your father's too. Not that you need it. You are your own woman, and anyone would be fortunate to call you their wife, or their daughter.

I hope that one day you will forgive me. Not just for those words, but for everything else.

With my love,
Your mother

Chapter 41

'And so the upshot is, I looked at the budgets and I'm afraid I just can't make it work. I can pay you to the end of the month, of course, and I hope you'll come in until then but I understand if you'd rather not, under the circumstances . . . I'm so sorry.'

I didn't really hear her at first, busy admiring my new hair in the darkened window that lined one wall of the reception. But gradually I began to appreciate Deirdre's remorseful expression, hands twisting in her lap just like Jette's used to in the cellars. *Luó; to untie, release.* They were letting me go. Seeing Deirdre's distress, I made sure to say that I understood and that it was completely fine; in fact I would appreciate the extra time to myself. Then I picked up my bag and left before she could see my face fall.

When the shock subsided, I tried to look on the bright side. The extra money had been very welcome, but it wasn't as if I was entirely unoccupied – I still had Otis to look after, and my friends, and of course Bobby. There was plenty to be grateful for. So I went and met Angela for lunch and she was gratifyingly irate, launching into one of her favourite rants about cuts, while I nibbled my salad and tried to stay positive, looking at my pearl bracelet as it caught the light of the spring sunshine pouring through the window of our café.

'Anyway, you could get another job,' concluded Angela, opening up her sandwich and systematically removing chunks of gherkin.

I paused, my fork halfway to my mouth. 'Not at my age! I'm eighty, for heaven's sake. Who gets a new job at eighty?'

'Who gets one at seventy-nine? You did it before, and now you know that computer system whatsit. See, you *can* teach an old dog new tricks!' chirruped Angela, through a mouthful of crisps.

I laughed. 'I think I'll stick to looking after Bobby and Otis.'

'Well, about that.' A crisp fell to the floor and Angela dived after it, but before she ducked under the table I saw a flicker of guilt flash across her face. 'I've managed to get Otis into an after school club, he's been moaning because all his friends go, and they had a space.' She came up from under the table. 'It'll free me up now I've got more work on. He starts next week. Stop me pestering you all the time.' Angela babbled on, avoiding my eyes, but when she finally lifted her head, I found I couldn't look at her, instead pushing rocket leaves around my plate, hunting for the olives.

'Well, that's nice. He'll enjoy being with his friends.' She was right; he didn't want to be with an old biddy like me, making twig houses for bugs. So that was the library and Otis gone, all in one morning.

'You'll still see him at weekends,' offered Angela. 'And there's always the school holidays.'

Ah yes. The holidays. I found a last piece of mayonnaise-drenched chicken and speared it.

'Speaking of which,' she continued, 'did Sylvie tell you, she's off to France for the summer?'

My dismay came crashing back. 'The whole summer?'

'Yes, her mother has to have an operation, and she's going to stay with her afterwards, help her out.' Angela reached across the table to touch the back of my hand but it was more than I could bear so I moved it away, wiping my mouth with my napkin.

'I thought her brother lived in France?'

'He does, but he's got too much on, apparently. Typical.'

'Oh dear, her poor mother.' I felt guilty that my first concern was my own loss, and envy of this off-stage presence who could summon Sylvie and be with her for a whole sun-soaked summer. If I had an operation, would Melanie come and tend me at my bedside? Of course she would, and probably Octavia too. Though they would both drive me mad. We'd come a long way since my mother marched for women's rights, but we still did the tending, on the whole.

The library, Otis, Sylvie. I sensed my fragile house of cards wobbling, and fingered my pearls nervously, remembering my New Year's resolution. Angela still wasn't smoking. She seemed much better though, and I was glad. She deserved a happy life, not one tinged with regret.

313

I went home, mainly to enjoy Bobby's vociferous greeting – she needed me, and I needed a reminder that someone did. But rather than hang around the house twitching, I decided to go for a walk, get us both a bit of fresh air. Once we were out, I found myself wandering towards Sylvie's house, and discovered her in her front garden, pruning the parterre. Seeing us, she ceased her ferocious clipping and beamed.

'Missy! How nice, come in for a coffee. I've just made some courgette cake in defiance of the shortage.'

'What about Aphra?' I gripped Bobby's lead.

'Don't worry, she's off somewhere butchering small creatures.' Sylvie threw down her secateurs on the front door step and led me in, where we were greeted by Decca and Nancy. They bore Bobby off for canine mischief, leaving us alone in the kitchen, which as usual smelt of a thousand indulgences.

An enormous sponge squatted on the peninsula, topped in a cream frosting and carelessly scattered with minuscule ringlets of lemon zest. Sylvie picked up a silver cake-shovel and plunged it into the middle, cutting me a huge slice, which she set in front of me with a spoon. 'Tuck in.' For a while we sat in silence, preserved in a kind of reverence for the cake, the like of which I had never tasted before. Each bite bounced around my mouth like an arcade ball, cherished by every taste bud. That hint of lemon sourness cutting through the sweetness of the frosting, its dense grittiness caressing my tongue. Sylvie *was* a genius, everything she touched turned to ambrosia. I noticed Bobby had re-joined us and was drooling at my feet. Usually I would have given her a morsel but this was too delicious to waste.

'God, I'm good,' said Sylvie, licking her spoon and sitting back on her stool with a sigh of satisfaction. I nodded, my mouth full of sponge. Bobby pawed at me, her claws scraping my leg and I shook my head at her, still chewing and relishing, so she scampered off to rejoin Nancy and Decca, casting me a slightly truculent look as she left.

'So, what's new?' Sylvie poured a cup of coffee from the cafetière and pushed it towards me.

'I've lost my job at the library,' I mumbled, scraping up a last spoonful.

Her mouth opened in surprise. 'No! How on earth?'

'Budget cuts. Deirdre was very apologetic.'

'Merde. You poor thing, are you sad about it?'

'Yes, a bit.' I paused. 'I'll miss having somewhere I need to be.'

Sylvie looked at me over the rim of her coffee cup. 'Hmmm. Talking of which, there's something I've been meaning to say. I saw Desiderata Haber last week—'

'Oh, the Habers were so lovely. Their poor son.'

'Yes, poor Sam, hopelessly indulged by loving and in-love parents,' scoffed Sylvie picking up our plates and walking over to the dishwasher with them. She continued with her back to me. 'Anyway, we got talking and Desi said . . . I mean, she mentioned – I hope you don't mind my asking . . .'

'What?' I spied a speck of cake on the peninsula and picked it up between my thumb and forefinger.

'Why didn't you tell me about Leo? I had no idea.'

I could hear the dogs scuffling in the living room, faint growls and whines as they wrestled and rolled. Even without seeing her I recognized Bobby's voice amongst them. The crumb of cake fell from my finger and I stared at it, fighting a rising nausea, the sickly sweet smell of the frosting assaulting my nostrils. I'd had too much. I could feel Sylvie watching me, and risked a sideways glance. She looked concerned, holding the cake shovel in one hand and a tea towel in the other. Still I said nothing.

'Missy. I didn't mean to pry. I'm just . . . so sorry.'

'No need. It's fine. I— I . . . must be going. I said I'd take Otis to the playground this afternoon.' I tipped myself off the stool, stumbling and fumbling for my bag and Bobby's lead. 'Thank you for the cake, it was delicious. I must get the recipe from you some time.' Gabbling, I just needed to get out of there before I embarrassed myself further. Hearing the clink of her lead, Bobby scrambled back into the kitchen, nose twitching. With shaking hands, I clipped it on.

'Oh dear, I'm sorry, I didn't mean . . . I just . . . Please don't go.'

'I must.' A solitary tear fell, but was absorbed into Bobby's thick fur. Head down, I made my way along the corridor to the front door, feeling Sylvie and her pity behind me.

'I shouldn't have asked,' I heard her say. 'But I just wanted you to know – if you ever need to talk . . .'

'Yes, of course,' I said. 'I must go.' I grappled at the latch and wrenched the door open, feeling the bile rising in my throat. Lugging Bobby along, we stumbled down the steps and between the neat hedges, where I could see the early weeds of spring poking through the soil. Hearing the door close behind me, I gagged and yanked Bobby's lead. We made it around the corner before I vomited, a congealed yellow custard that projected from the back of my throat, splattering onto the pavement, where Bobby sniffed it cautiously and looked up at me, her expression alert and curious.

'Don't worry,' I gasped, groping for a nearby railing to hold on to. 'I'll be all right in a minute.'

I heaved a few more times, then, checking that no one had seen my indignity, used a few leaves to cover the offending cake-mix. Seeing her favourite urinating patch, Bobby promptly crouched and did her business, causing me to retch again. I could feel the sweat beading on my brow, legs still trembling from the purge. As I began to totter towards home, my mobile rang.

'Listen, I feel bad about your job and the after-school thing,' Angela said as soon as I answered. 'I wasn't going to ask you coz kids' birthdays are so fecking hideous, but do you want to come to Otis's party on Sunday? You don't have to do anything, just hang around drinking Prosecco and listening to balloons popping, but you might like to see him get his cake.'

I thought of Sylvie's cake, gleaming on the peninsula, and then oozing on the pavement like a gross yellow toad.

'I'd love to,' I said, my voice croaky. 'Thank you for asking me.'

'No problem. Though you won't be thanking me on Sunday when you're dodging those little bastards. I'll text you the details.' She hung up, and I put my phone back in my bag, trying to focus on this one thing I could look forward to – to banish the ghost Sylvie had just raised. If I could do that, perhaps the feeling of doom I'd had of late would dissipate eventually. I was sure Sylvie wouldn't mention Leo again, and we could just forget it ever happened. Sometimes it was better not to think about things – bills, phone calls, arguments – because that way you could hold them at arm's length, maybe indefinitely. If I could just hang on a little while, things would get better again; I could forget again. Just for a little while.

Chapter 42

Sunday dawned bright and clear, one of those beautiful days when you could feel the world opening up again after the bolted door of winter, tender shoots curling out of the damp ground, the earth unfurling beneath us as the tide surged back in. When I walked Bobby that morning, greeting my fellow dog walkers and sucking up the fresh air like a tonic, the spring was back in my step. After the unsettling episodes of the last few days, I was glad to be going to Otis's party, to clap as he blew out his candles, to give him the present I'd spent so long pondering, see him with his friends. I would absorb their youth and energy and let it recharge me. What did the job, the bills, the phone calls, the creaking bones matter? The day was young, the sun was warm, and with Bobby by my side I was raring to go.

Six hours later, I was raring to leave. I had no idea children's parties were so ghastly. In my day they were much tamer affairs – a few friends, sausages and pineapples on sticks and a Victoria sponge with the age dotted out in Smarties. I remembered one of Mel's parties, the dim light and breathless anticipation when I carried out the cake, her little face screwed up in concentration as she waited. She was always worried about blowing out the candles. 'What if I don't blow them all out at once? Will my wish still come true?' She would fret about it for days beforehand.

For Otis's party, Angela appeared to have invited thirty chemically-fuelled gremlins and their Prosecco-powered, utterly disinterested zookeepers. The little fiends raged around the cramped church hall while their parents necked fizz and prattled about house prices, ignoring their appalling offspring entirely. Poor Angela was scurrying round filling up people's glasses, offering olives and removing sharp kitchen implements from tiny hands.

I stood in a corner, thinking that in many ways it reminded me of the St Botolph's party where I met Leo. Too hot, and loud, and things being thrown around while people talked nonsense to each other. Still, at least I wasn't going to get overlooked in favour of another woman this time. I snatched a glass from Angela and took a sip, ducking as a carrot stick whizzed past my ear. One of the beasts reared up in front of me, roaring, his face covered in hummus like a kind of war paint. Holding my glass above my head, I roared back at him, earning myself a few disapproving looks from the zookeepers. Briefly chastened, he soon recovered and continued his rampage, kicking over a chair and felling a younger child with a well-timed punch. 'Horatio!' rebuked one of the women vaguely, before spearing an olive and resuming her conversation about council planning laws.

Feeling the urge to escape, I made my way to the back of the hall in search of the kitchen, and found Angela seated at a small table with her head in her hands. She looked up as I entered.

'Oh, it's you. Aren't you glad you came?' She sank back down again and pressed her fingers to her temples. 'I told you it would be horrendous.'

I fetched her a glass and poured her the dregs of a Prosecco bottle.

'I can't drink, I've got to clear up after and pay for it all. I should have booked an entertainer but I can't afford it. Most of them get in these guys called Jackanapes, they turn up and do everything, flap a big rainbow sheet about and keep them occupied, but they cost, like, hundreds and I thought *"I've got this covered, I'll do a Pass the Parcel and we can make our own entertainment."* What a fucking joke.' She took a slug of the Prosecco. 'I've got five kids whose parents didn't RSVP so I wasn't expecting them and now I haven't got enough party bags, I'll have to hand them fucking fivers on the way out. Jesus Christ.' She took another gulp. 'And none of the mums like me because I'm a single mother and they think I'm going to steal their husbands. As if. They're all wanker bankers who stay late at work to avoid bedtime and train for marathons at the weekend so they don't have to help with childcare.' She drained the glass. 'Why did I do this again?'

'Mummeeeeee.' We both turned to see Otis at the door. He looked slightly woebegone and my heart jumped in my chest at the sight of him in his new robot costume. 'Can we do Pass the Parcel?'

'Yes, love, is it that time already?' Angela got to her feet, smoothing down her tousled hair. Otis wandered around the kitchen, idly exploring.

'Where's the cake?' he asked, poking his head in the fridge.

'Over there by the sink,' returned Angela, putting empty bottles in a bin bag.

'No, it isn't.'

Angela turned and looked at the counter. Next to the sink was a foil-covered cakeboard, entirely devoid of cake.

'Where's the fecking cake?'

She started to stalk around the room, pushing paper plates and napkins to one side, opening the fridge, peering inside the bin bag in increasing desperation. Having searched through all the cupboards, she returned to the table and gripped one edge with both hands, staring at me with wild eyes.

'Where's the cake?' she breathed.

Otis's lip started to tremble. 'Where's my cake? Did you forget it?'

She turned to him immediately. 'No, sweetie, of course I didn't. Mummy will find it. Why don't you go and play out there and we'll start Pass the Parcel in a minute?' She bundled him out, ignoring his protests, and turned back to me, panting.

'So the cake's fucked off. We need another one.'

'Where did it go?'

'One of those little bastards will have nicked it. Slimy little feckers, I hope they choke on it. Listen, we've got half an hour, maybe forty minutes. If I give you some money, can you get in a cab and go and buy me another?'

'Of course.' I felt daunted, but also delighted to have a genuine reason to escape this hellhole. Angela delved in her purse and pulled out a wad of notes.

'Right, here you go, that should be enough. You need to be back by five, otherwise the sugar withdrawal will kick in and they'll run amok.'

Feeling slightly hysterical, I giggled as I took the money and put it in my bag.

'Oh, and Missy? It needs to be a robot cake.'

I turned back, perplexed.

'A robot cake?'

Angela nodded grimly. 'He's really into robots now. I was up 'til 3 a.m. painting the icing silver and making antennae out of Satellite Wafers. WE CAN'T LET HIM DOWN.'

I took a deep breath. 'One robot cake coming right up.'

Luck was on my side. A black cab pulled up across the road with its light on just as I emerged from the hall, blinking in the sunshine. Hurrying forwards, I hailed it and waited as the driver made a U-turn to come and pick me up.

'Where to, love?'

Settling in the back, I hesitated. Where did one go to buy an emergency robot cake on a Sunday afternoon? I took my phone out of my bag and told the driver to head towards Upper Street, then called the only person I could think of who could rescue this situation.

'Darling, I'm so glad you called,' said Sylvie. 'I'm so sorry about the other day—'

'Never mind that,' I barked. 'I need your help. Otis's birthday cake went missing and I need to get him another one, but Angela says it must be a robot cake. I've got some money but I don't know where to go.'

'Where are you?'

'In a cab going towards Upper Street. I need to be back by five o'clock.'

'Give me two minutes.' She rang off and I sat back and put my seatbelt on as the streets of Highbury flashed past.

'That's a new one,' observed the taxi driver, eyeing me in his mirror.

'Children's birthday party.'

'Thank Christ I'm past that,' he replied, turning towards Canonbury. As we thudded our way over a series of speed bumps, my phone rang and I snatched it up.

'Right,' said Sylvie. 'Listen very carefully, I shall say this only once. There's a little place near Angel, owned by a friend. He owes me a favour. I'll text you the address, and he should have something for you by the time you get there.'

'Thank you so much.'

'Don't thank me; thank Etienne Durand, one of the finest pâtissiers on the planet. Goodbye and Godspeed!'

We raced through the streets of Islington, my driver now thoroughly committed to the venture, promising to wait outside the shop while I went in to collect the goods. He told me his three children were grown up, scattered across the globe in diverse lives and professions – 'that's what it's about isn't it? They're off, doing their thing' – while he and his wife lived in Enfield and waited for grandchildren. 'I know we won't see them much, them all living all over the place, but they're nice to have, aren't they? I'll like seeing the photos.'

Having received the address, we turned into an expensive-looking Georgian terrace where every window had a Juliet balcony, and then turned again, squeezing down a narrow cobbled mews. At one end was a tiny corner shop that looked like it should have been in Diagon Alley. A sign above the door read 'Durand's' in flowing script.

'You sure this is a cake shop?' queried my driver, pulling up outside.

'I'm not sure that's what the owner would call it,' I replied, getting out and checking my roll of notes.

Taking care not to trip on the cobbles, I knocked on the shiny black door and stepped back. After a few seconds' agonizing wait, it opened and a tall dark man poked his head out and regarded me solemnly.

'I'm Millicent Carmichael,' I stammered. 'Sylvie Riche sent me.'

'I am Etienne Durand,' he said, bowing and gesturing me in. I waved to the cab driver and stepped inside.

It looked nothing like any kind of shop I'd been in before. There were no cakes on display. We stood in what appeared to be an elegant sitting room with a chaise longue at one end and a round oak table in the middle, surrounded by chairs. For some reason it reminded me of a funeral parlour. I repressed a snigger.

'Sylvie did explain? We need a cake. An, um, robot cake.'

He made a little moue of distaste. 'Yes, she explain. It is not what we usually do, but she is very great friend.'

'What do you usually do?'

He indicated the table. 'People sit there. And I bring them . . . les gateaux. If you wait 'ere, I will bring you yours.'

He disappeared through another door at the far end of the room and I waited, checking my watch and tapping my foot. We had twenty minutes. Forty foot taps later, he emerged, carrying a huge box.

'You don't know what I 'ad to do to make this 'appen,' he said, resting it carefully on the table. I stepped forwards and reached out to open the box. He slapped my hand away.

'Do not open until you get to your party.' I shrank back, chastened. He was very forbidding. I'd always imagined cake shop owners were jolly.

I paused. 'But . . . I just wanted to check that it's . . . a robot.'

He snorted. 'It is robot. It is best robot you ever see. Trust me.' He handed me a separate paper bag. 'This is a little flourish I add, make sure you don't forget.'

'What do I owe you?' I asked, feeling faintly sick, sure Angela's roll of notes couldn't possibly cover this. But he brushed away the question as he'd brushed away my hand.

'There is no money required. This is favour for my friend Sylvie.' I felt dizzy with relief and embarrassment.

'You 'ave car outside?' he asked, interrupting my halting expression of thanks. I nodded, and he picked up the box again, ordering me to open the door for him. Together we manoeuvred it into the back of the taxi. I checked my watch. Fifteen minutes. We could do it, but we'd have to drive slowly. As the engine rumbled, Monsieur Durand's face loomed at the window. He tapped at the glass and I opened it.

He leaned forward menacingly. 'You tell Sylvie we're even now, yes? No more favours?' He smiled and his teeth gleamed in the gloom of the cab. They were slightly pointed.

'Definitely. I'll tell her,' I gasped, and the head retreated. He smacked the side of the car and we were on our way. 'Drive carefully,' I said to the driver and saw him nod, his eyes on the road.

My heart leapt at every speed bump on the way back, but the box remained upright. We pulled up at the church hall at 4.56 p.m. Angela was hovering outside. As I got out of the cab I saw she was holding an unlit cigarette.

'Just holding it for comfort,' she said. 'How did you get on?'

'I'm not sure,' I said, turning back to the driver. 'Derek, how much is that?' But once again, my roll of notes was pushed away. 'No charge,' he said cheerily. 'I haven't enjoyed myself so much since I picked up a bloke dressed as Batman and he pointed in front and said "follow that car."'

'Oooh,' said Angela. 'Was he chasing a baddie?'

'Sort of,' said Derek. 'He was on his way to a stag do.' He got out of the taxi and picked up the cake box. 'Now, where do you want this?'

I leaned forward and kissed him on the cheek. 'Thank you so much.'

'Come round the back,' said Angela.

Together we carried the cake round the back of the building and through to the kitchen. The empty silver cakeboard was still next to the sink.

'Any sign of the original?'

Angela shook her head grimly. 'It's that little fucker Horatio, I know it. He's got silver paint in his hair.'

Derek put the box on the table, Angela took the lid off and we all looked inside.

'Holy shit,' she said.

Nestled in the box was the most glorious robot cake I had ever seen. Well, I had never actually seen a robot cake before. But none could live up to the splendid beauty of this one. It was a vivid blue, sitting up with its legs out, with bright red buttons, and a TV screen across its chest that read 'Otis'. Its liquorice and icing grille mouth was smiling at us.

'That's some robot cake,' said Derek, stepping back to admire it.

'Fuck, I haven't got any candles,' said Angela, scrabbling around in drawers.

I remembered the 'flourish', and looked in the bag I was holding. Inside there were five candles and two sparklers.

'Here you go.' I stuck the candles on the robot's outstretched legs, and arranged the sparklers either side of his head, as antennae. Looking at my watch, I saw that it was 5.02 p.m. 'Time to go.'

'You should take it in,' urged Angela. 'You did it all.'

'No, I want to watch.' I shook hands with Derek, telling him I hoped his grandchildren came soon, and he left via the back door, while I slipped back into the hall and went in search of the light switch.

As I'd watched my own children decades before, I kept my eyes on Otis's little face in the darkness, alight with excitement and anticipation, tiny body shivering with the joy of it all, gremlin-friends surrounding him as he waited. Even the parents stopped gassing about loft renovations long enough to appreciate Angela's entrance. Her face was illuminated by the sparklers, grinning at the 'ooohs' and 'aaahs' of the assembled party, her eyes softening and blinking rapidly as she saw his reaction, his gasp of astonishment and wonder as everyone began to sing. He blew out the candles, his eyes screwed up with the effort of huffing and wishing at once, everyone cheering as the flames were extinguished, the smoke carrying our prayers to the heavens. I thought about what Derek had said. That's what it was about, them doing their thing, and you just enjoying it. Why had I waited so long to be able to do it? I clapped and cheered along with everyone else, and then, as the lights came on again, there was a piercing scream from one of the mothers.

'Horatio Lysander Swinton!' she bellowed. 'What on earth is this?'

We all surged towards her as she held out her bag, her tan buckled leather bag that looked like it had cost several bonuses, and was now filled with the crushed remains of one home-made robot cake with Satellite Wafer antennae. As the other mothers crowded round her patting and sympathizing, I could hear Angela's cackles from the kitchen.

The parents began their goodbyes, and the children clamoured for party bags, so Angela hastily re-emerged, buckling under a tray of them, eyes rolling as she totted up children versus bags. She moved through the throng pawed by eager mites, little claws snatching, each retreating to inspect and compare their hauls.

A wilting Otis was curling around his mother like a kitten while she rifled through her tray, patting cheeks and tweaking pigtails as she distributed her largesse, a lolly stick jutting out of her mouth. She still hadn't smoked.

'Wonderful cake,' said one of the mothers, as she left.

'I made it myself,' said Angela, poker-faced.

Later, while Otis opened his presents on the floor, we sat in the kitchen polishing off the last of each Prosecco bottle and bitching about the other mothers.

'Some terrible parenting going on there,' drawled Angela, watching Otis crowing as he ripped the wrapping off a Star Wars sticker book. 'One of them – Tybalt or Gawain or whatever – bit another so hard he drew blood. And his mum looked at the bite mark and said "the trouble with gifted children is they have such *energy*."'

I giggled and then checked my watch. 'I must be going, it's nearly six and Bobby will be wanting a walk. Shall I help you clear up some more?' The robot cake's remains were lodged next to the sink, ruthlessly denuded to bulk out the goody bags.

'No, don't worry, there's not much more to do, and besides, you saved the day today.'

'Not really. It was Sylvie.'

'I've saved her a slice. It's bloody good cake.'

'*I made it myself,*' I mimicked.

She winked. 'Got to get some credit since mine ended up in Mamma Swinton's Hermès.'

I said goodbye to Otis and wandered home, relishing the brighter nights now we were edging further into spring. As I unlocked the front door, I steeled myself for the usual ecstatic greeting from Bobby, Bruce Bunny hanging out one side of her mouth.

We set off on our walk together, and since it was such a lovely evening I treated her to a quick turn around the park, where she could have a more leisurely sniff, soaking up the new smells of the season. As usual I wished Leo were here to enjoy it with me, and thought how much he would have loved Bobby, grown to adore her as much as I did, her quirks and idiocies, her head-long tilt at life.

As the sun set over the thickening greenery, I chewed over events of the day, chuckling to myself at the thought of Horatio stashing the cake, and my flight into the shady world of French pâtissiers. Then the laughter died in my throat as we turned out of the park and with a sudden, blood-curdling howl Bobby launched herself forward. Across the road I saw a cat, her deadliest enemy, tail flickering as it gazed at us impassively from its vantage point. With another strangled growl, Bobby wrenched back, and, just as she had at Mel's wedding, slipped her collar and dived out into the road in search of her foe.

It all happened very quickly. The car came out of nowhere, Bobby a blur of brown and amber as she hurtled across the road, snapped up by the flash of scarlet and silver metal as it smashed into her. I stood on the pavement, rooted in shock as I struggled to process what was happening, then gave up, sinking to the ground, gravel grinding into my knees as the car screeched to a halt and the driver got out, circling his vehicle in growing horror to find Bobby's poor crumpled body. I thought of the robot cake, pristine in its box, then in pieces by the sink. One minute something was intact; the next, shattered. Untied, released, destroyed.

Someone screamed on the other side of the street, and a figure darted forwards to bend over my Bobby. Then I was able to move; no one should touch her but me. I rushed into the road, crouched at her side and cradled her bloody and broken form in my arms, rocking her to sleep like a child, crooning over the silken ears and burying my face in the lustrous mane for one last time. Her eyes were open; those lovely chocolate eyes that melted me, begging for her treats. She was still warm, the warmest thing in my life. My Bobby, the dog I didn't want, didn't own, but who was truly mine in a way that no one else ever had been.

'I love you, I love you, I love you. Please come back.'

I sobbed into her soft neck, but there was no answer, and I could feel the very essence of her gone, a vapour-thread that swirled and faded into the spring breeze.

We stayed like that for a while, the driver stuttering his apologies over our heads while we rocked together, cherry blossom drifting around us like snow. Eventually someone – was it Phillip? Or maybe Simon – appeared and helped me up, promising that he would bring Bobby home to rest. As they led me away, I saw the cat, still sitting there, looking at us, its tail flapping like the stingray under the sand.

Chapter 43

A week after Leo's diagnosis, we decided to go and watch a firework display.

We'd spent days stagnating in the house, Leo in his study and me in the living room, occasionally loitering in the hallway, my hand hovering above the handle of his door, wanting to go in but unsure of what to say when I did. I could hear him moving around in there, shifting papers and books, playing Bach, and sometimes – horrifyingly – weeping. I should have gone in then, but I had no words to comfort him when the void overwhelmed me too. What could I say to my husband of over fifty years who was being ruthlessly shredded by this terrible disease? So I cleaned the kitchen, and made hearty stews whose scents pervaded the house, but didn't tempt him out.

So much unsaid between us. As I ferociously scrubbed and stirred, the words echoed in my head, fighting to get out. But I knew they wouldn't come out right, so I swallowed them down as I always had. Hearing the tinny twitch of the letterbox, I marched out to clear up the post, stuff it all away, get rid of it. The local *Gazette* lay on the doormat and I swept it up, ready to decant into the recycling, but instead found myself sinking into a chair at the kitchen table, idly leafing through it. The bustling, mundane concerns of the community soothed me for a second – someone, somewhere was worrying about school children loitering outside a public swimming pool; someone else was campaigning for extra lighting on an estate; an article about the lack of dog waste bins. Life went on, even if in our world everything had stalled.

A local Residents' Association had organized a firework display in a nearby square. When we lived in Cambridge, we'd gone to the Midsummer Common event, and I remembered leaning against Leo's reassuring bulk in the spicy cold, both our breaths mingling as we gazed up. It felt like a heartening image to hold on to, and maybe even one to resurrect. So I took the paper in to him, and found him sitting at his desk, his head in his hands. When he looked up, his expression was as desolate as I'd ever seen it. I wanted to take him in my arms, smooth away the lines of despair and rebuild his shattered self with nuts and bolts to make it secure. Instead I waved the paper in his face and said, 'we should go to this.'

'Upwards and onwards,' he said, like he always did. Except he'd got it the wrong way round. I tried not to wince.

On the night of the display, we walked slowly towards the square, taking care not to slip on the pavement's carpet of mulched leaves. Eventually Leo took my arm, and I didn't know whether it was to stop me falling, or to stop himself. 'Nice night,' he said.

I looked at the sliver of crescent moon glowing against the black. Like Leo, slowly disappearing until there was only a tiny crack of light left. Soon it would be too late. All the unsaid things between us.

We arrived to find that the whole neighbourhood appeared to have descended, bustling about the square clutching plastic cups of punch. Some had sparklers, bright batons bristling in the darkness as they gesticulated, like a series of mad conductors. I could smell hot dogs, and smoke and bonfire toffee and was grateful for the assault on my senses. The same smells, same traditions, same expectations, year after year. Something to cling to, when everything else was falling from my grasp.

As we had for so many years – as newly-married sweethearts, as harassed young parents surrounded by shrieking children, and now, as an elderly couple sheltering from the storm of diagnosis – we leaned against each other and looked up when the sky began to snap and crackle above us. As always, my mouth fell open and I allowed myself to sink into the primal delight of those bright particular stars that sparked and showered and faded, the accompanying fizz billowing round the square as the crowd oohed and aahed.

And as my heart began to throb in synchrony with the detonations, I felt a demon take root. The fire and immediacy of the moment. So much left unsaid. I found I couldn't bear not to say the most important thing, the thing I'd carried all these years – suddenly it was imperative that the unshareable should be shared, before it was too late. My mouth was already open – all that was left was to say it. Say it. Bertie.

His name bubbled in my throat as I contemplated the act. My legs felt weak. I could feel Leo behind me, looming above, and half-turned to look at him, to see if it was in fact, the moment. His head was thrown back, his eyes fixed on the flickering sky, and he looked so much like the Leo of his youth, the one who walked away, oblivious to the wreckage, that once again I pulled back from the precipice.

It was over in twenty minutes. The fireworks, and my moment of madness. The show ended in a volley of cracks, bangs, and whistles, a chorus of 'aaahs' from the crowd and a final barrage of dazzling shots. Leo took my arm again and without a word we began to walk back, as fireworks elsewhere boomed and snapped around us. The lingering terror of the almost-confession and the noise of the rockets made me think of those nights in the cellar with Fa-Fa, thrill and horror, darkness and light, shelter and peril, fiction and reality all merging and swirling together until you didn't know which was which.

Back home, we stopped at our front gate, savouring the icy stillness of the air and the anticipation of a warm house, but as Leo put out a hand to push our way in, I blurted: 'I need to tell you something.'

The hand paused in mid-air and in that split second before he turned, I suddenly felt that he knew what was coming. His question hovered unspoken between us but I'd gone over now, so I carried on: 'There was a baby. Or at least, the start of one.'

His expression in the darkness had the shuttered quality of a house boarded up for the holidays. I stumbled on, 'In 1956. You left. And I . . . didn't realize.'

He took his hand away from the gate, but still didn't say anything. 'I was terrified. You know what it was like back then. And I thought I'd never see you again. So I never said. And then you came back . . .'

His eyes were slits in the dark, slivers of crescent moons. 'What happened to it?'

I'd gone over the edge but now we were teetering at a deeper abyss. I swallowed. 'I . . . we . . . got rid of it. Mama and I. That summer after we first . . . I thought you were gone from me forever.'

He pressed his thumb and forefinger to the bridge of his nose, trying to process the information.

'Why are you telling me this now?' he said, his shoulders lifting in a defeated kind of shrug.

'I'm sorry,' I faltered. 'I had to tell you. Before . . . before it's too late.' Crying now, my hands twisting round my scarf. 'I called him Bertie,' I whispered. 'I won't ever forget. Or forgive myself. But I felt you had to know.'

'Before I go?' he returned harshly. 'Some send-off.' He passed his hand across his face, as if erasing the memory.

'I'm sorry,' I sobbed. 'But it tore me apart. Doing it. And then not telling you. I don't want there to be any secrets between us now. I'm sorry. I . . . I love you.'

The fireworks, raging around us throughout, suddenly ceased, and silence hung in the air, only interrupted by the catch in my breath. Leo's eyes were closed, then he sighed, and it was like a great oak shaking off the last leaves of autumn. 'I'm sorry,' he said, finally looking at me. 'It's just . . . such a lot to take in. I don't know what to say. I don't know what you want me to say.'

I reached out my hand. 'I don't know what I want you to say. I just know I needed to say it.'

The bangs started up again. After a second's hesitation, he took my hand and held it. 'It was never fireworks with us, was it, Missy?' he said, almost to himself. 'It was always about coming home.' I nodded, not trusting myself to speak. He squeezed my fingers. 'Come on, let's go inside and have a hot drink. I can't think straight out here.'

We went indoors, stamping our feet and rubbing our arms against the cold as we took off our coats. Leo went off to put the kettle on, and, more for something to do, I went to the living room and started to build up a fire, scrunching newspapers and arranging kindling as if the careful positioning would restore order to everything. It was just catching when Leo came in to the room, holding two steaming mugs, which he set down on the side table by the sofa. Pushing me to one side, he stiffly lowered himself to his knees to attend to the fire, holding out his wrinkled hands to the leaping flames. Ham-fists, just like Fa-Fa.

I stood up, equally stiffly, and went to sit with my drink, watching him as he busied himself with the poker, adding another log. Then he got to his feet, and rubbed his hands together. 'Let's have that drink, shall we?'

He joined me on the sofa and we sat for a while in the fire-light, sipping our cocoa. Outside the pops and squeals continued but we were snug in our cocoon. Eventually Leo drained his cup, set it down and turned to me expectantly. 'Well, Missy? What was it you wanted to tell me?'

A volley of shots outside accompanied the blow. I pretended to sip my drink, although it was also finished by then. So much unsaid. Then said. Then unsaid again. The bitterness and shame coursed through me as I stared at the blazing fire, blinking back tears and then turning to Leo with a crooked smile.

'Nothing, my darling,' I said, taking another fake sip. 'Nothing at all.'

Chapter 44

Phillip brought Bobby home to me and we buried her in the garden by my roses. Denzil dug the grave, and we stood in a circle as she was laid to rest. Sylvie brought a small cypress tree, and we planted it above her though neither she nor I would ever sit in its shade.

Angela brought Otis as she wanted him to know about death, but I couldn't bear to see his pinched little face as he watched us shovelling earth over the small mound. So I just looked down at a worm burrowing through the overturned soil, and thought about cutting the crusts off the sandwiches I would serve later.

Bobby would have enjoyed her small wake, wandering around nosing for crumbs. I gave my few guests ham sandwiches and sausage rolls, because they were her favourite, and we talked about what a wonderful dog she had been, which she would also have enjoyed, head on one side, listening out for her name.

The worst moment came when Felicity arrived. Angela had rung to tell her the news, and my grief was now spiked with guilt because I was forced yet again to accept that Bobby was not my dog, that I'd been *in loco parentis* and failed in my duties. I was worried she would be angry with me, but as we stared at each other in my hallway, her cheeks streaked with mascara as they had been the first and only other time I'd seen her, I realized that she was holding out her hands, and after a second I took them, though I feared what she said next would break me.

'Millicent, I'm so sorry.'

Angela appeared from the kitchen, but seeing us there put a finger to her lips and pointed in the direction of the living room. We sat on my sofa, and in a prim little voice, I told her what had happened. She wasn't as thin as I remembered, and she'd lost the dead-eyed look she'd had in the café. I suppose I'd gained it.

I couldn't bear that she was so grateful. She kept thanking me for taking Bobby in, like it was a huge burden; like I'd done her a favour rather than the other way round.

'The other thing I wanted to thank you for,' she said, after Angela had tiptoed in with cups of tea, 'is what you said to Adrian.' She looked at my bracelet of pearls as she spoke, but I was embarrassed rather than gratified; the Missy who had confronted her husband was a wholly different woman from the stiff, formal creature who sat opposite her now. I felt shamed by the pearls – to think that I, an eighty-year-old grandmother, stood in the street and bared my breast to all and sundry. The very idea was vulgar and nonsensical. She talked about how empowered she'd been by the story, while I cringed and wondered if I should put more sausage rolls in the Aga.

Then, as she sat, twisting a tissue round her fingers, I found myself saying, in a broken whisper that seemed to come from someone else: 'I talked to her.'

Fix leaned forward to hear better. 'Sorry?'

'I talked to her. Bobby. Bob. We talked . . . I told her everything. She listened to me. She understood.'

She took my hands in hers again. 'Oh Millicent. The best dogs *do*.'

I'd let my tea go cold; when I took a sip, it made me choke, which brought on a coughing fit, and the tears I was working so hard to contain fell freely as I hacked and retched, bringing Angela back in to find out what all the noise was. She led Fix away to meet others who had known and loved Bobby, leaving me to compose myself.

When they'd gone, I sat for a while thinking about Leo and the latest letter that had arrived that morning, and then when I was done thinking about that I got up and went back to the kitchen, where Angela and Sylvie were tidying up. I put the unheated sausage rolls in the fridge and wrapped some leftover ham sandwiches in foil, thinking they'd do for dinner later. One of Otis's most recent pictures fell off the fridge door as I closed it – a drawing of Bobby and me standing outside our house. With a child's disregard for perspective, the dog was as tall as the second-floor windows. Would she always loom as large in whatever life I had left? He still drew me with long hair.

Angela and Sylvie left, with hugs and promises I barely listened to, so anxious was I to have the place to myself again. As soon as they'd gone, I went back to the kitchen and dug out the sherry bottle, hearing the tick tick tick of the clock, and the silence behind it. I poured myself a glass, and then another and another.

I took the bottle and sat in Leo's study, in his chair, stroking his desk as I sipped. On a whim, I went over to the shelves and started pulling out his books – *Killers of a Queen*, the one he called his 'blockbuster'. Pressured into writing it by his publishers, he hated the process and the result. Then *The Three Ambitions of Archibald*, about Archibald Roseberry. Another of Queen Victoria's prime ministers, the more he found out about him the more he claimed to dislike him. Then *The First Victorian*, his Disraeli biography – some said his best work. They all came out, one by one, until I reached *The Bedchamber Crisis*, his first book – the one that bought us our sofa. As I pulled it from the shelf it slipped from my hand and crashed to the floor, the pages opening and fluttering, a piece of paper falling from the leaves. When I saw Leo's handwriting spidering across the pages, I felt simultaneously hot and cold, hopeful and despairing, desperate to read and terrified of seeing more.

I took it back to the desk and unfolded it fully, my hands shaking.

'Dear Missy,' I read. Then stopped. A letter to me. His last letter.

Chapter 45

Dear Missy,

There are so many reasons I wish I didn't have to write this. The first is obvious — I have to write it while I still can. Eventually, the mists will descend and swallow me whole, and then the Leo you know will be swept away for good. So while I have this brief and terrible period of clarity, I have to say the things that must be said. Forgive my poor scrawl — this is written in haste. Not to get it over with, but to make sure it's done properly, before it's too late.

Firstly, the money. Horace Simmonds will keep an eye on our investments, and we should muddle along for a good while yet, but if it comes to it, you must do as you see fit. Don't worry about me; I will cease to have any say in the matter anyway. But know that whatever you decide, you have my blessing.

Secondly, Melanie and Alistair. I am sorry I never warned you of Alistair's plans, which were evident to me. I thought it might not come to pass, but now that it has, please, Missy – when they finally go, send him off with a smile. That day when we took him to those grim digs in Selly Oak – I can't remember what I had for breakfast this morning, but I remember your face that afternoon, your fingers clutching his sweater. You smiled then, so bravely, and you must do it again. Because if you don't, you will lose him anyway.

When he is gone, lean on Melanie. She was always my girl, wasn't she? From the moment she was born, my little curled-up hedgehog. But I know her spikes have irked you. You find her difficult for the same reason I admire her so: she reminds us both of you. Try to recognize Mel's fine qualities as your own, and rely on them to carry you through this. She will be your rock.

I don't deserve such an accolade. One of my greatest regrets is not being a truer and more devoted husband to you. Now I sit amidst all the books I wrote, I wonder if I couldn't have written a little less and attended a little more. You were always there, always present, always loving, however hard you tried to hide it, while I . . . well, perhaps my fate is a fitting one, to be forever absent.

My other great regret – the main reason I wish I didn't have to write this letter – is that I failed you. I remember Bertie. That night you told me – I did everything wrong. The shock of it, the anger, and the grief . . . and then it was blown away in one of those hideous blizzards where everything blurs and I can barely hold on to who I am. But it came back, bit by bit, and I pieced it together again. So I remember you telling me about him. And I'm so sorry I wasn't able to say then what I can write now: let it go. The guilt, the pain, the loss – anything you are carrying with you is not yours to bear alone. I shoulder it now, and when I go I will take it with me.

We had such happy times, you and I, and that's what I want you to hold onto. More than half a century rubbing along, and that's something I don't regret. You were always the one, Missy. The one I saw across the room at the St Botolph's party, sipping your wine and looking so out of place. The one walking down Sidgwick Avenue with the sun in your curls. The one swaying in my arms in the cellars of the Union, with tears on your cheeks. You thought I didn't see, but I did. I just never said. I never said.

I'm sorry for all the things I didn't say, all the things I wasn't. But I hope you're not sorry. Don't spend what's left of your life feeling guilty or apologetic – move on. Onwards and upwards, Mrs Carmichael. I'm going to forget about you; you have my permission to do the same. Let go. But know this: we may have sung different songs, and sometimes we were out of tune, but I think we harmonized rather well, in the end. Don't you?

Chapter 46

Sherry has always been my nepenthe, the anti-sorrow drug of choice, to quiet all pain and strife. After reading Leo's letter, I drank another glass, put on my coat – the old black one, not my Christmas parka – and set out.

It wasn't a long walk, and besides, it was one I did quite regularly. The usual route, down the little alleyway and along the boulevard until I came to a low, long building, wooden-clad on the ground floor with red-bricks on the second storey. We'd chosen it together, and Leo had joked about the red bricks; he still made jokes then. He always made me laugh, from the very beginning. Even when I'd been annoyed with him, he was able to tease me out of a bad mood, coax me to an unwilling chuckle. They say laughter is the best medicine, but that couldn't save him in the end.

'Good evening, Mrs Carmichael.'

I didn't say hello to Rachel as usual, because I had to get in and get it over with before I lost my nerve. So I marched straight past, down the soft carpeted corridor to the last door on the left. At the back, with the big window overlooking the oak. That was the one he wanted. I turned the handle and went in, breathing in the faint scent of the daffodils I'd brought a fortnight ago. They'd be wilting by now.

'Hello Leo, my darling.'

For a moment he sat in profile; that corrugated forehead, jutting Roman nose, firm chin. Such a strong, beloved face. Then he turned and gave me a hazy smile, lifting a finger from the arm of his chair before bending back to his cards. The Goldberg Variations were playing softly in the background; they were very good about ensuring he was always listening to music – it had been one of his stipulations. I joined him and sat down in the chair next to his. For a while I watched him laying out his cards in a vague approximation of Patience, but of course when you looked more closely you could see that there was no rhyme or reason to the order, just like there was no rhyme or reason to Leo any more.

He was still handsome, my husband of nearly sixty years. Still upright, with a full head of hair, mostly silver but threaded with the gold of his youth. He'd aged so well, in body. Such a tragedy, because I knew which he would have preferred, sitting there in his chair, turning over the same cards, looking at the same tree, day after day. After a while I cleared my throat and began my speech, wanting to get it all out before the effects of the sherry wore off.

'Leo, there's something I want to say to you.'

He turned again, and his striking blue eyes focused on me

for a moment. Not the piercing gaze of his prime, of course, but still it was unusual, and I took heart from it.

'That night, when we went to see the fireworks. I told you . . . about Bertie.'

Leo frowned slightly and tweaked an errant card back into place.

'Leo, listen to me.' He turned back obediently, and fixed me with that bright blue gaze again.

'And then you forgot. Just after I told you, just after I'd plucked up the courage, you forgot. And I just shrivelled inside, because I thought I'd failed. Then I got Bobby the dog – I told you about Bobby, didn't I? And it felt like something had healed a little. Like I might be loveable after all. Only now she's gone, and I didn't know what to do. But then I got your letter. Leo, you remembered! You remembered! And you wrote to me, and that letter, that letter . . . It was everything.'

'Walnut,' said Leo, sadly.

'What?'

'Walnut,' he repeated. 'Shrivelled. Like a walnut.'

'He was called Bertie,' I said, my voice trembling with the effort. 'I called him Bertie. I always thought of him as a boy. With your eyes.'

'Bertie,' he said. He looked at me with those eyes, those beautiful, blank eyes, and then suddenly he took my hand in his, which he hadn't done in months – years, even. He held my hand, and stroked it, and then he said:

'I love you, Missy. You know that, don't you?'

I looked out at his oak tree framed in the window. He gazed

349

at it every day, and while people came and went, the leaves unfurled, curled and fell, the trunk stood fast. Something to cling to, when everything else slipped from your grasp.

'I love you too, Leo. So, so much.'

There didn't seem to be much more we could say, so I stroked him back, and we sat there, hand in hand, until visiting hours were over. Then when it was time, I gently prised his fingers from mine and let go, leaving him sitting in his chair, my bright gold chain, looking out at his green oak.

Chapter 47

I missed the old Leo so much it was like a constant throb in my throat, and most of the time I could only bring myself to visit the new one in the hope of seeing some glimpse of the man he'd been. Once, when I was arranging his flowers, keeping up a flow of inconsequential chat, he suddenly looked up at me and said, 'Missy, really! Stop jabbering!' and it was so close to the kind of thing he would have said in the old days that I was jolted, my garden roses pricking my fingers as I clutched them. I sucked the blood away and stared at him hoping for more, but he just turned back to the book he was reading. He still read books; he had a little pile of them on the table next to him, and he would sit and turn the pages, carefully, considerately. Sometimes he would be holding them upside down. The light had gone out, and no one was home, no matter how often I knocked on the door.

Sometimes I would allow that thistle of tears to bubble up after I left him, and weep all the way home, back to that silent empty house with memories everywhere I looked. But the night after I visited Leo and he said he loved me, I walked out dry-eyed. As I stalked through the reception Rachel called out 'Mrs Carmichael!' but I ignored her, like I'd been ignoring all those letters and phone calls from Horace Simmonds for months. I knew the money was running out, but like everything else I thought that perhaps if I looked the other way then it would be all right. *Semper eadem.* Except that nothing did stay the same, did it? Hair got cut, cake got eaten and dogs ran out into the road. So I was going to have to accept that the money was almost gone, and come to terms with what that meant.

I was going to have to sell my house. My huge, prime location asset in Stoke Newington was going to have to go on the market to pay for Leo's care. I would have to buy a tiny flat somewhere, probably quite far away if the house prices round here were anything to go by, and use the remainder to repay our debts and keep Leo's precious status quo. I had to make a change, so he could carry on as he was.

I couldn't bear to lose my home. I knew it would be snapped up by some bright, ambitious family with 2.4 children, a hybrid car and Cockapoo. I'd been reading Sylvie's magazines - they'd rip out my kitchen and put sleek units in, replacing the back wall with toughened glass and laying those indoor/outdoor tiles that make the space 'flow'. Meanwhile I'd be stuck in some godforsaken bit of North London that estate agents optimistically refer to as 'up and coming', in a flat that would make Angela's look like a penthouse.

I'd lose all my friends. No one would be bothered to trek out there, so I'd be left, withering away, occasionally embarking on the trip back to see the husband who didn't recognize me. Contemplating that fate, it was little wonder I'd tried to pretend it didn't exist.

But it didn't matter how much I stopped myself from thinking about it, it turned out I'd been thinking about it all along and had it all planned out. So I arrived home and went straight back to the sherry. I took a glass and the bottle into the living room and sat on my sofa looking at Bobby's bed next to the fireplace. That beautiful, sumptuous bed the dog walkers bought me. The fleece was flattened in the shape of her. I drank a glass, and then another, and then I went to the kitchen and got two bin bags from one of the drawers.

Back in the living room, I stuffed Bobby's bed into one of them, pushing it down hard so it all squashed in. Then I did the same with all those stupid knick-knacks Sylvie had cast about the place – the photos, vases, pens, ornaments all went into the other bin bag until the room was clear again. All that clutter. The pettiness of it all. I stood in the middle of the room, breathing heavily, still dizzy from the alcohol. The ring of the doorbell interrupted my stupor. I imagined Bobby barking furiously, dancing into the hallway, at once excited and outraged at the intrusion. It rang again, and again I ignored it, looking around the room for more things to put away.

Angela's voice floated through the letterbox. 'Missy! Let me in! I know you're in there.'

I sat down on the sofa and poured myself another sherry as

I considered my next move. I wasn't sure I could get the bureau up to the attic on my own, but it would have to go.

'I can see your light on! Let me in, please!'

I looked up at the portrait of my father, his clever, sensitive face half-smiling down at me. I could probably take that with me to the new place. Nothing else though. It all had to go.

'I've been talking to Sylvie. She told me about Leo. Why didn't you tell me?'

Desi Haber told Sylvie about Leo, just as I feared she might, and Sylvie had told Angela. I supposed the world of historians was a small one. Not that it mattered now. I thought of the terrible row I'd had with Melanie. We didn't speak for months afterwards, then one day she called, and I'd thawed enough to talk. But then she couldn't resist broaching Leo's care again, refusing to believe that we had enough in savings to cover the cost, suggesting that I move him to a home she'd found in Cambridge and then buy a flat nearby for myself. Sheltered accommodation, she called it. I hung up on her.

'We can fix this, Missy. I promise.'

I switched the light off in the living room and sat in the gloom until Angela went away. Then I rolled up the Aubusson rug like I did all those years ago, and lugged it up to the attic. I was far too old for this. When I'd finished the sweat was pooling between my ribs, and I had the beginnings of a headache. So I went downstairs and got ready for bed, taking paracetamol in anticipation of the inevitable hangover. I had work to do tomorrow. Although Bobby wasn't there any more, I didn't bother to do my round of checking – who cared what was in the cupboards? As I got into bed and pushed my feet down, I felt a lump under the duvet and, reaching down, unearthed Bobby's rabbit. We should have buried him with her. Too late now. So instead I held him and stared at the wall, making shapes out of the shadows, until it was too dark to see any more.

Chapter 48

I didn't leave the house for three days, sitting in my dressing gown on the sofa staring at my father's portrait, reading more of my mother's letters and looking at photos of Arthur. I wanted to absorb everything from my past, to help me come to terms with what lay ahead. Periodically someone would knock at the door or yell through the letterbox, but I learned to tune it out, and when a face appeared at the window I simply closed the curtains and carried on as I was.

I ate the remains of the wake-feast, curling ham sandwiches and cold sausage rolls. The pastry was greasy and flat; shards of it fell on the sofa, and there was no Bobby there to hoover it up. I was alone as I'd always been, unknit and in flux, a mess of tangled thoughts and random impulses. The alcohol had run out, and so had the milk. When I'd finished the sandwiches and sausage rolls, I ate dry cereal and called the estate agent to arrange a value estimate. Hearing the excitement in his voice when I gave him the address and the thought of him salivating over his fee made me unusually curt over the phone. Afterwards I had to go and clean the kitchen, savagely washing down units and scrubbing the floor until the whole place gleamed like a newly-fallen conker.

It was late afternoon by then and, feeling drained, I drifted upstairs towards the attic, drawn to my mother's old trunks. In the half-light I sorted through some dresses, running my hands along silks and chiffons, letting the feathers and beads trail between my fingers. On a whim, I selected a long, high-necked Edwardian dress and held it against me, looking at myself in the tilting mirror in the corner. It was lilac, the colour of mourning. Shrugging off my dressing gown, I slowly pulled the dress over my head and it fell in silky folds around my shoulders, settling into the grooves and curves of my body like it was made for me. In the gloom I looked like my grandmother, restless hands plucking at the full skirt. Jette and her Singer, distracting herself with the thrash and hum of the machine, trying to ignore the ghost in it. It didn't work in the end – the only thing that worked was putting yourself out of your misery altogether. Like Jette. Take the pills, give up the ghost.

'Missy.'

I gave a shocked cry. In the mirror behind me was Angela, white-faced and red-eyed. I whirled around, and there she was, standing in my attic.

'How did you get in here?'

Wordlessly she held up a key – the one I'd given Sylvie. Then a clattering up the stairs, and there was Sylvie herself and – I drew a sharp breath – Melanie. Her eyes roamed around the rooms, before resting on the dress I was wearing over my night-gown.

'Come downstairs and let's talk,' she said.

I thought about refusing to come down, and spending whatever I had left of my life stalking these attics, the kind of ghoul I checked the cupboards for, but a glance at Sylvie and Angela's set faces suggested they would be perfectly capable of physically dragging me downstairs. So I picked up the train of my dress and sailed past them, my head held high.

Down in the kitchen I set about making tea, then remembered there was no milk. Seeing me hesitate, Melanie reached into her bag and pulled out a carton. I took it from her, feeling resentful. While the three of them talked about the lovely weather we were having, I made up a pot, put everything on a tray and carried it through to the living room. Sylvie cast a quick glance at the bare walls as she went in, but said nothing.

'Tea, anyone?' A perfect hostess, in my elegant day dress, I poured us each a cup and settled back on the sofa, steeling myself for a lecture. Once they were gone I would call another estate agent – best to get a variety of estimates before we fixed on a price. I raised my eyebrows at Melanie, but for once she seemed at a loss.

Instead it was Sylvie who put her cup down, got up and walked towards the fireplace to look up at the portrait of my father.

'William Jameson,' she said, patting the frame. 'I've been reading about him. You didn't tell me he was a war hero.'

The teacup trembled at my lips. 'He wouldn't have wanted

anyone to make a fuss,' I said, and took a sip to steady myself, burning my tongue.

'He rescued twenty-three British and American soldiers from a Ukrainian barn. They all escaped, but he was shot by a Russian guard. The war was already over. He could have gone home. But he stayed.'

'He hung on,' I whispered.

'And your mother, Helena Jameson. She ran self-defence and driving classes for women – secretly, so their husbands couldn't find out. She taught hundreds of women to drive and defend themselves. She never took payment. All those women, safer and more independent because of her. She was a hero too.'

'What's your point?' The tears were threatening but I swallowed them down with the boiling tea.

Angela took my cup from my hands and held them in her own.

'Her point is that they helped people. People help other people. You've helped me. Now we want to help you.'

'No one can help me.' I didn't see why anyone would want to. I wasn't a war hero like William Jameson. Or an activist like Helena Jameson. I was just Missy Carmichael.

'Wrong,' said Sylvie, slapping her hand on the mantelpiece. 'I have an idea, and as you know, my ideas are always excellent.'

'It's too late. You don't know the mess I'm in.'

'Au contraire. I know exactly what kind of a mess you're in, and I know how to get you out of it.'

Melanie, sitting in her father's chair, intervened. 'I told them everything, Mum.'

I glared at her. 'We've been through this before. I'm not moving to some dreadful bungalow in Cottenham, playing bridge with old biddies and getting bussed to the seaside.'

'Dear me, no,' said Sylvie heartily. 'Melanie, I must say that was a terrible plan. Mine is much better.'

'Dad's care home costs are huge,' explained Melanie. 'Ali and I are happy to contribute, if she'd let us, but even with that . . .'

Even with that, we couldn't afford it. I'd done the sums when I started getting the letters from our bank, and knew we wouldn't be able to manage for much longer.

'I don't want to move him,' I muttered. 'He's happy there. In a way.'

'You won't have to move him,' said Sylvie. 'He can stay right where he is. And so can you.'

I raked a hand through my shorn hair and heard the dress rip under my armpit. 'How?'

Sylvie smiled. 'It all starts with the attics,' she said.

I'd always thought of my house as an asset, but only in the sense that it could be sold, and thus its riches would be realized. Sylvie saw something else. All those rooms, all that space. All that potential to make money in a different way.

'We're going to renovate your attics,' she announced. 'I have all the contacts, the labourers, the decorators. I'll design it all. We'll put a little en suite in, and then you can rent it out, and use the money to pay for Leo's care.'

'But who's going to live in it?' I asked.

'I am,' said Angela. 'Me and Otis, we're moving in. I'm sick of my landlord. I'd much rather pay you rent. Plus I'll have a live-in babysitter on hand, Otis will have a constant supply of biscuits and best of all . . .' she tailed off and looked at me from under her lashes.

'Best of all, what?'

She grinned. 'We can get a dog.'

All at once I felt a quiver in my heart, and caught my breath, transfixed. 'A dog? Of my own?'

Sylvie butted in. 'And there's your spare room too. We can spruce it up a bit, you can get a student in there. More money. More company.'

'But, how will I pay for all that? I haven't got the money to renovate a loft, or redecorate, or add bathrooms or . . . anything. There's nothing left.' I slumped in my seat, deflated once again. For a moment I'd had a sliver of hope.

'You *will* pay for it all. For now, Denzil is going to give you a loan. No, wait!' She held up a finger as my mouth fell open to protest. 'A loan. He can afford it, and besides, you're going to pay him back. We're going to sell things. All the stuff in the attic, for starters. And Leo's books. They're worth thousands.'

'Leo's books? But . . .'

'But nothing. The money will do him much more good than the library. Phillip Kingston is a second-hand book dealer, he's got a shop on Charing Cross Road and he's going to get you a good price on all of them. They're worth a fortune. Simon Charles is a builder, and his wife Maddie is a plumber. They're waiting to measure up the space, see what they can do. We're all ready.'

'They're waiting . . .?'

'They're all outside, in your garden. Go and look.'

I stood up and walked out, through the hallway, into the kitchen and to the back door. Opening it, I saw a crowd of people and dogs on my lawn next to Bobby's cypress – Denzil with Badger and Barker, Phillip and Dexter, Simon and Maddie with Tiggy and little Timothy, Octavia, Hanna, and Otis with Decca and Nancy, all standing and chatting in the sunshine. Seeing me there in the doorway, they all waved and cheered. My heart swelled again and I put my hand over my mouth. Here was my Gordian knot, nonchalantly untied, released, destroyed, in a single stroke, by the people I loved, who loved me. They didn't say it; they didn't have to, because it shone in everything they did.

'See?' said Sylvie in my ear. 'It's a pretty good plan, isn't it? What do you think? Can they come in?'

She, Angela and Melanie were all looking at me expectantly, waiting for a response. But I couldn't speak, I could only look. Their faces, alight with excitement and affection, bubbling over with their ideas and schemes. I gazed out at all my friends in my garden, ready to devote their skills and their time to me. Help was on my doorstep, and all I had to do was let them in.

'I think,' I said finally, turning to smile at Mel and cupping her cheek in my hand as I slowly found my voice, 'that we're going to need a lot more milk . . .'

Chapter 49

'So the whole top floor has been transformed, you wouldn't believe the difference. Just washing the windows changed everything – they were absolutely filthy. But now they're gleaming and the place is so much brighter. We've made one side into bedrooms for Angela and Otis – they've got one each now, though of course Otis's is quite small. And then the other side is a little sitting room and bathroom. It all looks simply lovely, Sylvie is so clever.'

I finished arranging Leo's flowers – honeysuckle from the garden – and stood back to admire them in their vase. He was sitting in his chair looking out as usual, one finger twitching to the Prelude that was playing. I knew he could hear me though, because sometimes when I stopped talking he would grab my arm and make a kind of rolling gesture with his hand as if to say 'carry on'. So I did.

'And downstairs we've re-painted the spare room and Maddie put a new sink in, so it's all ready for the young man, Aleksander, to move in. I was hoping Hanna would want the room, but she just moved into a new place with her boyfriend. Aleksander is a friend of hers, he's studying at the Royal Academy of Music and plays the cello. I must say, it will be quite helpful to have a man about the house again, though of course he's only twenty. We were worried he'd be practising day and night but she says he does all that at the college and just wants somewhere to sleep and eat. Maybe he'll play for us in the evenings though, that might be nice.'

After giving him his drink, I stacked Leo's books on the table next to him, and opened a window to let some fresh air in. It was still warm and there were a few hours of daylight left. Smoothing back his unruly hair, I kissed his forehead, and picked up a card that had fallen on the floor, adding it to one of his rows. Then I sat on his bed and, since it was a kind of bedtime, began to tell him a story.

'Apollo was a handsome god, used to getting his own way.'

The breeze shifted outside, as though the gods were on my side, urging me on.

'Eleni was a beautiful young girl, but very shy, and one day she was walking in the forest when she bumped into Apollo, who was hunting there. He'd missed everything so far that day, but he took one look at Eleni and decided to make her fall in love with him. He pierced her with one of his arrows and she was instantly smitten, following him round and offering him gifts. But eventually Apollo had to move on, leaving Eleni alone. Devastated by the loss of her love, Eleni became mute and from then on was unable to speak a word.'

I wiped away a rogue tear that threatened to fall and continued. 'When she was hungry, she couldn't ask for food. When she was thirsty, she couldn't ask for water. When she was lonely, she couldn't ask for company.'

Leo lay back, his hands stilled. 'Eleni roamed the forest, getting thinner, thirstier and more miserable. Until one day she met a dog called Skyla. Skyla was a good and loyal hound, and she joined Eleni as she walked through the forest. When Eleni was hungry, Skyla would bark at the farmers until they gave her food. When she was thirsty, Skyla would lead her to a stream so she could drink. When she was lonely, Skyla would curl up with her in the moonlight to sleep. Gradually, Eleni grew stronger. She and Skyla became inseparable. But Apollo's sister Artemis, watching from above, was jealous. She sent an arrow down to Earth and it killed Skyla instantly. Skyla died in Eleni's arms. But as she wept over the dog's body, her voice returned. Another passing goddess, Achelois, heard her cries and stopped to listen.'

I took a deep breath. 'Incensed by Artemis' cruelty, Achelois turned Skyla into a constellation, and if you look into the sky at night, you can see the Dog Star up there, even now . . .'

At last, Leo's eyelids began to droop and his breathing settled into a regular rhythm, so I allowed my voice to lower until it was just a hum in the cosmos. Darling Leo, whose arrow still pierced my heart, a wound I would always live with. And Bobby, my guiding star. Both of them whispering my heart's song as they always would.

For a while, I sat there watching him sleep and listening to the great oak outside, leaves sighing in the breeze. I imagined, one day, Leo's spirit might weave its way to join the whispering force, soaring up into the heavens, free at last. Before the tears came, I let myself out and headed back down the corridor, waving to Rachel and walking out into the balmy summer evening.

Rooting in my bag, I fished out the postcard that had arrived that morning. Sylvie was still looking after her mother in the South of France, though the operation had been successful. She'd invited me to go and stay with them for a week and I thought that after we'd got Aleksander settled, a trip to Provence might be just the kind of adventure I needed. Thinking of French bread and cheese, my stomach rumbled and I remembered Angela had said she would try to make a Sunday roast tonight. It was good of her, though the kitchen always looked like a bombsite after she'd finished.

We hadn't got round to getting our dog, though Angela regularly trawled rescue home websites and showed me pictures of ones she liked the look of. In the interim, we had acquired a cat, Angela bringing him home one night just after they'd moved in. A family nearby were moving up north, and couldn't take him with them. An enormous ginger tom with wild yellow eyes and a nick in one ear that told a tale, he was called Sourpuss, and lived up to his name – aloof, unfriendly, and occasionally vicious. We were all devoted to him. I still wanted my dog, all the same. We weren't sure how Sourpuss would react to an interloper, but they'd just have to learn to get along.

I walked up the path to my house – our house – and stopped for a second to gather myself. 'Move on,' Leo had written in his letter. 'Let go.' *Luó* – to untie, release. I was getting there.

'Hello, I'm home!'

As I opened the front door, I could hear Otis making engine noises, just like Alistair used to. Little boys are all the same. Hanging up my coat, I threw my keys on the hall table and went to see what they were up to. I found them in the living room; my rug had been rolled up and shoved to one side, and they were both on their hands and knees, holding pieces of chalk. The wooden floor was covered in white marks. As I looked around and made sense of it, I realized they'd drawn an enormous racetrack, weaving its way all around the room.

'Look!' yelled Otis. 'We've drawn roads for the cars!'

'Don't worry,' said Angela. 'It'll wash off.'

'It's a vast improvement,' I said, rolling up my sleeves. 'Now, who's going to give me a car so we can have a race?'

'Brum!' growled Otis, sliding one in my direction. And off we went.

Acknowledgements

Back in 2014, I spent New Year's Eve with some very dear old friends in Whitley Bay. During the evening we each made three resolutions. Mine were something along the lines of 1) eat less meat, 2) have a baby and 3) write fifty thousand words of a novel. I accomplished the second the following year, but didn't manage the third until 2016. Still working on the meat thing. But I want to thank those friends – and *all* my friends – for egging me on. Like a marathon runner nearing the end of a race, any writer needs encouragement to keep them going, and I had lots of flag wavers who were excited simply by the idea that I was giving it a shot. Thank you for that excitement, that enthusiasm. It really made a difference.

To the dog walkers of Clissold Park, bless you for opening up a new world. Before we got a dog, I was barely aware of the park's existence; now it frames my days and I've met so many interesting, funny and brilliant people there, all with leads around their necks and poo bags in their pockets. What a great bunch you are, though you know I'll always prefer your dogs to you.

To the nursery and primary school staff who look after my sons while I work – thank you for providing the security for me to lose myself in a café for a little while.

Cheers to everyone at RDF, my telly family, and the best training ground any writer could hope to have. And to Jack – you spurred me on; hope I can do the same for you.

A huge thank you to my former Director of Studies at Newnham, Jean Gooder, who hosted me in Cambridge one morning and regaled me with glorious anecdotes to inspire the St Botolph's party scene, and life at Newnham generally. Jean also directed me to the fascinating Newnham College Library archives, where the staff kindly helped with my research.

Marianne Levy, a fantastic writer and excellent friend, took my submission in hand and gave me wise and robust advice about how to sell my book. It was invaluable. And the marvellous Meg Rosoff, who I've idolized ever since I devoured *How I Live Now*, was kind enough to read some early chapters and critique them. Her encouraging, bracing insights were heartening and helpful in equal measure. Thanks also to Alison Carpenter, who let me text her random queries about various classical references and Latin verbs. To preserve her reputation, any mistakes are mine and mine alone.

I am indebted to the Greek poet Maria Polydouri, who wrote the beautiful poem 'Because You Loved Me' that Leo puts in a cracker for Missy to translate. I hope she wouldn't have minded the liberties I took with my own translation.

To my wonderful editors, Martha Ashby at HarperCollins and Tara Singh Carlson at Putnam: you joined forces in the finest possible way and every note you gave me opened up a shaft of light. Thank you for your pushing, your pedantry, and your occasional 'tumultuous rounds of applause' that made the editing process a total joy. Thanks also to the teams alongside you – the publicists, copy editors, designers and many others who come together to create a book.

Then to Madeleine Milburn . . . Wow. Personally responsible for two of my best days on the planet (behind getting married, getting a dog and having children, but only just), you are the empress of agents, and quite possibly have supernatural powers. Thanks so much to you, Giles, Alice and everyone at the agency, slogging away to bring our books into the world. You all work miracles.

Edging closer to home, thank you to my mum and dad for providing unfailing support and steadfast devotion to your spoilt only child. Dad, thank you for reading the manuscript and giving your notes, especially the one to lose the last chapter. You were quite right.

Obviously I couldn't get through this without giving Polly a mention. To my favourite girl, the apple of my eye, my guiding star and muse, thank you for being the world's best dog. And to my favourite boys, Wilfred and Edmund – the loudest, craziest, funniest and best boys. Thank you for keeping me in the moment, and making those moments utterly awesome.

Finally, to my husband, Tom: I don't say it enough, but you are also the best. Quite simply, this book would not have been written were it not for you. Not just because you helped make it happen, giving me the confidence and the opportunity to go for it, but because when you've run the marathon, you need someone to come home to who'll rub your feet and say you did great. There's no one I'd rather do that with than you.